KLR Covers designed the book cover.
Illustrations from Century Library.
Margot and Nikolas Character Art by @amaya_maria

Software and tools used:
Scrivener
Obsidian
Post-it notes, notebooks, and journals.

ISBN 978-1-0699767-1-0

To Piper,

For all my minxes,
who revel beneath the moonlight.

Author's Note

Hey friend,

This novel came kicking and screaming out of my head, refusing to stay quiet. It was inspired by chilly autumn days and warm summer nights. Jazz music, wine, and boozy spirits. Poetry read in hushed voices. History, artefacts and art viewed in museums. The stories we tell in libraries for our future generations. And, by one more chapter before bed.

This book contains violence and death with vulgar and unbecoming language. It also contains some very flirtatious, and sometimes sexually explicit scenes that are always consensual. It's recommended for readers over the age of 18.

I hope you have as much fun reading this as I've had writing it.

With love, Anika.

Encyclopaedia of Torresium

This is a general guide for new readers.

Spirit Wielders — Lucerna.
They hear what others cannot — the *whisper* of Spirits moving through the world, and the unspoken current beneath a mortal's thoughts. They are drawn to confluences of power — the crystallised leylines of *mana.*

Ignis — Fire.
They shape and throw flame, but their more useful gifts are the *Azure Flame* — a cold blue fire that Spirits instinctively avoid — and *heat sight,* which lets them read the world by warmth rather than light, seeing through darkness by the faint glow of living things.

Terra — Ground.
With the ability to move stone and soil, they listen to the slow whisper of roots, the memory of bedrock. Their *vibration senses* extend into the leylines themselves, feeling the pulse of *mana* like a heartbeat beneath their feet.

Soul Wielders — Nox.
They sense the aura of *mana* within every living thing and can sway those feelings quietly and without a trace.

Aer — Air.
They control currents, stop breath in lungs, and leap distances that shouldn't be mortally possible. They carry their voices across vast terrain and track the world through *scent*. Some possess the *breath of life* — the blessing to heal minor wounds.

Aqua — Water.
They command the flow of rivers and tides. Their voices can bend a mortal's will so smoothly that it goes unnoticed until it's done. Their *hearing* reaches extraordinary distances.

The Little Girl's Dreams

"Quiet," the teacher called out to her class.

A loud wooden snap rang out beside her — she jolted and gripped her report tighter, nearly crumpling the page. As she cleared her throat, the weight of her classmates' stares and silent snickers filled her with dread.

*Margot took a breath and continued, "This excerpt was found preserved in the archives. '*The Fundamental Principles of Mana,*' by Professor Olivia Brown, Department of Animus Bestiary Studies, Historia.*

A flash of white caught the corner of her eye. A paper crane flew directly at her head — she ducked. A hot flash of fire landed on her woollen skirt. The laughter of two boys, her constant tormentors, rang in her ears. She slapped at the burning paper and stormed toward Quentin, or at least she tried to before her teacher pulled her back.

"Quentin! That's it! Go stand in the hallway." The teacher pointed to the door, shut it behind him, and motioned for her to keep reading. The same report her mother had forced her to rewrite three times.

Her hands still ached as she gripped the page tighter.

"It is said that when mana split in two, the Alignments were born. Some within our society claim it was deliberate – a calculated act of destruction. Others insist it was the first and only accident of creation. Regardless, that fracture began the ebb and flow that shaped Torresium's landscape.

The Mind and the Heart: Spoken before mortals transcribed their old tongues as Lucerna and Nox — and now known to us as Spirit and Soul."

The class was silent. She caught her breath.

"When the Two became Four, balance found form in the physical. From their union emerged the elements: Terra, Ignis, Aer, and Aqua. And the seasons: Spring, Summer, Autumn, and Winter. Mortal and Spirit alike follow the rhythm of the Alignments. Each carrying an eternal well, a shard of that fallen star."

Part One

Library of Historia

PROLOGUE

The Nox Protectorate

☾

Chilling nightmares haunted him. *The girl's dreams again, always that girl.* Suffocating fear seeped into the edges of his sleep, drowning him in icy waters.

His eyes snapped open. Damp air filled his lungs, thick with rot. Branches arched overhead, leaves crowding the sky until it broke into fragments of dimming light.

Shrubs choked the clearing, the one he remembered. In the centre stood her tree. It had been a spring sapling when they planted it. *A marker. A promise.* Now its trunk was wide enough to split the light, its roots buckling the ground as though they had been protecting him.

Pain flared through his bones, sharp as needles driven behind his eyes. He lay still, breath shallow, staring up through unfamiliar leaves.

Ceramic cracked as he lifted his head. The shell that had sealed his fur broke apart in dull flakes, drifting to the ground with a soft clatter. He stood with stiff muscles and shook the debris from his coat.

Older memories had thinned during his sleep. Colour leeched from them until only shapes remained. What was once warm and intimate now felt cold, like ink faded by rain.

The afternoon light dimmed beneath the canopy. *Autumn.*

He sensed it in the air even before he saw falling leaves. The frigid air carried an edge he used to relish when he curled beside his bonded in the library she had loved.

The endless dark had stripped his last memories to bone. He could feel the shape but nothing else. Voices. The Council, maybe? *Rest,* they had said. *Let us rule for a while.* He must have agreed. Their faces washed into nothing.

Why did he have to linger? The days felt empty and grey without her. When her heart stopped beating, his rule ended with it. Reduced to managing their trivial mortal concerns.

A snap of twigs and a mortal voice cut through the haze.

His ears twitched toward the sound. His *mana* answered with a low hum in his chest as it reached her heart. A young mother. Her love burned bright and afraid, close enough to ache. The delicate nature of mortals always fascinated him. Their lives were a brief symphony of smells and sounds that still stirred him, even when it hurt.

He studied her, her heart hammering with the particular terror of someone who had come too far to turn back. She had not found an easy path here. She had found the only path, and she had taken it for a child who was not yet old enough to take it herself.

"Please. You have to protect her." She stood at the base of the ancient tree, hood drawn low. His bonded had planted that tree long before he fell asleep.

"How long has it been, mortal?" His voice, rough as stone, cracked with each word.

"Sixty-five," she said. She bowed low, gripping his staff with white-knuckled hands.

Sixty-five years. Long enough for rot to spread.

He closed his eyes and pushed his *mana* into the ground. The living web of roots and mycelium stirred beneath him, a subtle tremor against his paws. His senses reached along forgotten tunnels to the heart of the city. The shields still held.

Historia remained hidden. *Asleep.*

He let out a ragged breath, changing to a low growl that resonated in his chest, then shifted into a purr that deepened within his bones. When he yawned, his teeth glinted in the dimming light.

She stepped back in fear.

Claws sank into the soil as he stretched, bones reshaping with a fluid ease that came from centuries of practice. Fur melted into skin. His height rose, and rose.

She tightened both hands around his staff. The hood slipped, revealing black curls tangled in branches. A hatchet and an open book lay on the grass near her feet. Thorns shredded the edges of her sleeves as she forced her way through the overgrowth.

Steam drifted from his skin, carried on the cool air. He closed a fist, the faint bite of his own claws dug against his palm. His bare feet pressed into the gravel that circled the tree. He clenched his jaw, swallowing acrid bitterness.

"Why should I allow you or the Council to live?"

Anger simmered beneath his skin, rain hissing into steam. They killed his bonded in a foolish and suicidal effort to control him and his city. Every day. *Every miserable day.* He couldn't bear to see the faces of her killers. He should have left them to rot in their cells.

They outvoted him. Five to one. Even those who had sworn loyalty to her.

She knew exactly what she was doing. She had always known, from the moment she stepped into the clearing. He could feel it in her heart — not cruelty, not ambition. Just a mother, down to her last option.

The mother whispered, "I am sorry." A tear rolled down

her face. "I have to do this. To protect her." Her lips trembled. She lifted his staff above her head and began to chant.

The words charged the air — leaves stirred, the tree groaned, static crawling over his skin like something alive. *She shouldn't have the power to do this. She shouldn't have known those words.*

Every small hair along his arms rose as the air charged. The ground vibrated beneath his feet. A weak pulse grew stronger, becoming a steady rhythm that moved up his legs and along his spine. "Stop!" he snarled.

She did not stop.

An icy wave of *mana* erupted from the ground. It slid into his bones with invasive precision. Invisible claws pinned him in place, his muscles locking tight. His breath left him in a sharp gasp.

The air thickened. The odour of petrichor sharpened, flooding his senses. The leaves overhead spun in violent spirals. The pressure increased. A prickling sensation began under his skin, thousands of tiny shards coursing through his veins. The current intensified until his nerves screamed. The *mana* wrapped around his ribs, squeezing, redoing the paths inside him.

His bones shifted with a sickening crack. His arms folded inward. Fingers shortened. Claws punched through skin in reverse, curling back into paws. His legs buckled, his form shifting. His spine arched as a tail forced its way into existence, vertebrae snapping together one after another.

He tried to roar, but the *mana* in his throat warped the sound into something small and broken.

His ears throbbed as cartilage twisted upward, reshaping and sharpening into feline points — sound distorting with each shift. His jaw reshaped in a series of sharp, nauseating pops. Heat steamed from his skin.

His own *mana* pushed back, burning hot in defiance,

fighting the containment. The surge held stronger, binding him, forcing him inward. He collapsed inward with a jolt, height draining from him in an instant. His limbs trembled under the weight of the transfiguration.

She held his orb, his *mana,* his power. His autonomy, contained in mortal hands.

His attempt to snarl "*crazy woman*" turned into an angry meow.

He could only watch.

Well. This was an unfortunate development.

NIKOLAS VENATOR

The Vulpine

✹

Nikolas' ass was numb and frozen stiff from sitting in the damn cart for hours. He exhaled a slow ribbon of smoke. The early morning air bit his lips, sharp with cold and nicotine.

The trees had long shed their leaves; a dusting of snow gathered along the ground. Wisps of pale light — Will-o-Wisps — stirred with his presence. The little predators flared brighter and drifted across the road. As one neared the Azure Flame, a morbid thrill ran through him.

Phut... Pop!

A tiny shimmer of blue puffed away. His stocky mount didn't even flinch, long accustomed to the wisps' dramatic little shrieks as they fizzled out in the flame.

We won't bite...

Come... show us how strong you are...

He huffed a laugh. Spirits always tried to seduce the exhausted.

Nikolas kept silent, letting the wisps glide past as they made their way toward the Gates of Fenn. The cart squeaked awfully under the weight of vegetables and spices. Beside him, Erik snored with his hands tucked under a thick blanket. He jabbed him with his elbow. *Bastard, how was he able to sleep?*

"We're almost there," Nikolas said, pulling his cloak tighter.

Erik's job was to protect the merchandise, and Nikolas was — according to their cover story — just the poor disposable soul hired to drive the cart from Kit Sun to a village outside the Gates.

"All right, al'right, you needn't strike me so hard…" Erik rubbed his side. "Anythin' abnormal?" His voice strained as he arched his back.

"Just a few wisps," Nikolas yawned. His eyes burned, tears forming in the corners. He had not slept for days while on the road.

"Good, good." Erik yawned and rubbed his eyes — once a Legionnaire, now a deserter.

Nikolas collected his coin from the merchant and pocketed the meagre earnings. He turned to face the village and remembered the first week Johansen and Estrid had taken him in — still mourning the son they had lost to a Soul creature.

The village had scraped together enough aureus to hire him. In return, he'd carved runes on every fence post and tree stump — barriers to hide the farm from hungry Spirits. They'd provided him with a sturdy bed, hot meals, and welcomed him with the warmth of a family.

When he stayed in a village for too long, he grew twitchy under the skin. Just last week, a pair of Canis eyes had gleamed at him from the darkness. It was time.

"Good girl," he whispered against her neck and fed her oats. *"Long road ahead."* He brushed a hand along her stripes and smoothed down the thick, curly coat. Lifting the beast's rear hoof, he checked her spurred metal shoes.

Snow was piling on the browned roof as he stepped back toward the farmhouse. *Shit.* He needed to go before the winter storm arrived.

Estrid was stuffing his saddlebags with supplies for the road. He'd risked sneaking into Kit Sun just for them — trading for the Azure Flame from a Vulpine dealer and bringing back Erik to wield it. Erik was stronger, quicker, and could fuel the flame himself — enough to hide the village from Spirit senses.

"Wouldn't you consider staying for a couple more seasons?" Estrid asked.

Nikolas shook his head and patted Erik on the shoulder. "He'll protect the village."

"I owe you a great debt for getting me out of Kit Sun," Erik said, though the smile never reached his eyes.

Estrid moved to the hearth and ladled fresh stew into a wooden bowl, groaning as she stood. "Are you sure they won't come looking? They don't take kindly to losing what they consider theirs."

"I've warded the village from their sight. They won't find Erik. You'll be safe — you have my word." He didn't need to push far with his *mana* to hear the notes of her dread.

Estrid sniffed and wrapped her arms around him. He held her until she released him. She had every right to be afraid.

Nikolas ate one last meal with them, rested his feet by the fire, and nodded off.

Just before sunrise, he checked the farm one last time. The Azure Flame flared at the village gate as he looked back. A dull ache settled in his chest.

He should be used to goodbyes. He pushed his beast into the thick snowfall and told himself it didn't matter.

Once, when he was younger, he'd ignored that instinct. Even the bigger cities, ruled by elder Spirits, proved no refuge. Their laws choked him as tightly as their expectations. Bennu would sooner break him than leave him be.

He exited the woods, the path bending left into a clearing where a Vulpine stood on a boulder, watching him. A mix of fiery russet fur, charcoal-dipped feet, and a creamy, proud chest stood out against the snow.

"Easy," Nikolas said, and tightened his mount's reins. The beast flicked its ears, alert. There shouldn't be any Vulpine out here, not this far from their city.

It paused, watching him with golden eyes glinting in the morning light, its twin tails flicking in challenge.

"Follow me," Nikolas heard the wind whisper.

The Vulpine held a scroll firmly in its teeth, and when he reached out with his *mana,* he sensed it did not wish him harm.

Easing his Equus over, he ducked beneath a heavy branch — CRACK.

Pain exploded across his face as the branch smacked him square in the nose. Blood dripped into the snow. "Spirits have mercy," he muttered, dismounting.

"Who are you, little one?" He crouched, one hand extended. With the other, he wiped the blood from his lip onto his sleeve. The Vulpine held its ground, scroll still clamped in its jaws. He led his Equus behind him along the path — low and passable, with pine saplings poking through the snow.

The Vulpine looked back at him, then turned and continued along the road.

"I suppose you can't talk with that in your mouth, right?" Nikolas chuckled.

The trees thinned out, opening into a clearing, just as the Vulpine hopped over a rock and disappeared.

A snap of twigs behind him froze him in place. Nikolas turned his head slowly, just able to see a pair of glowing blue predatory eyes staring back.

A Canis.

Soul Creature

✷

Abyss take him. The Canis' eyes locked him to the spot, its long muzzle sneering into a low growl. Making enemies with Fenn was not part of the plan.

"You are far from your path," the Canis whispered as it stalked closer.

"I can go where I please," Nikolas retorted.

"It would be wise to turn back." It growled, lowering itself to the ground. Its grey quill hackles raised, ready to charge.

Nikolas reached back and unsheathed his sword. He unhooked his shield and looped it onto his arm. "Leave me alone."

His beast snorted, stamping the ground. He gave her a sharp slap on the rear. The Canis's glowing eyes never left Nikolas as the Equus fled back along the trail. It bared its sharp teeth and licked its lips. The rattling of its quills reverberated through the ground and up through his feet.

"Foolish. Your kind are too easy to kill," it growled, lunging forward.

He brought his sword along its side, cutting through fur and muscle — not deep enough. His arms strained under the weight of sword and shield. "Tell Fenn I am not interested in his offer." He spat out blood.

"Why don't you tell him yourself when I drag you back to him?" the creature snarled.

Up onto two powerful legs it rose, its forelegs twisting and reshaping into clawed arms, its spine straightening upright with sickening cracks. The creature shook and shuddered, its lithe body warping before his eyes.

The wound shifted along its protruding ribs, the seeping garnet-black slash standing out against its snow-grey fur. The stiff quills on its back made it a formidable opponent.

Nikolas shifted his weight back, shield snapping up just before the blow landed. His sword caught its claws, and he shoved — muscles burning, boots sliding in the snow.

It howled and swiped a clawed paw. His sword scraped along its quills, and he felt the vibration rattle through his grip.

Getting near it was the only option. He threw the shield into the snow.

It leaped, claws ready to sink in. His back throbbed when hit the ground hard, sword raised as the Canis's jaws snapped shut — metal clashing with teeth. He thrust upward, using the creature's weight against itself.

Nikolas's free hand found his boot and drew the dagger, driving it between its grotesque ribs. He *lifted* — piercing its heart. It writhed and growled at him.

Teeth clenched, he growled back.

The Canis' slashes were growing feeble as Nikolas struggled to hold on to the sword lodged in its maw.

His vision snapped back when it finally stopped.

On the frozen ground he lay, inhaling the icy air, feeling the snow fall on his face. He freed the dagger from the Canis and wiped its garnet-black blood off with his cloak. *Great. Now he'd have to smell dead Canis for hours.*

He was nowhere near Renhold, as he had planned. The wind blew, seeping right through his cloak. His Equus had run off along the other side of the clearing. Nikolas sighed and stomped across the snow to collect his startled mount.

Shhh… It's okay. He soothed his steed and ran a hand along its thick neck.

Its scent still lingered in the air — iron and wet fur and rot. Old habits told him to burn it. Spirits could follow a trail of their own dead, and Fenn's creatures were no different. To leave it was an invitation. To burn it was sensibility dressed up as ceremony, which suited him fine.

He gathered dry brush and kindling — flint against his sword, a small tear of cloth — and the oily pelt went up in flames. He warmed his hands by the fire, watching it burn, and dug an apple from his supplies. A small victory meal.

His neck tingled as he sensed the Vulpine's return. Its long, bushy tails swept the snow as it curled up beside him, drool coating the scroll held in its teeth.

"You could have warned me." Nikolas chucked the core into the fire, listening to it sizzle and fizz. He warmed his hands, the heat returning to the tips of his fingers.

"Follow… out of… snow." The Vulpine's tails twitched before it trotted down the path.

Well then.

The path through the woods tightened. The Vulpine kept looking back, the scroll still in its mouth, as it trudged forward. Nikolas grew more impatient with every step in the wrong direction.

As the sun set, sticky, billowing snow swirled around them, leaving a frigid wash on the ground. Nikolas observed the odd movement of the tree branches ahead, shifting and marbling with an invisible rainbow. The Vulpine passed through a tree trunk and disappeared.

Surely he didn't see that. He rubbed the snow from his eyelashes — a trick of the dimming light, it must have been — then stretched out his hand and felt nothing where the bark should have been. Weightless. *Tingly.*

Nikolas closed his eyes and held his breath. His whole body tingled with static as he stepped through the shield. Gasping, he tried to pull air into his lungs, his chest aching as if he'd surfaced from the depths of the ocean.

Trees gave way to fields and towering stone — a

battlement carved straight into the mountain, its gate watched by twin turrets, an immense fortress city rising beyond with edges glowing in the fading light.

He had not expected *that.*

His hand brushed along the wall. It stretched far in both directions, constructed from smooth, slate-grey stone. No handholds to climb over.

The gate was more rigid and stubborn than he was. He kicked it hard enough to feel it in his teeth. The gate didn't move.

Nikolas cursed, breath fogging and lungs aching in the frozen air. He had to get his mount and this damn Vulpine out of the storm before it claimed them.

MAYA IYER

Library of Historia

△

A knock sounded at Maya's door.

She ignored it. She had the grim task of allocating precious resources. Anthony would be furious if she didn't complete this on schedule. This was not the time for distractions.

She picked up the next requisition slip, Sophia's delicate handwriting immediately recognisable. *Coffee beans. Nutmeg.* Far beyond her weekly allotment by a scandalous margin.

The snap of her fingers produced a small flame. She touched it to her cigarette and inhaled, letting the warmth settle before releasing a slow ribbon of smoke toward the ceiling.

Sophia knew better than this.

The slip moved toward the *Deny* pile. Rules existed to protect the city, even from small indulgences. *Especially from small indulgences.*

And yet.

She remembered the sugar-dipped cookies delivered after hours. Still warm. Sophia lingering only a moment before retreating down the corridor, as though the offering were an afterthought. Maya had eaten them alone at her desk, brushing crumbs from council decrees and telling herself it meant nothing at all.

The parchment hovered.

The knock came again, firmer this time.

Maya studied the numbers once more. With a quiet sigh, she adjusted next week's shipment in careful increments. The difference would go unnoticed.

The slip settled into the *Approve* pile.

"Enter," she said, smoothing the edge of the ledger before looking up.

"Ma'am." Matthew stood at attention in the doorway. "There is an urgent matter that requires your presence."

"What is it at this hour?" Maya checked her pocket watch. *Was it that late?* She rubbed her eyes, blinking to refocus.

"I just received word through a porter stationed at the Western Gate," Matthew said, sounding winded.

She jotted a note to add double laps around the shields to their regimen.

"We have a newcomer," he said, smiling.

They hurried along the hallway as he filled her in. A lone male on a beast, coming through the shields, with a Vulpine in tow. If his intentions weren't good, the shields would have stopped him.

But Maya didn't fully trust the shields. Just last week, she'd incinerated rot that had crept into the lemon orchard. Theodore had cried over losing his prized lemon tree. She could still picture his face as they felled the tree and burned the roots.

Matthew stood beside her on the battlement wall, shivering. *Ungifted weakling.* Her palms instinctively warmed against the ice-covered stone. Maya leaned on the battlement and gazed at the newcomer.

"State your name and intent, or we will take action!" she yelled above the wind.

Snow crusted the stranger's hood. The Vulpine sat patiently at his beast's side, tail wrapped around its paws.

"I need shelter and a good meal." His lips moved. The howling storm made it almost impossible to hear.

"Do you know where you are, boy?" Maya called out.

"I mean no harm," he said, lowering his hood and raising

his hands. "And my name is not boy. It's Nikolas."

Maya extended her senses through the blizzard, taking his measure. Long, slicked-back hair tied at the neck. An untrimmed beard. Exhaustion marked every line of his face — the particular kind that came from months of not sleeping in the same place twice. She knew what a man running from something looked like.

"If you step through these gates, you are bound by the rules of the Twelve Tables." She studied him closely. He looked scrawny and gaunt, with deep bruising beneath his eyes. "If you cause any trouble during your time here, your punishment will be swift and deadly."

"I accept, under the condition that I may leave when I wish. Many have tried to contain me. None have succeeded."

Maya signalled the guards to unlock the gates. "Welcome to the Library of Historia."

The metal groaned as it opened. The Vulpine trotted in with them and dropped the scroll it carried with a wet, drool-soaked slap in the snow.

Disgusting. She did not have the time to deal with that.

"Matthew, clean this up for me. I need to have a little chat with our new friend."

The Vulpine panted. She knew many descended from Kit Sun, but there was a lineage loyal to the Library. They spread and travelled through cities and villages, gathering every genre of book, tome, and grimoire, and, to the joy of the researchers, any other mouth-sized objects that took their fancy. If he'd come through without the Spirit, she would have been more cautious.

Maya met the newcomer at the gates. He gave a curt nod and allowed a guard to take his beast to the stable to be fed and brushed.

"I'm afraid we have to confiscate your weapons and belongings. Standard procedure. I promise they'll be returned when you choose to leave."

He unclasped his sword and daggers. "I assume I can't object. Just be sure to give them back. I'd prefer not to fight you over it."

Let him try. She would give her life to defend this city.

The guard hesitated, brows scrunched, eyes flicking between Maya and the stranger. Maya met his look and gave a single nod. That was enough.

"I stick to my promises," she said as she turned away. "Come. We should dress those wounds and get out of the blizzard."

Nearby guards began to tremble and brace against the ceaseless winds. Except for her and the newcomer.

"This blood does not belong to me," Nikolas added. "I felled a Canis."

Maya stopped. "You… killed a Canis?" *Had she misheard him?*

"I burned the body," he said, brushing snow from his cloak. Torchlight lit his tired features.

Blizzard winds whipped her onyx hair into her face. He seemed too weak to lift a spoon.

"I suppose a hot meal and a bath are in order," she said, masking her surprise.

"I'd be quite grateful, thank you…?" The newcomer removed his glove and held out his hand.

"My apologies. Where are my manners?" She shook his icy hand with a slight smile. "My name is Maya Iyer. I am the Commander-in-Chief of the Library of Historia."

She ordered Matthew to secure a room as they walked toward the Southern Mess Hall. A newcomer was rare. One escorted by a Vulpine was rarer still. She needed to understand who, or *what*, he was.

She twisted her ruby-and-gold ring. When had their last newcomer arrived? A season ago? Longer? *Spirits have mercy, it had been too long.*

Supper time was long past. Maya barked orders to rouse a chef and have food reheated for her guest.

"So," she said, settling across from him. "Tell me your story."

The newcomer stiffened, glancing upward. "Not much of a story. I left my village at fifteen and never stopped moving. Spirits are drawn to me, so I won't be staying."

He tore off a piece of bread and dipped it into the juices.

Her face remained neutral. "They are drawn to you?"

"Like a wisp to a flame."

She held his gaze a moment longer than necessary. *Interesting.*

"You're safe here. The shields hide Historia. Only those with permission to leave can remember the route."

"I don't know how I ended up here. I just followed the Vulpine." He scraped the bowl clean. "Wonderful stew." He wiped his mouth with his sleeve.

The newcomer was uncultured.

"The Vulpine brought you here for a reason," Maya said. "As part of our laws, we will take care of you."

If the shield ever dropped, it would be her worst nightmare. Kit Sun sought to bond with every Ignis wielder in Torresium. The Spiritless city of Historia should not exist. Yet here it stood, hidden from the eternal storm of warring Spirits.

Maya cleared her throat. "The chefs here have lived and worked their entire lives inside these walls. We are one enormous family."

"How many people live here?" The newcomer lifted a curious brow.

"Around three thousand. Most unblessed. Some aligned," she said, holding his gaze. She bore responsibility for each mortal in Historia. It was a heavy burden, one she carried with pride. Every single soul within the city upheld a duty. She was no exception.

His lifeless eyes roamed over her. "This place is a wonder," the newcomer said, rising from the bench.

"It is. We're blessed to be guarded by a Spirit who was kind." Maya gestured to Matthew. "He'll show you to your room. Rest. I'll meet with you in the morning."

Maya nodded in thanks to Matthew. She had much more paperwork to finish before the sun rose.

He was trouble. She was almost certain of it. The question was what kind.

Just a few more hours.

NIKOLAS VENATOR

Custodian

✷

Nikolas held his hands toward the fire and waited for the feeling to return to his fingers. It came slowly, in small, aching pulses. Outside, the blizzard clawed at stone that did not yield. In here, the air smelled faintly of wood smoke and something spiced.

The largest bed he'd ever seen took up most of the room, four posts holding up a red velvet cloth tied back with rope, an ornate green rug covering the foot. He sat on the edge and pulled off his boots, the thuds echoing off the wooden floor. His shoulders sagged with relief when he saw his saddlebags placed on top of a trunk at the end of the bed. He made sure his supplies were intact: his pipe and tin of tobacco, a small pouch of salted and smoked nuts, a few apples, and a few glass jars of spices he'd lifted in Kit Sun.

His finger slipped through a hole in the bag. Bitten through.

No, not the notebook. Teeth marks scored the spine, the pages warped where blood had seeped through, ink bleeding into muted shadows. He turned one page, then another — a sketch of a warding sigil blurred into something unrecognisable.

He closed it carefully and slid it back into the bag. He had redrawn worse. By the fireplace, two leather armchairs flanked a small table with a decanter of brown liquid and glasses. *Yes — liquor.*

Maya's aide walked around the bed and gestured to a

door. "This is the bathroom. You can run hot water and take a bath."

"You have running water?"

"Yes, here." The aide reached for the left handle. Steam rose within moments as water spilled over his hand. "This handle is for cold water. Soap's on the shelf."

Nikolas watched the steam curl and vanish. He had paid extra coin for hot water before, but never like this.

"Fascinating." A small sink with the same handles, a mirror above it — and his own reflection staring back at him, a tired, unkempt stranger who had no business still being alive.

The aide stood with his hands behind his back. "Clean clothes from the laundress are on the bed. In the morning, someone will knock to collect your dirty garments. They'll be washed and returned to you."

"Thanks." His mind was racing. He was standing inside the Library of Historia. A Spirit city thought destroyed a thousand years ago. He'd always dismissed the whispers as legend or a trap.

"Rest up." The aide went to leave, then paused. "One more thing. We don't receive newcomers often."

Nikolas pushed *mana* into his eyes.

"They'll be excited," the aide stated with a shrug. "A few might be startled. Try not to take it personally."

"I will keep that in mind." Nikolas couldn't sense any animosity from him.

When the footsteps faded, he locked the door. He strained to move the heavy trunk in front of it, muscles burning. The wood scraped loudly against the floorboards. His jaw tightened at the sound. Hated that he had nothing sharper than a fireplace poker within reach.

Nikolas survived by blending in. Predicting which Spirit was going to take a bite. Fenn's city had been the easiest to enter and leave, relatively speaking. They only wanted to harvest his *mana* for potions or transmute his bones into weapons. He preferred his organs where they were.

Kit Sun was no better. They wanted him trained in their Legion, a prizefighter destined for a glorious death. *He wasn't fond of that choice either.*

As Nikolas turned the left handle, hot water rushed out within heartbeats. He turned the right handle to temper it and eased his sore muscles into the tub. He washed his hair and beard, sinking into the warmth. *When had he last bathed like this?*

He dried himself, retied his wet hair, and ran his hands through his beard. The red tinge in his eyes had softened after the soak. He eased into the bed, listening to the fireplace crackle, savouring the softness of the mattress.

A knock at the door woke him. The trunk scraped awfully against the floorboards as he moved it.

A wide-eyed woman greeted him. "Good sunrise. I'm here to collect your — your garments." She looked young, wearing a uniform with a pinned coat of arms on her chest.

Nikolas gathered his dirty riding clothes, folding them as neatly as he could. "Return them as soon as you can."

She held out a fresh set of linens. "These are for walking around the grounds." She darted off with her cart without another word.

The pants were black wool and too wide; he pulled the straps to cinch them to his waist. The cream linen tunic fit snugly, and the vest matched the pants but restricted his movements further. *Not designed for fighting.* He fastened it regardless. *Better to blend in than stand out.*

He put on the woollen coat next. *No. Too tight, too constricting, he'd die in a fight wearing it.* He reached for his riding cloak instead. The shoes were too small. His riding boots would have to do.

Another knock sounded. Maya strode into the room with controlled grace. "I see you've made yourself comfortable."

The Commander-in-Chief appeared in her mid-thirties, with shoulder-length black hair and warm olive skin, dressed in the same uniform. Young for someone in her position, but he could sense she'd earned it.

"Yes. I appreciate your hospitality. I've stayed nowhere with these amenities."

"I felt the same."

"You also travelled here?"

"Yes, a very long time ago. A story for another time, preferably over hard liquor. Would you like breakfast? I have an offer," she said in a quick, matter-of-fact tone.

He felt the jaws of a trap tighten. "Lead the way."

Maya greeted people by name as they walked.

Quite impressive, that she knew everybody. Some stared openly, others pretended not to, and a few offered polite nods as they passed.

"This is the Southern Mess Hall," Maya said. It bustled with people eating or leaving with plates piled high. "You may eat as much as you need," she said, handing him a plate.

Nikolas inhaled the delightful smell of fresh bread and porridge. He piled scrambled eggs, a thin slice of salted swine, and an apple. People seemed to eat well here.

Maya sat across from him with a bowl of dried fruits and tree nuts. "I've been thinking it over. You should stay." She leaned her elbows on the table.

"Stay?" *Why would she want that? Unless she knew who he was.*

"You said you killed a Canis on your way here. I would like you to help defend the Library."

Defend? Canis were a growing threat. They bred fast, ate livestock, and assaulted villages. Fenn used them to control mortal populations. "I'll give it some thought."

"Understandable." She crunched a single nut between her teeth. "I believe we can come to an agreement."

"An agreement? I don't work for Spirits."

According to legend, Historia was either a benevolent Spirit or a tyrant, depending on who told the story. Standing beneath the shield made his skin prickle, regardless.

Maya speared a dried fruit between her nails. "Come work for me as a Custodian. I'll offer permanent lodging and a stipend."

"A generous offer." *Almost too generous.* He reached out with his *mana*.

The connection flared — hot and bright, like reaching too close to an open flame. He withdrew quickly, pulse hammering. "I don't live by tyrannical Spirit rules." Pain rang between his eyes.

Maya did not flinch. *A boundary.* "The Council makes the rules, and I enforce them."

"That is unlike any other Spirit city I've known," Nikolas replied. He would have to study this place carefully, in case they changed their minds and handed him to Fenn — *or worse.*

"I was once like you," Maya finished slicing her apple. "I know our people. Most are survivors, travellers, orphans, or descended from them. We all sought the same refuge. I have no wish to see you harmed."

Nikolas paused, considering her words. If Historia's shields had kept them hidden for centuries, maybe they could hide him too.

"If it's agreeable to you," he said, "I'll stay a few more days and consider your offer." *A few days wouldn't hurt. Not with a blizzard raging.*

"Take a week," Maya said, rising. "Explore the grounds. No one will bother you. You have my word."

She turned and left.

His hand had drifted to where his sword should have been. He pulled it back. *A week was not a promise.*

MARGOT WILSON

Wayward Soul

Margot couldn't reach the top shelf. She rose onto her bare tiptoes atop a rickety old chair.

Her apartment door burst open.

"Good morning, Sunshine!" Sophia beamed.

"Spirits have mercy!" Margot squealed and jumped out of her skin. A sickening smash against the floorboards made her heart sink. She let the felis figurine drop to steady herself. The last thing she needed on her gravestone was *R.I.P. Margaret Wilson: Death by Bookcase.*

"Oh my, Margot! Are you okay?"

"You damn near killed me, Sophia." There was more bite in her words than she had intended. Sophia held her hand as she stepped down.

Oh. This was Mum's.

She bent down and winced as pain shot through her finger. The sharp edge bit her skin. *Clumsy as ever.* Mum gave her the figurine right before she —

Tears pricked her eyes as she sat on the edge of the bed.

"I'll take care of this," Sophia said and put the empty wine bottles in a crate. *"Who are you, my love? Oh, that was a nice one,"* she added, swigging the last few drops.

Margot sat on the edge of her bed with the figurine resting in her lap. Tears gathered before she could stop them. "She gave it to me," she said, her voice thinner than she liked.

Sophia's expression softened. She lowered herself beside her without speaking and wrapped an arm around her shoulders.

"I know," she murmured.

Margot stared at the chipped ear. She had only just begun sorting the shelves. "I just started organising," she whispered. "I thought —" She swallowed. "I thought I was ready."

Sophia tightened her hold and rested her chin lightly against Margot's hair. "You don't have to be."

The words undid her more than the fall had.

Margot's shoulders shook once, twice.

Sophia pulled back slightly. "Let me see your hand."

"It's nothing."

"Let me."

Margot held it out. The cut was shallow but sharp. Sophia closed her eyes, her brow knitting in concentration.

Warmth spread beneath her skin, soft and almost ticklish, and when Sophia released her only a faint pink line remained.

"There," Sophia whispered.

Margot blinked. "You've been practicing."

Sophia tried to look modest and failed. "The recruits at the custodian barracks are terribly clumsy. Maya lets me help."

"Maya lets you?" Margot managed, her voice thick but steadier.

"I bring cookies," Sophia said, as though that explained everything.

Margot huffed a small laugh despite herself. "Of course you do." She shook her head, a smile tugging at her mouth. *Sophia never changed.*

"Your mother would not like it if we sat around all day crying about her. Let's get some lunch. I have some hot gossip." Sophia got up and dodged a few crates.

Her stomach shifted and growled. When was the last time she ate anything? "Lunch? Give me a minute. I have to feed Orion before we leave."

At the word lunch, Orion leapt onto the bed with offended urgency, meowing as though neglected for weeks rather than hours.

Margot smiled for real this time.

"All right," she grumbled. "First, I feed the tyrant."

She filled Orion's bowl and scratched beneath his chin. His fur shimmered faintly in the light. He was the one constant thing after her mother died, a tenth birthday gift. *His name is Orion, and he's yours.*

After being covered in dirt and dust from cleaning all day, she went to the bathroom. She let her curly, bobbed hair fall free of the silk scarf. Tugging through her brown-amber knots, she brushed it back and rolled a pin into the curls the way her mother had taught her. She added rouge to her cheeks. Wetting a spooled brush, she rubbed it across the solid mascara cake and applied it to her lashes. Her mother would turn in her grave if she went out into society with anything less.

She changed into a white blouse and wool skirt, pulled on tights, thick wool socks, and her snow boots.

No more crying, she could almost hear her say. She forced herself to smile in the mirror for the first time in a while.

At her mahogany dresser, she adjusted the gold locket with her mother's picture and a lock of black hair, nestled against the onyx ring threaded on the chain so it rested over her heart.

She lifted her timepiece and traced the inscription on the back: *You deserve it* — she remembered the day he pressed it into her hands — then clasped the buckle closed.

Opening a smooth lacquered box, she lifted her crest from the ruby velvet and rolled it in her hands. The rejection letter lay where she had left it: *we promoted a more qualified applicant.* She crumpled it and tossed it into the bin.

The crest weighed heavily as she pinned it to her blouse.

She was stuck cataloguing and translating, running errands for the elemental societies.

"All right, I'm ready." Margot pulled on her cosy emerald cardigan and tweed overcoat, both somewhat outdated but sturdy. She wound a scarf around her neck and slipped on the hand-knitted gloves Sophia had made her, neat and tightly stitched like all the stylish Aerian ladies wore.

"Be a good boy and don't cause any trouble while I'm gone," Margot said, steadying herself as she petted Orion one last time.

Filthy Mud Trekker

Margot followed on Sophia's heels as excited chatter rippled through the corridors. Clusters of people leaned together, voices low and eager. She had not seen this much commotion since the theme announcement for the upcoming Brumalis celebration.

A poster caught Margot's eye. Love in the Midnight Snow. The Aquaan Society promised the transition from Autumn to Winter would be more eventful than last year. Brumalis was nothing short of dramatic.

"The Northern Mess Hall is this way," Margot said, pointing in the opposite direction.

"I know." Sophia spun, hands clasped behind her back, a sharp harpy's grin curled on her lips. Her smooth citrine hair swished around her head. "We're going to the Southern Hall."

Margot frowned. Why was she going there?

"You'll see," Sophia said.

Snow crunched underfoot as they crossed the commons. The Library Guild had granted Margot a few extra days away from her duties while she grieved. Her mother had died in the middle of Autumn, nearly a full season ago.

The world had moved on. *She had not.*

Sophia's head bobbed, searching for someone within the bustling Hall. She called out to the baker and chatted away to him in her usual friendly manner. If Margot walked up to a stranger and acted like that, they would probably think she had gone completely mad. Of course, she had her librarian duties, and that involved talking to people, but it was more transactional than a genuine connection.

A new poster caught her attention: *78 years since the explosion. A trip back on time. The lessons learned.*

Margot muttered, "Looks like the Historical Guild and the Mycology Department have collaborated again. Great." She paused before the poster longer than she had meant to. *Seventy-eight years?* They always misprinted the dates. With a small, irritated sigh, she eased it from the wall and slipped it into her bag. She would correct it later.

Sophia sped toward her, floating on the wind. "I found him!"

Margot's heart leaped into her throat. "Found who?" She held her beating chest as Sophia glided through the air, feet light as paper.

"The newcomer." Sophia's grin was wide, which meant trouble.

"No wonder people are excited." Margot chewed her lip. What awful stories does he bring?

Sophia was ready to explode with excitement as she entered the Art Gallery. Margot followed with significantly less enthusiasm, her stomach growling in protest.

"Oh," Margot muttered. *"That explains the drama."*

His wide, strong shoulders made him impossible to overlook. A man who had dragged the weather in and deposited it among delicate, perfumed academics. A cloak stained in ways she did not want to imagine. Hair tied back with a leather cord, the aftermath of considering grooming and discarding the notion entirely.

He stood with still, focused intensity. Studying *The Happy Accidents of the Swing* with his hands clasped behind his back. The wanderer had good taste. Unfortunately, he looked as though he wrestled creatures in the dirt for a hobby. The man turned toward them — *oh.*

"Good afternoon," he greeted.

"I'm Sophia," she said, gesturing to Margot, "and this is my best friend!"

"It's a pleasure to meet you both," the newcomer smiled.

Mercy. A devastatingly warm smile hid in his wild, tangled hair. "I hope we are not bothering you." Margot cleared her throat.

"Oh no, not at all." His hair brushed his neck, long enough to be braided. Mud streaked the floor beneath him, threatening the fresh wax polish.

"Do you like this painting? It's one of my favourites," Sophia asked.

"The way the light hits the pink maiden on the swing captures the eye." He pointed to the shading.

"The pink maiden?" Sophia chuckled.

Ugh.

"Is that not what she is?" He blinked between them. "Should it be something else?"

"No," Margot said. "Ignore her. She's… whimsical." She nudged Sophia in the ribs. "Maiden is an apt descriptor."

A small, grateful tilt softened his stern brows.

"Have you checked out the Study Hall yet?" Sophia winced and tried to recover from her nudge.

"Not yet."

"That is a shame. Margot offers tours." Sophia patted her back, pushing until she stumbled.

His eyes glanced between them. "I would like to see everything."

"Are you not staying?" Margot said abruptly, then glanced at the wooden floor pattern.

"The weather is rather horrible. Ms. Iyer has offered me lodging for the time being." He shifted his cloak higher on his chest.

Margot caught the faint scars along his knuckles — pale, crisscrossing stories she did not want to imagine.

Sophia's grin was all mischief. "That's perfect then! Margot will give you a tour."

She opened her mouth to reject him. She disliked it when Sophia volunteered her for things without asking. Her own apartment had become a cocoon, too easy to hide in.

Margot's stomach growled again. She wouldn't even be here if Sophia hadn't lured her in with promises of lunch. Sweetness sharpened her voice. *"I will murder you."*

The man raised his brows. "I don't want to cause trouble."

"Oh, you already have," Margot said. "You trekked mud through a building dedicated to fine art."

She hadn't been that quick since before Mum died.

He looked down at his boots, then back up at her, utterly calm. "I'll clean it," he said. "If you give me a tour?"

Sophia quietly squealed behind them.

Margot huffed and blew a wayward curl out of her face. "Fine. I'll show you around. Someone has to make sure you don't wander into a restricted section, read something you shouldn't, and summon Discordia."

This could be the perfect opportunity to get back into the swing of things. She wanted to make sure they hadn't recategorised her collections.

His smile sharpened, intrigued by her chaos. "I keep hearing that it's… labyrinthine."

"I know it like the back of my hand." She smirked right back.

The newcomer tilted his head. "From what I have seen so far, it will exceed my expectations." He gave her a coy smile and adjusted his cloak.

"So," her eyes dropped to the scars on his hands before she caught herself, "Sophia mentioned you're deciding whether to stay?"

"I am."

"Oh, good." Margot said. "That you have lodging. Not

good that you are… here." She winced.

He huffed a quiet laugh. "I haven't even unpacked, and you're already trying to send me back out there?"

"No," she blurted. "I'm just trying to make conversation."

His gaze flicked over her, curious. "Tell me more about Historia."

She licked her lips. "Well… if you stay until Brumalis, the festival's worth seeing. Lights, wine, garnet — lots of people pretending they're having fun. To celebrate the death of Hiver and the start of a new cycle. It is always worthwhile to go."

Margot's chest squeezed for the first time in a while. From this close, she could see his eyes were a dull grassy-grey; his hair was dark as half-burned wood. Tall, with a slender frame and a good nose. A bit rough around the edges, though, with all that hair.

He stepped closer. "How much wine?"

"Enough to justify terrible decisions."

"Will you be there?"

"Unfortunately."

"*Good,*" he whispered.

Her pulse jumped, her neck tingled.

Sophia cleared her throat, breaking the moment. "Well! That's settled then! Margot will give you a tour and take you to the festival."

"I did not agree to —"

The man smiled devastatingly. "I will have to go then." He ran two fingers down his beard.

Margot hated how her chest clenched. *Hated it.* She loathed attending the festivals, only appearing to steal a few bottles of wine after finishing the setup.

As the newcomer watched her, Margot sensed that leaving would not be as simple as she wanted it to be.

The Bond Between a Lady and Her Felis

Margot returned from lunch and collapsed. Orion leapt onto the bed and curled over her chest, purring like a tiny furnace. Each pass of her fingers down his back eased her tension.

Of course, Sophia had volunteered her for the tour. *Of course she had. It was so painfully Sophia to pretend it was spontaneous.* Margot knew she'd been planning this from the moment she'd mentioned the newcomer's existence. She loved her, but it was like loving a whirlwind that changed her life.

Orion's purr deepened, vibrating straight through her ribs. She let her eyes close. At least he expected nothing from her except head scratches. Her eyes grew heavy and tired.

She felt his weight leave her chest.

Thunk thunk thunk.

Groaning, she rolled over and peered over the edge of the bed.

It was the trash can. The figurine was rattling against the metal as he pawed at the top edge.

"Oh, honey, no. Don't play with that." She groaned and bent over, picking the broken figurine out of the trash.

Mum.

Sorrow struck back mercilessly, and a cold, static feeling prickled along her fingers — a faint glint of a gemstone catching the light inside. "That's odd."

She lifted it toward the window. *What was inside it?* In a moment of pure impulse, she lifted a heavy bookend and shattered the head against her desk.

Sorry, Mum.

An Orb. Dark, swirling colours of onyx and amethyst, glinting in the sunlight — and as she held it up, a rush of static ran along her arm.

What the – The Orb slipped from her fingers with a heavy thunk and rolled across the floorboards, just as she noticed a shape appearing on her right inner wrist. It resembled the —

"I thought you might never find that."

She gasped, pushing herself back against the desk. *Who said that?* She spun around the room, seeing no one except Orion sitting by the trash can. He leapt up onto the bed.

"Margot, it's me, Orion."

That voice was speaking to her? *No. Impossible.*

Orion's amethyst-tipped tail curled around his paws. *"I am your familiar,"* he said. *"I've been observing you for some time now."*

She choked on air. "My familiar? My pet is a Spirit?"

"Felis," he corrected. *"A very dignified one. It has been many years since I have spoken to anyone."*

Margot squeezed her eyes shut. "So I just picked up a rock and now you live in my head?" *Maybe she'd dozed off while lying on the bed. She must have.*

"You are awake."

Feeling faint, she went to him. How was this possible? All she did was —

"When you touched the Orb, we bonded," Orion said. His mouth didn't move.

"Bonded?" Her voice cracked. "By accident?" She paused, stopping herself from reaching out and touching his head. *This was real.* And a significant breach of privacy.

"I assure you, I have been a perfect gentleman for fifteen years. I have never once gazed upon you inappropriately," he clarified. Orion's voice in her head sounded deep and soft, fitting his onyx-and-amethyst fur.

Margot choked. "That's not reassuring! Abyss take me, Orion, were you there for everything?"

A soft rumble of laughter rolled through her skull. She clutched the desk to steady herself. "Wait — can you read my —?"

"Yes," he said, his tone bordering on amusement. *"I can read your mind."*

"Oh no. No, no, no. You should not be inside my head when I'm thinking things."

"The Orb is my conduit. I chose you."

"You chose me? Without asking? That's emotional kidnapping."

He tilted his head. *"Margot, you don't care for me?"*

"Well, sure, as my pet, not… whatever you are." Her voice climbed several octaves. "This is too much."

Margot rubbed her temples and glanced at the stub of a candle on her desk — half-melted, blackened wick. She had never managed more than that, while Sophia could fling leaves around the room without blinking.

If there was a shard of mana in her at all, it learned to stay buried. She could spend hours untangling dead languages. Books never asked her to be more than she was.

When her mother died, the guild arranged a stipend, a quiet apartment, and a bed wide enough for her and Orion. It was enough. It had to be. She twisted her fingers and glimpsed an inky-black mark on her wrist. It felt hot and painful against her sleeve, like a bad sunburn.

She gazed at the faint mark, anger blooming beneath her skin. "Did you brand me?"

"You now bear my insignia."

"Is it possible to break it?"

"Your death will undo the bond." He sat with his tail curled around him.

"Comforting," Margot said. "Just how old are you?" It was

odd that he'd never gone grey around his maw.

Orion's amethyst gaze tracked the Orb in her hand as she chewed on her thumbnail. *"Older than most of your histories. I have lived long enough to watch mortal cities rise, fall, and rise again."*

She threw up her arms. "Of course you are older than civilisation. Why not?"

Orion was a constellation, the grouping of stars known as The Hunter. Well then, this would be a change, having a *thing* in her head, hearing her every thought. Now he could just talk back.

"I'm not a thing, and furthermore..." Orion jumped onto the desk. *"I need to mention something else."*

"There's more?" She picked at the cuticles of her nails, her heart going to give out at this rate, and sprawled onto the floor, the wool carpet scraping her back.

"Your alignment has now been brought to the surface."

"Alignment?" Margot huffed. "I remember that day. They tested me. When I failed, I cried so hard Mum gave me ice cream for dinner. I was very dramatic."

"Soul alignments only rise through strife," Orion said. *"I felt drawn to you when you were a child. You have great power, and I will be your guide."*

"You're telling me I'm a Soul wielder?" She laughed a short, broken sound. That shouldn't be possible.

"Do you doubt me? I will prove it to you. Let's go for a walk, shall we?"

☾

With great reluctance, Margot put on her wool coat and wrapped Orion in a blanket — she did not have to go very far before she felt the rush of emotions from every living thing, the scarf around her neck becoming too tight and hot almost immediately.

It was overwhelming.

As people carried on with their lives around the square of her apartment building, she could sense what they were feeling.

"It's… terrifying. Beautiful and chaotic at the same time."

Each mortal she focused on had an ever-shifting light within them that changed with their moods, their hearts.

Their beating hearts had colours.

Tears welled up in her eyes.

"Let's go inside. I am cold," Orion purred through her knitted sweater.

As they made their way back inside, she sensed the auras dim.

"Please. Please tell me you can help me before tomorrow. I cannot show a stranger around while eavesdropping on everyone's emotions."

She set Orion down, crossed her arms over her eyes, and lay on her bed to block out the light.

Her lunch churned in her stomach. "I cannot go back to work. Everyone will think I'm insane." She hugged her legs. "I will never get laid again." A bit of the ache in her chest eased.

"I can teach you to hone your alignment, only feel the hearts of mortals when you want to," Orion said. *"I have done this many times, and I will do it again for you."*

Work in a few days. Twelve-hour shifts with people's feelings bombarding her, like they had in the square. She could not handle it.

It would be torture.

"All right. Fine. Let's do this. But if I explode, I'm haunting you." She reluctantly sat up on the bed.

Soul Wielder

☾

Her back ached, the cushion she was sitting on was lumpy, and the floorboards were unforgiving. The candle beside her had burned low, leaving a curl of smoke and a wax puddle hardened in the saucer. A half-read journal rested on her knee.

"Just breathe in, and out," Orion purred, his amethyst eyes closed in blank meditation.

She flipped over the torn poster she'd tucked in her bag. Soul wielding: taboo, dangerous, and apparently something she could do now. Her throat tightened. *Wonderful.* What happened to Soul wielders? Nothing good, judging by the Council's fondness for rules.

She would have to research more when she returned to work.

Orion had not been very helpful; he refused to answer her questions. He'd only warned her not to share her newfound alignment with anyone. *"Focus."*

She shut her eyes. "Easier said than done."

Her apartment smelled of old paper, lavender soap, and a trace of ink that always stained her fingers. She could sense the flickering pulse of Orion's aura in the candlelit dark.

She'd been practising for hours. Her stomach squelched, a stubborn reminder that she was supposed to have dinner with Sophia. *"Refocus,"* Orion repeated. *"And then you can leave."*

Bossy little star-beast. She inhaled and focused on the amethyst glow around him. The soft sheen around his heart when she reached for it with her *mana.* She pushed at it, willing it to dim. To disappear. *For goodness' sake, just be quiet.*

Orion huffed. *"All Soul wielders use this technique when their alignment first surfaces. Just push the aura back."*

She clenched her jaw and concentrated. She forced her mind to be clear, quashing the glow. She kept others' feelings at bay unless she willed them. Not on the ticking clock. Not on the fireplace crackle. *"Imagine the shove of the ocean,"* Orion said. *"The slam of a door."*

A wave of quiet washed through her. An inner space opened: stacks of books, a cosy chair — her mental equivalent of a broom closet. Margot opened her eyes. "I did it!" She'd done it after hours of effort and two mental breakdowns.

Orion climbed into her lap. She stroked his soft fur, half-expecting him to scold her for treating him like a regular house pet. He didn't; he purred instead. *"Well done,"* he said. *"You are quite a talented Soul wielder when motivated."*

"I wouldn't be able to do it without you," she said, continuing to pet him. "Or rather, the threat of disappointing you."

"I will teach you many things in time."

"Like what?" Margot asked, fingers still at his chin.

"I suppose we begin with simple glamouring. Then emotional influence. And eventually, alchemy."

Well, damn. That all sounded… interesting. She blinked. "You're starting me with becoming a shapeshifting, emotionally manipulating alchemist? Not a single warm-up exercise?"

Glamouring, the art of masking and concealing. "Maybe I could use it on an irate researcher after I mis-catalogued their book. Or when I'm trying to sweet-talk the elder Librarians into giving me an extra-long break."

She felt Orion's deep laugh echo in her head. Even though his face stayed blank, she knew he was amused. *"We shouldn't get ahead of ourselves."*

Alchemy, though. The whispers of Fenn and his Canis soldiers made her stomach churn. Researchers pretended the art was dead, yet Historia Weekly had reported sightings along the city's borders were becoming more frequent. *Mercy.* "I'm not someone who could make Soul creatures," she said. "I can barely make tea without scalding myself."

Orion jumped off her lap to face her, his black tail curling around his feet. *"Soul wielding is the art of transformation,"* he said. *"You can turn what mortals sense — what they smell, hear, feel — into something else. It is not evil unless you make it so."*

Her stomach squelched.

"You may go to dinner," Orion said.

"About time." She glanced at the clock on the mantelpiece. Another charming thing she loved about this apartment was the ornate, carved marble fireplace, shaped by a master Terra wielder. Six Spirits danced along the stone — three in white, three in black — intertwined in exquisite detail.

One for each alignment, she mused. Margot chewed her lip and decided she had time for a bath. Keeping this secret would be harder than she'd thought, especially from people who knew her better than she knew herself. She'd promised Sophia they'd meet for dinner at her family's estate, a new tradition that had started after her mother died.

She hadn't expected that tradition to come with secrets. She was a terrible liar. *What would happen if anyone found out? Would the Council lock her up?*

She sank into the bath and let the hot water soak the day from her bones. Orion's lessons dulled the noise at the edge of her mind. She pressed against the mental shield she had built — closing the door on auras, on hearts, on anyone else's feelings.

Quiet. For the first time since the square.

She got out of the bath. After wrapping a towel around herself, she found Orion sleeping in his nest by the window.

She couldn't hear his voice as she stroked his head. He chirped in his sleep.

Good. She could still sense his aura, but it was manageable. She dressed in a long plaid skirt and a black turtleneck jumper. She did her best to hide the new mark on her wrist.

Frustration grew as she saw a new scratch on her weathered bag. To celebrate Margot becoming a Maven, her mother had gifted it to her. She slung the leather bag over her wool coat and tucked in a scarf. She kissed Orion's forehead. *"Won't be long."*

As she stepped into the hall, her mind was quiet, but her secret thrummed within her.

Aerian Estate

☾

She paused near the abandoned estate on her way to Sophia's, drawn to it the way she always was when her thoughts felt too loud. It was one of the oldest in Historia, and it looked it.

Weeds overgrew the gate, the diamond panes on the windows were always dark, and the chimneys never smoked. A shame — rain had darkened the intricate carvings in the stonework, and vines of ivy climbed the grey brick walls.

The wind hissed through the cracks in the shutters and cut straight through her coat, needling her bones.

Sophia's family's estate was among the biggest in the city. Home to over five generations of Aerians seeking refuge from Alces, the great Elk Spirit of the East. In their youth, Sophia told horrible stories of how her ancestors were ordered to wield the very air in a person's chest.

She pulled her sleeve over her hand, steadied herself, and lifted the harpy doorknocker.

Sophia opened the door and gave her a warm hug, then pulled away to examine her. "You look different."

"Do I?" Margot removed her coat, hung it, and attempted to appear composed, as though she hadn't just bonded with a Spirit after lunch.

Sophia came closer to her, her eyes roaming over Margot's face. "Have you been using a new moisturiser? Your skin looks great."

Margot chuckled. "No, just the usual." She ran a hand through and shook out her curls, smoothing her still-wet hair. Her hair was a fickle thing with a mind of its own, not drying the same way twice. She tugged her sleeves and folded her hands together.

Hide the wrist. Hide the crisis.

She followed Sophia through the ornate archway from the foyer into the formal dining room, greeting Mr. and Mrs. Meyer with kisses on their cheeks. They had always been kind to her.

The aroma of dinner filled the room as she took her seat. "Smells wonderful as always, Lenora," Margot said, scooping mashed potatoes.

"Oh, thank you, darling." Lenora took a sip of her wine.

Sophia's classical looks perfectly matched her mother's. Lenora was wearing a striking deep blue that brought out her pale aquamarine eyes, contrasting with her straight, greying-citrine hair. She always wore expensive fabrics, something Margot could not afford and would only end up spilling ink on.

Lenora sat across from Margot. She caught the faint flicker of Lenora's heart before she could stop herself. It was black-green and soft at the edges. *Lovely.*

"Are you excited to get back to the Library soon, Margot?" Anthony Meyer Sr. said. He took a measured sip of red wine and pierced her with his gaze.

She pushed out her shield, cutting herself off from the auras. She hadn't meant to slip. "Yes, I am. I am taking the newcomer on a tour tomorrow."

Anthony was a quiet man, his one passion was keeping the city running smoothly and on time — short salt-and-pepper hair swept back from his widow's peak, rounded glasses framing his face. He had the air of a man who could reschedule your life with a single memo.

She took another forkful of garlic mashed potatoes, the creamy texture melting in her mouth. *Spirits have mercy, this is good.* The food at the Mess Hall was okay, but she wished she could eat like this every day.

Anthony's shoulders relaxed. She could sense a faint blue aura coming from him. "Oh, wonderful. I hope you can convince him to stay. We need his expertise." He continued to cut the roasted vegetables. "I heard from Maya that he killed a Canis on his way here."

Margot's pulse lurched. She shuddered at the thought of seeing one of those Soul creatures in the Taxidermy Hall. "He does not look strong enough to take down a Canis," she said, spearing a buttered carrot.

On a good day, maybe shred a book. But a Canis? Perhaps the newcomer was hiding muscles under his cloak.

"Looks can be deceiving." Sophia looked at Margot.

"I will do my best to show him the best this city can offer." She took a big sip of her white wine. She could at the very least guide him to the epic adventure books.

After dinner, Sophia herded Margot upstairs.

Margot envied Sophia's wealth in the way one might envy a particularly well-fed house pet. Her rooms were an autumnal paradise of garnet, sapphire, and emerald — the bedroom alone was bigger than Margot's entire apartment, with two large adjoining rooms. Margot sat and picked at the gold leaves embroidered on the cushion.

"What was that?" Sophia crossed her arms, shutting the door behind them. "Don't hide it. You've been out of sorts since you arrived."

She had her usual *Sophia Scowl Face* on. Margot knew she couldn't hide this from her. "How could you tell?"

Sophia scoffed and pointed. "You're wearing your watch on the wrong hand."

Margot uttered a silent *fuck.* Once, she lied about sneaking one of Sophia's cookies before they were done. Sophia just glared at Margot with her arms crossed in the same way.

Pout and all. Some things never changed.

She sighed, pulled up her sleeve, and took off her watch to reveal the mark. "Orion is a Spirit. We are now bonded, and I can communicate with him." There was no use in trying to deny it.

Sophia took a step back, blinking a few times before opening and shutting her mouth. "He… what…"

Margot collected her thoughts and tried to explain as best she could. To her credit, she only got sidetracked once, going on a tangent about heart reading.

Sophia took everything in stride. "Margot, that's quite overwhelming." She took a breath and thumbed over Margot's Rune mark as if she were trying to erase it.

"I know… it just happened after lunch." Margot picked at the cushion, the threading coming apart in tiny ribbons.

Sophia said, "You're a…" but stopped herself.

"I am a what?" Margot pressed.

Sophia swallowed. "You're a protectorate now."

Margot stilled. A protectorate. Her mother had known. Orion had been waiting. All of it — the figurine, the Orb hidden inside it — suddenly felt less like coincidence and more like a path she had been walking without knowing it. She pressed her palm flat against her knee to stop her hand from shaking.

"A protectorate? But that's impossible…"

"Evelyn came over. I didn't know she could climb that high…" Sophia cleared her throat. "She came through my window, speaking of the previous Council, before they had a voting majority eighty years ago."

Margot's breath caught, her heart leapt. "My mother?" She asked, taken aback by the information her friend had been keeping from her.

Sophia took a shuddering breath. "Before the Council came into power, a group of six wielders — *the protectorate* — bonded with Spirits to protect the city. Back then, Aerian councillors erased the Spirits' names from records. I remember thinking as a wieldling that it was odd your mother named a felis after Orion."

Her anxiety curled in her stomach. "How…?"

"She stole something from the Council and told me to protect you. I think she always knew Orion was a Spirit."

"When did she say this to you?" Margot got up and started pacing, shuffling her feet on the cream carpet.

"Around a week before she…" Sophia stopped. Tears welled in the corners of her eyes. She sniffed. "Before she passed away."

Margot's heart was beating wildly in her chest.

Sophia turned to her shelf and pulled a notebook free. "Eve wanted you to have this. She visited and told me to protect you, then gave me this — to give to you."

It had the same looping symbol that was on her wrist.

"Her words were: *Margot will know it when she sees it.*"

Margot untied the ribbon lace. Handwritten in Old Frianc, a beautiful looping script. Of course, her mother left her homework. She translated the first few lines. "*…Orion said the expedition will take several months. I am hesitant to leave the shields, but he has put together a team. Theodore, two Aerian combat doctors, and three Ignians. Hopefully, I can make it back in time for Rich's birthday…*"

The handwriting wasn't her mother's, nor anyone she recognised. She'd have to read this later, when she wasn't one revelation away from a meltdown. She tucked the notebook into her book bag. Her fingers buzzed, and a tingle ran over her arm.

The Orb's *mana* chilled her hands. Without a second thought, she hid the Orb in her bag. It felt wrong to leave it at home. She showed it to Sophia. Perhaps she knew something about the glowing thing.

"What's this?" Sophia said.

Margot sensed Sophia's aura change.

The power slithered under Sophia's skin — then recoiled, glowing a pale blue. Sophia handed it back. "That wasn't meant for Air," Sophia said as she rubbed her hands together, a faint glow fading with each shake.

A flicker of pride warmed Margot's chest. The Orb had chosen her. Finally, something had. "I'm going to do research soon. Until then, can you keep this secret?" She pleaded.

Margot knew she could trust Sophia.

Sophia sat with her on the bed. "Of course. I just want you to be careful. Do not say a word to anyone."

It had been a long and strange day. She wanted to go home and nap for a week.

As they hugged, Margot reached out with her *mana*. Sophia's aura flickered, tight and shimmering. *Fear. Worry.* Margot knew there was more information Sophia wanted to say. The Aerian Society would shun her for telling any secrets.

Sophia pulled back first, clearing her throat. "Are you excited to show our newcomer around?" she asked, her voice too bright, too quick. Sophia's attempt at changing the subject.

Margot blinked. *Books.* It would be nice to smell paper, ink, leather, and dust again. Her thoughts drifted through the to-do lists that had been piling up: shelves to reorganise, collections to catalogue, languages to translate. *A nice, normal avalanche of work.*

She nodded. "It would be good to see the Library again."

Amelia, the newest Inkling graduate, had just passed the exam before her mother died. Margot hadn't had the strength to give her the proper training. A pang tightened in her chest. "I hope they haven't changed the system too much on me while I've been gone."

Sophia giggled, the sound trembling at the edges. "That

isn't what I was trying to say," she said and stroked Margot's arm. "I meant… what do you think of Nikolas?"

Oh, this again.

"I'm looking forward to talking to him too," Margot answered. She had honestly forgotten him until Anthony brought him up at dinner. He seemed friendly. He was interesting only because he was a newcomer. *Well, that and the whole Canis-killing rumour.*

Sophia hesitated, then pressed on. "Make sure you show him around. And maybe… convince him to stay? Father was saying earlier," her voice wavered, "before you arrived — that we need him. His strength could bolster our defences." A flicker of pain rippled through her aura.

She reached over and touched Sophia's hand, wanting to test her powers — wanting to understand. Her aura glowed a quiet blue. *Sadness? Or something else tugging beneath it?*

"I'll give him a tour," Margot said. "I promise."

NIKOLAS VENATOR

Six Alignments

✹

Third time's the charm.

Nikolas climbed the steps toward the Library again, boots scraping ivory stone worn smooth by centuries — the marble and inlaid brass foyer opening around him in a sweeping circle, twelve pillars forming a perfect ring beneath the coloured glass dome, light spilling and splintering into shifting blues and greens along the walls.

He paused beneath it every time. *Mortal hands weren't supposed to build things this beautiful. Nothing mortal felt this grand.*

Nikolas had spent hours trying to track the librarian, approaching the circular desk each time expecting to be turned away. The guards had rejected him twice, and both times she had vanished into another corridor the moment he arrived.

"Against protocol," they said.

"No unauthorised mortals," they repeated.

He braced himself for round three until she stepped through the fractured light. She looked as though she had walked out of one of the stained glass panels, curls bouncing, gold spectacles sliding down her nose. The last time he had seen her, she had been sharp and wary. Now, her face warmed the moment she saw him.

"It is alright, Glenn. I've got this one." She patted the guard's arm and hung her glasses from the chain at her collar. Her warm eyes lifted to his. "Good to see you,

Nikolas."

The way she said his name sent shivers crawling up the back of his neck. Absurd for a man his age, over a librarian with ink on her fingers. "I... thank you for the opportunity."

A tiny twitch pulled at the corner of her mouth. "Yes. Protocol. I am sure you understand."

Her eyes were a stunning mix of emerald, gold, and amber. She looked away first, turning toward the circular desk beneath the dome. Behind it stood a marble statue of a woman holding an open book and lifting a staff skyward.

The librarian collected her leather bag. A curl slipped forward. She tried to tuck it behind her ear, failed, and let it fall with a small, embarrassed huff.

He huffed a silent laugh.

Around him, workers in coordinated emerald knitted sweaters and vests moved with quiet precision and speed. Nikolas felt feral by comparison, a wild thing that had wandered into a gentleman's parlour.

"I put together a route," she said, pulling a leather-bound notebook from her bag. "It has been a while since I visited each Hall. Shall we walk through them?"

"That sounds good."

Her brows lifted. "Most newcomers try to skip sections."

"I am not most people."

"That remains to be seen," she said, tucking the same curl behind her ear. "The Study Hall is a maze. People get lost."

"I have a good sense of direction."

"Is that what you call it?" Her tone was mild, dipped in amusement. "Confidence disguised as skill?"

Nikolas fought a smile. "You wound me."

She peered over her spectacles, far too knowing for someone he had only met once. "You will survive." She adjusted the strap of her satchel and walked ahead, giving him a small, restrained smile.

Nikolas felt rewarded by it.

Her heels clicked across the polished wooden floor as she fell into a guide's cadence. "Four Halls divide the second floor, one for each alignment."

They stepped beneath a shimmering white-blue arch. "This is the Aquaan Hall," she said.

Pale stone carved the Hall's pillars, the roof casting a cerulean light that ebbed and flowed. "We have an impressive collection of preserved sea creatures. The Vulpine bring back skeletons from their trips."

He looked at a painting of a Selkie carrying a severed head. "That's dramatic," Nikolas murmured.

As she walked, the stained glass cast waves of azure across her face, brushing her cheeks and catching in her curls. "Aquaans can influence emotion through their voices," she continued. "Compulsion, if they are skilled." She paused, eyes dragging over him for a fraction too long — his shoulders, his jaw, the way he stood. She lifted her hand toward the painting of half-human creatures with long tails and haunting expressions. "Halfway people can be calm one moment and violent the next."

He cleared his throat. "Are there many Aquaans here?"

"Oh yes. Aurora, our head councillor, has the most beautiful voice. If you decide to stay, you will hear her at Brumalis."

"That sounds enticing," Nikolas blurted. He smoothed his beard to cover the slip.

Her lip quirked. "*Enticing?* You say that like the singing alone might persuade you."

They moved into ruby light. Intricate stained glass depicted a flaming feathered Ave fighting a reptilian creature with clashing claws and teeth. Nikolas could have stared at the window forever and still uncovered a minor detail that shifted with the sunlight.

She stopped in front of a glass case with legionnaire armour. "This armour belonged to *Acer the Swift.*"

Nikolas' jaw tightened, old memories flaring hot — Kit Sun had trained Ignian legionnaires to the bone, only to send them to slaughter Fenn's soldiers. He still remembered the haunted look on Erik's face the day he'd pulled him out.

"People celebrate the Summer Solstice of Calor with a dance festival from sunrise to sunset." The librarian lifted her arms and gestured toward the painting of naked women dancing around a pyre.

"The Ignians know how to party," Nikolas chuckled.

A quiet laugh escaped her lips. "They do," she said, nudging his arm with her elbow. "They can be rash if they are not careful."

Nikolas knew Ignians who brawled in taverns and got tossed out before they set fire to the roof.

Soft amber lighting cooled the Hall. The librarian reached up toward a book on a tall shelf, her fingers brushing the spine, and let out a soft whine of protest.

Without thinking, he reached up and took it for her. "Here," he said.

She locked her eyes on him, not the book. He noticed the sweet smell of white florals mingled with the woodsy sandalwood of her perfume. Her ears flushed red. "Thank you."

He stepped back, though not far.

She cleared her throat. "Aerians specialise in strategy, research, and can shape storms."

"And you?" he asked. "Do you have an alignment?"

She froze for a single breath. "No. I am ungifted."

She was lying. He felt the shift hit him like a bruise, tender and unmistakable — and let it go. *Mortals lied for odd reasons, even when they didn't intend to.*

Emerald light washed the shelves. Petrichor clung to the

air.

"These were so caked in mud they took months to restore," she said, stroking the book spine. Dirt smudged her finger, and she wiped it on her skirt with a huff. "Terran-aligned mortals can live beyond two hundred years."

"I have never met a Terran," he mused.

"They are introverts. They prefer plants and rocks to people." She laughed behind her hand.

"I can understand that," Nikolas said, trying not to smile.

"People can be the worst sometimes." She gave him a sly smile.

He hoped she smiled like that again. "I hope I am not one of those people."

"Oh, you are perfect company." The compliment slipped out. She realised it too late, cheeks flushing.

He swallowed. He should not want her flustered, yet he found a quiet pleasure in causing it. He opened his mouth —

She stepped back. The moment snapped.

The librarian looked away, pretending to examine a crooked statue.

He turned to study a painting, yet his mind drifted.

Between the shelves, statues of Terra creatures stood like guardians. Lumps of moulded stone that might have been rodenta, hares, or moles. Above them hung paintings of grassy fields, lakes mirroring the sky, and people dancing around a pole.

Nikolas wanted to ask about it, but they'd never leave. Not that he would have minded. *She talked like each detail mattered. Like each fragment of lore deserved love.* He realised he was watching her more than the artefacts, measuring the rhythm of her steps beside his.

She looked up at him, and for one suspended heartbeat, neither of them moved.

Anika Nagy

Day and Night

✹

"Would you like to see the Day and Night Halls next?" the librarian's voice cut through his thoughts.

Nikolas blinked. *Had they made a full loop?* His feet did not want to stop. "Lead the way." Dust motes danced, reflecting the light from the windows. He gazed at the grand, towering statue in the centre of the Hall.

They walked down the stairs in comfortable silence.

Night, or Soul, as the adorable librarian called it, had a soft, dark glow, shifting through various shades of amethyst pricked with pinpoints of light.

"This place is my favourite," she said, her lips parted, the starlight catching in her eyes.

No wonder this was her favourite. He could have stood there for hours, watching the colours shift and melt, creating new hues and shades. "The Night Hall has most of our mortal history books and family lineages within Historia." She tilted her head up to the ceiling. "This is where we store any research on Soul creatures." Her soft smile scattered his thoughts.

It was unfair how lovely she looked, lost in wonder.

The Study Hall was the second most impressive thing he had ever seen. He sat beside her on a bench — closer than he should have been.

Fatigue settled into his bones, heavy and familiar. Nikolas had encountered plenty of Soul creatures in his life — none of them friendly, all of them eager to take a bite. If a Canis got a whiff of his scent, he had to move.

Again.

He rested his head against the wall, wishing Fenn would leave him alone after so many years of running.

The librarian sat in silence, her hand resting on her chin in thought. He had never encountered a mind like hers — overflowing yet steady, a river with hidden depth. The notes in her head were chaotic and layered, melodies colliding while others looped far off, unresolved, and yet she seemed perfectly calm.

"Tell me what you're thinking."

"None of the other librarians will have the guts to tell you." She paused. "They outlawed Soul and Spirit wielding eighty years ago." Her voice dropped. "Alchemy too."

Nikolas stopped breathing. His heart was in his throat. *They outlawed Spirit wielding here?* "Why?"

She leaned in, close enough that her breath brushed his jaw. "I don't know. Nobody will tell me."

He reached for his sword. *Shit.* Confiscated. He did not want to fight innocent mortals to escape — and leaving now meant the blizzard, numb fingers, whiteout skies, another night measured in heartbeats.

He took a measured, calming breath. "Sounds like a question I'd want to answer." He buried the instinct that reared its ugly head, the dread coiling in his gut and urging him to escape and hide.

"Exactly!" She beamed at him. "I knew you were a smart one."

Nikolas' heart gave a too-quick stutter that he was not expecting. *Brute or beast* — that was all he ever was to them. Her praise slid under his ribs. He cleared his throat and stood, holding out his gloved hand. "Want to keep going?"

She pinned him with her eyes. "I'd like that." She grasped his hand.

As they moved from under the mezzanine and into the circular space, the quiet chatter grew louder. Overhead, the midday light dimmed, and the sconces glowed with amber warmth.

She gave a brief nod and a shy smile to a coworker as they passed around the desk and into the Hall. A beautiful, slow-shifting glow shimmered across the roof with a rainbow haze. "The Day Hall is where we keep our information about Spirits."

Nikolas clenched his fists. "Superior Spirits think we are nothing more than tiny, fleeting things that do not deserve mercy." Bennu once said Nikolas was no better than bugs crawling in dirt.

"I suppose you'd be the expert."

"I did not mean to say that." He shuffled back.

She shook her head. "I just meant that I have seen nothing outside the walls. I have spent my whole life in the Study Hall or at home reading."

"You'd want to leave?" he asked, too interested.

She twisted her finger around her gold necklace and rubbed the pendant before answering. "I have everything I need here."

"Trust me, you are much better off living here." He kept the Interwilds to himself. He didn't want to scare her.

Beyond the stacks, Nikolas noticed a map at the back of the Hall. It was a perfect recreation of Torresium, spanning wide and reaching the top of the wall. The circular borders of Spirit cities shifted and blended together. Kit Sun's bubble was the largest, with Fenn pressed against its southern border. Bennu's city sat high on Mount Ophion. *Aquila* stood out in red, moving along a mountain ridge before stopping, then disappearing.

Despite its detail, Nikolas could not find his hometown. A familiar hollowness opened in his chest. "Where are we?" he asked, before he could stop himself.

She stepped beside him, their shoulders brushing. "We are located here."

It was an ideal position, with a thick forest on one side, two layers of walls, and an ocean beyond the cliffs. "Is this map current?"

"Yes. A powerful Terra wielder created it over four centuries ago."

He followed the librarian down the corridor, weaving through the stacks. In the corner of his eye, he saw it. A marble statue tucked into an alcove, sitting upright with tails wrapped around its legs on a pedestal.

The sculptor captured the several fluffy tails and individual fur strokes. He ached to touch it, to feel how soft it was, knowing she'd slap his hand. Instead, he read the plaque: *Vulpecula Vulpina Adamantina.*

"Someone discovered it in an old annex," the librarian said. "I have tried translating. Unfortunately, it's in a dead script, which could have multiple interpretations."

"It's a Vulpine, right?"

She nodded, excited.

Nikolas stared into the Vulpine's eyes longer than he should have. It captivated him, pristine except for a single battle scar revealing long predator teeth. "So you truly have never met Historia?"

"No, of course not. They died in the great cataclysm. It is said that before Historia died, they created the Twelve Tables."

"The Twelve Tables?"

"I will show you. Follow me."

The Twelve Pillars surrounding the Study Hall each bore a plaque. Nikolas had assumed they were decorative. Each brass etching was no larger than an average book, detailing the governing rules for all mortals living within Historia.

He struggled to read the symbols. They seemed familiar. Nikolas realised Kit Sun and Fenn were bound by the same laws. Superior Spirits tried to twist the Twelve Tables to their advantage. Historia's law applied to them as well.

It had grown dark. His stomach growled as he rubbed it.

"Hungry?" the librarian chuckled as she checked her timepiece. "Spirits have mercy, I have talked your ear off for over four hours."

Nikolas met her eyes. "I savoured every second."

She looked away, a hint of blush warming her freckled cheeks. "I can show you the Mess Hall." She tucked a wayward strand of hair behind her ear, the same one that kept slipping free.

He nodded. "I'd like that."

She steered them toward the Northern Mess Hall without hesitation.

✷

Talking to Margot did not feel like work, and that alone made him wary — she had endless knowledge and fantastic stories about the city and its people, and yet she avoided discussing wielding entirely. Which was odd, because she was lying about having an alignment.

"Can I ask you something?"

"Anything," he replied, removing his gloves to eat.

"What is it like living in the Interwilds?"

Ah. There it was.

He sighed, breaking crusty bread and soaking it in his stew. "If you are fortunate, you live in a warded village, protected by a couple of wielders. Outside the boundary, you fight Soul creatures. You can also live in a Spirit city, under their protection, but you live by their rules."

"That doesn't seem so bad." She leaned in, her attention fixed entirely on him.

"Well," he dusted his hands. "There is the Superior Spirit Kit Sun, the Emperor and Empress of the North. I have helped fire wielders escape their city."

"They want to escape?" Her fork froze halfway to her mouth.

"And Fenn, the Wolf of the South. If you wield, they indoctrinate you into their army. Kit Sun and Fenn wage constant war, forcing their wielders into battles that have lasted years."

"Alces looks elegant," Margot said. "But pretentious?"

Nikolas let out a low laugh. "Pretentious is a polite word for him."

She tilted her head, curious.

"I have passed through once or twice," he said. "You do not need sharp ears to hear complaints."

Margot snorted into her potatoes. "And their complaint was?"

The sound tugged a smile from him before he could stop it. "That their Elk lord demands order," he said. "Everyone competes. Expensive fabrics, rare gemstones. Polite to the point of suffocation in public, backstabbing in private. Alces encourages it and forbids anyone from eating something with a heartbeat."

She scoffed. "Strict vegetarians? Really?"

"It is not the food," he said, his voice cooling. "It is class warfare. Everyone desperate to impress a Spirit who barely acknowledges them." He rubbed his thumb over the scar on his knuckle. "It is exhausting."

Margot stifled a laugh. "Have you ever seen any Spirits that won't form bonds with mortals?"

"I can think of one."

She perked up, mouth half open. "Which?"

"Historia."

Her spoon stilled. *"That is right. We do not have a Superior Spirit,"* she whispered, the realisation settling over her.

From what he had gathered, the city had survived something vast, a catastrophe burned into its bones. Historia emptied their well eight hundred years ago to raise a shield and hide the city from the Interwilds.

And it worked too well.

How had it stayed hidden for so long? Why were there no stories, no warnings? Cities did not vanish without reason.

She went silent, thinking.

On instinct, he opened his senses. His pulse jumped. Her thoughts burst into sound, too loud and layered, a dozen melodies clashing at once. He cut off his senses.

Margot inhaled and nodded to herself. "I'm staying in Historia."

"I am considering staying, too," he said. The words escaped him, heavier than he had intended.

Nikolas shouldn't have felt anything for her — certainly not the low ache curling under his ribs. And yet he waited for her reaction.

"I get it. You need to trust us first." Margot smiled, warm enough to disarm him. "If you ever want company, I have weekends off, and my shift ends at five." She reached out and touched his hand.

His pulse tightened. *Shit. He might actually stay for a while.*

MARGOT WILSON

Hearts and Dreams

☾

Margot was back in her apartment, having a small meltdown. *"This is bad. Oh, this is terrible."* She paced the room. *"When I touched his hand, I sensed his aura. Night cloaked him."* Shadows slithering under his skin — something was going on beneath that calm exterior.

"Calm yourself." Orion had been happily sleeping in his perch bed by the window before she arrived.

Margot was breathing hard, chewing her thumbnail to the quick. "The newcomer." Her voice dropped. "His aura was terrifying. Blood-red eyes. A black mane." She swallowed. "A beast."

"Interesting," Orion murmured, unconcerned.

"What does it mean?" she asked Orion, who watched her pace back and forth with amethyst eyes.

"You connected with his heart. It was merely a vision." Orion yawned and scratched his ear.

"Wonderful, so now I can't touch anyone?"

"Your alignment is new. This was going to happen."

"How much longer?"

"You cannot master this overnight. It will take patience and hard work."

Great. Just great.

After a long day, Margot was sticky. She showered, changed into flannel pyjamas, and sat at her desk to review the notes she'd taken before meeting Nikolas. A newspaper article reported the Council outlawed Soul wielding after two prominent wielders died, providing little information on the subject.

They moved all Soul wielding knowledge to a secure archive — even as a Maven she'd need a special permit, and the Curatrix monitored every request. Her stomach sank. She could not risk drawing attention to herself.

Margot sighed, leaned back in her chair and stretched until her back popped. *So tired.* Her throat felt raw; she had talked the newcomer's ear off for hours, and he had listened to every word — asked the right questions, noticed the right details.

When she rattled off facts or stories, the only people who really listened to her were the wieldlings.

Rummaging through her book bag, she took out a battered tome: *Asterism Scientia: Celestial Rune Spirits.*

Margot considered herself lucky to have found the only reference to Rune Orbs in the entire Study Hall — she'd gone looking for Soul wielding books, found no reference cards in the catalogue drawer, and only stumbled across the little tome by chance, tucked near the back and covered in thick dust.

During the purge, the Council must have overlooked it… or someone had tried to hide it.

Another unsettling detail snagged at Margot's thoughts. There was not a single reference to Spirit wielding anywhere in the Library catalogue. If Soul wielding was its natural opposite, then why did they erase them too? *Historia was home to four, not six, wielding societies.*

She pushed her reading spectacles up and scribbled notes in her leather journal. *The Astra Lapidem, commonly known as Rune Orbs, are a collection of six gemstones that serve as conduits for the essence of Spirits. These Orbs are carriers of cosmic energy, granting vast amounts of mana and elevating the wielder's power tenfold.*

"Well, damn."

"I could have told you that." Orion stretched, his tail curling.

"It's still nice to know," she retorted.

She continued reading. *They are selective, only bonding with those they deem deserving. This society knows little about how Spirits choose their wielder, but theorises the mortal must align with the Spirit's own mana.*

Her *mana* aligns with Orion's? "So you are a Soul creature."

"No. I will allow no one, not even you, to compare me to those creatures."

She gasped and leaned backward, sensing the shift in his aura from amethyst to a darker onyx — her fountain pen dropping onto the notebook with a dull thud.

Orion hopped from his perch and leaped onto the desk, letting Margot look into his swirling eyes. *"I will not lead you down a path of evil. Soul is the other half of Spirit's coin."* His eyes burned deep. *"Heart, not Mind."*

She shuddered a breath — Orion wasn't dangerous, even if he was holding back details. "How can you be a Soul Spirit? That seems contradictory."

"Spirits have an alignment, just like mortals. Kit Sun's alignment is to Ignis, and they bond only with fire wielders."

His lecture was not over. Orion leapt from the desk and claimed his spot again — *so cranky* — and the hairs prickled on the back of her neck.

"Grab that mana crystal from the shelf."

She sighed. Orion was worse than her mother.

"I disagree with your comparison. I am a fine teacher. Now hurry."

With a scrape against the floorboards, she slid the chair out and went to her bookshelf, glancing over the many objects her mother had left her before grabbing the crystal. It was a clear prism no bigger than her hand. "Got it."

"Good. Do you see that rainbow? No clear border, just a spectrum? That is the alignments coming together."

She nodded. Spirit wielding is the light, and Soul is the dark that shadows it. She sat back at her desk and continued to read, jotting notes in her notebook as she went. *Many people have long sought Rune Orbs not for their material worth, but because they increase mana regeneration when a wielder touches them, feeding their well.*

Too tired to continue reading. She took off her spectacles and rubbed her nose — her studies could wait until tomorrow.

"I believe," Orion said, *"it's time we found your staff."*

"My staff?"

"Yes, it's essential for your training."

"Was it stolen or lost?"

"You ask many questions, young one."

"I work in a Library," she said, her voice flat. "Curiosity and a thirst for knowledge is in my nature."

"Very well. Eighty years ago, the Spirit wielder that carried the Lucerna Orb caused an explosion. My previous bonded, Olivia, died in the blast. The Council, in its infinite wisdom, stole the power of the well for themselves, waiting until two bonded remained."

"The Council covered up the real reason for the explosion and banned Spirit and Soul wielding too?" She opened her senses to Orion's sorrow. *"I am sorry you've been suffering."* She reached over and gave him a quick pet on the head. He didn't object. He moved to rest on her lap. "So, what are you saying? I need this staff back?"

"As my second, you will use it to maintain your position within Historia. Nobody will stand in your way once you do. Until then, we are both vulnerable."

"What does the staff do?"

"The Anima Staff is a powerful tool and is the key to the vault."

"Which vault?"

"Are you a glossy crimson lory? No. Stop parroting questions and focus. The archive vault contains my grimoires, including decades of research on the ley lines, and I cannot continue my work until I open it."

Margot racked her brain, putting bits and pieces together. Her mother and the senior mavens only discussed the sealed door in the museum basement during annual inspections. Margot had inquired once before, but her mother dismissed her, ordering her to continue translating a tedious journal from a Terran herbalist.

"How did you become a felis?"

Orion went still in her arms, then moved to his nest beside the window. *"Your mother did it to me."*

"How? She was not a Soul wielder."

"Yes, she was."

Her heart stuttered. *Mum lied to her?* There was a bigger story, and she was determined to find out. She was unblessed two days ago, but now she had power.

"Did she seal away my wielding?"

"She went to great lengths to shield you."

What? Margot turned. Orion was curled into a ball, eyes closed, already sleeping — or pretending to. He always did that when he wanted to stop talking. Frustration bubbled up, hot and familiar.

Her eyes drooped and she stifled a yawn — she'd have to get used to the exhaustion again. Sleep came to her swift and heavy.

NIKOLAS VENATOR

Shield of Historia

✷

Nikolas slept exceptionally well — the best sleep he'd had in ages, on a bed that didn't have sticks and hay digging into his bones.

He had to uncover why the Council banned Spirit wielding, even if it meant sleeping under a Spirit's protection, a thought that bothered him more than it should have.

He felt stripped bare without his weapons: no shield, no daggers, no reassuring weight of a sword across his back. The Council and the elemental societies had created their own laws and had no intention of letting that power slip — he understood why they kept the city hidden. He just didn't like it.

He was more intrigued by that librarian than he wanted to admit. *Why would she lie about being a wielder?* He had a talent for sensing lies, and hers struck him harder than it should have.

To settle his thoughts, he leaned over the battlement wall. Heavy snow blanketed the slopes below, an impenetrable forest of pine stretching beyond. Nothing was getting through until the thaw. He couldn't have predicted the blizzard that froze the entire peninsula solid — pure luck he'd crossed that Vulpine, luck that led him here before the cold claimed him. He still didn't know why it had helped him. Now, he just had to keep himself alive inside the walls.

Historia was strange, unlike any Spirit city he had seen — housing and farming dominated the land, the Study Hall standing where a palace should have been, Aquaan mechanics pumping fresh water through underground aquifers while Ignian engineers harnessed natural gas for heat and light throughout the maze of buildings.

He learned most of this by asking the right questions, or looming until someone answered. Being six-foot-two with a beard and a short temper usually helped. The Chief vouched for him, but he treated Historia like any other city: *with caution.* He still needed to understand who held the leash.

He walked into the Administration Building without hesitation, and as he neared Maya's office the corridor grew tense, eyes tracking his every step.

"Sir, you can't go in there!" the clerk yelped, scrambling after him.

Nikolas opened the door anyway.

Maya looked up from her desk, glasses perched on her nose. Not even a flicker of surprise. "Ah, Nikolas." She gestured to the chair opposite her. "Sit."

He did. There was no point in pretending she couldn't snap him in half with a single command. "I've considered your offer," he said, voice clipped. "I'll stay until Spring." Every instinct screamed run, but the blizzard outside screamed louder.

Maya leaned back, fingers interlaced. "Good."

"I had time to explore the grounds," he said. "I am… impressed."

"It pleases me to hear that. I'll arrange permanent lodging in the custodian barracks. Are you comfortable where you are now?"

"That will be fine." His shoulders remained tense.

Maya studied him. "There is one thing you must know."

His pulse tightened. "All right."

"If you choose to leave," she said, "every memory you have of Historia and everyone in it will vanish the moment you pass through the shield."

He went still. "How is that possible?"

"It's a defence mechanism," Maya replied, as if commenting on the weather.

He leaned forward, gripping the wooden arms of the chair. "So… I can never leave?"

"You may leave," she corrected. "You just won't remember that you ever lived here." She tapped two fingers against the desk in a walking gesture. "Someone else will walk out wearing your face."

Nikolas pushed on his senses and felt hot, blistering truth. His stomach sank. "Why does the shield do that?"

"It is… inelegant," she admitted. "But brutally effective. It ensures Historia stays hidden. No loose threads."

No survivors with memories.

He sat back, breath tight, instincts slithering beneath his skin. *Run. Run now before it's too late. But run where? Into the blizzard? Into Kit Sun's grasp? Into Fenn's jaws?*

"I see," he said, voice rough. "I suppose I have no say in the matter anymore."

He stood and shook Maya's hand. A formality. Nothing more.

"Experience has taught me that newcomers react more rationally once they've had time to see what they stand to lose."

He froze. The room seemed quieter.

Maya rounded her desk and opened the door. A timid worker lingered nearby. She barked instructions about housing and clothing.

Nikolas stepped into the hallway. He had planned to stay for a season. Now he wasn't sure he'd ever leave.

✷

He found himself drawn to the Day Hall, where the Vulpine statue rested. Staring into its white-rainbow gemstone eyes, he admired the detail carved into the fur. At the reception desk, he found a stack of notebooks and a box of pencils. An older librarian with greying hair nodded, so he took one and drew.

His hand drew clean and confident lines — he had drawn hundreds of beasts like this, and it had always calmed him.

He was finishing the statue's tail when he sensed Margot nearby — heat creeping up his spine, ending in a tingle at the nape of his neck.

"Hello." He lifted his gaze and met her wide doe eyes.

"Hello," she squeaked, clutching a stack of books. "I'm sorry if I disturbed you." She set them on a wooden cart. "I didn't realise you were drawing." Her hazel eyes darted to the page.

"I'm trying to keep myself occupied while they prepare my room at the barracks," he said, closing the notebook and setting the pencil aside.

"Oh, so you stayed?" A smile tugged at her mouth.

He nodded.

"Well, that's good," she said, arranging the books. "Everyone in Historia will be glad to have you protecting the walls until then." She hesitated. "I won't keep you." She pushed the cart away.

"Have a good day," he said.

She paused, glanced back, and nodded. Nikolas watched her go before returning to his sketch.

Time dragged. He kept her in the corner of his vision as she worked, pulse jumping each time her heels clicked closer.

He tried to keep drawing. He failed.

She had lied to him and hidden her alignment.

Perhaps he could tug at one loose thread and see what unravelled — perhaps she knew how to get past the shields. Information was worth the risk.

She stood behind the reception desk. Time stretched as he

worked up the nerve. If he didn't speak now, he'd keep staring like a fool.

Fuck it.

Margot looked up, tucking a curl behind her ear. "Hello again."

Before he could answer, a short, greying blur slammed a book onto the desk.

"Give this to Ob and be quick."

Margot jumped. "But he likes you more than me!"

The older woman planted her hands on her hips. "That's a lie and you know it. Go now, before I assign cleanup duty in the children's section." She stomped away.

Margot groaned. "Fine."

"Something wrong?" Nikolas asked.

She removed her glasses and rubbed her nose. "It's nothing. I just don't enjoy the trip. It's at the far end of the grounds, and the basement gives me the creeps."

"Then let me escort you." *And ask about the shields.*

Her mouth twisted before she smiled. "Company will be lovely." She ducked under the desk, retrieved her worn book bag, and slid the volume inside. "We'll need to make a detour."

They gathered their coats and navigated the maze of corridors, past dust-choked corners that had gone untouched for decades.

Nikolas tried to bring up the shields, but the words never landed. They walked through the cold in silence until they stopped at a small restaurant called *Revana*. The bell chimed as she stepped inside. She asked him to wait while she ordered. Smelling basil, tomatoes, and fresh bread made his mouth water.

"Please tell me you ordered for both of us," he said.

"I did, my treat for walking all this way." She slid onto a stool.

When her name was called, she returned with a large box.

"What's in the box?" he asked, stomach growling.

"A surprise. Come on. Ob doesn't like his food cold."

They left the restaurant. Instead of turning back toward the Library, she led him to a grey stone building marked: *Mathematics Building*.

MARGOT WILSON

Ob, the Mathematician

☾

Inside the Mathematics Building, polished black-and-white stone flooring stretched into gloomy darkness, the lingering smell of chalk dust thick enough to make Margot sneeze. She hated going down there — the Ignis lights seemed dimmer, only turning on when someone drew close.

That made it worse. Her shoulders tightened. *Of course, he didn't flinch.* Nikolas' attention drifted instead to the warm box in her hand.

"We have to go to the basement." She adjusted the book bag on her shoulder. "It's this way."

He nodded and followed behind her to the eastern side of the building and down the double doors.

The basement was eerily quiet — Ob the only one who stayed behind after most researchers and professors had left.

Margot took a breath and stepped forward as the Ignis lights flicked on ahead — snap, buzz, hum — each activation scraping across her nerves.

Just as she reached the next light switch, she felt him lean in. *"I can see why you don't like this,"* he whispered.

Her neck tingled, and she nearly dropped the food. Her heart tried to escape through her ribs.

His mouth quirked. He was enjoying her suffering.

She reached over and punched his arm. "No one likes this task," she said. "And I'm too much of a pushover to give it to anyone else. Just so you know, Ob has a temper. Don't take it personally." She rubbed her chest, trying to calm herself.

Nikolas murmured, "I rarely do."

Great. He had a sense of humour.

She knocked on Ob's door before she could embarrass herself further.

A hunched and cantankerous old man answered the door. He straightened and pushed his glasses up. "Come in, come in." He grabbed the box out of her hand and opened the lid before closing it with a flick.

His office was a shrine to numbers and nonsense. Margot took her usual stool, avoiding the geometric nightmares chalked across every wall — give her books, journals, dictionaries, fiction, anything else. Numbers made her eyes cross.

"I got your favourite and the research you requested." She set her bag down at the square table, buried under stacks of paper and notebooks dense with formulas.

Nikolas looked out of his depth, glancing around the room before sitting beside her. "I know that symbol…"

"Ob is the department head mathematician and engineer in Historia. He invented the Ignis lights."

"My team helped somewhat," he huffed before flipping the lid of the box and taking a piece.

Nikolas looked like he was about to die of hunger, so she slid the box closer and told him to take a slice. A smile flashed beneath his scraggly beard. "*Thank you,*" he whispered before taking a bite.

She took a slice and tried not to stare as his eyes fluttered closed — content, at ease, vulnerable in a way that caught her off guard, his head tilted back with a sigh.

"You've never had this?" she asked between bites.

"No… never. It was always too expensive in other cities." He finished his slice, dusting his hands together as flour fell onto the table.

"I will take you along with me then. It's much less scary

with you." Her thumb brushed sauce off her lip — his gaze dipped, following the motion, and didn't look away. She tried to ignore the thrill that coursed through her as she licked it.

Ob ate in silence, either oblivious or ignoring them, writing equations on the board as he took bites. He was mild-mannered enough with her, but he had a reputation for yelling at Inklings who brought him books. Margot always volunteered for the job — and always took her time doing it.

So what if she pocketed a few gold aureus from the new Curatrix to buy food? Could she not take any breaks?

Nikolas paced the room, looking at the plans for a new aqueduct system. Ob barked at him, warning him not to smear the board's writing. "Do you know anything about the shields?" he asked, too casually for the weight of the question.

She stopped chewing her food. *Why that question? Why now?*

"Not much," Margot answered, "just that it keeps us safe. Ob?"

Ob was writing odd symbols and numbers on the board. "That was before my time, and those before me. We don't ask those sorts of questions here." He stared up at Nikolas over the glasses hanging on the tip of his nose.

Nikolas continued pacing and flipping through Ob's notes. Another few minutes of silence stretched. She was due to go back, but she was enjoying her time away from work, even if the company was less than favourable.

"So… do you have any siblings?" he asked, flipping over a paper that was thumb-tacked to the wall.

She opened her mouth to answer before her heart dropped.

"No, no actual family left." Sophia was a sister, even though they weren't related by blood.

He stopped pacing. "*Oh, I am sorry,*" he whispered. "And

your father?"

"He died before I was born... and you?"

"I have ten brothers that I know about," he shrugged.

Her mouth dropped open. Ten? "That's a lot of siblings."

"More have been born by now."

What kind of life did he have outside the shields? "What made you leave?" she asked before thinking.

"I... had to." The shadows on his face deepened, the light draining from his eyes — the pain old and sharp, hooking beneath her ribs and pulling.

Silence filled the room, broken only by the scraping of chalk as Ob worked. She knew the complicated pain of losing the people she loved. Her hand lifted. *The need to soothe. To take. To heal.*

Margot stepped toward him, looking into his dull green eyes, wanting to ease the pain she felt in his heart.

He took a step back, brushing against the chalkboard.

Shit, what was she doing? She jerked her hand back, bumping the desk. It scraped against the floor. Ob pursed his lips, displeased. "Sorry."

She brushed her fingers through her hair and stepped back, face flushing. She didn't know what came over her — his pain was heavy, layered with years of guilt she had no right to feel.

Margot took the research questions from her book bag and set them on the table, then turned to leave, hoping to avoid Ob's anger.

She had nearly exposed her wielding to a stranger.

Her hands tingled. Margot checked her timepiece. "So sorry, I have to go. It's getting way too late."

"I will escort — " He moved toward her.

"No, no, you don't have to." She moved toward the door.

Ob huffed, quite done with them. "Can you two stop flirting and leave already?"

She sprinted away, her heart thumping, refusing to glance back.

☾

Margot's hands were freezing by the time she got home. Sophia was sitting by the door.

"What are you doing here? Why didn't you go in?" she asked, fishing the keys out of her bag.

"I lost my key, and… Orion scares me."

"Why would you be afraid of him?" Margot turned her key and stepped inside.

Sophia shucked off her coat and hung it. She spotted Orion watching her and bowed her head.

"You don't need to — "

"He's the protectorate," Sophia cut her off.

Margot clenched her jaw tight, hating the way people talked over her. She had stopped counting how many times it happened, the frustration of it too much to bear.

Sophia pulled a thick burgundy book with gold looping accents from her bag and let it thud against the desk. "I started researching in the Aerian archives for anything that might help and came straight over when I found this."

Black censoring marks littered the pages as Margot leafed through *Protectorates of Historia,* lineages dating back over a thousand years — her fingers aching to translate it. Perhaps Sophia's great-uncle or grandfather worried that someone would use this knowledge as a weapon.

"I intended to explain this once you had the staff," Orion said.

"I hate it when you keep things from me, Orion," she replied.

"So you can talk to him… interesting." Sophia crossed her arms.

"You cannot hear him?"

Sophia shook her head.

They both stared at Orion, expecting some flicker of

remorse, but he curled into a ball and tucked his head under the blanket. *"I do not answer to mortals or wielders."*

Sophia returned to the book. "I can't give this to you. My father would know, but I had to show you what I found." She flipped through the forbidden pages.

"Check out the last recorded entry when the Council took over the city. Before that, Protectorates made the rules and bonded with only one mortal. You are Orion's protectorate. His second. *His shadow.*" Sophia looked up, waiting for her reaction.

"I already know," Margot said, biting her lip.

Sophia's eyes narrowed. "Did you know what he was before he became your felis?"

Margot shook her head, guilt tightening her chest.

"He was a tyrant," Sophia said. "He ruled the city with an iron fist until he bonded with Olivia Brown."

Margot swallowed the lump in her throat.

"Orion has a mortal form." Sophia flipped to a detailed illustration of a mortal with onyx hair and amethyst eyes wearing a flowing, inky purple robe. It shimmered and shifted under the light. Orion's mortal face still kept the feline features, but he was handsome.

She had wondered if he could take mortal form — most research illustrated Spirits as creatures or beasts, nothing like this.

Her stomach twisted. Perhaps he was different now? *No. He wasn't evil. At least, not in the way tyrants usually were.* She'd felt his grief, his guilt. Monsters didn't sound that tired. *A tyrant? More like her bossy little star-beast.*

"I will assume my role as bonded protectorate once I have that staff," Margot said. "Until then, we are vulnerable."

"...Staff?"

Margot tapped the illustration. It had a unique curve and wasn't what she was imagining when Orion first mentioned it. "This. I need to get this."

Sophia stepped back and sat on the couch. "All weapons are kept in the custodian armoury. I cannot get you access."

"True, but I can do this now." Margot took Sophia's hand, sending her fluttering thoughts of pigeonhawks.

"How did you do that?" Sophia gasped.

She thought back to earlier that evening. Orion launched into her training the way he did everything: without warning.

"Again," he ordered from his place on the windowsill, tail flicking. *"Your eyes slipped."*

Margot exhaled hard and tried to steady herself. Her reflection in the mirror shifted from brown to hazel and snapped back. "This is impossible."

"No. You are unfocused. Your emotions control the glamour, not the other way around."

He made it sound easy. It wasn't. Her scalp tingled as her eyes opened — her hair had lightened to a citrine shade.

"Better. Hold it."

She held it. Five seconds. It wanted to snap back.

Frustration flared in her ribs and the glamour fractured. Her hair bled back to amber-brown.

"You cannot glamour with an emotional mind," Orion tsked.

"I'm trying," she snapped.

"And failing."

The memory faded just as quickly as it came, leaving her breathless.

"Emotional manipulation," Margot said, rising from the couch. "I can also glamour myself." She ran her hands through her hair. It straightened and lightened to Sophia's exact shade of blonde.

"Oh, what! Margot!" Sophia exclaimed.

"I am still practicing. Orion has been a wonderful teacher." Margot clasped her hands behind her back, grinning. She had never felt special before — always envious of Sophia's wielding, never quite enough. Today she did.

The rush crashed like a wave of bone-deep exhaustion. She slumped onto the seat beside Sophia.

A huff blew past her ear. *"You used too much too quickly. Using mana exhausts the wielder if their mana well depletes completely."*

"So tired…" Her eyes drooped.

Sophia shifted on the couch, letting Margot rest in her lap. She stroked her hair and hummed a soft melody as Margot drifted into sleep.

Henry House

☾

She drifted in the space between waking and dreaming, weightless and warm. A body lay beside her, heat radiating steadily. She rolled toward it without thinking, her hand sliding over a firm stomach, then higher over ribs and the defined curve of muscle beneath soft skin.

Her fingers brushed a beard. A breath caught.

Lips found hers. Slow at first. Testing. A low sound vibrated in his throat as she kissed him back, a sound that went straight through her.

She had fallen asleep alone. *This had to be a dream. A wicked, intoxicating, utterly decadent dream.*

His mouth moved against hers with a coaxing rhythm. She opened for him when his tongue brushed hers, every part of her leaning into the slow rise of desire that had been dormant for far too long.

He groaned against her skin, the vibration chasing sparks down her spine. She felt herself arch toward him, greedy for more.

She wanted him. She wanted the weight of him, the scent of him, the warmth and the heat and the relief of finally being touched again. His surprised chuckle warmed her throat as she kissed his neck, tasting the salt of his skin, teasing with deliberate nips along his collarbone and chest.

He rose to meet her, fingers sliding into her hair, pulling her back into another kiss. His other hand gripped her hip, their bodies finding a rhythm that made her gasp.

And then she woke.

She sucked in a ragged breath, heart racing, and looked

around in the dark silence of her bedroom. Her skin was hot, her lace shift sticky with sweat.

What the fuck was that — an intense dream?

She sat up and gazed out her bedroom window — the inky black of winter, snow falling in slow silent flurries, dawn just breaking through a horizon of pewter clouds.

She rolled out of bed, grabbed a glass from her bedside table, and went to the kitchenette sink. She gulped the water and slipped back under the blankets — warm on her preferred side, cold on the other. No weird kissing men in her bed.

Definitely a dream.

She tossed in bed, pulling the cool sheets over her body, heart still racing as her thoughts drifted to the last person who'd made her feel like that.

When Emile heard about Mum's death, he stopped by just once to offer his condolences with a few wilted wildflowers and a brief visit. He sat awkwardly in her living room chair, not knowing what to say while she cried.

She wiped away a single tear, her hands clenching into fists against the soft mattress.

Her chest got tighter.

It began last summer, around the solstice. He was charming, and his stupid custodian duties always conveniently overlapped with her librarian duties, and they got to talking. But when he stopped by and left, saying nothing, she knew it was over.

The stupid bastard hadn't looked her in the eye since then.

She knew some people couldn't handle grief. They chose avoidance with too-quick, awkward glances and pitying half-smiles before walking away. *Why was she waiting for him to come back?*

Emptiness throbbed in place of her heart. She had a talking felis hissing in her ear, ordering her to steal a staff. Perhaps it was a good thing that he wasn't coming back.

She could definitely use a stiff drink.

☾

The smell of stale beer wrinkled Margot's nose as she walked into Henry House — the usual Custodian guard hangout — and unwound her scarf, breathing in the warm air lit by the fireplace.

Margot had been secretly visiting after her shifts every night, working a plan to steal the staff from the Custodian Armoury — she just needed more information from the right personnel.

Sophia was waiting in a booth tucked into the corner. She wanted to be included in Margot's plan to steal the staff back and insisted on coming this time.

Unease settled low in her stomach. Margot didn't want her getting involved in this. Sophia's father was the Aerian Councillor; he'd shun her. The last thing Sophia needed was more trouble.

Margot was also dealing with a vexing issue — visions kept intruding upon her thoughts during every shift. Pushing out the auras was easy, but the moment she touched someone, her senses opened to the unique space inside them.

A heart signature.

She kept herself occupied researching Soul wielders as quietly as she could.

"I never thought I'd see you here again," Sophia said, sipping white wine. "I assumed you and Emile had broken up."

Her heart sank. Stupid Emile. She had been having dreams every few nights and did not want to be dreaming of him. "We are. I made it very clear," she said, hooking her coat up beside the booth. "He's a fool if he believes he can leave me for two months while I'm heartbroken and then come back expecting everything to be fine."

When she returned to Henry House, he sauntered over with a cocksure smile. She brushed him off with a scowl and unleashed a tongue-lashing that was as cutting as any lecture from her mother about overdue books. After that, he'd steal glances, but he left her alone.

Good riddance.

"Why not Hex and Bone?" Sophia asked.

Their old haunt — Margot missed the comfortable leather chairs and the bartender who knew her favourite cocktails. Could she get the password? Sophia would know.

"I like it here," she lied. It would be hard to sway them while Sophia was there. Perhaps they could escape to Hex and Bone and lose themselves in the loud jazz and the smoky, hazy atmosphere.

Margot turned. She'd come back here another time.

"What has been going on? You can tell me." Sophia grabbed her hand, her brows knitted together.

Margot connected with Sophia's heart. "I just want to forget all about Emile. Mabel has given me the day off tomorrow," she said. Sophia's worry flooded her senses.

It was difficult to lie to Sophia's kind grey-blue eyes — Mabel had not given her the day off. Margot had been here after work each night, trying to find a connection in the Armoury. Someone she could sway into loving her so much that they couldn't help but give her the codes. *Anything for you, my love! You have my heart for all time!* She'd listen to their pledges of eternal love before callously abandoning them in the cold, unforgiving snow.

Sophia's heart shifted from worry to relief. "Well, if that's all, then let's flirt with the boys," she said.

A gust of icy wind and the chime of the door drew Margot's attention — and she locked onto those familiar dull green eyes. Her heart raced. She blinked, slack-jawed.

Nikolas walked in with Emile and John — shorter hair, a

trimmed beard, a new suit and overcoat. *Spirits have mercy.*

"Oh… look who the Canis dragged in," Sophia whispered.

Too good. Under the shaggy beard was a straight jaw and perfect lips.

No. No. No. She remembered the vision. Inky mane, ruby eyes, onyx fur. He glanced in their direction.

Shit. She had been avoiding him.

"You're drooling," Sophia whispered, waving over Nikolas and the others.

Nikolas brushed the snow from his dark brown hair and swept it back, smiling and waving at Sophia before encouraging Emile and John toward their booth.

"Hello, boys," Sophia said with a smile. "What brings you in here this fine evening?"

"I could say the same for you," Emile said.

Margot snapped out of her daze. "Nobody asked you," she scowled.

Emile shuffled backward. "I'll just go then," he stuttered. John followed a moment later, claiming an empty booth at the far end of the alehouse.

Before he could walk off, Sophia caught Nikolas by the sleeve. "Sit with us."

Next to Margot.

Nikolas looked back at his new friends before sliding into their booth.

Damn, it was empty. Margot slumped down, holding her nearly finished cider.

"Do I want to know?" Nikolas' eyes danced between them.

He was sitting so close she could smell warm amber and vetiver from his knitted sweater.

"They used to date," Sophia said, breaking the awkward silence.

"Oh, I'm sorry." He paused, leaning back. *"Or not,"* he whispered.

Margot snorted. "Definitely not." Her neck tingled when she tipped her head back and finished her cider.

"What he did was awful."

She never said what Emile did. She doubted he had the balls to admit it — not to anyone, let alone someone he was trying to impress.

"How are things with you? I hope everybody has been treating you well." Sophia gave Margot a wink, tipping back her wine.

He nodded. "They've got me protecting the Armoury," Nikolas replied.

Margot's ears twitched. *Oh, that was how he knew Emile — he worked with him. Perfect. She could use him.*

"Oh, that's an important job!" Sophia added.

"It is. Quiet night shift."

Margot tapped her glass, catching Sophia's attention.

"Oh! Look at that — I've finished my wine," Sophia said as she scooted to the end of the booth. "Would you like another, Nikolas?" She winked at Margot.

"That'd be nice," Margot said as she gave her empty pint glass.

Sophia left Margot alone in the booth.

A terrible, wicked idea. A perfect idea.

Her pulse thudded, ringing in her ears. The Custodian grey of his uniform brushed her hip — he wasn't a newcomer anymore. He was a guard assigned to the Armoury. An enforcer of the Council's laws, including the one that'd see her imprisoned for the rest of her life.

Margot steeled her nerves. This was why she was here. Codes. A way into the Armoury.

Before she could think twice, she reached out and touched his hand, controlling her *mana* to connect to his heart. "So… handsome, tell me about the Armoury." Her voice sweetened, her fingers brushing over his shirt.

It was too easy — she needed only a few heartbeats, and they always forgot what she had asked them afterward.

Nikolas was as still as a marble statue. Other hearts softened under her fingers. Warmed. Leaned toward her. He resisted — inhaling sharply, his heart stuttering under her touch.

His eyes went lazy and glazed over.

It was working.

"What do you want to know, darling?" His eyes were dropping, sleepy and heavy-lidded. "I'll tell you whatever you want to know."

A flutter bloomed in her chest. She was grasping his chest, pulsing her *mana*. His hand reached up and tucked a loose curl behind her ear and stroked her cheek.

She swallowed. *All part of the plan.*

Nikolas' eyes dropped to Margot's lips. She licked them. Yes, it was working. He was copying her movements.

"Where can I find the passcodes for the vault?" This was a risk. She leaned into him, tilting her ear so it brushed his lips. Heat coiled in her stomach. Too intimate.

He leaned in, lips grazing the shell of her ear. "*Anything for you, my love. You have my heart for all time.*"

Her anxiety spiked.

His grip did not loosen. His pulse steadied.

"I'd prefer it if you stopped with that little trick of yours."

Blood iced in her veins. Was he not swayed? How did he resist it? He could arrest her — should arrest her. She jerked back, pushing him away. "How did you do that?"

She was so fucked.

Nikolas smiled wickedly. "Few have manipulated me so easily. Fewer still walked away afterward." He chuckled low. "You almost got me."

Margot needed to leave. Run. Pack quickly. Grab Orion and the essentials.

As she moved to get out of the booth, Nikolas grabbed her wrist like a shackle. "Don't panic." His voice was a whisper. "I have no desire to hurt you. I believe I'm understanding who you really are." His voice deepened, calm and sultry. "You wouldn't be sitting here if I wanted to arrest you."

Her heart skipped a traitorous beat at the low quiet of his voice. She pulled at her wrist, trying to free it. "So what, you've been stalking me?" she bit out.

Where was Sophia?

"No…" Nikolas said. "You have had my attention since your lovely tour of the Study Hall. I've been… curious." His eyes wandered over her face.

Curious? "I — what do you want from me? Are you going to arrest me now, hand me over so they can kill me?"

His laugh was louder than she expected. "No, I'm not in the business of killing people." He leaned in. "Not unless they deserved it."

"What are you?"

He leaned over, lips kissing the lobe of her ear, sending a shiver down her spine. "*Now is not the time for this conversation. Invite me back to your place,*" he whispered, eyes darting away.

"I — what?"

As Nikolas leaned back, Emile and John walked over with Sophia following behind, carrying a tray of drinks. Her red wine was half finished. The tops of the ciders had gone flat.

"Emile! Sorry, Margot was just perfect company. We were talking about how fascinating bookbinding is. Thank you for the cider, Sophia," Nikolas said in his usual friendly manner, not at all the same man she'd been speaking to a second ago. He reached for the tray and passed the other cider to Margot.

"Would you like to join us at my quarters for a game?" Emile asked, with a slight scowl. Annoyance flaring brightly in his aura.

"Actually, he was going to come back to my place, right?" Margot said with a saccharine smile, placing her hand on Nikolas' thigh, digging in her nails.

What are you doing? Are you crazy? You can't just invite a man over to your house. You live alone.

Margot knew exactly why she'd said it — she wanted Emile to watch, and she'd already exposed herself, so she might as well control where the next move happened.

Sophia sprayed wine upon hearing the statement.

Emile's eyebrows shot up in surprise. John chuckled softly, hands tucked into his pockets.

"Well… okay then. Goodnight. See you in the morning, Nikolas." Emile turned tail, walking away with his shoulders slumped.

Serves him right.

"Oh… are you now?" Sophia chuckled. "I was only gone for five minutes."

"I was just inviting Nikolas over so he could look at my first edition collection of Molesloth Poetry," Margot lied. *She was way too tired for this.*

Sophia clasped her hands together. "Ask her about Page 134," she teased.

"Do I even want to know?" Nikolas asked.

"Only if you're lucky," Margot said, wiggling her eyebrows. Molesloth Poetry was the least interesting book she owned. *Not even a first edition.*

"Now I'm more interested in hearing about this book," he said, reaching his hand across and placing it on the top of the booth behind her.

Margot smelled his sweater again. *Fuck.* She liked that smell. Perhaps Nikolas had secrets of his own to share.

She drank another cider in the loud and stinky alehouse, listening to Nikolas and Sophia chat. So much for getting the information she needed — when her cider was done, she declared she was going home to sleep.

Sophia nodded and went to the bar to pay the tab.

Margot stepped outside. The cold air felt good against her flushed skin. "Look, I am not in the business of bringing strange men into my apartment."

He raised his eyebrows and put his hands up. "I have a few questions for you. Sophia would suffocate me if I hurt you, trust me."

Sophia would, too.

"Fine, but don't be an asshole." She pointed a finger at his hard chest.

NIKOLAS VENATOR

A Deal Between Friends?

✸

He had followed her anyway, despite her best efforts to convince him to return to the barracks and forget their little conversation. She had no intention of letting him in, but he had no intention of leaving either.

"Wow, nice place." He stood in her foyer, wiping the remnants of snow from his boots on her jute rug.

"Come on in, but don't make yourself *too welcome.*"

A black ball of hissing fur and claws. He almost smiled.

She shucked off her coat and hung it on the hook. "Leave your wet, muddy boots by the door and don't make a mess."

She dropped her keys into the bowl and twisted the dial on the wall — the gas sconce lamps humming to life, bathing the room in warm light, the glow curving over her cheekbones and catching in her hair.

Abyss take him.

He couldn't have made a mess in here even if he'd tried — frankincense and myrrh coiled through the air, and her apartment was far nicer than his barracks room.

Her space was an eclectic nest of beautiful, strange things — tapestries, paintings, and *drawings* covering the walls so thoroughly he couldn't see the deep green brocade wallpaper beneath. Crates and half-unpacked knick-knacks crowded every surface. *Had she moved in recently?*

She stood in the middle of her living room with her hands on her hips, shifting between offensive and defensive stances. "Well?"

Nikolas kept a careful distance, giving her space. "I haven't seen a room with this much stuff in it."

"I collect things from outside the shields." She picked up an object from a crate, unwrapped it, and set it on a bookshelf. Her eyes went soft, her mouth curving. She was reliving a happy memory that had turned bittersweet.

He knew that feeling well. *Grief.*

From a perch on the windowsill, a black tail flicked once, slow and displeased, violet eyes narrowing as it watched Nikolas watch her.

"Why do you want the Staff?"

She glanced at her small pet, biting her lip. "I… can't say."

"It's okay, Margot. You may tell him." A deep voice whispered in his head.

He stumbled back a step, tripping over a crate, his hand going for a dagger that was not there. "It just spoke…" Any time he faced a Spirit, it never ended well.

"You're a seeker, aren't you?" the creature said. *"I am known as Orion. I am Margot's bonded and Soul Protectorate of this city."* It jumped from its perch by the window and stretched. *"You have nothing to fear from me."*

Nikolas stared at the creature, slack-jawed. "What are you?"

"You do not know?" It tilted its head. *"Interesting."* It used a back leg to scratch its ear.

"I've never met someone who could talk to Spirits." Margot's fingers tugged at her sleeve, unravelling a loose thread.

Of course he could hear it — Spirits always found him first. He dragged a hand through his hair and rested his fists on his hips. "What's the Staff for?"

"It's part of my training. I am a Soul wielder," she said.

He stopped breathing. Soul wielders were rare — across this desolate continent he'd only met a few, and most of them had wanted to bleed him dry.

His defences snapped up, and he turned toward the door.

The creature's voice dropped. *"I will not harm you, and neither will she. I have tasked Margot with finding the Anima Staff because it's hers by right. However, we must be very cautious."*

"Cautious?"

"The Council," Margot said. "They murdered the previous Protectorate and banned Soul and Spirit wielding. They'll do anything to stay in power here."

He decided sitting was better than bolting and moved to the couch, its leather creaking beneath him. "I knew there was something odd," he said. "Too many unbonded wielders hiding in plain sight."

Maya had been trying to assess him from the start. "I will help you get the Staff if you help me figure out how to leave the city," Nikolas said.

Margot's lips pursed tight. She rolled an orb between her palms. "You want to leave? Why?"

Nikolas gathered his courage. "Almost every Spirit in the Interwilds has hunted me my entire life. They want to use me for one reason or another." He gazed at his scarred hands, tracing a deep scar on his palm. "I cannot risk them finding me."

"You have been hunted because you are a Spirit wielder," Orion said, his deep amethyst eyes fixed on him.

"Yes, I am." His greatest secret, bare in a single sentence. The Spirit took one look at him and knew — his blood carried condensed *mana,* and Spirits could smell it in the air, track him by it. Even most alchemists didn't know what that blood could do.

Spirits fed on *mana*. He knew that much: they forced bonds, clung to near immortality, hunted what they could not control.

Nikolas had never forced that bond on anyone. He'd

refused to give in to his nature, isolated himself, and became a mercenary who haunted Spirits as much as they haunted him.

Orion's pupils thinned to slits. "A Spirit wielder's blood is potent."

Nikolas met his gaze. "And none of you are getting a drop."

"Good," it replied.

The look it gave Nikolas was not friendly. *Possessive — of her, of what she could become.* He'd met Soul wielders before. Margot was the first who looked afraid of herself.

"So, you're like me," she whispered, one hand covering her mouth, her hazel eyes darting back and forth as she tried to absorb it.

"We're opposites. And yet… not so different." He cleared his throat. "Look, I can't stay in Historia. I don't want to spend the rest of my life locked in a dungeon. Especially for being born this way. I want to leave with my memories intact."

"Afraid of losing your memories?"

He huffed a laugh. "All of your memories, good or bad — they make you who you are."

They were his only map: every Spirit, every cult, every village and hidden tunnel. Without them, he'd be stumbling prey in the Interwilds; he wouldn't last the winter.

"I get it. When I was a kid, my mother threatened to throw me out a few times."

"That's awful," he chuckled.

"She was a fierce teacher." Margot rose from the couch and wove through the maze of crates without looking down. "Would you like tea?" she called from the kitchenette.

"Yes, thanks." Nikolas was still turning everything over in his head. *Was this why the Vulpine led him here?*

The rhythmic sounds of her kitchen filled his ears: the

creak of the cupboard doors, the soft clinking of mugs, and the gentle rush of boiling water.

"I have a trusted source who can help me research the shields," she said, her voice carrying over the clink of porcelain. "She's an expert on Spirits and Soul creatures, but you can't come with me."

She handed him a steaming cup. Her fingers grazed his as he took it. The gentle touch made his heart leap.

Margot settled onto the couch beside him, legs tucked beneath a blanket, the soft lamplight turning the edges of her hair to gold. He inched closer, drawn by the quiet of her voice, the heat of her presence.

A low rumble rolled from the windowsill. The creature's tail flicked once in warning.

"Who is your expert?" Nikolas asked, ignoring the Spirit.

"I can't say. It's a secret." She bit her lip, tracing the rim of her cup with one fingertip.

Nikolas stopped just shy of brushing her knee, pretending the creature's stare didn't make every instinct in him bristle, waiting to see if she would move first. "A secret expert," he said, taking a slow sip of tea. "You enjoy keeping me on edge." The tea smelled like her apartment.

It smelled like her.

She blew on the surface of her cup and took another sip. "Seriously, I'm sworn to secrecy." She wiped her palm along her skirt and held it out. Her hand hovered between them, steady despite the tremor in her shoulders. "I will aid you in finding a way for you to leave the city with your memories. If there's a loophole, I will find it."

He clasped her hand. A tingle skimmed up his arm as their palms met, just as it had at the tavern. "And in exchange, I'll help you get your staff. Just don't sacrifice me to Malum."

Her hand jerked back, and she let out a breathy chuckle. "I don't even know what that is."

"Malum is a Spirit of wrongdoing," he said. "I had to take down a cult of wielders who worshipped them."

"Oh... my." Margot placed her mug down and began rubbing her hands together. Not absent-mindedly. Frantic. Small, tight circles into her palms. Her breath shortened. The notes in her head, the ones he always sensed humming, grew louder, more chaotically layered.

"You've killed people?" she whispered.

Sensing her growing distrust, Nikolas tried to steady her. "It's kill or be killed outside the walls. I don't regret a single life I've taken. They deserved it. They were trying to use me to revive Discordia. It would've been catastrophic."

That did not soothe her.

Margot recoiled, hands now pressed tight against her chest. "Kill or be killed? You speak as if that's normal. As if it's routine." She took a shaky step back, bumping into a crate. "I live in a library. I shelve books. I catalogue manuscripts. I don't—" Her voice cracked. "I don't know people who kill."

He opened his mouth, but she cut herself off with a trembling laugh that held no humour. "What am I doing? Bringing you here? Talking to you? I invited a murderer into my home."

Nikolas flinched. She did not know what survival had cost him.

Carrying both empty mugs to the kitchenette, he leaned against the counter, putting distance between them so she wouldn't feel cornered. He wanted her to trust him.

He gazed at the half-organised bookcase that took up half the wall. Reading had never been his favourite — he knew enough to manage, but books were heavy and took up room. More than once he'd used one as kindling.

Margot had retreated to the couch, a palm-sized book held like a shield between them, her fingers trembling around the worn edges.

He walked to the shelves and pulled out books, flicking through pages filled with tight, unreadable script. *"I'd like us to be friends,"* he whispered. He cleared his throat. "I'd like your help. But I fear I have a special set of skills that are useless to you right now, and I can't help you with researching."

Margot stayed rooted to the rug for a few heartbeats before she grasped the tiny book and approached. "So, what are you suggesting?" she asked.

His own pulse kicked up at her nearness, at how good she smelled — his gaze dropping to her mouth, then rising to her eyes. He could get lost in those enormous hazel eyes, spend hours counting the freckles scattered across her nose.

Words jammed in his throat. "Teach..." he stuttered, then forced the rest out. "Teach me how to read Laetin?"

A soft laugh escaped her, surprised he'd ask for something so... ordinary. "Two favours for one? So needy."

He stood up straight. "The heist is a colossal task. The logistics alone will take weeks to prepare."

She held out her hand. "You have yourself a deal."

As he clasped her hand, a shiver ran through him again — his thumb almost tracing the line of her pulse before he thought better of it and let go.

Margot exhaled, the panic loosening from her shoulders.

Nikolas remembered the icy touch of her hand all the way back to the barracks and the choice it sealed.

SOPHIA MEYER

The Triad

✦

Sophia steeled her nerves as she waited her turn. Here, in the cavern beneath Aerian territory, Anthony Meyer was not her father; he was her commander. Her judge and punisher when he wished to be.

Every Aerian in the cavern lived and died by his judgment — his voice could tilt votes, end alliances, and silence dissent with a single decree.

A limestone stalactite dripped, a slow patter that made her skin crawl, and her father's voice rose above the hum of the gathered Aerians, calling her name with the same bitter tone.

No. She was not his daughter here.

Her heart was a drum in her chest as she stepped forward, the crowd parting around her — friends and families shifting aside to form a path.

She bowed on one knee, her voice steady only by force. "Yes, Father." She could never look up. His icy grey gaze was a weapon sharper than any sword. Meeting his eyes without permission was a transgression that left five lashes across her back.

They'd heal the wounds, of course, leaving her skin unmarred, but the hour of searing pain was the lesson.

"What have you decided?" His voice boomed through the cavern, filling the Aerian secret meeting place.

She told the truth. "I want to become a baker, Father." Her eyes did not leave the cave floor, but the stirrings of disappointment and disdain from the crowd told her enough.

A murmur rippled through the crowd. *Guild crafts were for ground-born families, not sky-blooded Aerians.* She heard a faint hiss of disapproval from her cousins.

Anthony inhaled.

Sophia's spine locked into place.

"You are a talented healer," he said, each syllable a precise cut. "Why not pursue a more noble cause?" There was no anger in his tone. No raised voices.

Every Aerian in the chamber stilled.

"There are many talented Aerian healers among our ranks," Sophia replied, her voice steady with practice. "I want to follow my passion." Her throat bobbed — if she said the wrong thing, she knew what would happen. Five lashes across her back.

"You are free to choose," Anthony said. A lie wrapped in silk — his voice serene, her stomach twisting. When Sophia's healing blessing surfaced, he had decided her future for her: the hospital, under her uncle's supervision. "Have you decided on your partner?"

Sophia froze, panic flickering like a trapped bird in her chest. "No," she whispered. "I have not yet."

Anthony hummed, a quiet, thoughtful sound that made her blood turn to ice. "Then let me make the choice easier. Stand, my child."

She rose. The crowd parted again. And then — a scent reached her. Juniper berries and clean linen. *Impossible.* She turned her head a fraction, and her breath lodged in her throat.

"Welcome back to Historia, Quentin," Anthony said.

"It is a great pleasure to be back in your presence, Your Excellency," Quentin replied, bowing.

Sophia blinked hard, her breath faltering, ribs tightening.

It was him. The boy she knew, the friend she lost. The third part of their triad.

Except he wasn't a boy anymore. His copper hair had deepened into auburn, his shoulders broadened — but his eyes, the brilliant cerulean she used to tease him about, were exactly the same.

Her body snapped back into neutrality, hands folded at her thighs, head bowed, obedient. "Are we to be matched then, Father?" she forced out.

"Provided you find no other male suitor and you both find it amicable, you may be wed by the Summer Solstice."

Her father's words settled over the chamber — a marriage between their families would bind two Aerian bloodlines in time for the election cycle, strengthening his claim to the Council seat.

"Yes, Father."

Six more months of freedom. Before she was born, it was decided she'd marry, bear children, and continue the family line — more freedom than many women received, yet she still chafed against the shackles.

She stepped back into the crowd as her father called the next family name. Her answers seemed to have appeased him.

She allowed herself a single, quiet breath of relief.

✦

"How long were you going to make us think you were dead?" Sophia shouted.

Quentin flinched. *Good.* She wanted him to feel that sting.

"Alces forbids any communication out of his territory without approval. I would've, if they had let me."

"And now you want to marry me? Why?" Sophia bristled.

"It was that, or stay as a political prisoner. You don't understand what it's like there. I had to get out, no matter the cost." His voice broke on the last word, thin and frayed.

Sophia swallowed hard. Quentin was not the boy she remembered — he was weary, the old wound in her chest reopening despite herself. The boy who used to leap over rooftops with her, laughing until they were breathless.

The boy who died. Or so she had believed.

Quentin was the third member of their triad — Margot, Quentin, Sophia, three tightly bound threads that together had once formed an unbreakable rope.

Quentin followed on Margot's heels, so close that her father and Quentin's father had spent years trying to separate them — and failed, again and again. The three of them always found each other.

Until the day they told her he was dead.

She remembered that bright Solstice day — the news hitting her so hard she thought her ribs had cracked, Margot collapsing into her arms. Losing Quentin had broken her. Regaining him could break far more than her heart if the timing was wrong.

"Margot is going to be devastated. She has grieved over you for years," Sophia said. She stitched her together with trembling hands because no healer had come fast enough.

"How is she?" Quentin asked, taking a tentative seat at the table.

"Her mother died recently, and I have been picking up the pieces. She seems distracted with…" Sophia caught herself.

A quick laugh escaped her. Margot was now a Soul wielder, bonded to Orion — she considered telling him, but she had promised secrecy, and besides, Orion had a plan she couldn't afford to disrupt.

And then there was Nikolas — Sophia had noticed the change in Margot the night she saw him at the bar. They'd been spending a great deal of time together.

"Evelyn died? How?" Quentin stood and paced. Sophia's parents had given them privacy in her rooms after the meeting.

"The newspaper wrote an article — I will find it for you.

Evelyn was discovered in an annex of the Study Hall, at the bottom of a rarely used stairwell." Sophia sank into a chair and covered her face with her hands to hide her tears.

They had not found Evelyn until morning — her ankle twisted, her arm broken from the fall. Sophia had never believed it. *Too clean. Too convenient.*

Evelyn had been the mother she wished she had. Her own mother was vain, concerned only with reputation.

Quentin slid a book from her shelf, pulling out a hidden bottle. "May I?"

She nodded. He poured them both a knuckle of liquor.

"To Evelyn," he said, raising the glass before drinking.

Sophia did the same, coughing as the burn coated her throat.

"So what now?" she rasped.

"The only thing we can do. Go with the wind and hope we land safely." He had abandoned his coat the moment they entered her room. Now he loosened his tie and rolled up his sleeves.

"The election cycle is happening this year. We can use it to our advantage." Sophia cleared her throat. "Aurora has held onto that power for too long. She cannot hold it any longer. The others will not allow it, no matter how much she sings to manipulate them. My father is determined to seize control but lacks the political sway he once had. Theodore and the other Terrans do not want it, and they do not have the numbers. I think Maya's society will take control."

Quentin hummed into his hands. "Does she still hold the custodians?"

"Yes. I have been getting close to her."

"So what are you proposing? An alliance?"

"For now, we keep low and pretend everything is moving in my father's favour. I have strings I can pull."

Quentin leaned back and interlaced his fingers, a boyish

grin crossing his face, the kind that always meant trouble. "I love pulling on people's strings…" A few heartbeats of silence stretched. "I should tell her," he whispered.

Sophia's head snapped toward him. "*No.* Not yet."

He blinked, startled by her sharp tone. "Why?"

Because the moment Margot sees him, everything Orion is planning could explode. She forced out, "She's fragile right now."

Quentin looked at his hands and nodded, the movement small and wounded. Once Margot saw him again, old wounds and old love would resurface — the triad never broke, it only frayed. Sophia let out a short laugh. She couldn't help it. The absurdity of it all.

✦

Quentin left her to dress for dinner.

Sophia stood at her window for a long time after the door closed, watching the last of the light bleed out of the sky. The toast still burned at the back of her throat. *To Evelyn.* She pressed two fingers to her sternum, as though she could push the ache back down where it belonged.

The triad was whole. She should feel relieved. Instead, she felt the weight of all the things she was still managing — Quentin's return, Margot's grief, her father's ambitions, the election cycle tightening around all of them like a fist.

Go with the wind, he'd said, as if it were simple.

She exhaled and opened the window a crack. Cold night air slipped in, carrying the smell of pine and fresh snow. She breathed it in slowly, letting it clear the liquor and the staleness of the room.

The candle on her desk fluttered.

Sophia glanced at it. No draught had reached that far. She turned back to the window, and the candle flame steadied — then bent sharply toward her, as though drawn by a current she couldn't feel.

She took a step back.

The air in the room shifted as if someone had walked in. A warmth moved through her palms.

Her breath caught.

Stop. She pressed her hands flat against her skirt and swallowed the sensation back down. Smoothing the fabric over and over until her heartbeat settled.

The candle returned to its upright flame.

She stood still for a moment, listening to the distant sounds of the city below — footsteps on cobblestone, the creak of a cart, someone laughing in the street.

Then she closed the window, latched it, and went to dress for dinner.

She told no one.

CLARA LOXLEY

Daughters of the Harpy

▽

Clara knocked once.

Then twice.

Then four times.

A slot in the door opened. "Password?" They asked her for the password every time; it was always different.

Spirit mana, we hear your whispers, she signed to the pair of watchful blue eyes — and heard the slide of a bolt as the heavy door swung inward.

Clara stepped through and lowered the hood of her cape. The speakeasy was a small hole in the wall, but it was home. She signed her thanks to the barkeep, who nodded and shuffled behind the bar.

She sat at the bar and eyed the barkeep. *Summoned,* she signed.

"Aye, your summons is sitting in the booth in the corner." He slid a letter across the bar.

She nodded in thanks and headed over to the booth.

M-A-R-G-O. It's good to see you, Clara signed.

"It is good to see you too, Clara," Margot said as she signed.

My condolences on your loss, Clara signed, sliding into the booth.

"It has been difficult, but I am keeping myself busy," Margot said, shuffling in her seat. She rifled through her book bag, sliding a gold Harpy token across the table. "I need to turn in a favour."

Clara picked up the small round coin and ran her thumb over the symbol of a feral-faced, half-naked, half-avian woman moulded into its surface.

Clara respected Evelyn — her death had shocked the elemental societies. She recalled the night Margot's mother passed: the Council's closed session, the stairwell's guarded entrance, the Library staff's early dismissal. By the time the story reached the public, someone had scrubbed the staircase clean.

Too clean.

Clara had watched the librarians exchange glances — the kind that meant: *we are not safe to speak here.* Everyone went along with the official story.

But Clara never did.

How did you get this? Clara signed.

Only those who helped their Society were granted a boon.

"My mother had it. I found it among her things. I know you work for the Daughters," Margot said, making Clara freeze.

Who told you? Clara signed. She'll kill them.

"I will not betray your trust," Margot said, rolling an Orb across the table.

An Orb. Clara picked it up — the glow ran over her hands and into her skin, then rejected her, the sting sharp enough to force her hand back. She hissed and flexed her fingers. *So, you are a Protectorate now. Who bonded with you?*

"Orion. That's not why I am here." Margot fidgeted.

If he had chosen now, then he was ready — Orion had slept through the Council's rise and refused every bond. *What are you here for, then?* Clara signed.

"I need information on the shields and how to bypass the memory wiping."

Of course, I can do that. But what about the Protectorate? Clara signed.

"I want to protect this city. I will assume the role of his second," Margot said as she tucked an amber curl behind her ear. "Right now, he is vulnerable. He is trapped as a felis."

Clara stifled a laugh, clearing it with a wince as she rubbed the old scar on her neck.

How? Clara signed.

"If I had to guess, the Council did it," Margot shrugged.

Understood. I will see what I can do for protection, Clara signed. The Daughters of the Harpy would have to protect both of them.

"Orion said it's unnecessary unless they find out who I am. I'm safer if we act as if nothing has happened," Margot said.

I'll get your information, if that's your boon? Clara signed, taking the token and tucking it into her pocket.

"That will be fine. Thank you, Clara."

Clara nodded and hugged Margot once more before waving goodbye. She adjusted her cape, checked that the space was empty, and stepped behind the bar to press a small button beneath the counter — a faint mechanical click sounding from behind the wall. She pressed her hand against the invisible door.

The wall slid open to reveal a metal spiral staircase descending into a dim space beneath the speakeasy — ribbons of white and red wax dripping from the sconces lining the walls. Clara paid homage to the Harpy, as required.

The robed figure pushed back her hood, revealing a sickly pale, bald head and clouded white eyes. "What brings you, Daughter?"

I bring news for the Magus, Clara signed.

Maeve nodded. "The Magus will come out soon. Take a seat." She shuffled forward, pulling a thick corded rope hanging from the ceiling.

A faint chime echoed in the distance. A shiver ran along Clara's spine as she sat at a table to wait. Maeve gave her the creeps — but she was a fellow alchemist, and alchemists were the only family Clara had ever known.

A door opened behind her, and Clara turned.

"Come in, Daughter," the Magus said. *Daughter.* That was what they called every member. Names were irrelevant.

The Magus' office was small and cluttered — a desk buried under alchemy tomes, parchments, and instruments, three paintings of her predecessors hanging along one wall, the current Magus seated in a worn leather chair beneath them.

A porter — a small child — stood facing the wall, waiting.

"What have you come to tell me? Is it about the summons?" the Magus asked.

Yes. Orion has decided to bond. He has chosen, Clara signed.

"Ah. It's time."

You knew? Clara signed, her hands fumbling.

"Of course I did. I know everything that happens in this city." She took a fountain pen and scrawled a note, snapped her fingers — the child turned, took it, and ran.

Why was I not informed? Clara signed.

"It was before your time. The fewer people who know Orion is awake, the better. He's a grumpy bastard and does not like being disturbed. He's been protecting that mortal for a while now."

M-A-R-G-O-T? Clara signed.

The Magus decanted liquor into her glass and leaned back, taking a sip. "Yes. It's cute watching the most powerful pure Soul look after a mortal girl, but that's his *thing.*"

He remains trapped in the felis' body, Clara signed.

"Again, I am well aware." The Magus took another sip.

Clara's hands slackened at her sides. They said Orion was grief stricken when the Council staged the coup and he lost his bonded — she couldn't imagine being so overcome that she would curl up and turn to stone for decades.

Shall I watch over her? Clara signed.

"No. She has protection. Supply her with whatever knowledge she asks. Dismissed, Daughter," the Magus said.

Clara bowed in respect. Orders were orders.

The Hex and Bone. We watch and wait, Clara signed, and left the office.

The cool night air hit her as she stepped outside, snow falling again in white flurries.

She had a new task: help the Protectorate. Margot, of all people.

Clara understood why Orion had chosen her. Quiet Margot, who brought her books to read in her language while she recovered from injuries and taught her to sign. Shy Margot, who had little to say until you mentioned something she loved.

She looked up at the night sky. The snow fell, indifferent and soft.

Ducking down a side street, she made her way to the graveyard — the eerie cold crawling over her skin, intensifying the moment she spotted it. A small Will-o'-Wisp, its blue flame hovering above a grave, illuminating the headstone's carvings.

She tilted her head, hearing the faint cry rising from the flame. A lure.

Not wanting to draw its attention, she took a longer path around to the mausoleum, wielding the snow beneath her feet to soften the crunch of her steps. The rusted gate creaked as she opened it — the wisp brightened in response. Clara slipped inside, muffling her panting breaths with her woollen gloves.

She stayed silent as the biting stone seeped through her coat, doing nothing to calm her racing heart.

Clara peeked out through the gate — the wisp hovered above its home grave. Her shoulders relaxed.

Feeling safe enough to move, she stood before the gargoyle

statue guarding two raised stone coffins, moonlight streaming through the gate and catching the ornate stonework.

The browned paper rustled as she drew it from her coat pocket. Instructions from the Magus.

She dug through her pockets and pulled out a small box of matches. After lighting a black pillar candle to pay her respects, Clara pulled the gargoyle's outstretched hand — stone sliding against stone as the coffins shifted along grooves in the floor. She stepped aside as a circular pattern descended into shallow steps, a low boom echoing through the cavern below when the stones settled.

Clara moved before she could change her mind, her footsteps echoing as she curved down the staircase into enemy territory, carrying the Magus' orders like a weight between her shoulders.

Ink and Parchment

▽

Stepping into the foyer of the society, Clara didn't have time to lower her hood before a bulk of muscle and momentum slammed her back into the stone wall — cold stone scraping her spine, the blow knocking the wind from her lungs. Her hand twitched toward her blade a heartbeat too late.

His forearm pressed across her collarbone, pinning her hard. "Who are you? How did you get here?" The depth of his voice vibrated through her sternum.

Clara grimaced and lifted her hands to sign — he shoved her back against the wall again, pain jolting through her shoulders.

Enough.

Instinct snapped. She twisted her free arm, fingers finding the small blade at her side, her other hand curling around the dagger's hilt — angling the weapon beneath his jaw, the point grazing his pulse. A vein throbbed in his neck. Frost bloomed along the steel.

That got his attention.

The man stilled, lifted his hands, and backed away. Clara stepped with him, keeping the blade at his throat long enough to study him — then nudged forward into the thickness of his beard, digging just enough to draw a bead of blood.

His hands rose higher.

Clara eased back and examined him. Broad shoulders. Firm jaw. Hazel-green eyes narrowed not in fear, but surprise. A full head of hair. Cedar, ink, and stone — she hadn't expected that. He might have been handsome if he hadn't slammed her into a wall.

She let the ice melt off her blade, droplets sliding down the steel as she sheathed it. Her breathing settled. She lifted her hands, palms up, mirroring his gesture — then swept her cape aside to show the long scar running from ear to ear. *No harm,* she signed, hoping he understood.

The moment stretched taut between them.

He nodded once, then moved to a desk, rummaging for a fountain pen and paper. He did not react. *Good.* She hated the pity looks.

His shoulders lowered. "Apologies." His voice still carried that deep vibration as he sat on the bench and gestured for her to join him.

Clara rolled her shoulders as she removed her cape, stretching her neck. He might have bruised her.

Few people ever caught her off guard.

She scribbled: *I am here on behalf of the Magus. My name is Clara.*

His expression stayed unreadable.

"What brings you here?"

She wrote: *I need information on the shields of Historia, as requested by the new Primis Protectorate.*

She slid the paper toward him.

His gaze flicked over her handwriting, something in his eyes sharpening, as if he'd learned more than she intended.

"The Sons are at your disposal then, *Harpy.*"

The title carried thick disdain, but she was used to that. A Harpy and a Gargoyle — not ideal company. Rival societies rarely bothered with courtesy; they'd sooner cut each other's throats than share a drink. Still, every society answered to one authority: the Protectorate.

"Where would you like to start?" he asked.

She blinked, unsure, and scribbled a single question mark.

"Do you think I'm giving you free access to our archives without an escort?" he huffed, crossing his arms.

I don't want to waste your time, she wrote beside the mark.

"You won't. This takes precedence. I will take you to the archive. Follow me."

He stood and passed her cape to a bald, robed man who emerged from a side corridor — Clara smothered a laugh. The fashion was the same everywhere: robes, hoods, grim faces.

They reached an ornate wooden door carved with a massive Gargoyle. Leathery wings tipped with bone. A snaking tail. A muscled torso rendered so vividly it seemed alive in candlelight.

The door creaked open.

A cold corridor stretched ahead, lit by candles — wax bleeding in long black trails, uncomfortably like her own society's passages. Another door opened to her left, revealing a library packed with tomes and heavy desks.

"Sit here," he instructed. "I'll bring you books that should answer your question."

Clara sat mostly because she didn't want to be thrown into another wall. She surveyed the underground library: warm golden light from an iron chandelier, shelves crammed with books, some chained to the wood. Probably to stop people like her. She noted every face, every exit.

Two thick volumes slammed onto the table — she flinched, pain rang in her ears. He flipped open the first, turning pages with practiced impatience.

Clara clicked her fingers and mimed writing. With a reluctant groan, he fetched paper and a pen. She mouthed *thank you* and got to work.

▽

The candles burned low. Clara's eyes drooped, her vision going cross-eyed.

The man yawned, stretching his long arms until muscle strained the fabric of his shirt. She absolutely did not mean to stare. *Damn.*

She scribbled a note before she could think better of it and pushed it toward him.

He read the note and replied, "Theodore."

She raised a hand in a small wave and wrote: *Find anything?*

He cleared his throat. "The Council scrubbed all records of the shields from the archives. However, a guild merchant who lived during their construction left one small journal entry."

And? she wrote.

"And," he sighed, "it notes six rings worn by the Protectorates to shield themselves. The account is likely a lie."

Clara tapped her pencil, dotting the page — letting her mind drift.

Ever since she had crossed the barrier, she had felt trapped. The Daughters kept her safe, but at a cost to her sanity.

Do you have any other texts that support this?

"I'll have to ask the Archivist. Can you wait here?"

Clara nodded. Theodore stood with a muffled groan and disappeared between the shelves.

The moment she was alone, she moved.

She didn't have long.

Darting through the stacks, she thumbed through titles, hunting for anything useful to the Magus.

This was her gift.

A slim book about Celestial Spirits and their progeny. Perfect size. Lightweight. She slid it into her blazer.

Her senses stretched toward the hallway. Fast footsteps echoed off the stone walls.

She slipped back to her table, soundless, reopened her

book, posture composed.

Theodore returned with a stack of journals under one arm — leaner than formal tomes, edges singed or warped by water — and set them down with less force this time.

"These are travel accounts," he said. "Mostly unreliable. Hunters, researchers, smugglers. People who liked to exaggerate."

Clara perked up — unreliable accounts were often the most honest. She slid the Old Frianc text aside and reached for the top journal, her fingers brushing Theodore's as she pulled it closer.

She flipped it open. Sketches filled the page — Spirits illustrated in half-formed charcoal smudges, drifting through margins like fever dreams.

Theodore hesitated, closing the book. "They're graphic. The man died shortly after drawing some of those."

Clara's pulse quickened — the macabre had always fascinated her.

Show me more, she wrote.

He blinked, startled. "Most people don't enjoy that."

She wrote again: *Spirits are complex. Unique patterns and morphology. There is always something to learn.*

Theodore leaned back, studying her with curiosity, unsure whether she was brilliant or unhinged. "You study Spirit morphology," he said. "By choice?"

She nodded, flipping the book open with restrained excitement.

"You're not afraid of Spirits?"

Clara looked up. *Afraid? Of learning? I respect them. Study them. Not fear.*

Theodore huffed a breath — almost a laugh, though he hid it poorly, his mouth twitching with begrudging admiration. "That's a dangerous mindset."

So is ignorance. Living under the dome. Ignoring the Interwilds.

He leaned in, close enough for her to hear his slow inhale. "You're difficult," he muttered.

You shoved me into a wall.

"That," he said, jaw snapping tight, "was a misunderstanding."

He set down another journal. She reached for it — before her fingers closed on the cover, his hand settled over hers. Firm and deliberate. A silent command to wait. His palm was solid, sun-warmed stone. Hers was ice-cold from ink-stained pages.

The contrast startled her.

"Go on then," he whispered. "Don't say I didn't warn you."

MARGOT WILSON

Scheming Between Friends

Margot was putting the last of the books on her shelf when she heard a knock at the door — she dusted off her hands, surveying the hive of clutter and half-finished attempts at cleaning.

She forced herself to face it. She didn't want Nikolas to think she lived like this, didn't want him to see the grief that still clung to her cobwebbed walls. She used to be organised before her mother died.

Each attempt at unpacking always ended the same way: Margot sitting on the floor in tears. Her bedroom was worse — he was never going in there.

She had been distracting herself from the Nikolas issue by translating the diary her mother had left her — the first thing she noticed was the embossed symbol on the cover, the same one on the inside of her wrist. Gold worn down to nothing. When she touched it, something under her skin stirred in recognition.

It was the last diary of Olivia Brown, Orion's previous bonded.

In her research, she had found three newspaper clippings. One for her birth. One for a brief two-season engagement to a mycology professor. One line announcing her death. No photos. No journals. Nothing preserved.

As though she had never existed at all.

An icy ripple skittered down Margot's spine. *Could that happen to her?*

She opened the door. Nikolas stepped in, gaze sweeping the apartment, then settling on her — that faint tug of want, a whisper of peppermint tea behind her ribs.

"Did you get the plans?" she asked.

Nikolas hung up his coat and held out a long tube, one corner of his mouth pulling into something slow and sly that tightened something low in her stomach. "Got them."

"Excellent. Let's get started." Margot exhaled and set her research on Celestial Spirits under her arm. She cleared several mugs from the low table. A few days had passed since she had tried to sway him at the bar. Orion had demanded they meet at her apartment after their shifts; he needed to watch both of them. Nikolas agreed. The Study Hall was too open, and his room at the Barracks was forbidden territory. She didn't want Emile to see her there.

Margot had plenty of space here, relatively speaking. She had visited Emile's room once — an ivory plaster room with a single window facing a brick wall, large enough for a bed and a desk.

She had ignored the signs. How wrong she had been.

Clara had stopped by earlier, promising to send information on the shields the moment she found it.

One illegal problem at a time.

"How did you get them?" she turned, impressed.

"If you can have secrets, then so can I." He winked.

Heat curled up her throat. She turned to the stove to buy herself a moment and lit the flame. She couldn't tell him about the Daughters of the Harpy; Orion had made her swear it. The peppermint tug brushed her again as she reached for the tea jars. "Peppermint? I don't have any orange pekoe left." Rations grew tighter every month. The empty jar felt heavier than glass should.

"Peppermint is fine," he called.

She knew he'd say that.

She had been practising on him, learning to reach toward the edges of his heart. Never with coworkers. Never with someone who could report her. Nikolas was dangerous — but different.

She handed him his cup, prepared the way he liked it.

"So, when can we get the staff?" she asked, tucking an errant curl behind her ear. She had been practising glamour on herself too, attempting to soften her forever-unruly hair into curls at her shoulders.

Orion perched on the sill, tail flicking in annoyance, watching everything.

Nikolas stared at her long enough for her skin to prickle, then cleared his throat and tapped the plans. "Getting in will be simple. Getting out will be harder. We slip into the armoury when the party peaks during the Brumalis festival. Everyone will be hungover or drinking for days."

Her brows pulled together. "The Study Hall is always full then. No one notices anything that night."

"Exactly," he said. "I can hold everyone in stasis."

Her breath caught. "You can do that?"

"Once," he said. "For a short time. It will drain me. You'll need to keep track." His gaze dropped to her wrist. "Your timepiece. Half an hour. I can only promise that much."

She nodded and forced herself to swallow the fear.

"Have you been working on the replacement staff?" he added.

"I think it looks good." Margot crossed the room to her closet. "I asked a craft guild for a wooden dowel, and Orion made me practise transfiguring it."

She lifted it, running a finger along the grain — she sensed Nikolas' heart quicken at the touch. "It has an interesting shape," she said.

He leaned closer, admiring her handiwork. The staff was deep brown, curved wood, polished smooth. "Not bad," he said.

His praise slid under her ribs.

"Have you been working on your glamour?" he asked.

Margot set the staff down and smoothed her skirt. "A little. It is hard to tell if I am doing it well." She closed her eyes and pictured the person she wished to be. *Become them.*

Her skin pulled and tightened, *mana* spreading across it in a warm buzz. Bones lengthened. Muscles shifted. She grew taller. Her face reformed.

When she opened her eyes, his shock was a thrill that skittered down her spine.

Nikolas' jaw dropped. "How did you do that?"

"Pretty neat," she said in his voice, taking a swaggering spin with her arms out. Holding onto the glamour was difficult.

She could change an object easily enough, but a body fought back, her *mana* well straining, every heartbeat begging her to snap back.

Nikolas reclined on her couch with a casual grace that made her stomach flutter. "I did not know I was this handsome in a skirt."

Margot snorted and tilted her head up toward him.

He rose and approached. She felt his rough, calloused fingers slide over her altered jawline, tracing the stubble. Her breath hitched as his thumb brushed her lower lip. Even through the borrowed skin, she felt the touch everywhere. He tilted her head from side to side, studying her, his gaze dropping to her lips.

Orion hissed from his perch.

"Excellent work," Nikolas cleared his throat.

Margot blinked and released the glamour — a crackle of static tingling across her body as she shrank and returned to herself.

The moment she snapped back, a tight flutter threaded

itself in her heart. He was rugged and scarred — but the scars were stories she wanted to hear.

Anxiety coiled around her throat. She knew better than to fall for someone who planned to leave the city.

Nikolas returned to the plans laid out across the table. "We follow this path." His finger traced the route from the main entrance to a basement corridor. "One guard on duty. I can get the keys and the code." He tapped a point near the east wall. "Security is relaxed, considering they house several *mana* weapons."

"How?" she asked.

"I can nudge the roster."

A weight settled in her throat. "Emile."

"Emile," Nikolas confirmed.

She pressed her lips together. "You will not hurt him?"

"I will not kill him," Nikolas said.

The answer was honest, which made it worse.

"It still feels too easy," she breathed.

"Our alignments make it possible," he smirked. "Are you nervous, soul wielder?"

She scoffed. "Of course I am. I have never done something like this." She fidgeted with her fingers and took a sip of tea.

"Don't worry."

"What if something happens?" Her fingers tightened around her mug.

"Then I will take care of it." His jaw tightened.

Images of Nikolas cutting down cultists flashed across her mind. The things people whispered about him. Her control slipped. She stood abruptly and paced, chewing her thumbnail.

These were her friends, her colleagues, her family. Margot felt everything in the room — Nikolas' concern, Orion's irritation sharp and stern as her mother's warnings. If anyone got hurt because of her, she'd never forgive herself.

Nikolas rose and stepped in front of her, his hands sliding gently up and down her arms, warming through the thin blouse. "Close your eyes and breathe."

She let the warmth of his hands steady her. The room was too loud. In through her nose. Out through her mouth. *Too bright. Too full.* But slowly, her panic dulled.

"Better?" he asked softly.

"Yes." She opened her eyes.

She fell into his dull green gaze — from this close, flecks of gold glimmered in the Ignis lights, the green sharpening each time she dared to let her glances linger.

Her breath caught as he leaned closer. He wanted to —

"Are you two finished?" Orion leapt from the windowsill with perfect timing and brushed against her leg.

Margot jerked back and scooped Orion into her arms. "Are you hungry, my darling?" she said, scratching his chin.

"I am," Orion said, purring into her arms.

Too close. She nearly let Nikolas kiss her.

Nikolas wanted to leave. He wanted to go back to the Interwilds. She could not allow herself to want him. She wouldn't survive being left behind again. Her chest ached.

Do not get attached. He will leave.

She hugged Orion even tighter. *Everyone leaves.*

Nightmares and Daydreams

☾

Every day Margot crossed off her calendar, the more her nerves frayed at the edges. Reality rolled endlessly through her mind every night as she tried — and failed — to fall asleep. Her new role as Orion's second meant she'd soon oversee and protect an entire city.

She couldn't look after them. She couldn't even look after herself.

When she got up for the third time, her feet didn't meet her apartment floorboards — they sank into grass and prickling dirt.

What the…?

A field of grass and trees surrounded her, tall grasses shifting in the wind. The bed was the only familiar thing left, and even that felt out of place — the tips of her white sheets muddy and brown, swaying gently in the dirt.

A low mist crept around her ankles.

The blue hour. Early dawn. She shivered in the gentle breeze, feet wet from the dewy grass. *It's not winter here.*

She paced around her bed, looking for any signs of life.

Or — any reason she was here.

A pinprick of light caught her eye, flickering beyond the thicket of trees surrounding her bed.

She could crawl back into bed, hide under the sheets, and hope this nightmare would end. Or she could move to the light.

The second choice terrified her.

Cursing, she pulled the top sheet off the bed and wrapped it around herself.

She had always felt safer in layers.

She stepped through the grass until she reached a dirt road: deep grooves from cartwheels cut through it, hardened by countless journeys. Beyond the path rose a makeshift village wall, built from tree logs packed with moss, mud, and sticks. Sturdy but crudely made.

A lantern hung above the gate, burning with a blue flame. The gate creaked softly in the morning breeze — crimson and ivory wax trickling along the walls, each drip like frozen blood.

"Get up and face me, boy," a deep voice thundered from within the wall — Margot flinched, yet crept closer, pressing her eye to a narrow gap in the logs.

Inside lay a small village built of stacked rocks and thick timber, roofs covered in grass, smoke curling from stone fire pits in thin blue ribbons. Bundles of dried herbs — sage, eucalyptus, and crimson root — hung over doorposts beside wood carved with runes she didn't recognise.

A tall, well-muscled man stood over a thin, trembling boy no older than ten — mud clinging to the boy's tattered shirt, red gashes streaking his sleeves, fresh blood dripping down pale skin.

"Pick up the sword," the man barked.

The child scrambled backward, shaking his head.

"Pick it up," the man roared.

"I can't! Please, Father, let me go!" the boy sobbed.

A strip of leather tied the man's long, white-citrine curls back — the boy had the same pale hair, the same delicate build. A miniature version of the man towering above him.

"You can, and you will."

The man swung the sword — the boy raised his hand to shield his face, and the blade sliced deep into his palm. Blood spilled freely. The boy screamed, clutching his injured hand to his chest.

Margot gasped, clapping a hand over her mouth, and stumbled backward.

As she turned, the hair prickled on the back of her neck, goosebumps skittering along her arms. Something ancient pressed into the air around her.

Ruby eyes flared open behind her, burning like coals pressed into her spine — pain stabbing through her skull.

She dropped to her knees, hands over her head, gasping for breath.

When she forced herself to look up, she froze.

Four long onyx legs, each one gleaming obsidian polished to a mirror sheen. The creature towered over her, its torso shifting with a fluid motion, its hide swallowing the light.

An Equus — but twisted, monstrous.

Its ribcage rose and fell with unnatural slowness, nostrils flaring and releasing a metallic mist that smelled of blood and iron. Where a beast's face should have been, there was only a smooth expanse of shadow — split in the centre by two burning ruby eyes.

The wall pressed against her back.

She couldn't retreat. Couldn't breathe.

The Equus reared, its forelegs slashing at the air — hooves cut from black stone, catching the light. The scream, warped and bone-deep, sliced through the quiet of the dawn.

Complete blackness crashed around her.

Margot awoke in her own bed, covered in sweat, tears streaming down her face, the sheets tangled around her legs. Her chest heaved.

The Cycle

☾

Margot glanced at her timepiece — two hours left. Her foot tapped in a constant rhythm. She had read that same passage at least four times.

Over the last week they had developed a routine: it started at the end of her shift and ended at midnight, when Margot couldn't keep her eyes open any longer. After a quick dinner in the Mess Hall, they sat in silence, Nikolas reading or practising the lines she had prepared for him.

He was a fast learner — Laetin and Angloic both, astonishingly quick. She felt envious of his abilities.

When he was done, he scribbled notes in a runic language she didn't recognise, or drew fantastic creatures in the margins — always obsessing over that particular statue in the Study Hall.

Her head hit the notebook. *So bored.* Someone tapped her with a paper flower, and several others giggled.

The Aquaan Council had demanded they categorise the rest of the books by the end of Brumalis; the Guild used the same intake procedure for every single volume, and the delay displeased Aurora.

Part of her duties as a Maven was categorising and translating volumes of books, tomes, and scrolls. She used to find it exciting — the thought of reading a text unseen for decades once thrilled her.

"What's got you lookin' so bummed, kid?" April, one of the senior librarians, squawked from across the table.

"Oh, nothing… just tired," Margot sighed, dropping the pen onto her notebook.

"That new fella's got you worked up, eh?"

Margot choked mid-swallow. "I do not have a new man!" She threw one of the paper flowers the others were folding for the festival at April.

"You sure, sweetheart?" April's amusement brushed against her senses, featherlight and bright as spring wind.

April glanced over Margot's shoulder.

She followed her gaze and turned. That familiar tug of want threaded through her ribs as she locked eyes with the gold-flecked green she had missed.

Missed? Oh no…

"Well, isn't it our newest member of the custodian guard coming to greet us oldies," April called as Nikolas approached, Mabel beaming beside her.

"Always a pleasure to see you, April," he crooned back with a sly smile. "I finished my training early. Since it's the last shift before Brumalis, I was hoping to take this lovely thing off your hands for the rest of the day." He held out his hand, topping it off with a wink at Mabel.

Both librarians melted instantly.

Margot's smile faltered when she caught sight of Emile standing by the stacks, pretending to read.

Oh, this was not a show for her — it was for Emile. She'd ask questions later. For now, she wanted to lean into it, if only to rub salt into the wound.

"Oh, my knight in shining armour! Coming to rescue the fair maiden from paper folding!" She held out her hand, the other pressed to her forehead in an exaggerated swoon.

A giggle escaped her as he lifted her off the chair with far more strength than she expected.

Margot turned to Mabel, who gave her a subtle nod of approval. She moved behind the counter to grab her book bag.

She dared not look at Emile again — his aura was a putrid

greenish-brown, spilling from his eyes and clinging around him in a rotting haze. His jealousy and hatred of Nikolas were consuming him from the inside out.

In a small, distant way, she pitied him.

It was dark by the time Margot put her coat on. The longest night of the year was rapidly approaching. She was going to make the most of it.

They used the underground pathways as much as they could, the snowstorm outside gaining severity.

Outside, the storm howled — Heims exhaling its final winter breath. High above them, a chilling wind swept through the stone as the Spirit's life faded toward its annual death. The Spirit would return to the ground in a matter of days, and Viridis would awaken again twelve nights later.

The cycle inched toward its turning point.

☾

"My hands. They're frozen!" Margot hung up her coat and blew warm air between her fingers. "I'll get the kettle started."

Nikolas moved toward the centre of the apartment. "Who are you?" he asked, staring at the figure sitting on her couch.

Margot's heart leapt into her throat — they were petting Orion.

"No need to be alarmed," Orion sounded too pleased as their fingers rubbed his ears.

The stranger was Clara. Orion jumped from her lap as she stood, brushing fur off her clothes. *I came to deliver my boon to you,* she signed.

"Nikolas, her name is Clara, and she is a friend. With your permission, I will translate for you," Margot said.

Clara nodded and handed over a notebook. Margot opened it and read through her notes.

"You are from Britannia," Nikolas stated.

Clara nodded. *How did you know?* she signed.

"Your eyes and hair," he said. *Sapphire eyes and onyx hair were trademarks of Britannian people.*

"Let me guess, Aquaan?" he added, looking at Margot.

"A long story, but yes," Margot said and stepped between them. "Come on, it's too late for fighting. Let's have peppermint tea."

Orion meowed and brushed along Margot's legs, purring. She scratched under his chin and filled his bowl with chopped, dried fish.

She dusted her hands and washed them in the basin as she prepared the tea. "Why did you not meet me at the Library?"

You are always with that one, Clara signed, pointing her chin at Nikolas. *You are making a move for the Anima Staff, and I want to help.*

"You have been watching us?" Margot's hands fell to her sides.

I have been keeping suspicious eyes off you. Protecting you.

Nikolas watched their exchange in silence, his only movement the slow rise and fall of his chest. She could sense his anxiety sharpening, coiled and ready. One shift of Clara's stance and he'd strike.

"Why have you come now?" Nikolas asked, his eyes never leaving Clara's hands.

I want to help you steal the Staff.

"What is in it for you?"

Change is coming. I can hear it. The new cycle begins soon. She paused to crack her knuckles. *And the power struggle means innocent people will get caught in the crossfire. I want to protect them.*

Nikolas stroked his chin. "The cycle?"

Margot answered, "As dictated by the Twelve Tables, the electoral cycle begins when Heims dies in the twelfth and final year and goes to ground. The Council will decide on a new leader. It ensures equality."

Nikolas never looked away from Clara's hands. "You're siding with us? Not the Council?"

It's time something exciting happened around here, Clara shrugged.

"Aurora is due to give up her reign of power. Who is going to replace her?" Margot asked.

That is an excellent question, Clara signed.

"I will." Orion trotted over, his tail swinging in slow, feathery arcs, and sat in front of Margot.

Margot had her back pressed against the kitchenette, her hands braced on the sink. *"You will what? Take over the Council? And what about me? I never asked for this."*

"And yet here we are, standing at the precipice of change, Margot. You have to get the staff and reverse the transfiguration your mother placed on me. You will begin your studies as a novice Soul wielder." Orion's tail curled around him and swayed, the faintest sign of irritation.

With the staff restored, the Protectorate could supersede the Council in a breath. One decision could reshape Historia for decades. He had mentioned this — her new role — countless times, but it had always felt distant. Now, with Heims dying and going to ground and the city caught in a never-ending storm, it sounded inevitable.

"What's in this for me?" Nikolas whispered.

Margot's pulse faltered. He fixed his gaze past her — toward Orion, toward the Interwilds that stretched beyond the shields.

Toward his freedom.

The thought throbbed behind her ribs as she felt that faint thread between them loosening, slipping through her fingers. Still, she forced herself to meet his grey-green eyes.

Orion twisted his head toward him, tail curling around his legs. *"I shall grant you passage through the shields."*

The air stilled.

Nikolas went quiet in that devastating way of his. *"Will that guarantee my memories of this place stay intact?"*

"Yes. You can cross the shields as you will it."

Margot's heart squeezed. There it was — the promise he'd wanted, the one that let him walk away without losing a single memory.

He could leave her and remember everything.

Nikolas nodded, slow and resolute. *"As long as you keep your promise,"* he said, *"I'll keep mine."*

Her breath hitched. She tried to steady herself, to hide it, to pretend she wasn't unravelling.

Nikolas must have felt it. He turned to her, brows drawing together, a flicker of something raw crossing his face as if her pain tugged at something inside him. *"Margot..."* he whispered, too softly.

She tore her gaze away before her eyes could betray a prickle of tears.

What was that? Clara signed.

Margot swallowed hard. "Nothing important." Another lie, one that settled under her ribs.

Clara accepted it and nodded. *Then bring me up to speed on your plan.*

Nikolas stepped toward her, close enough that she sensed him watching her, trying to decipher the flinch she hadn't meant to show.

The distance stretched between them anyway — opened wide by choices he had made.

All Margot felt was a deep ache and a sense of utter helplessness.

She Aimed for His Head

Margot smelled the fresh pine garlands as she walked into the Study Hall. Love in the Midnight Snow was a dumb theme — who needs love when you can just read about it instead?

"Good morning, Margot, excited for tonight?" her co-worker April said, her wrinkled hands twisting the garland along the banister of the staircase.

"Morn'in," Margot replied with a yawn.

"Long night?"

"No, just... odd dreams."

Odd dreams was an understatement. She'd been having another round of sex dreams for the past few days and could not get them to stop. She shook her head. If he wanted to leave, *fine.*

She tried to believe it. She really did. But even thinking of his face made her chest pull tight — she'd agreed to help him find a way around the shields. And then... *No.*

Margot started unpacking festival decorations out of the box and let out a heavy sigh. She can't get hurt again. She isn't strong enough to survive that again.

"Odd dreams, eh?" April peered at her from the ladder and pushed up her glasses. "You're a terrible liar."

Margot shook her head. "I can't say."

"Yes, you can. You can tell me anything."

Margot stopped unpacking the decorations. April stepped down from the ladder. "I have seen boys buzz around you your whole life, and none of them have made you feel this way."

Tears pricked Margot's eyes. She refused to cry again, closed her eyes and took a hard swallow.

"Margaret Wilson, don't be silly. You're young and beautiful. Don't let one stupid boy ruin it for every other one that comes your way." April waved her hand. That prompted the other librarians to leave and decorate another part of the hall.

"He…" Margot tipped her head back. "He isn't committed to me." She lied — *sort of.* Nikolas was as clear as *mana* about his wish for freedom.

"Then he's an even bigger idiot than that dolt who got you all knotted up last time." April took off her glasses and rubbed her eyes.

Margot tried to stop the prickle of tears forming. She never used to cry — now she seemed to cry over meaningless things. *Crying is for the weak.*

"Or you could just fuck him and move on, as I did with my last three husbands." April pulled her into a tight hug. "You're a survivor."

"I wish Mum was here."

"I know, bug."

She was helping April hang more garland when a gust of frigid wind made her shiver. Her neck prickled with awareness. The double doors had needed maintenance for weeks —

All thoughts emptied from her head. She looked at the face of someone she had thought was dead — her knees buckled, her senses narrowing sharp and ringing, as if refusing to believe what she was seeing.

Qu.

He couldn't be standing there, shaking fallen snow off his mahogany hair. Their eyes met. His smile was brief — a quick nod as if to say, *Yes, I am alive.*

The nod hit her harder than a blow to the gut, heat

flooding her palms. Every buried feeling surged at once, raw and wild — the kind she had shoved so deep she thought they'd never surface again.

She crossed the room in a trance and slapped him straight across the cheek.

☾

"You—"

Quentin caught the glass headed directly at his head with a whoosh of air — the third one Margot had thrown at him, and she was not stopping.

"Darling, I need you to stop doing that," he said, remaining where he was, determined to take whatever punishment she demanded as penance.

Margot wasn't done. She moved to pick up her mother's fountain pen and tossed it as hard as she could at his chest. It bounced off him and landed on the deep ruby carpet between them.

He picked it up and approached, so slowly, as if she were a caged animal ready to strike.

She was out of breath, papers and books and mugs and glasses scattered across the room between them. She leaned back on her mother's desk. There was so much left to do downstairs, but she did not care one bit.

"Why…" Her voice cracked. Too many questions choked her throat. *Why did you leave? Why did you stay silent? Why did you let me grieve you? Why did you come back now? Why does this hurt?*

"Just breathe, my love…" Qu demonstrated with his own breath. He smelled different, yet the same as she remembered — the evergreen leaves of Autumn, the warmth of nutmeg and cardamom, the powdery smell of fresh linens.

"Do not call me that. I will never allow you to call me that again," Margot said as a tear fell.

He captured her hand, so warm as he turned it over and

wiped away the other errant tear.

The contact struck like lightning, his breath staggering. Margot felt the shock travel through him, raw and unguarded.

Relief. All of it burst across his aura, aching in a way that cut through her.

"I see you never took this off." He glided a hand over her timepiece — a generous gift on her name-day, the back engraved with a token of a promise they could never keep. She had told no one who gifted it to her.

"Yes, well," she cleared her throat. "I couldn't let such a useful tool sit in a box unused."

He was way too close, his body caging her in, pinning her back to the desk. She didn't feel trapped — not with him. His intoxicating scent coated the back of her throat as his nose glided along her neck, his short stubble kissing her cheek.

"I am still mad at you," she whimpered.

Part of her wanted to shove him away and demand why he had ripped her open again. Another part remembered the nights in the dormitories, their whispered futures, their stolen kisses.

She had loved him with her whole young, reckless heart.

"No, I don't think you — " Their lips crashed together, and he lifted her onto the desk. His lips felt exactly the same. His stubble was thicker, his chest stronger. Not a teenager anymore.

His moans were just as hungry as his hands, grasping and pulling her closer. "Fuck, this is going to be harder than I thought," he ground out.

She was eighteen when her mother told her. *A freak training accident.* Her mother had lied to her about a lot of things.

"I need to tell you something, but you have to promise not to freak out," Qu said, his eyes squeezed shut.

"I will not promise anything," she said.

He eased her off the desk, letting her stand, pulling down her skirt and fixing her blouse. The shift in his posture cut through the haze. *What was he doing?*

Qu grasped her hand and placed it on his chest. "I've returned because my father and Sophia's father have arranged a marriage. If I don't marry soon, I'll be sent back to Alces. I was going to tell you — "

He tightened his grip as she tried to pull free. "Listen, I didn't — "

"I cannot believe you have the audacity!" She swung at him, but he stepped aside before it made contact. Betrayal cracked through her chest, hot and humiliating.

"Sophia's not thrilled with the arrangement either. In fact, she has fewer options than I do. You know how she is."

Margot had just seen Sophia that morning at breakfast, sensed nothing out of the ordinary. *How long had she been hiding this?*

Boiling with embarrassment, Margot could no longer look at him. She pushed him back, wiped her face, smoothed her hair — returning to the icy, detached pose her mother often took.

She opened the door. "Leave now." Her tone was pointed, one she did not use often.

She needed him gone. Needed the room empty before she shattered. Needed space to remember that Nikolas existed.

She wasn't supposed to fall apart for Quentin Atticus anymore.

"I understand why you're upset, and I'm here to listen whenever you're ready to talk. I'm very sorry for your loss." He glided out the door, his scent following him — juniper berries and powdery musk.

Abyss, fucking take her.

She closed the door, slamming it shut. Her heart was too confused to choose one grief. Everything pressed in until she could barely breathe — tears stung, but none fell. She was so reckless and impulsive.

Her mother would be ashamed.

She felt burdened, as if she were born with the yoke tipped heavily to one side. Constantly moving through life, judged by an invisible rubric that everyone else seemed to know.

She hated failure — it clung to her chest, aching and sticky. And yet she had only herself to blame when it all came crashing around her.

Why did it have to be this way?

She wanted to be productive, to find value in her work, but there were so many other creative things she could do. Instead, she had been forced to follow in her mother's footsteps since birth.

Evelyn Wilson's office — her office — was a chaotic mess, worse than her apartment.

Margot picked herself up and cleaned.

The Heist

☾

Margot smoothed her new silk dress, glancing at herself in the mirror — she'd had just enough coin to buy the material. She layered it with one of her mother's slip dresses, the lace hem gracing her calves.

While the garnet piece was nice, it never stood out. She liked to press her back against the wall and watch — to be seen briefly, make polite conversation, find someone to pass the time.

She chewed the special leaves she'd taken from the Conservatory and stashed the rest in her purse, then adjusted the coat of arms pinned on her left shoulder.

Tonight, she was going to break into the Armoury and steal the staff.

"*You are beautiful,*" Orion said, prancing into her bedroom.

"Wish me luck?"

"*Break a leg.*"

☾

The Library was a stunning sight, bathed in the soft glow of the moon. Garlands of weeping pine twisted around the rails, decorated with white candles and red ribbons, filling the space with warm, ethereal light.

Protected by the librarians' round oak desk, Historia's statue — the only one with their face intact — stood proudly in the centre of the Study Hall, reaching for the sky with Margot's staff, holding an open book. The Anima staff was Historia's before it passed to Orion.

Margot took a slow breath to calm her nerves. She spotted Sophia making her way down the stairs — their eyes locked, and Margot's racing heart collided with thoughts of kissing Qu on the couch.

Margot immediately regretted kissing him — guilt ripped through her. She never intended to stretch out her *mana* and connect to Qu's heart. She felt everything, and it was overwhelming.

"I'm so — "

Sophia's arms came crashing around her. Margot connected to her heart instantly — heartbreak coursed through her at once. Their triad was unshakeable, even from themselves. Margot understood why Sophia had agreed to marry Quentin; her family would shun her otherwise.

"How are you doing?" Sophia asked.

"Ready to take my position. I just hope we can pull this off."

Sophia nodded. "You'll be needing this." She handed Margot a note — the rest of the code needed to open the Armoury Vault door.

Relief flooded through her — Sophia had done it, had risked enough stealing the paper from Maya's breast pocket. "Keep your father and Aurora busy. They cannot know that I have the staff until I have freed Orion. Then, it's up to him."

Sophia's father would let them starve in the damp, dark cells below the barracks if the guards caught them.

"Can you trust Orion?" Sophia asked.

Margot paused. She had to do this — it was an order from her bonded. Of course she could trust Orion. "I can," she said.

Sophia let out a soft whistle and jutted her chin toward the stairs.

Margot spotted him descending the steps in his finest custodian uniform — no patches or proper crest yet, hair slicked back, face shaved clean.

Though Nikolas appeared weary — the stress of the heist

likely affecting him too. Margot loosed a sigh, nerves bubbling up in her stomach.

"Have you seen the latest piece in our gallery?" Nikolas said as he handed Sophia a flute of champagne. *Is everything in place?*

"I particularly like the new oil painting in the Aerian Hall," Margot said, her eyes already darting to a guild member holding a tray of champagne. *The exit is clear. The uniforms are secure.*

She tipped the first flute back, bubbles pricking her tongue. It had been a while since she'd had any wine — Orion forbade it. *Just this once. He won't know.*

Margot had another after enduring an hour of small talk with April and Mabel, and a particularly nasty exchange with Delia about proper protocols for artefact cleaning.

She assured herself three was fine after a droning conversation with Garry about how the rodenta were chewing holes in the third floor's tapestry collection.

By the fourth drink, all the nerves were gone.

Orion would be livid.

A rousing few notes played nearby on the quartet — her favourite. She tilted her head back, slightly buzzed, the room too small, her eyes prickling with memories of other celebrations with her mother. Perched on her toes, dancing to the music. This song belonged to them — the anthem of a love cut short.

Nikolas grabbed the wine from her hands before she could take a long sip and placed it on a nearby tray. "Dance with me?" he asked, his hand outstretched, eyes pleading.

Fuck it. One tiny dance wouldn't hurt with someone you have limited time with. She'd savour every second.

She placed her hand in his, warmth meeting her palm as the quartet's song shifted into something soft and winter-sweet, a quiet melody threaded with longing. He pulled her toward the centre of the room, his movements careful, as if she might slip through his fingers if he held her any tighter.

He spun her away. A wide smile broke across Margot's face, matching his — her dress flaring around her legs, silk catching the light, and for a moment she felt weightless.

He drew her back, slower than before, stretching the distance — their chests brushing together, a soft collision that stole her breath. One gloved hand held hers, the other settled at the small of her back. His touch was gentle, but his fingers pressed with the careful pressure of him memorising her shape.

Her pulse thrummed, light enough that she might float. He stepped in; she stepped back, a slow sway that felt more intimate than any moment they'd shared. His breath warmed her cheek, and she let herself rest against his temple for a single moment, hidden in the moving crowd.

The quartet's music swelled, then dipped into a held note. She could have lived in that moment, suspended in his arms. He tilted his head; their cheeks brushed. Her lips parted. He spun her one last time, her hair swirling around her shoulders — and when he brought her back in, his heartbeat drummed against her chest.

The music ended. They paused, the lingering melody hanging in the air between them.

"*Ready*?" he whispered in her ear.

Her breath caught as she looked into his grey-green eyes — they softened, bright as grass on a spring day, his hand tightening as if he wanted to linger for one more second.

One more breath. One more heartbeat.

His smile struck her spine like lightning.

She felt it happen the instant he let go. *Statues*. Every dancer halted mid-twirl. Her pulse pounded in her ears. She hadn't thought he could actually do it — the sheer strength of it staggered her. For one suspended heartbeat, she wished he had frozen her too, frozen her in that moment with him.

Their last dance before everything shattered.

They snapped into action, moving to the fire exit at the back of the Library. Margot had been surveying the Aerian Hall for days — she knew every way in and out.

They had limited time to reach the Armoury before everyone unfroze and their absence was noticed. She glanced at her timepiece.

Twenty-nine minutes remained.

Nikolas pulled at his tie and undid his vest, letting the fabric fall to the floor. Margot shimmied out of her dress, leaving a white silk camisole and tights.

She glanced at his back and anger flared in her chest. She recognised one scar as a whiplash mark — some were new and red, others silvery and aged, deep purple and yellow bruising raised and tender across his skin.

Did the guards beat him?

Margot pulled on the custodian uniform hidden between the stacks.

"Ready?" Nikolas huffed.

Margot nodded, fixing the cap on her head, tilting it sideways.

This part disgusted her — transforming into him. She made her body more masculine, increased her height to match Emile's, felt her face tingle as she replicated his features.

She had to pick a guard she knew well — unfortunately, that meant Emile. She could replicate skin tone, height, hair, and eye shade, but not clothing; those had to be worn. Nikolas had done his part by ensuring Emile was on duty that night.

She tied the guard's shoelaces and stood. "Do I look okay?"

"You're getting better at this." Nikolas smiled, hid a

bundle of rope in his jacket, and headed for the exit.

Her boots hit the gravel. Twenty-one minutes remained. They hustled across muddy ground — a pleasant run of warm days had melted the snow on the commons, leaving piles of dirty slush and slick patches along the paths.

"Evening, gentlemen," Nikolas said.

The two boys snapped to attention at the Armoury doors, saluting with hands placed below their coat of arms. Margot and Nikolas returned the gesture and moved past.

She was prepared for every movement to this point — anything beyond those doors was unknown. She relied on Nikolas to get her the rest of the way.

Emile stood from behind his desk, blinking at Margot wearing a copy of his face — Nikolas came up behind him instantly, pressing a cloth over his mouth and tying him to the chair.

"You—fu—" Emile's muffled curses grated on her nerves.

She placed two fingers at his temples and lulled him into dreamless sleep — at least until they were done. Nikolas searched his pockets for keys and the code. Emile's head lolled to the side.

Margot checked her timepiece.

Eighteen minutes remained.

☾

Nikolas memorised the rest of the route.

They reached a heavy door sealed with a rolling combination lock — the code changed daily, one half carried by the guard on duty, the other kept by the Commander-in-Chief.

Sophia had ensured their victory when she lifted it from Maya's breast pocket, doing *practice runs* for weeks leading to this single moment. A councillor's daughter was the last person anyone suspected of theft.

The dial shifted as Nikolas turned it, stopping at symbols,

then rotating in the opposite direction. He pulled the lever — it clicked, opened smoothly, stale air rushing out with a spill of dust motes.

Margot rushed inside, scanning endless rows of unused weapons. Nikolas drifted toward a suit of armour, tracing the hole in its chest plate with a finger — something had caved it in like a tree stump or a massive blunt weapon.

"It's not time to touch. Let's move." She checked her timepiece.

Ten minutes remained.

I am here…

There — displayed on the wall like a trophy. The staff whispered as she connected to it. She dragged a chair across the stone floor.

Come to me.

The chair creaked beneath her weight.

Mine.

She reached up and grasped it.

Margot placed the replacement where her staff had been. She needed more time to undo the transfiguration. The cycle had to keep the Council distracted long enough to give it to her.

She jumped down, warmth radiating from the Orb in her pouch, its longing to reunite with the staff pressing against her palm.

"Let's head back," she said.

Five minutes remained.

Broomsticks

☾

They ran back through the maze of hallways and up through each checkpoint, returning at last to untie poor Emile from his desk.

She placed two fingers on his temples and pushed a bit of *mana* into him — he would wake soon, thinking only that he had nodded off at his desk. Distant laughter echoed down the hall. The last obstacle remained: the guards at the entrance.

Nikolas tripped, bracing his hand against the wall.

"Almost there," Margot said, catching her breath. *Shit.* He was fading fast, *mana* reserves running low. She adjusted the staff slung across her back — her hands tingling as her form began shifting. Her time was running out.

Soon, she would succumb to *mana* fatigue too.

She opened the pouch tied to her waist, grasped the orb, and fed off its *mana*. Strength flooded back, washing away the ache in her limbs, her chest suddenly lighter than air.

Resting her back against the door, she edged her vision through a stained-glass window — the guards were playing a round of cards.

Three minutes before everyone would unfreeze. She tucked her nerves beneath her ribs and nodded to Nikolas.

They walked through the doors — just a few more steps.

Chairs scraped as the guards stood at attention. "Have a wonderful night, gentlemen," Nikolas said, and Margot forced her eyes forward, keeping the staff tight to her back and out of view.

The sharp, freezing air hit her lungs. She made it.

"Just wait right there!" one guard called out. Her heart

hammered as the others followed.

No, no, no.

"What is that?"

She shuffled backward until the door slammed against her back.

A roar of water surged past them — Margot gasped, throwing an arm over her head. It happened so fast she only felt the sting.

The wave curled mid-air, freezing into jagged ice as it struck the guards, the impact lifting them and slamming them against a building. An instant later, frost spread over their bodies, sealing them to the wall.

Clara stepped forward, boots crunching over frozen puddles, and flicked her wrist to lock the last sheet of ice into place. Her sapphire eyes glinted in the moonlight as she glanced back and nodded.

Clara had saved them.

"Keep going, move!" Nikolas grasped Margot's hand and pulled her toward the fire exit.

Margot looked back, her curls falling into her eyes. Fatigue was setting in — she willed her feet to carry her, limbs leaden, lungs burning.

She felt grit bite into her palms as she climbed the rusty ladder. At last, they reached the third level and paused, recovering their strength.

One minute remained.

Easing through the window, she slid it shut. Nikolas rested his back against the wall and slid to the floor, his tired eyes struggling to stay open.

"Look at me!" Margot cried and slapped him.

Nikolas snapped his eyes open, briefly shifting to ruby-red. He grasped her hand, and a familiar, eerie sensation washed over her. *Inky mane. Ruby eyes. Onyx fur.*

Her chest ached with hollow emptiness — she couldn't

stop thinking about the way his hand felt on her waist during their dance, the way his breath warmed her cheek, the stupid little smile he gave her before he froze the entire room. She swallowed hard, trying to shove the memory deeper.

Nikolas blinked slowly, still dazed from *mana* fatigue, a faint tired laugh escaping him — barely a breath. His gaze snapped to hers.

Her stomach dropped.

"Margot," he murmured, voice rough from exhaustion. "You think too loudly."

Heat shot up her neck. "Stop listening."

"I try," he whispered, *"but you make it impossible."*

She nearly choked and stepped back.

He pushed a hand against the wall to steady himself, still watching her with that devastating mix of affection and restraint.

She wanted to be furious with him, but her heart refused to cooperate.

"Margot." His voice was rough, but warm beneath the exhaustion. *"It was a wonderful dance."*

Her face burned hot. *"Shut up,"* she muttered under her breath.

His smile deepened, turning roguish.

She swallowed. "We have to go," she said, holding out her hand and pulling him up.

He changed first, his back turned. The quartet's music swelled as she was halfway through changing, a crowd of voices echoing through the Aerian Hall.

She smoothed her dress, adjusted the staff on her shoulder. "I will meet you back at the apartment, okay?"

Nikolas nodded, rubbing his chest. "I will find a way to distract them. Give you more time."

☾

Margot moved through the stacks on the balls of her feet.

She spotted a couple coming toward her down a rarely used service hallway and rummaged through her purse for the cleaning closet keys.

Her shoulders sagged, exhaustion dragging at her bones.

The couple's laughter echoed as they bumped against the cleaning closet door.

She was going to get caught.

She opened her pouch, grasped the orb, and willed the staff's shape to sag and warp into the mundane lines of a mop, placing it with the others.

The door opened, and the couple stumbled in. The woman wiped red lipstick from her chin. "Oh! Sorry, I didn't know anyone was in here."

"Someone dropped a glass. I was just about to clean it up," Margot lied. "If you're looking for a place to snog, this is not it."

"Right, sorry… we'll just be leaving," the man said, backing away.

Margot ushered them out and rested her back against the door, breathing in fresh air.

Clara strode up to her. *Successful?* she signed.

Relief loosened in her chest — she could give the staff to Clara. Her hands shook with fatigue. She grabbed her orb, but it didn't replenish her energy. *Shit.* Her knees threatened to buckle.

This was going to get messy.

Clara's eyes widened as she reached out to steady her.

Margot swallowed hard, forcing her spine straight. "Can you help me with one last favour?" she slurred.

Her vision blurred to black.

CLARA LOXLEY

Hot Drunken Mess

▽

Margot tilted her head and slurred, "You know that old wives' tale about the broomsticks?"

What?

Margot dug through her purse, found the keys, and fumbled putting one in — nearly breaking it off. She twisted the knob, felt resistance, stumbled back, and threw her shoulder into it. "Stupid thing always jams when it's cold out!" Clara stepped in to stop her from hurting herself further.

"Owwww..." Margot stumbled into the cleaning closet and fell to her knees.

Clara rolled her eyes.

Margot writhed on the floor, a drunken, *mana*-drained mess draped in garnet silk. She mumbled incoherently, "Shhhhiiitt... I ripped a silk stocking! No, no, they're soooo expensive. Fuuuckk — "

Clara had been waiting outside the staff corridor for the signal when she spotted Margot's pathetic attempt to shoo away a clumsy couple. They'd stumbled off giggling while she watched from the shadows.

But why the cleaning closet?

Giving Margot a moment to collect herself, Clara closed the door behind her.

Margot leaned against the wall, a mess of flipped-over, frizzy amber curls, using it to hold herself upright.

Clara mouthed *where is the staff?* and grasped both sides of

Margot's face, shaking her gently, hoping the shock would give her the focus she needed.

Margot made a noise that was part moan, part burp — it curdled Clara's stomach.

Frustration clawed at her chest. *Fuck.* She couldn't communicate with her like this.

Clara held the struggling Margot upright and looked around for the staff — she'd gone in here for a reason.

What did Margot say… broomsticks?

Clara spotted the collection of brooms and mops in the corner. Which one? This was ridiculous — she had no way to detect the odd handle with her senses.

She held one. It felt ordinary.

She picked up another. Also plain wood.

Clara shook her head and took the heaviest, nicest broomstick, trusting the drunken hint. If she was wrong, she'd come back.

She grasped the broom and lifted Margot off the floor. Margot had slipped into *mana*-drain and would have to sleep it off.

Orion definitely owed her one after this.

Clara exhaled through her nose, steadying her pulse, then brushed her *mana* outward, coaxing and pulling the water in Margot's blood to rise and lighten. The weight lifted from her shoulders at once, Margot's body going feather-soft against her back.

Clara closed the cleaning closet door, mapping out the fastest route out of the Study Hall and back to Margot's apartment.

This was not part of the plan.

As she drew closer, the crowd was… odd. Drunk, delirious, some sitting on the floor giggling. An Aquaan woman — a high-ranking one — swayed on the ground, singing as she waved her hands.

Margot mumbled along to the melodic tune coming from a group of Aquaan that passed them.

Clara knew this tune — a hymn sung by the first halfway people to connect with Historia, rather good at putting mortals into a state of drunken bliss. They swayed together, hands on each other's shoulders. A rowdy sailors' tavern tune, not something a fine society Aquaan would sing in polite company.

The Brumalis festival celebrated an end and a new beginning. Perhaps a researcher had found the tune and sung it to the crowd without realising what it did.

Hopefully, none would remember.

She rested Margot against a nearby pillar and collected their coats — even underground, it was freezing outside at night.

She coaxed Margot to put on her coat, not letting go of the broomstick.

Icy-hot pain gripped her as Margot grasped Clara's arm.

Margot tipped her head back in a delirious gasp.

No, you don't.

Clara ripped her hand away. "*I cannot believe you tried to drain me*!" she coughed out, her throat raw, a wave of grating pain tearing through her neck.

"Fuck, that was…" Margot clutched her own hand, sobbing. "Sorry, Orion told me. I didn't believe him."

We have to keep moving, Clara signed, threading Margot's arm through the coat and ignoring the stinging pain.

Margot snapped out of her daze, smoothed her coat, and took out two leaves — placing one in her mouth before handing the other to Clara. "The leaf blocks pain and boosts *mana* for a few hours. Just don't eat too many," she yawned.

I forgive you, but you owe me one, Clara signed, chewing on the minty-basil taste of the leaf as she pushed Margot onward.

☾

They made it to the front door.

Clara gave Margot a thorough pat-down and found her keys tucked inside her coat pocket. She turned the key and peeked into the apartment.

Margot sat on the hallway floor, her head lolling to the side.

Clara set the broomstick by the fireplace in Margot's living room, not loosening her grip until it was safely down.

A dark, mortal-shaped lump sprawled on the carpet.

She tilted her head as the lump jerked and snored softly.

Nikolas couldn't have…

Clara stepped back into the hallway, collected Margot off the floor, flopped her onto the bed, filled a cup with water, and placed a bin beside it.

She snooped through Margot's bathroom, rifling through the medicine cabinet — pushing aside cosmetic jars to find dried hallucinogenic mushrooms and a small jar of pain-blocking leaves. She left one beside the water, just in case.

Orion jumped up and curled between Margot's legs.

How should I handle the other one? Clara signed.

Orion blinked and rested his head on Margot's leg.

Clara eased off the bed and patted Margot's leg, adjusting the blanket over her chest. She exhaled and cracked her back.

Finally.

Time to report to the Magus.

MARGOT WILSON

Animus Staff

The blinding winter morning light penetrated beneath her eyelids with a wash of red. Margot's head throbbed, her mouth dry and dirty. A rhythmic bang complemented the pressure behind her eyes.

She rolled over, thoughts coming back in waves, and pulled at the silky fabric covering her chest. Who had changed her last night?

The taste of bitter bile at the back of her throat brought back a vague memory of retching — a trail of peeled-off clothing led to the bathroom.

Goosebumps skittered along her skin. The fire had gone out — snowflakes landing on the flipping pages of an open book, the thumping coming from a window left open overnight.

She stumbled out of bed, climbed over a stack of books she had been meaning to read, and closed the window. The sun shone high against a vivid blue sky.

It must be noon.

She shut the curtains against the light and stood in the freezing quiet darkness, rubbing her temples until the pressure lessened.

She took a deep breath and eyed the body sprawled along her couch.

Boots still on, hanging over the armrest. Covered in a blanket hand-crocheted by one of her mother's coworkers. His mouth wide open, snoring against the leather.

Nikolas.

Relieved, she knelt beside him, moving a curled lock of hair to watch him sleep. She cupped his cheek and brushed her fingers over his short stubble — before, she'd not dared get this close. Now she noticed the way his beard comprised different strands of colour. White, grey, reddish-brown, and black twisted together to make a shade that was uniquely his.

His grey-green eyes opened — and a familiar vision of the pitch-black stallion flashed before her, inky mane, deep ruby-red eyes. She yelped, falling backward and bumping her shoulder on an antique ceramic vase.

"Are you okay?" he drawled, sitting upright and covering her with the blanket.

She moved to sit next to him on the couch. "Just sore… everywhere." She tucked the blanket tight — still warm, still smelling of vetiver.

He shivered, running his arms along his uniform. "Do you mind if I start a fire?"

"Yes, please." She held her head in her hands, covering her eyes — the leather sprang back when he stood, and panic surged through her. He was in her bedroom.

When he began meeting her in the apartment, she had set a rule that her bedroom was a 'Margot Only Area' — a boundary Nikolas had always respected. Until now. She didn't want him to know how messy she was.

He will leave –

Nikolas draped the duvet over her shoulders, his arms wrapping around her as he embraced her from behind the couch. "Tea?"

She nodded again.

The sound of the kettle was an unpleasant reminder of her headache as she let Nikolas free-roam her apartment — she hadn't allowed it since their first meeting, had tried to keep a healthy distance, strictly professional. But the lines were blurring.

Warmth crept back into her fingers, the fire heating the air, smells of burning wood enveloping her. She lay with her eyes closed, letting the ache roll through her temples, until the sound of a mug on the low table made her sit upright. She reached for it and took a long, warm sip.

It was perfect.

She adjusted the duvet, tucked her legs under her, and hummed with satisfaction as she took another sip.

Nikolas smiled over the rim of his mug. "I'm glad you made it back."

"I owe Clara a boon in return for helping me. My *mana* drained faster than expected. I couldn't make it to my office in time..."

"So what happened to the staff?" he asked, taking another sip.

"I... I left it back in the Study Hall, in a closet." She moved the blanket higher over her bare shoulders.

His face fell. "Then we can go get it, right? Everyone is home, sleeping off a nasty hangover or resting."

The mourning period for the death of Hiver — fourteen days of rest that Margot planned to use as cover to break the seal on Orion's transfiguration.

"Where is Orion?" He wasn't in bed with her when she woke.

She got up and paced, checking his favourite hiding spots — under the bed, tucked away in the corner.

Where was he?

He always napped in the pile of her mother's fur coats. Not there either. This was an important day. Why hadn't he woken her?

"Have you found him?" Nikolas' voice echoed from her bedroom.

"No..." she sobbed.

Beside her fireplace, she spotted a broom laid against the wall — Clara had brought it back.

She picked it up and focused her *mana* on the wood.

This was… not her staff.

"Oh no, oh no, this can't be happening." She threw the broom in frustration and balled her hands into fists.

Nikolas dodged the projectile. "Your *mana* reserves may just need more time to replenish. Are you sure?" He cupped her cheek, getting way too close.

She flicked his hand away. One crisis at a time.

She stepped back. No, she was sure — it was not her staff. It had weight when she first held it.

The broom lying on her living room carpet was a regular, light brown wooden broom.

She remembered transfiguring it into a —*fuck.*

She stopped pacing. "When Clara brought me back to the apartment, she picked up a broom, not a mop."

"Why in the abyss did you turn it into a mop?"

"I don't know!" Margot tore at her hair. "I was going to stash it in the office like I planned, but — "

Nikolas crossed his arms, his brow creased. "New plan. We eat to recover our strength and figure out where Orion could've gone."

"I don't need food!" She wrapped the blanket around herself and moved to open the door.

Nikolas planted a hand, stopping her.

"Get out of my way!"

"No."

What an asshole. Is he scowling?

Margot pulled on the door. His hand stayed firm. She pulled again, harder. "I have to find him!" Orion always slept between her legs — he never went outside. It was too cold.

"We will, but I won't let you go outside like that." His eyes darted to her chest. The blanket had slipped off her shoulders.

Her lace shift barely covered her chest. She was never shy around Sophia — but around men, good-looking men, handsome men with hunger in their eyes, she felt shy.

"Don't be a perv," she scoffed.

She shut the bedroom door without looking back and changed: a loose linen shirt and pants, thick woollen socks, a white robe tied at the waist. She washed her face, cool water soothing her headache.

A knock sounded at the front door.

Dread washed over her. No one came so early, especially not during Brumalis. She steeled her nerves and ran her hands through her cropped hair — it could just be Sophia checking in. No reason to panic.

Nikolas remained out of sight.

She opened the door. Her heart rose into her throat.

It was worse than Sophia. Worse than the Curatrix. *Fuck.* Worse than a Council member.

Qu.

"Hello, darling. May I come in?" He smiled. His reddish-brown hair was damp with sweat.

"No — d-did you run here?"

"I'm afraid I must insist."

"It isn't the right time," she said as he pushed past her with a gust of wind.

"Ooh, hello…" Qu said to Nikolas.

Margot closed the door slowly, regretting every choice that led to this moment.

Nikolas shook Qu's outstretched hand. "I'm Nikolas, a friend of Margot."

The two men stared at each other.

Qu looked unbothered. "A friend. Interesting. Yes, I remember Sophia mentioning you once or twice in passing."

Why was her heart pounding so fast?

Margot tied the belt tighter around her waist. "Nikolas stayed the night, as we both don't have family. Now, I'd like you to leave."

"Ah, I see," Qu interjected. "Well, it's good to know. I was hoping to speak with you…"

Nikolas moved in front of Margot. "Say it now, then leave."

Qu stared at him. "It concerns you both."

Margot peered around Nikolas' shoulder and folded her arms. "Alright then. Spit it out."

"In ten — maybe fifteen minutes, a custodian guard will knock on that door and arrest you, including anyone associated with the crime." Qu pointed at the door. "The Council has summoned you to atone."

Margot scoffed. "The crime being what? Stealing the staff? How did you know?" She chewed her thumb. "Sophia told you, didn't she?"

"Yes. Sophia panicked and told me after Maya issued the warrant."

"I had to steal the staff to break Orion's transfiguration. I had no choice."

"Now I'm stuck in the middle again, cleaning up your mess. I see not much has changed," he seethed. "I arranged for your arrest to be coordinated with my assistants. Sophia turned herself in and is under house arrest."

"You want me to turn myself in too?" Margot cried. "And what happens to my staff? To Nikolas?"

"I don't know. I'm sorry. I did everything I could to protect you."

"But not anyone else."

Qu shook his head. "Sophia is safe."

Margot turned to Nikolas. In the bright, unforgiving light, his expression was unreadable — but she felt it. Betrayal, cold and quiet, settling between them.

The Council

☾

She threaded her mother's ring onto her finger.

Margot stood before the Council Chambers, waiting for the whispers to stop. She pushed her senses inward, connecting to her heart — her well had replenished to full in the days after her arrest.

Almost full — Orion was still missing. Not hiding. Not asleep. Gone. If the Council had him, they'd never give him back.

Maya went out into the blizzard and captured them after they escaped down the fire ladder of her building. It happened so fast it was embarrassing.

She had dragged Nikolas into her mess.

The memory twisted like a hook behind her ribs. They were ill-prepared to be running in the snow — they collapsed from the freezing temperatures within minutes. During the Mourning Period of Hiver, even a short time outdoors was a gamble with death.

The guards knocked on the door.

"Come in."

"Hello, Maya," Margot said with a cautious smile.

"It's Chief Iyer in here. If you could please sit."

Margot had little choice. She sat politely at the semicircular desk.

"Margaret Wilson," Maya said — Margot's full name ringing in the Council Chambers for what felt like the hundredth time.

She wasn't a stranger to the people in front of her. But today their gazes felt colder, appraising her *mana*, her breath, her pulse.

She felt flayed open under their scrutiny.

"The Council summoned you to stand trial for theft. How do you plead?"

Margot summoned her strength and stared at the four Council members. "Not guilty, Chief Iyer." A small smile kicked at the corner of her lips.

Chief Iyer leaned back with a mask of indifference — Margot sensed surprise in her aura. Aurora glanced at Anthony as he choked back a scoff.

Anthony's knuckles whitened around his stack of papers, his contempt oozing.

The other member, Theodore, looked unamused. "I thought you were going to plead guilty. Did you not liaise with…" He drifted off as he shuffled through his papers. "Nikolas Venator and break into the vault that contained the staff?"

"Yes, but it's mine by right." She fiddled with her mother's ring. "I am the Soul Protectorate of Historia, chosen by Orion to be his wielder and his second."

An uneasy ripple of sighs passed through the Council Chambers.

Anthony's jaw tightened. "You still broke into the vault, hurting three people and knocking two unconscious. The injured require penance under the laws of the Twelve Tables."

Margot grasped her Orb through the pouch at her side. She would make it through this alive. *She had to.* Her heart pounded as she remembered Nikolas being dragged away, barely conscious. *She could run — perhaps she could make it to the Barracks and break him out.*

Aurora's hand rose. "Margaret Wilson, you are to serve the remainder of the Mourning under house arrest. The Council regrets its actions that befell your predecessor, Olivia

Brown."

"That's it? Just wait out… what, three more days?" Margot's palms prickled with sweat.

How could she be free? Her instincts screamed: it's a trap. Be ready to bolt.

Anthony lifted a piece of paper. "We had an interesting letter from an Emile Pendergast who insisted on your, quote, immediate termination."

Aurora interrupted him. "Firing the late Curatrix's daughter? Not a chance — I'd prefer to keep my head on my shoulders." She held up a firm hand. "The librarian guild threatened to strike if you were not released. Nothing will get done!"

Anthony scoffed and sat back, scowling.

Her vision blurred. "They demanded my release?"

Theodore added, "Yes. Chatty ladies, they are."

Aurora laughed. "We can begin the elections soon. I sense a change in the flow of ley lines."

"So, what… the Council has allowed Soul wielding again?"

Margot doubted it was generosity — they must be terrified of Orion's wrath.

Aurora continued, "The Council has come together, and we voted to allow Spirit and Soul wielding again. The actions of the last Council were ill-advised and regrettable."

Her chest loosened. "What will happen to Nikolas?" she blurted out.

Aurora leaned back. "Nasty business with the guards, I'm afraid. Most of them are angry that he hurt them. They're demanding at least a month in the cells."

A month? The guards were blaming him and not Clara?

She bit her lip. Clara had saved her life and carried her home — if the Council learned of her membership in Hex and Bone, they would put her on trial.

Or she could free Nikolas.

Guilt flared in her ribs and unsettled her stomach. She couldn't expose Clara as the wielder who hurt the guards. Margot leaned back and kept her mouth shut.

Nikolas would understand. He would forgive her.

Aurora picked up her glass of water and took a sip. "Where is Orion now?"

"I'm not sure. The guards have been keeping me locked in my apartment. I should be asking you." Margot shook her head — she had tried to sway the guards, but they were prepared and shackled her wrists.

Aurora sighed.

Perhaps Aurora knew less than Margot did — but one of them had to know something. Margot reached out, trying to sense Anthony's heart. A reckless and stupid thing to do, but she needed to know if he was involved in Orion's disappearance.

The window slammed open — a blast of frigid air rushed in as Anthony bellowed, "Enough! I am adjourning this meeting. We will reconvene in three days."

Cold air needled through her clothes and iced her breath. Anthony's glare speared her from across the room.

"Am I able to visit someone?" Margot asked Chief Iyer.

Chief Iyer studied her. "I suppose we could allow a brief visit. Who are you going to see?"

Margot forced her breath steady. "Nikolas," she said — her voice cracking on his name.

Theodore's brows lifted. Anthony's jaw flexed. Aurora hid a smile behind her hand.

Margot didn't care. She needed Nikolas to know that he could still trust her.

NIKOLAS VENATOR

Betrayed by Her

✷

He felt pathetic gazing at the black mark on the wall. A deformed face looked back at him — then appeared again on another part of the wall. Footfalls from porters running above him made him lose concentration. Where was he…?

Ah yes. The crack in the plaster that reminded him of a black stallion.

Water cascaded from the window and trickled along the wall. A broom swept by two, three times before the smudge eddied and washed away.

Why did they take everything from him?

The guard's footsteps came from beyond the cell, growing more metallic as they got closer.

A guard unlocked the door, and Quentin strolled in, hands clasped behind his back.

Anger flared hot in his chest. Nikolas concentrated his remaining *mana* and reached for Quentin's thoughts — he needed to act fast, he could only —

Nikolas's chest constricted, his breath halting. His lungs clawed for air, each gasp sending waves of agony through his spine. He couldn't inhale. Couldn't exhale. Something inside him pulled tight, restless and hungry.

Fuck. He let go of Quentin's mind.

Quentin held up a finger, panting. "I believe we started on the wrong foot." He coughed. "I come as a friend."

The Aerian was stronger than he expected — so much for making an escape. He rested against the wall, steadying his heart.

Quentin smoothed his coat. "I was supposed to be your representative, but it seems I was mistaken." He pushed his hair back. "I was doing it as a favour for Margot."

Her wide amber eyes flashed in his mind — the guilt and regret on the day they were captured. "Who are you to her?"

"I am a friend." Quentin's eyes softened.

"Bullshit." Nikolas straightened. "Who are you to her?"

"It's a long story." Quentin cleared his throat and held up his hand to show his ring. "I'm engaged to Sophia. I have known them both my entire life."

Engaged to Sophia? Nikolas remembered sensing the tension between Margot and Quentin — palpable when she looked at him. Years of unspoken feelings in a single glance.

"You look… familiar. Now that I've had a proper look at you… have you been part of Alces' herd?" Quentin asked.

"I've had the displeasure of being in his presence."

"Were you involved in the vermilion pheasant incident? Yes, I remember seeing a poster on the streets. Alces was pissed for months."

Nikolas huffed a tired laugh. "The stupid thing squawked for three blocks before it realised we were trying to save it." Alces kept a menagerie of different species in gilded cages, on display for his herd to gawk at and poke. Nikolas couldn't stand by and let it suffer.

Quentin crossed his arms. "And now you are here, in Historia. Quite the traveller, aren't you?"

"You could say that."

Someone rapped on the door.

"Time's up," Quentin said. "Keep your mouth shut and let me talk."

The heavy door opened on squeaky hinges.

The Commander-in-Chief strolled in, hands tucked behind her proud chest. "Come on, gentlemen. Let's get going."

Nikolas walked to the Council Hall in silence, head down and without resistance. The custodian guard followed behind him — a good man. Nikolas could not fight them. He had eaten, laughed, trained, and struggled with them.

He reached out with his senses to connect to the guard's mind — a quick stab of pain at his side. Quentin had stopped him.

The Council Chambers were opulent and stifling — wood, leather, and heat from the raging fireplace, four Council members standing behind a lacquered desk.

The Chief pulled out a chair opposite and forced him to sit. She rounded the desk. "You have five minutes to plead your case."

Nikolas opened his mouth to speak.

"Thank you, Your Honour," Quentin interrupted and stood next to him.

Shit. His life was in the palm of this man's hand.

Nikolas nodded, letting him continue. He would trust Margot.

"What evidence has the Council brought to the case?" Quentin asked.

"Four eyewitness testimonies and two written statements from his conspirators."

Nikolas' heart dropped. Sophia and Margot betrayed him for a lighter sentence? Signed their names and handed him over without a fight? *A velvet noose was still a noose.*

Quentin asked, "What penalty has the Council decided?"

"Most waived the right to penance. However, I have a statement here from Emile Pendergast, who demands the penalty of five lashes," the Aerian Councillor read, "and one more month in solitary."

Five lashes. One more month. All thoughts crumbled through his fingers — his vision blurred, sweat dripping down his back.

Maya sat up. "Five lashes? That seems excessive."

The Aerian Councillor scoffed. "Not severe enough. He has been here less than a month, and he used his alignment to break into a vault and assault three members of your guard."

"Five lashes is excessive," Quentin said. "I agree with the Ignian Council Member."

"No son-in-law of mine will disagree with me!" the Councillor snapped. "Five lashes, and that is final."

The chamber dissolved into bickering. The Chief argued with him, but eventually she sat back, unable to convince him.

Nikolas heard none of it. Margot had given him up to this air wielder — a man she trusted to speak for him while he rotted in a cell.

The betrayal twisted a slow, hot sting behind his ribs.

He'd stood beside her. *Risked everything... and for what?* Something inside him curled, restless, hungry for an outlet.

The meeting was over in minutes — the Council had decided his fate long before he entered the room.

✸

The jingle of keys made him turn. He locked eyes with the succubus in a librarian's skin — she dared to look guilty, tucking that loose curl behind her ear like she thought it would work on him.

"What do you want?" The words scraped out of him. He hadn't spoken in days. His throat felt raw, too dry.

Abandoned in this cesspit, starving in the darkness, with only the threat of whipping. She used him, took what she needed, and now she was here to throw him away like everyone else.

"How are you doing? I finally have some freedom," she said, voice trembling, glancing around the four bare walls that had been his prison. It was her fault — her master's fault.

He should have known better than to trust a Soul creature.

"Don't even finish that sentence." He forced himself to stand on unsteady legs, every joint throbbing. "That Aerian man got you a lighter sentence. You served me up on a silver platter." His voice cracked with the bitterness burning through him. "Get out."

Her face crumpled and she backed away, putting what little space the cell allowed between them.

Good. She should fear him. His heart pounded — the walls closing in on the edges of his vision.

Why did he always have to fight to survive? To breathe?

Dark thoughts slithered along his spine. *Grab her. Pin her. Make her scream for help. Use her like she used you. Do it. Do it now. Don't let them leave you here to rot.*

She swallowed hard and slammed her fist against the door.

Guards yanked it open. She slipped out, shutting him behind thick iron and oak.

⁕

Moonlight shone through the barred window and painted a shadowy picture of the barracks above him. The custodian guards did their nightly rounds with perfect timing — he'd memorised the schedules not long after deciding to stay for the winter.

He shouldn't have stayed. Pain radiated from his fist, blood coating his knuckles. He slid his back against the stone, prickling hay digging into his skin.

Should've kept moving.

The librarian looked up through the window. *That lace shift. The one from that morning*. What a taunting mirage she was, baring four feline fangs.

Her skin gleamed where the moonlight kissed it, long black hair flowing over her face, curling along the mud as she hugged her legs and rested her chin on a knee. Deep amethyst eyes glowed. Her lips curled, and her fangs glinted.

She tilted her head, studying him as if selecting where to

bite, then leaned forward. *"Hello, seeker,"* she spoke in his voice.

"I don't care what you have to say," his exhausted voice called out.

A soft, sultry purr slid out. *"Oh, that's a shame..."*

The mirage slipped off the bucket and prowled closer, hands and knees gliding over the muddy stone. *"I came to tell you that your imprisonment is almost over,"* she pouted.

She took a long breath starting from his legs and along his body. *"You smell rank,"* she said, her breath forming a misty cloud in the frigid air.

He pushed her away, surprised at how close he had let her get.

Moonlight showcased how little the librarian wore — just like the morning he awoke to her perfect, peaked nipples pressing through the lace shift. He remembered rushing to cover her. The mirage in front of him, snarling with four feline teeth, was nothing compared to the vision that had taunted him in the days that followed.

"It's your fault I am in here, Orion." Nikolas dusted himself.

Orion tsked — the mirage melted, and he sat there still in the body of a felis. *"I suppose I have to apologise for your accommodations, or lack thereof."*

"What do you want?" Nikolas hit the wall and collapsed to the floor.

"I am here to give you a choice, seeker. Option One: Leave Historia and never come back."

"Okay. Easy. Let me leave."

"Are you sure? I haven't presented my second option." He purred.

Nikolas nodded and licked his chapped lips, letting his head fall back against the gritty stone. "Fine. What is my second option?"

"Stay and help me protect her."

Nikolas let out a barking laugh. "I have to leave. If I stay, I will just bring my baggage to you — and to her."

"I am one of the first Souls to hear the whispers of mana's creation. I was a simple creature back then."

"Stop talking in riddles and get to the point," Nikolas interjected.

"The shields around Historia have long hidden a deep mana well. I've kept it hidden with my kin for a very long time. I want you to help me protect it."

"Protect it from what?"

"Historia is slumbering, in a… forced hibernation, for several thousand years. Lately, they have been rather fitful."

A forced hibernation. "Historia is sleeping beneath the city?" *They're not dead?*

"Yes, and awakening will be disastrous."

"You make it sound like that's happened before."

"It has. That's a story for another time."

"Let me get this straight. You want me to protect the city from Historia waking up? After imprisoning me for… days!"

"Precisely." Orion blinked.

"You promised me I could leave," Nikolas grumbled.

Orion's tail whipped around — the silver flash of a ring against the stone echoing in the quiet air. Nikolas tracked the rustling, reached into the damp hay, and blew the dust from the ring.

"I will allow you full access through the shields — Historia will stay a safe harbour for you. As long as you pledge to me, you will return when I call."

Held up to the moonlight, the silver ring with its inlaid gemstone emitted a soft, ethereal glow — perfectly clear, but sparkling with colours when he turned it. "Is this what Clara found? The boon?"

Orion blinked.

Nikolas cursed. "You could have given this to me at any time!"

"I cannot just give this away. I need assurance that you will return. And I had to find it first — took longer than expected because of my lack of opposable thumbs."

"I've been stuck in this hole for days. Why didn't you tell me where it was? I could've gone and — "

"You needed to be elsewhere, to help my bonded get the staff. You had to get caught." Orion's voice rumbled through his temples.

The heist was a distraction? He put the ring on his pinky finger — felt the clay beneath his feet rumble in response.

His heart felt heavy. To Orion, he was just a game piece to be moved along the board — Nikolas knew his place on it, at the very least. He could leave and never come back. Spirit wielders could ignore the pull of a bargain.

This pull was not a bargain being called.

Nikolas closed his eyes and listened to the *drip… drip… drip* of water. He followed it through the alleyways to the sewers, felt a pull toward an object, a whisper calling to him.

The instant Nikolas raised his father's sword, he set his life on a short, bloody path. Patricide was a grievous crime, no matter which Spirit you were born under.

He would carry that mark with him wherever he went.

When he left Johansen's village, his borrowed time ran out — he'd be nothing more than frozen remains on the trail without the Vulpine.

His bones ached, muscles strained. No matter how warm the weather, he was always freezing — it vexed him to be at another Spirit's beck and call.

Nikolas had struck that bargain with Bennu when he was younger and easily swayed by Spirits — since then, he'd travelled many roads, seeking fire wielders in exchange for safe harbour.

Nikolas threaded the ring from his pinky, ripped the side

of his mattress open, and wrapped it in the torn cloth. He untied his shoes, loosened his socks, shoved the ring deep, and retied everything back into place.

"What do I have to do? Tell me the rest of this plan you've got."

"Stay and pay penance to the victims." Orion licked his paw and rubbed it along his face.

"You want me to stay and get lashed?"

"You have survived worse. It's written all over your body."

Nikolas pulled at the sleeves of his fleece tunic. He could handle a few lashes — Bennu had done worse, called it training, and expected gratitude.

His head found a comfortable spot on the stone. Five more lashes in exchange for safe harbour.

"Okay, I will…" His eyes dropped, and everything went black.

A dark laugh rumbled in the distance.

MARGOT WILSON

Regretful Choices

The bowl was heavy in her hands, the fire held by the custodian guard reflecting off the water.

"Thank you," she said as she stepped into Nikolas' cell.

The floor beneath the Custodian Barracks wasn't a floor at all, just hay and crumbling dirt, damp with cold. Nikolas lay belly-down on the thin mattress pressed against the wall — they had discarded his shirt, not bothering to cover him afterward.

Sophia had told her Maya whipped him. Guilt dragged her forward even as every instinct screamed that Nikolas hated her for dragging him into her mess. She set the bowl beside him and dipped the towel — the warm water rippling with the tremor in her hands.

"Don't." Nikolas' eyes snapped open — he sneered, a vicious look that promised retribution she deserved.

"Please… let me," she breathed, reaching again.

Five long, striped gashes carved across his back. Blood still trickled down his ribs. Dumped here afterward, left to heal alone.

Nikolas inhaled sharply and nodded. So she worked — wiping the blood from torn skin, the water running red down her forearms. She had watched Sophia tend to the guards. She knew how to do this.

She should have known how to protect him.

Carefully, she smoothed the balm over his wounds. "It has arnica and yarrow. I picked and mixed it myself, so it might… sting."

Why did she say that?

Biting her lip, she pressed clean gauze over the wounds. "Can you sit up for me?"

Nikolas nodded, eyes closed.

"Arms up, if you can."

He lifted his arms, pulling the wounds tight.

She unrolled the bandage. His chest was a landscape of scars: old and new, healed and rebroken.

Stories she wanted to ask. Stories she didn't deserve.

She wrapped him as gently as she could.

"Done." She didn't dare look at him. "I'll leave a few leaves. Chew them, they'll dull the pain."

The towel fell back into the bloody water as she packed her bag — Nikolas' hand clamped around her forearm before she could stand.

The connection hit instantly — his heart, that stallion black as ink, flooding her vision. She jerked away, pulling his hand off. "I'm sorry, I — "

"Don't apologise," he rasped. "I shouldn't have touched you."

Her throat squeezed. "I should apologise for, well, everything." Shame sat heavy, a hot stone in her stomach. "I can come back tomorrow to change the bandages — or I can leave the supplies, if you'd prefer."

Nikolas lowered himself back onto his stomach.

Fine. He could ignore her too — she deserved it. "I'll be back tomorrow."

She knocked on the cell door and stepped out, wiping away an errant tear.

☾

Margot was under escort everywhere she went — the Study Hall, Sophia's estate, the Mess Hall. The "approved" places, sunrise to sunset.

She was adrift and unmoored without Orion. He'd been missing for days. She had to break the transfiguration on him — not being able to complete her orders was excruciating, hot and too tight.

She pleaded with Quentin to let her search — his assistants kept a close eye on her instead, taking her straight back to her apartment after she visited Nikolas. After she'd heard what his penance was, what pain she'd caused him, she'd begged Maya to let her see him.

She was tired of pleading, of begging, of being escorted.

What if Anthony captured Orion and locked him in a cell like they did Nikolas? Blood and gashed wounds filled her vision — guilt and shame coiling in her stomach as she fought the tears.

Two days to keep herself occupied. The abandoned and unread books piled alongside her chair were tempting her.

At a time like this? No.

She grabbed a palette knife from her mother's stash of painting supplies and jammed it into the crate — wood splintering, nails groaning as she lifted off the cover.

Where was it? She lifted a few bottles from the crate, inspecting each label.

Ah, there you are.

A feral grin spread across her face — an ancient bottle of single malt that dated back past the explosion.

Fuck it. Her mother wasn't alive to lecture her. Sophia was engaged to Quentin. Orion wasn't here to scream in her head, either.

Her apartment was eerie and lonely. She took the palette knife to the wax covering the mouth of the bottle and ripped the stopper off with her teeth — the warm burn sliding down her throat, smoky flavour hitting her nostrils.

Fuck, that's good.

Her night descended into a fragmented kaleidoscope of

colours — spinning, twirling, dancing with the bottle in her mouth. If she stopped moving, the thoughts came back. She dug through the crates, pulling things until they tumbled and crashed around her.

She found it tucked in the corner and slid the leather case toward her, the hardness of the floor not mattering at all. She flicked open the brass clasp, laughed with glee, and took another burning sip.

She inserted the handle into the crank and wound it until it wouldn't go any further. She dug through the crates — the wood biting into her stomach as she clumsily brought the remnants of her mother's life out into the light. She took the record from its protective sleeve and placed it, aiming the needle so it wouldn't scratch.

Lying on her mother's rug, she let the music fill the void — she needed someone, something, to fill the space inside her. Soon, tears ran down to her ears. She leant up and took another long, gulping burn of her liquor.

☾

The cold porcelain was a welcome reprieve from her heated skin as she retched one more time. She flushed last night's regrets and rinsed the taste out of her mouth.

"Could I not leave you alone for a few days?" Orion said into her mind.

Relief flooded through her as she took in his long onyx fur, the tip of his tail bleeding into amethyst, his proud chest seeping violet.

She missed him so much.

"Orion... I..." Her head swam with rather unpleasant images that she tucked away, never to be thought of again.

"Clean yourself up, and then we can talk."

Margot nodded and turned to the mirror. She turned on the faucet, letting the steam rise over her face, and brushed her teeth — enjoying the spicy-mint flavour that washed away the gross.

Orion was waiting in his usual lecture spot. The living room fireplace crackled. She tightened the sash on her robe and sat on the couch, her head hung low.

"Progress report," Orion said.

Margot's head snapped up. "Excuse me?"

"Nikolas. How was he?"

"Horrible. They whipped him five times."

Orion blinked. *"I am disappointed in the punishment the Council gave. His Spirit is strong regardless — he'll be out of our hair soon."*

"What do you mean? Is he going to leave?" Margot fidgeted with her fingers.

"I made a bargain with him — he can leave if he wants to, or live here. Historia always believed in freedom of choice, of movement. I try to follow their ways, but sometimes I have to bend the rules to get what I want."

A small smile bubbled up within her — she hugged a couch cushion. Nikolas got what he wanted; he could leave. "That's good. And if he stays?" She picked at the embroidery.

"Focus on your studies. Once we have the staff, we will unseal the vault. I need your mind sharp and on task. No more late-night benders."

"The vault?" Her brow furrowed. "You mean your grimoires?"

Orion sighed. *"Yes, the grimoires that were stolen from me and sealed away. Have you not been paying attention?"*

"I'm sorry, okay? It's a lot to take in, with the Soul wielding, the heist, and—"

"Stop making excuses," Orion interrupted.

"What does that even mean?" Her voice cracked raw. "I've been through a lot."

"Sit now," he commanded. *"I need your well full, so rest. Eat something. You are depleting your reserves, and your mana is*

compensating."

"Okay." Margot could only nod.

She had her orders.

The Nyxmara

☾

Margot adjusted the worn leather strap on her shoulder.

The custodian guard unlocked the gate — a hollow, metallic groan echoing around the stone hallway.

The warm torchlight drifted away. The chill seeped into her bones the moment she stepped through — damp clay and old straw.

Nikolas was in the same position she'd left him, stretched belly-down on the narrow mattress, shirt discarded, one arm dangling off the side as he idly drew patterns in the packed red clay.

The light caught the dried blood at the edges of his bandages, turning rust to garnet — his fingers pausing mid-circle when he heard her.

He didn't look at her. He stilled, inhaled sharply, his shoulders trembling. "Come in." When he pushed himself upright, his breath hitched in a strangled groan.

The guilt lodged in her throat as she set her bag beside the mattress, careful not to disturb the odd, swirling clay pictographs.

She knelt beside him, the straw crackling beneath her knees. As she peeled the bandages back, cracked scabs tugged against the linen, releasing a faint herbal bitterness from the salve. The gashes were clean but deep. She doused the fresh pad. "This is going to hurt."

Nikolas didn't speak. He only braced.

Margot wiped the wounds. His back shivered beneath her touch, a ripple of muscle tightening against the sting. She spread the salve, warming it under her fingers, then placed gauze and wrapped the bandages tight around his torso.

"All done," she said, packing the bandages, the metal clasps clicking shut. When she rose, his hand shot out and closed around her forearm.

Her breath punched out of her, *mana* surging wildly, instinctively — her mind slamming into his heart space.

A black void.

Four hooves pounding through her mind. A scream that split her skull. Nyxmara, the night stallion — a predator of despair, snarling at the edges of his soul like a parasite.

Not anymore.

Garnet and onyx shadows writhed under Nikolas' skin as he tried to pull away from the icy burn of her *mana*.

"Don't." Her voice broke. "Let me do this for you..."

She seized the inky tendrils of the creature's mane — it thrashed, burning ice beneath her palms.

She pulled, ripping it out from the roots of his heart. The thing screamed, vibrating through her teeth. "My Orb — get it!" she gasped.

Nikolas moved through the agony, hands shaking as he dug through her pouch and pressed the Orb into her palm, their fingers intertwining.

The stone glowed — a violent, blinding violet bursting outward, spilling between their knuckles, searing up their arms. Light surged beneath their skin, racing like molten gold along their wrists, curling around their forearms, climbing their shoulders in mirrored spirals.

Her breath faltered. His breath hitched.

They connected. Two heartbeats slamming into the same rhythm. Two minds colliding. Two souls bursting, pouring into each other.

She fell inward.

Margot sensed fear that wasn't hers — it was his.

His memories spilled into her, eddying through water:

loss, raw and bleeding. Loneliness settled like dust in forgotten corners. Pain carved into the map of his skin. *Running. Running. Always running.*

Her heart lurched in the endless darkness — cold winter flurries falling, blanketing everything in white.

A flicker of light — of warmth — drew her.

She came to a wall and smoothed her hand over the green, flowery, brocaded paper — a punctured hole spilling light.

Margot ripped the wallpaper down and stepped into the light. Warmth embraced her, a room full of plants and vibrant green leaves, sunlight filtering through tall glass panes and painting the air with shimmers of gold.

Where are we?

Thunder grumbled overhead. Grey clouds rolled in, and rain started as drops, then thickened into a roar, slamming against glass.

His Solarium.

She stepped outside into his mind's storm. The Nyxmara waited for her in the downpour.

Tall and silent. A shadow with teeth.

It's time to let him go.

It screamed — a shriek, metal tearing through her skull.

She held on and inhaled, reached inward, and pulled the creature under her skin one last time, its icy grip stinging along her arm, her fingers burning violet. She forced the writhing thing into the orb.

Their ragged breaths were the only sound in the silence.

Margot opened her eyes — her vision wavering, then snapping into focus.

Nikolas stared back at her. His eyes were *green* — not the tired, muted grey-green she'd first seen in the gallery, not the sick ruby flicker that had haunted him. Vivid as the forest after rain.

"*Sorry,*" she whispered. "*That was —*" She stumbled back,

legs trembling and buckling from fatigue.

Nikolas panted hard, rubbing a hand over his chest as if learning how to breathe without that thing coiling inside his heart.

He moved slowly — fingers tucking a curl behind her ear, then sliding to the back of her head.

"What are —"

Nikolas tilted her head and kissed her.

Everything else fell away.

Part Two

The Interwilds

NIKOLAS VENATOR

The Pull

✷

Nikolas was kissing her. Abyss take him — the moment his lips met hers, every restraint he'd ever learned cracked.

It tore through him like floodwater bursting through a dam he'd reinforced his entire life, sealed with discipline and the instinct to stay unnoticeable. He'd wanted her for too long and finally let himself taste it.

Her lips were softer than he'd imagined.

She made a small sound against his mouth, surprise melting into want, palms curling against his chest. He pulled her closer at the back of her head, wanting to sink into her curls.

A sharp spike of panic flared through him.

What the hell was he doing? If anyone walked in, they'd both be in trouble. He tore his mouth from hers — breaths shaking between them.

"That was..." Margot said, a stunned smile tugging at her lips.

That freckle on her cheek moved when she smiled.

He had no defence against it. Words tumbled out too fast. "That was unbefitting of a gentleman." His heart hammered — he would rot in this cell if she even hinted he had forced himself on her.

"It's okay," she murmured, lashes lowering. "I enjoyed it."

His heart lurched, breath hooking behind his ribs. *She was a temptress.* He swallowed hard. "What did you do?"

"I pulled the Nyxmara out of you and trapped it in here."

She slid the glowing orb into her pouch.

A palm-shaped burn flickered with pain along his arm — the price he paid. "I didn't know how else to thank you..."

"So you kiss me?" She touched her lips, the faintest curve pulling at her mouth.

He nodded before he could even think to stop himself.

"I have always been exhausted. I thought that was normal."

"It's possible it fed from you for years," she said. "It was old — but you kept it alive. It must have fed on your well."

The truth hit hard. Years of bone-deep exhaustion. Nightmares he could never outrun. That bitter cold in his fingers and toes.

It had been death chewing on him, savouring the marrow.

"Oh." Her voice softened. "And your eyes changed colour." She reached out but stopped herself, fingers hovering inches from his cheek. "They're lovely and bright green."

Lovely.

His heart ached at her words, a molten sensation pulling him closer, yearning to kiss her again. He looked away before he ruined everything.

Now is not the time.

Now is not —

He shifted, heat curling under his skin, and sat on the mattress. His ribs expanded for the first time in months.

He felt... warm.

Margot tucked a curl behind her ear. "So... what now?"

"Look for another guild to take me in, I guess," he said.

Her eyes widened. "You want to stay?"

Nikolas nodded. "I just need to finish my isolation."

For the first time, he wasn't running.

"You have three weeks," she said, guilt tugging at the corners of her brows.

"I forgive you. Those leaves helped."

A blush crept up her neck. "I'm glad they did."

He hesitated, then let the question tumble from his mouth before fear could stop it. "Will you visit me?"

"No." Her brows furrowed, and she chewed her thumbnail. "I have to break Orion's transfiguration. I can't lose focus."

The ache behind his ribs sharpened. He shouldn't cling to things too tightly — he nodded, keeping his expression neutral. "See me when you can."

She stepped back and lingered, caught between leaving and staying. Her gaze drifted to his mouth, then snapped back up. "Okay," she said. "I will."

And for once — she didn't run. He kissed her again, just in case.

*

Nikolas spent his waking time reading the same book Margot gave him. His wounds were healing — now he had to sit and wait for his isolation to end.

His cell door opened once a day for dinner. Maya had discovered the guards hadn't been feeding him and came by to offer her apologies, fixing the oversight with her burning words.

Nikolas didn't blame Maya. The Aerian Councillor had demanded the penance — as Chief, she had to follow through. He knew she could have whipped him harder, but she pulled back just enough to make him bleed.

Enough to make a show.

Today, however, the footsteps were heavier. A burly man walked in — enviably long beard, a mane of hair dark as soil. Nikolas had seen him once before at the Council meeting.

He held the tray steady. "Figured you'd want a hot meal."

Nikolas stood. "Thank you… ah — who are you?"

The man blinked, offended. "Name's Theodore," he

rumbled.

"Nice to meet you, I guess." The man did nothing to help him at the Council meeting — why was he helping now?

Nikolas sat and lifted the dome — steam curling upward, rich and salty, thick chunks of meat and potatoes and carrots. A basket of warm rolls sat beside it, wrapped in a towel.

He hadn't eaten proper food in days — just what Margot had stashed in her bag, and one cold meal a day.

"Maya told me they hadn't fed you," Theodore said.

Nikolas shook his head, chewing slowly, letting warmth spread through him. "Emile has this vendetta against me."

Theodore leaned back, arms crossed. "Explains the letter he left — it was full of expletives, if you're curious. And his insistence on five lashes."

Nikolas huffed a laugh. "I can handle it."

"I thought Maya would go easy on you," Theodore said. "Did somebody heal the worst of it?"

Nikolas hesitated — he didn't know if calling out Margot would stir up trouble. He nodded once. "Some blonde Aerian woman. Quick with her hands."

Theodore hummed. "Sophia. I know her well."

Nikolas said nothing.

"Well," Theodore continued, unclasping the leather satchel slung over his shoulder, "I came to drop these off as a favour." He set the bag down and took out a small collection of books.

Under the top cover, Nikolas found a folded note. He recognised the disciplined, elegant handwriting:

Don't think you can get away without doing your homework. Complete every translation of the text before you get out. — M.

"You know Margot?" Nikolas asked.

Theodore barked a laugh that echoed through the stone.

"Yes, I've watched her grow up here. Capricious little thing. Wild as a Vulpine. Her mother spent more time chasing her than raising her, I swear."

Nikolas smiled despite the throbbing in his back. "She gave me work to do."

"She's a genuine believer in the Twelve Tables," Theodore said. "She'll roll up her sleeves and muck in with the rest of us."

"So what's your role?" Nikolas asked, studying him again. He hadn't met many Terrans up close.

"Me? I keep everyone fed and healthy. My tonics are the best you'll find — we send them north on ships, trading with Britannia." He puffed out his proud chest.

A healer. That explained the air of grounded calm around him.

"How come I haven't met you before now?"

"Busy," Theodore said with a shrug. "We've had many fresh faces over recent years. Hard to keep up."

Nikolas leaned back against the wall, warmth filling his stomach in a way he'd forgotten. Nikolas leaned back against the wall, warmth filling his stomach in a way he'd forgotten. "The food… helps."

Theodore pushed to his feet and knocked on the door. "No need to be polite. Just hang in there."

MARGOT WILSON

The Antitransfiguration Method

The staff was heavy in Margot's hands, the weight of her task pressed on her chest. Her mother transformed Orion for a reason. The Council appeared eager to please him now — they probably figured their punishment would be milder if they appeased him.

Orion was her teacher, her guardian. She steadied herself on the memory of every lesson he'd taught her — he loved this city and wanted to protect it from other Spirits.

She exhaled, letting her shoulders lower. Her new role was to be Orion's Shadow.

She could do this.

She'd trained for weeks in preparation for this day. And yet those vibrant green eyes were all she could think about — she was pleasantly surprised when he leaned in and kissed her, at how easily she let him. His lips were just rough enough to linger.

Orion refused to let her see him until she had undone the transfiguration — so she kept practicing, kept meditating on the *mana* deep within her well.

The Study Hall was her heart space, her inner sanctuary — old paper and leather-bound books soaking into the air. Tomes towered around her, lined up alphabetically and categorised by decimal number.

Pulling the orb from the pouch at her side, she placed it on top of the staff — it fit together with a simple click and shift of the wood. *Complete.* She realised it then — her staff wasn't quite a staff. It was a curious shape, curved as if made for swinging.

This was no ordinary staff. *It was a scythe.*

Light filtered through the knot as she focused her *mana* into the wood — it flowed outward and became a weapon of shimmering violet.

Orion sat in front of her with his tail curled around his legs. Her vision blurred — tears spilling, a shudder moving through her, the grip of anxiety tightening with each uneven breath.

"Do it, my little soul wielder."

His command sank into her bones, and she obeyed.

Slicing downward, she reaped his soul from his felis form. She glided beside him, scooping out his aura and holding it in her arms — so light, still just a warm, purring ball. She hummed with him, lulling him in her embrace.

This was her gift.

Humming the tune her mother used to lull her to sleep, she realised the days of being a bratty little girl were long behind her. She transferred the love she had for her mother — sending Orion visions of being full after a good meal, the warmth she felt when she was around Sophia.

The aura leapt out of her arms and sat beside his body — Orion was free. Its form shifted, reshaping from felis to something much more mortal.

A very naked mortal. His endless ebony skin shimmered with *mana*. Margot covered her eyes and turned away. "Put clothes on!" she squealed.

"I am decent," Orion said, his mortal voice rumbling with a tone that vibrated the windows. Thunder rolled outside in answer. Long, pointed ears slanted backward, the Ignis lights reflected in his amethyst eyes — their upward tilt mirroring the graceful lines of his felis form.

"What are you wearing?" she said, suppressing a giggle.

"Hm, I suppose these will be out of fashion." He snapped his fingers, and the long, flowing robes that grazed the floor dissolved into a black suit that complemented his towering frame perfectly.

"Much better," she said, yawning as fatigue washed through her. Her feet throbbed, her back ached, an insistent ringing in her ears.

Every part of her felt hollowed out.

Orion moved, catching her before she toppled — he scooped her up as if she weighed nothing and deposited her in her bed, tucking her in as bone-deep *mana*-drain swept through her.

It dragged her consciousness into a deep sleep.

Margot lay cocooned in softness for a long time. She found no reason to open her eyes.

She drifted and drifted and drifted in an endless expanse of blackness and quiet.

Sophia's voice woke her — sleep tugging her from the darkness she wanted so desperately to stay in forever.

"Hey, sunshine." The brush of Sophia's hand and the smell of freshly brewed coffee coaxed her eyes open.

"Please tell me that is coffee I smell." Margot's voice came out dry and papery. Sophia must have pulled strings to get fresh beans — that was worth waking up for. "How long have I been asleep?"

"Drink up, then we can talk."

Muscles ached as Margot sat up and stretched. Warm sunlight spilled through the open window, freshly cut flowers in a vase on her bedside table. Veridis should wake soon —

Wait.

She rushed to the window and stared into the quad. Fresh patches of grass were sprouting along the pathways — in the centre, the great oak tree shot out its first few crimson shoots.

"I was asleep for a while, huh?" Margot said and took a coffee mug.

"I healed you once a night, but you still took longer than expected," Sophia said, sipping her own coffee.

Margot hummed, savouring the milky-bitter taste while the heat spread through her — a deeper, aromatic flavour lingering on the tongue. Perhaps Sophia had added medicinal herbs. She remembered flashes of Sophia's glowing *mana* filling her reserves.

Margot looked around her apartment. "Where is Orion?" The smell of fresh soup wafted from her kitchen.

Sophia was a talented healer, even if she hated being one.

"Off running the Council to the bone. They've got eighty years of penance they've inherited," Sophia said.

Margot sat up sharply. "But Orion promised to let them get off easy. They had nothing to do with the Explosion."

Sophia shrugged. "My father needs to be whipped by someone. He was the only one who insisted the Council take Emile's statement seriously."

Margot inhaled so sharply that coffee spilled.

"Whoa, calm down, Margot!" Sophia snatched the mug out of her hands.

Emile was the reason Nikolas got whipped?

A tremor, soft as a heartbeat under stone, shivered up her spine.

She will kill him. Slowly.

Another voice, soft and feminine, whispered: *Lady of Wrath and Patience.* The words echoed in her ears, ringing until they snapped into silence.

Patience. Yes, that is what she needed.

Sophia's eyes widened. "Your — your eyes looked like Orion's for a heartbeat."

"Did they?" Margot breathed.

"Was kinda hot," Sophia muttered under her breath.

They both giggled for a second before the weight of her newfound powers settled under her ribs.

Her well felt full again, ready to uncoil — a new plan blooming in her mind.

Sophia shuffled through Margot's kitchen and ladled a bowl of soup, making sure Margot ate every drop.

She had missed this — missed her.

Her Reward

Orion walked into her bedroom without knocking. "There you are."

His mortal form was going to be an adjustment.

Sophia got up from the bed. "I hope you are giving my father a hard time," she said. Orion nodded and crossed his arms at the foot of Margot's bed.

Sophia crossed her arms and scowled.

Orion blinked back.

"I will leave," Sophia said, sighing. She kissed Margot on the cheek. *"We'll talk later, okay?"*

She bowed before she closed the door behind her.

Margot scoffed. "I told her not to do that."

"In exchange for her services, I have promised to help with her... *marital issues.*" He ground out the last two words.

Her breath loosened. Relief flooded through her. "That's good." She stretched and flexed her hands — bones and muscles aching.

Orion outstretched his hand. "Would you like to go for a walk?"

"Absolutely," Margot yawned, feeling the warmth of the sun on her face. "I've been sleeping for too long." She tossed the covers aside, freshened up, and changed into something simple and easy to move in.

Orion was waiting at the door, holding her arm in the crook of his the entire way down the stairs. The morning spring light was blinding — the last remnants of winter melting on the corners of the paths.

They walked along a familiar route, heading towards

Sophia's estate.

He paused at the gate, one hand resting on the iron rail. "Fifteen years is a long time to be small," he said. "Thank you for ending it."

Scaffolding covered one side, tarps over the windows. A carpenter carried a piece of lumber into the rundown estate she always passed on the way. "Orion—"

Tears pricked her eyes.

Margot stood in the grand foyer, taking in every detail. The paint was peeling, the deep brown wood needing care, dust accumulated on every surface.

"This was once hers," Orion said, leading her through the kitchen — old spices and wood smoke clung to the air. "And now it's yours."

"Mine?" The sunlight filtering through the stained glass windows made her apartment feel laughably small — light shining along the walls in fractals.

They walked through in silence, their footsteps echoing as they opened every creaky door and inspected every shadowed nook.

It needed work. A lot of work. Dusty and old, but with good bones. "It's perfect in every way."

The empty bookcases in her new *personal library* could finally display her mother's collection the way it deserved — she loathed the sight of those unopened crates gathering dust.

"Can I trust you to take care of yourself for a few hours?" Orion said.

Margot nodded. "Of course. I'll go right home."

He paused at the door. Then, he pressed his forehead briefly to hers — the way he used to butt his head against her cheek. He said nothing — didn't need to.

He squeezed her hand and kissed her cheek before leaving.

☾

She wandered the corridors for ages. The excitement waned when it got too dark, so she went outside to wander the grounds, walking where her feet wanted — *seeking retribution*. The Custodian Barracks was a short walk from her new house. She'd make a detour on the way home.

Margot had a score to settle. Orion didn't have to know.

John jogged over to her. "What can I do for you?"

"I want to talk to Emile. Where is he?"

He scratched his head. "He's at the Wielding Hall."

"Tell me where."

He tilted his head back and groaned a curse. "Follow me."

She followed John into the impressive ivory building — a gymnasium the guilds used to train. Margot never went, she got enough exercise from walking the Study Hall.

She spotted Emile sparring with the other guards.

Emile stopped — got a proper hit to the chin after spotting her. "Are you crawling back to me?" He grinned from ear to ear and adjusted his jaw.

She scoffed. "Not in your wildest nightmares."

Emile nodded to John. "Boys, let's take a break." The guards walked out of the training hall.

Good — she hated confrontation. She didn't want an audience for this.

"If you're not here to beg for my dick—"

Margot put her hand up, silencing him. "What is it with men and their obsession with their cocks?" She adjusted her glasses. "Why did you insist on his penance?"

"He used me," Emile scoffed. "First, he goaded me into fighting him so I'd be on guard duty that night." He stepped toward her, cold malice radiating from his aura. "Then he ties me up."

Margot stepped backward — he kept coming. *Shit, not good.*

Emile yelled, "Next thing I know, I am waking up with

Chief Iyer screaming at me. I have been on cleanup duty because of him."

Anger bloomed in Margot's chest and she stomped toward him. "Nikolas is rotting in the cells right now!"

He crossed his arms. "And he can stay there."

"You're such an asshole."

"You like it though," he said, leaning in to her eye level.

She sensed his lust as he wet his lips. The sick bastard was enjoying this. "You're rotten on the inside," she said. His heart was a sticky, dilapidated tavern — dimly lit, reeking of stale beer and regret, the kind of place only the grimiest of people enter. That part of him used to draw her in. Now she could see exactly how disgusting he was.

He pouted and put his hand on his chest. "You wound me."

She was never a violent person, preferring to bottle her rage up in a small glass jar — but she desperately wanted to wipe off the smirk that said he'd won.

So she reached out and put two fingers on his temples.

Emile's eyes rolled back, his jaw going slack. He fell backwards with a fleshy smack onto the mats.

Margot sauntered off, feeling rather proud.

NIKOLAS VENATOR

Lucerna Orb

✷

The Study Hall breathed with life.

In the early hours, it inhaled — the soft shuffle of boots on stone, the murmur of sleepy greetings as mortals trudged in from the cold. By evening, it exhaled them again, leaving only dust motes and the low hum of Ignis lights.

Today, the air carried something else. Her new perfume — faint, resinous, and floral — threaded through the stacks, cutting through ink and old paper.

He followed it up the stairs before he even realised he was moving.

She was there. Of course, she was.

Margot lounged at a familiar desk near her favourite nook, glasses perched low on her nose, gold chain glinting at her throat, brows knit in concentration as she worked through a stack of forms — the tip of her pen tapping an impatient rhythm. A tin of Sophia's cookies sat open at her elbow.

He leaned on the bannister above, letting himself just look at her.

Three weeks in the cells had rubbed him raw. The sight of her smoothed him.

"You're staring," came a cool voice at his side.

Sophia slid into place against the rail. "She wanted to see you — Orion kept her busy. She was worried."

"It's all right," Nikolas said, forcing his gaze away. "I had plenty of time to think." And to sense the pull of the ring on his finger — thrumming, the strange tug in his chest dulled to a low ache.

Nikolas remembered the day Orion had given it to him — the way his feet itched to move, the pull dragging him back to one place, to a particular statue in the Study Hall.

"You look good," Sophia said, tilting her head. "The streak is new."

He rubbed his temple — the white in his hair catching the Ignis light, shimmering with an iridescent sheen. "It can stop any time now."

Margot shifted, the air catching her scent and sending it drifting up toward him. He swallowed.

Sophia's grin sharpened.

"Don't you—"

"Margot! Nikolas is here!" Sophia wielded the air, her voice amplified and spread across the entire Study Hall.

Every head turned.

Margot froze. The flush started at her neck and climbed, blooming over her cheeks and the tips of her ears. She shot Sophia a look that could flay skin — then packed up her things with stiff, murderous precision.

Sophia patted his shoulder. "Good luck. I'm rooting for you," she said, drifting away before he could protest.

Margot trudged up the stairs. "Why do you two embarrass me?"

"It wasn't me," Nikolas said, hands lifted in surrender. "I'm innocent."

Margot's lips twitched as she fought a smile. "What do you want? I'm busy."

Oh, he liked it when she snapped at him. A loose curl had escaped and fallen over her brow — she puffed it out of the way. The pencil tucked behind her ear didn't help.

He took a breath, easing his nerves. "Would you mind," he said, voice hoarse, "if I asked you to walk with me?"

"Walk with you?" she said, suspicious. "Where?"

He glanced at the hallway where her shadow waited — the custodian guard sat in a chair, reading the paper.

"If you could spare the time," Nikolas said.

She chewed her thumbnail, eyes flicking between him and the guard. "I'd like that. But he —" she jabbed a thumb toward the man — "is making my life insufferable. Hard to do my job when I can't even sneeze without an audience."

Nikolas knew the guard — he took Margot's hand before he could overthink and led her down the stairs.

"Jim," Nikolas said.

The man jerked upright, pastry dangling from his mouth. "Nik—"

Nikolas clapped a hand on his shoulder and slipped into his mind. It was a colourless place — neat stacks of ledgers, a window that never opened, the endless rhythmic tick of a clock. *Take the day off, Jim. You've earned it,* he whispered.

Jim's shoulders sagged. He blinked owlishly. "I need a break," he muttered. "I'm going to feed the pidgehawks." He tucked the paper under his arm and wandered away.

Margot watched him go, eyebrows raised. "If I knew it was that easy, I would've done that weeks ago."

Nikolas caught her hand and, on impulse, brushed his lips over her knuckles. "Would you still like to go?"

"Of course," she said. "I'd love to."

Love to. Those two words speared through him. He let go of her hand once they reached the Vulpine statue — white marble, primly atop its plinth, teeth bared.

"This is where it pulls me," he said.

Margot tipped her head, curls falling over her brow. "What do you mean?"

He slipped the ring off his pinky and held it out to her.

She took it and twirled it in her fingers. "How did you get it?"

"Orion gave it to me," Nikolas said. "So I could walk

through the shields."

"And instead, you stayed." Her gaze flicked from the ring to his face.

"I sensed a pull," he admitted. "Like a bargain being called. It dragged me through the city until I ended up here."

"To the Vulpine." She looked up at the statue and slipped the ring onto her finger, frowning. "I don't sense it."

"Maybe it only reacts to Spirit wielders?" he said. "Your Orb only answers you."

"So this ring is connected to the Lucerna orb?" Her eyes lit up with hungry curiosity. "The Spirit Wielder's orb. The pull brought you here."

"I've got a theory that the annex has a connection to the statue."

Margot smiled. "Let's go solve a mystery?"

✸

The annex sat at the far edge of the Study Hall — the further they walked, the more polished stone gave way to scuffed floorboards and peeling paint, the Ignis lights flickering, their bulbs left unchanged for decades.

Margot scribbled notes as they went, marking turns in a battered notebook. "This is it — annex three, lower wing, sub-hall two," she said.

"Damn thing won't budge," she muttered, pushing against the sliding door. It creaked and moved a thumb's width.

"Allow me." He pulled, and the door slid open with ease. Her glare could've cut diamonds. "You loosened it for me," he said.

"Hold this?" She was already digging through a side pouch. He took the empty glass vial while she uncorked two small vials with her teeth, poured them together, and shook them until the liquid inside glowed an emerald green.

The cramped, stale office lit up with an eerie wash of colour. "You're prepared, aren't you?" he coughed, waving dust away.

Margot squinted into the room. "The Mycology Department closed it decades ago. I checked the records."

The office was a disaster — rodenta had turned the cushions into nests, springs bursting from collapsed chairs, a fireplace choked with ash. Bookshelves sagged along the wall, empty except for one lonely volume caked in dust.

Nikolas ran a finger along the shelf. The wood beneath his fingertip was lighter in one rectangular patch — where the Vulpine plinth must have sat, the floor bearing a faint arching stain of black dirt. Only one book? He tugged it free — something clanked behind it, the bookshelf shifting forward with a metallic hiss.

"Oh, that is nasty," Margot said, clapping a hand over her nose.

"Rotten eggs," he agreed, wrinkling his nose.

"I wonder who built this," she said, scratching dirt onto her chin.

He reached out and wiped the smudge away with his thumb. "Let's find out," he said, and pushed the shelf farther aside.

A narrow stone passage yawned beyond, swallowing the light. Margot lifted the glowing vial, casting emerald shadows over the walls.

Their footsteps echoed, the air colder and drier with each step.

"Thanks," she said after a long stretch of silence. "For the door… and the dust."

Nikolas allowed himself to grin like a fool in the dark.

The passage split. Someone had cut handholds into the wall. Faint, bright light bled through the canvas panel.

"No way!" Margot opened her mouth, a gasp forming.

Nikolas turned and pressed her against the wall, resting his finger on her lips. *"We don't know who's on the other side,"* he whispered.

"Don't shush me," she whispered back, flicking his hand away.

He climbed the handholds and pushed the canvas back — a glimpse of a furnished room: deep red carpet, a mahogany dresser, a brass sculpture, the sound of pen on paper, the quiet roar of a fire. A Councillor's private office, maybe?

His hand slipped on the stone — he swallowed a curse and dropped, landing with a muffled grunt. He caught Margot's hand. "Wrong turn," he said, pulse thudding. "Let's go."

Her giggles followed him as they ran together.

Smugglers Tunnel

✹

"No!" She held her notes away from the sudden burst of salty water from a hole in the passageway.

He burst into laughter.

A feral sneer crossed her nose. "You're enjoying this?"

"Of course. I'm breaking rules with a librarian. It's thrilling."

"Librarian? That's blasphemy. I'm a linguist," she muttered, but she was smiling. She stopped. "Do you hear that?"

He listened. "The sea." Ocean waves crashing, the calls of Aves, the smell of salty brine and algae.

Her head turned. "We could head back."

"Do you want to go?"

She shook her head. "It's been a while since I visited the cliffs."

Relief loosened his chest. The stairs cut steeply upward through the opening, worn smooth by centuries of feet. He glanced at her skirt. "I'll be a gentleman and go first," he said, and winked.

Her gaze dropped to her hem. "Yes, that would be best."

"Later," he added with a wicked grin, and started climbing.

"Don't you dare," she hissed.

The stairway opened onto a stone alcove carved into the cliff face, wind rushing through with salt and the distant roar of surf. Just beyond, a circular tower jutted out from the cliff, ringed with narrow windows and banded in weathered brick.

They followed the exposed path, the drop yawning to their right where the old handrail had crumbled — Margot edging along the cliff side with her back against the wall.

Nikolas pushed the heavy wooden doors — they protested and swung inward with a groan. "Not much to look at." The tower's interior was a hollow cylinder of stone, cracks splintering through the mortar, windows rattling in the wind, a fireplace choked with rubble.

"I think it's neat," Margot replied, stepping into the centre of the room. "Patch the holes, reseal the windows, lay a rug." She turned in a slow circle. "The view is stunning. You can see the whole bay."

He moved behind her, the wind tugging her curls free, her cheeks flushed pink from the cold.

He slid his arms around her waist, slow enough that she could pull away.

A thrill ran through him when she didn't. *"Do you want to keep going?"* he whispered.

She swallowed and nodded, shivering. He slipped out of his coat and settled it over her shoulders — the icy wind didn't affect him anymore. Without the Nyxmara feeding on him, his body burned warm, alive in a way he hadn't felt in years.

The ring tugged at his hand again — he followed it, palm gliding along the stone until it came to rest over the fireplace.

He crouched and tapped the cracked mortar — a thin howl slipped through. "Something's behind this."

Margot's eyes widened. "No way. It keeps going?"

"Whatever's hidden here, someone didn't want us to find it."

Margot dug through her bag and found a letter opener. "Here."

He picked at the mortar, levered a loose brick, pulled a few more free — the sooty back of the fireplace gave way, revealing an iron grate and a tunnel below it.

The smell of sand and salt billowed up. "Looks like a

crawlspace," he said, voice echoing.

Margot was beside him, peering into the dark. "Could be a smuggler's tunnel?" she said, excited for someone faced with a death trap.

"Is there nothing that doesn't excite you?" he asked.

"Paperwork," she answered. "I hate paperwork." She swung her legs into the gap and dropped onto the stone. "Come on, let's go."

Nikolas followed her on hands and knees, trying very hard not to stare at her as they crawled — the tunnel narrow, the ceiling low, sea air seeping through hairline cracks.

The sound of open water echoed somewhere ahead.

"It's a pulley," Margot said. "Look."

He squeezed past her enough to see thick ropes and iron wheels bolted into the stone. "If we follow this, it should lead to something that opens or lifts."

"Or drops," she added. "Or collapses. Or floods. But, you know. Options." Her eagerness was infectious.

The tunnel ended at another grate. Margot rolled onto her back and kicked — it popped free and fell with a clang. Nikolas slid out into a circular stone chamber, bare walls rising around him like the inside of a well.

A metal cage sat in the centre on a low marble pedestal. Inside lay the thing that was pulling him.

The Lucerna Orb.

Nikolas circled it. The cage was seamless — smooth bands of steel with holes no wider than his eye, no hinge, no latch, no obvious trap.

A sign that there was one.

"You could try lifting it?" Margot suggested after a few beats.

"And trigger a mechanism that floods the chamber and drowns us?" he said. "Tempting."

She snorted. "Better than standing here staring at it until

we starve." She dug in her bag and pulled out a small cloth pouch. "For the orb."

He weighed it in his hand. "Seawater will come in fast. There are pressure points in the floor — twelve, at least."

"I'm a strong swimmer," she said, backing toward the tunnel.

Her wink undid him. He drew a breath, braced his feet, and lifted.

The cage rose on hidden chains with a grinding squeal, nearby cogs turning with a shuddering noise that echoed through the stone.

He plunged his hand inside, grabbed the fractured orb, and shoved it into the pouch — a sharp spark climbing his arm as the fabric closed, bright and hot.

"Nikolas!" Margot's voice rang from the tunnel. "We have to go!"

Cold water lapped over his boots. He bolted, diving back into the tunnel as water surged behind him, rocks slicking under his palms, salty spray cooling his face.

The roar of rushing water thundered closer.

"Turn this way!" Margot called. Her hand shot back, and he grabbed it. She hauled him along the slipway. Together, they slid through the narrow space, then tumbled through the final grate and fell.

Into freezing, churning water.

He surfaced with a gasp — the reservoir deep and bitterly cold, the shock of it stealing the air from his lungs. Bright Ignis lights glowed somewhere above them, warped and smudged by the sloshing surface.

Nikolas swam hard for the edge, hooked his elbow over the ledge, and held out his free hand. "Come on, ladies first."

Margot grabbed his hand — he levered her up, water streaming off her clothes and hair. His coat was long gone, vanished somewhere in the tunnels. She shook herself like a wet creature, curls clinging to her forehead, blazer lost somewhere along the way.

Her blouse was frustratingly see-through.

He looked at the far wall. His own dripping sleeves. The ladder. "Not exactly what I imagined for a first date."

She laughed, a breathless, bright sound that warmed more than the water had chilled. "Are you joking? That was fun."

Her teeth chattered, betraying her.

"Where are we?" he asked, scanning the stone walls.

"Underground," she said, climbing the nearby ladder. "But near the surface. This feeds the upper apartments. Follow me."

She pushed the grate aside and peered out.

They slipped into an empty utility corridor, boots squeaking, passing no one on their way back through the underbelly of the city. When they reached the street near her block, the sky above was bleeding into evening.

They stopped outside her door.

She was still shivering, the ring gleaming on her finger, the pouch with the orb tucked into her bag. The smell of her perfume clung beneath the salt and damp. "Would you like to come in?" she asked. "Get warm?"

The word *yes* roared through him.

"I would," he said. "Very much."

MARGOT WILSON

His Solarium

Margot slumped her soaked leather book bag against the wall of her foyer. It made a sick, wet squelch as the contents hit the floor. A problem for the future.

She peeled her blouse out from her skirt and unbuttoned the bottom, leaving the middle few in place. Rips and snags tore through her tights in jagged stripes. A frustrated, feral little noise escaped her throat.

Her shoes were ruined, soaked through, leather warped, one heel smashed inward. She was filthy and streaked with sand, grit, dust, and smudges — palms burning with angry red scrapes. She rubbed her aching hands.

And yet… she'd never felt more alive.

Nikolas hovered in the foyer — damp, rugged, in as much disrepair as she was, his hair dripping with dark curls, the streak of white catching a glint of light. Several cuts still glowed pink along his shoulders.

"I'm going to shower," she said, carefully trying not to drip on her mother's rug.

She pulled on his *mana*. "*Want to join me*?" she whispered.

Her heart thudded. She didn't wait for his reply, didn't want to acknowledge what she'd learned to do in the tunnels. She left a trail of wet clothes behind her, each piece peeling away like a strip of skin.

The Ignis lights hummed louder as she turned the knob — the pipes shuddered, then expelled a blast of freezing water through the brass faucet.

She unclasped her brassiere and let it fall to the tile, shivering as she removed the last of her soaked clothing. Tossing the curtain aside, she let the water run over her fingertips until it began warming, then pulled the stopper — the shower burst to life, warm steam curling upward and fogging the mirror.

Nikolas' hands found her waist.

His palms left heat in their wake. Her breath hitched, skin prickling with goosebumps, her head tipping back on instinct as his lips brushed her ear, then along the curve of her shoulder. "I see you joined me."

His approving hum vibrated against her skin.

She turned, steam swirling around them. He looked different in the warm light — no longer the gaunt, shivering man from the cells. *Stronger. More alive.* His vivid green eyes flashed with hunger, the white streak in his hair glowing like moonlight, his chest broader, ribcage no longer visible.

Was he always this handsome? Or was she seeing him without the shadow of the Nyxmara draining him?

Nikolas held her chin and wiped dirt from her cheek with his rough, calloused thumb. This time, instead of pulling away, he leaned in and kissed her — exactly how she wished he'd kiss her earlier.

She rose on her tiptoes, pressing closer. *"I want you."* She slid her hands into his shirt and ripped it open — buttons skittered across the floor.

A growl rumbled from him as he lifted her.

She wrapped her legs around him, fingers burying in his hair, nails scraping just enough to make his breath hitch. *"Fuck yes, more,"* she whispered, kissing him deeper.

"With pleasure," he answered, kissing her before lowering her to the tiles. She whined in protest — until he grasped her hips, stripping away the last scrap of clothing she had left and guiding her into the tub.

Hot water seared her skin, washing off the grit and salt.

She tipped her head back beneath the cascade, letting the warmth soak through her hair. When she wiped water from her lashes, she found him watching her.

Watching her as if he'd been starving. He peeled away his shirt, then unbuckled his belt. Slowly, deliberately. His socks followed, his pants dropped, then his cock sprang free.

A thrill rolled through her at the sight of it. "If your plan was to torture me," she said, "you're doing an excellent job."

"Just a little payback," he grinned, stepping in with her.

She didn't want to think about what she'd done to him. She didn't want to think about him leaving. Wanted nothing to ruin this moment.

Nikolas reached for a soapy tonic on the shelf, lathering it between his palms. "Want me to wash your back?" he asked.

She could stop him. *Right here. Right now.*

Instead, she nodded. He turned her, hands gliding over her back in slow, languid strokes. Making sure each inch of skin was clean. He turned her around and knelt in front of her, his breath warm on her skin.

His hands slid lower. Down her thighs and calves. Back up again.

Closer, closer, until he lifted one of her legs onto the wide rim of the tub, his fingers digging into the soft flesh of her ass. Her moans echoed off the tile. Steam curled around him like smoke.

His vivid green eyes glowed. "*May I?*"

"*You may,*" she smiled.

A trail of lightning sparked from her nipples straight to her clit the moment he touched her breasts. His hands trailing her side to her hip. Then his mouth was on her, a hot tongue circling and sliding through her. Sucking that perfect bundle of nerves. Fingers working her open with exquisite precision.

She was gasping, moaning. *Fuck me.* He played her like a

well-loved instrument. Her moans were the melody. His tongue was the bow. His fingers moving with her rhythm.

He wasn't just devouring her, he was learning her, reverent with every slow, maddening flick of his tongue. Pleasure surged through her in spikes of lightning, waves of heat.

Her thighs shaking, her spine arching, her breath turning to desperate little sounds she couldn't control. She grasped his hair, clawing at his back. Steam blurred the world as she came apart against his mouth.

Margot rode through the waves, basking in the glow. She rolled her hips as he held her through it, fingers steadily moving in and out of her. His tongue slow, savouring every tremor.

Her orgasm built and grew deliciously until it crested over and crashed through her. When her legs finally gave out, Nikolas caught her, scooping her into his lap.

They sank into the tub together, listening only to their ragged breaths and the hiss of falling water. He held her, kissing the side of her neck and grounding her back into her body.

"That was… fun," Margot panted and barked a laugh. "Round two?" Her smile was soft now, drunk with pleasure and something dangerously close to affection.

"Oh, absolutely," he murmured — a wicked smile tugged at his lips.

She didn't bother drying. Didn't bother hiding how badly she wanted him again. She left a trail of wet footprints for him to follow as she slid back onto the bed, leaning on her elbows, legs open as he stepped between them.

"Like what you see?" he teased, cupping her jaw.

She bit her lip and slid her hand down, cupping his balls, stroking the length of him. His head snapped back, a deep groan vibrating from his chest.

"I'll take that as a yes," he moaned. He kissed her again, pushing her back onto the bed.

They kissed, scooting backwards. She guided him back until her head hit her pillow. Her fingers tangled in his hair as he pressed the tip of him inside her so easily, so perfectly that their breaths mingled together in the quiet, stolen moment.

He stopped for one heartbeat. He stared as if she was the first warm refuge he'd found in years. He opened his mouth.

Before he could speak, she bit his neck. She bit him to pull him deeper and to silence whatever frightened words she sensed forming behind his eyes.

He groaned, thrusting deep. "*Ow…*" He pulled out, letting the emptiness drive her mad.

He teased her with agonising slowness.

"Fuck this," she growled, hooking under his arm and rolling him beneath her.

"Little minx," he gasped.

She sunk into him. Resting her hips against his. Their hips found their rhythm, a desperate, rolling grind, and his cock slid in and out of her with perfect friction. She lavished in the way he filled her.

"Clever minx," she corrected, riding him harder. She dug her nails into his chest, her head rolling back.

She connected to his heart. Her awareness slipped sideways.

The room got brighter — she was suddenly being pleasantly fucked on the couch inside Nikolas' Solarium.

Keep going.

Their pleasure tangled with the memory of his grief, and her longing folded together in the bright, impossible warmth. She didn't want to stop — it was so achingly perfect that she didn't want it to end.

Don't stop. Another wave of pleasure coursed through her

body, her ass now touching soft velvet. *Fuck.* The tips of her toes glided along his back, pulling him deeper.

Nikolas looked into her eyes. *So beautiful.*

A hot wave of pleasure hit her. His panting and moaning became quicker. He was so close. His hands gripped her hips, guiding her harder, deeper. Heat gathered between her legs until the orgasm washed over her, ripping the breath from her lungs.

He followed seconds later, thrusting hard, moaning her name into her neck as he spilled into her.

She collapsed on his chest, panting, trembling, satisfied. She lay in his arms for several heartbeats, catching her breath, as he brushed a damp curl from her cheek.

He rolled away to the bathroom, bare ass glowing like a final parting gift. She rolled onto her stomach, opened her desk drawer, and pulled out a half-forgotten pack of Woodbine.

Score.

She lit one, inhaling the burning smoke deep into her lungs, exhaling toward the bathroom door.

Nikolas poked his head out, eyebrows raised.

She held the cigarette between two fingers, motioning: *Come get it.*

Vulpecula

A knock at her front door startled her.

It came louder. "Margaret Wilson! Are you in there?" the guard said.

"Shit," Margot coughed on the smoke and wafted her hands in the air. "I'll be right there!" she shouted.

"You have two minutes."

The guards argued about the semantics of legal entry into protectorate-owned property as Margot ran around her apartment, looking for clean clothes. Orion had run her ragged with training, study, and endless meditation — when Nikolas asked her, she was so relieved to be doing something, anything else.

She tied the band around her robe tighter and opened the door. "Yes, gentlemen?"

"Orion has been looking for you. You weren't at the Study Hall."

"He doesn't need to be aware of my every movement," she said, smoothing her hair. "I wasn't feeling well, so I came home."

"Right. Well, he requests your presence at the barracks. He said to bring the Sun Wielder with you."

She knew Orion wanted Nikolas. Did he know she had just got pleasantly fucked by Nikolas? *Is that why he called her?*

She chewed her thumbnail. She really needed a different hobby.

"Tell Orion I'll be there as soon as I can. Thank you." She closed the door in their faces before hearing their reply.

Oh, she was in deep shit. She smoothed her hands over her

hair, walked to the vanity, and ran a brush through the tangles.

She had to see Orion as soon as possible.

Nikolas came out of the bathroom. "Any regrets yet?" he asked, picking up his damp shirt and flicking it.

"I keep a stash of men's shirts in the closet," she said, eyeing him in the mirror. She finished brushing out the last knot, walked over, and let her robe fall to the floor. "And no, not yet."

The walk to the barracks was torture, her mind running over every scenario. Orion should be in a Council meeting.

Margot checked her timepiece. "Orion's meeting was supposed to go for two more hours." The guards led them to the cells in the same row where they had kept Nikolas — a wave of anxiety tightening her throat.

Was this a sick game to Orion?

Orion stood waiting at the cell door.

"I'm here!" She tried to put a chipper tone in her voice.

It failed.

Arms crossed, the usual scowl on his face — the one that showed when she got an equation wrong. "What did you get up to?" he said.

Nikolas piped up. "Why did you bring us here?"

Orion shook his head and motioned for the guards to open the door. Contained within was something she couldn't have imagined — cowering in the corner, a ball of snowy-white fur. *Trembling.*

"What is that?" Margot rushed into the cell — the fur changed with a symphony of colour, so beautiful she didn't notice Orion's ebony hand on hers, pulling her away. "What —"

She shook his hand off.

"She is Vulpecula, the Lucerna Spirit of Historia."

Vulpecula — the name sounding so familiar, yet she could

not remember. Long fur, short triangular ears, a long snout. Compared to the other Vulpine in Historia's service, she was ivory white.

A faint tremor rippled through the air, brushing over Margot's skin like a chilly wind. Instinct made her reach back — Nikolas' hand found hers. She glanced at him.

His vivid green eyes weren't on the creature; they were on her.

"Did you know she would awaken?" Margot whispered.

He looked stunned — as if the Vulpine statue he was obsessed with had come to life in front of him. She was damn sure it had, because it had the same gaping gash that exposed the statue's canis-like teeth. She turned his wrist over — a new welted mark shaped like the sun was on the same spot as hers.

Vulpecula had awoken and bonded to him when Nikolas touched the Orb, just as Orion had bonded to her.

Only when he tore his gaze away did the trembling little Spirit lift its head. Their eyes connected to Margot's mind. *"Oh, hello. You must be Orion's new bonded."* She shivered — the voice in her mind was gentle, but ancient.

"Why in Historia's name are we keeping her in the cells? Isn't she a Protectorate?"

Orion seethed. "She attacked several workers and guards when she woke up in the Study Hall — I only realised it was her when I was dragged out of the meeting."

"I was not myself when I woke." Vulpecula's voice was now a cool summer wind in her head. Her eyes — bright red, wobbling.

Albino. It explained the lack of pigment in her coat.

"Orion, I'd like to speak to my bonded in private."

Nikolas sucked in a sharp breath as Vulpecula shook and shifted.

Glistening, icy alabaster skin, long crystal-white hair

flowing down her back. She wore a grey linen dress tailored to her lithe shape, the hem grazing her mid-calves and showing off her naked feet.

Not a single spot, mole, or freckle graced her skin.

Nothing except a healed gash in her lip that showed her teeth.

NIKOLAS VENATOR

The Bond

✹

"You will do no such thing," Orion's booming voice echoed. "You will escort Margot back to the Study Hall."

A sharp, instinctive heat rose beneath his skin when someone tried to command him. His childhood had been the sound of orders barked into his ears, followed by bruises. When a voice boomed like that, he braced for impact.

"Orion, that's not fair!" Margot let out a whine of protest and stomped her foot.

"I'm going to talk with Vulpecula, as is my right as the Lucerna Protectorate." He crossed his arms, letting his legs spread out.

"Orion, must you be so… you?" Vulpecula rolled her red eyes. "And you may call me Vix." Her smile was lovely in theory — twisted viciously around the scar that cut through her lip.

The room was silent except for Margot's nervous shuffling. Orion insisted. Nikolas kept himself planted.

Bonded to a Spirit.

He had made bargains, sure — those can be bartered, broken, and fulfilled. But the bond between mortal and Spirit is a lifelong, permanent connection.

To bond is to serve.

Nauseating dread coiled in his stomach. Serving meant yielding. Yielding meant vulnerability. And life had always punished him for his vulnerability.

His fingers curled, nails biting into his palms.

The silence stretched. He could wait — Margot pleaded with Orion, but he stood firm.

Vix sat perched on the edge of the makeshift bed, her legs crossed. She checked her nails, flicked a piece of that white-rainbow hair through her fingers, or waited with a subtle smile for one of them to crack.

Nikolas refused to budge. He'd lived too long letting the creatures run him from one tavern to another.

If bonding was inevitable, he would face it.

Margot couldn't handle being around conflict — he could sense the anxiety rising within her. Orion would cave and go after her.

Almost on cue, Margot threw up her hands in frustration and stomped out, the cell door slamming shut behind her. She screamed about the stubbornness and audacity of men, her agitation echoing along the hall.

Orion broke eye contact first and closed the door with a soft click behind him.

The silence that followed was thick.

Nikolas relaxed, letting out the *mana* he was holding. "You wanted to talk?"

Vix let out a quick giggle. "She's fun."

"Fun doesn't even begin to describe her," he said — thoughts of her skin through the translucent white blouse, her hair curly and drenched, her laughter, the taste of her skin, her breathy moans against his throat. All of it flickered through his mind like a wildfire he couldn't smother.

"Oh no, stop that," Vix wafted her hands in front of her face. "Please, for the love of Historia."

Fuck — the bond. His jaw clenched, heat flushed through him.

"Yes, the bond," she said dryly. "Now, let's get to business." She circled him, her eyes roaming over every bruise, stretch mark, scar, freckle, and mole on his body. "Not what I was expecting, but you'll do nicely."

Nicely?

She hummed excitedly. "You have lived an interesting life, haven't you?"

"Between the running, fighting, and losing the people I love, I wouldn't exactly call that interesting," he grumbled.

Vix's face shifted. "I have bonded to many mortals in my time, and you, Nikolas Venator, have suffered at the hands of my children. And for that, I am sorry."

Every body he'd left behind. Every scream. Every time he'd run while someone else didn't make it. The weight piled behind his ribs until his breath stuttered. "Your children?" he asked.

She clasped her hands. "Some Spirits are my progeny. Is that not taught?"

He crossed his arms. "I suppose my village taught me strength over knowledge, so my education wasn't thorough."

Kill first, search the bodies later.

"It is still my burden to bear. You were just eight when your father brought you along on your first raid, and you ran?"

He remembered the smoke, blood, his father's laugh, the icy terror of the Interwilds swallowing him whole. The bite of winter wind on bruised skin, his mother's voice begging on her knees.

Nikolas blinked hard and nodded. "I lasted three days in the Interwilds before I came back. My mother took a beating for coddling me — I was forced to keep watch on the tower for three weeks."

"You were… sixteen when you killed him?" she asked without blinking. "And have been running ever since." She paused, adjusting her dress. "You would've died in one or two years if it wasn't for your friend."

If he hadn't stumbled into Historia… If he hadn't met her… If Margot hadn't pulled the mara out of him.

Vix tilted her head. "Your well was dry. Years of depletion..."

Nikolas snapped his fingers in front of her before she could finish. "So what now? I just work for you?"

"Of course. You are the Spirit Protectorate now. We will have to focus on getting your physical and mental wellbeing back into balance before I can trust you to rule in my stead, though."

"And if I want to leave?"

"Want to leave?" she scoffed. "Didn't you just decide to stay? Honestly, you have been running for so long that the minute you get uncomfortable, you run faster than she did, damn the consequences."

"Those consequences are people dying! Because I am a *beacon of fucking light* for them, a delicious snack they'd just *love* to eat, and the Canis take others with me. So yes, I *run*." The words tore out of him. He clenched his fists, breath shaking.

Running wasn't cowardice. It was survival — for him and everyone else.

Nikolas sat, his head falling into his hands. *I am safe, I am safe.* He repeated it until the tremor eased. Vix sat beside him, his pulse thudding.

He was so tired.

Vix offered him training and education, a place to stay better than any ramshackle village or tavern. A role beyond running and fighting, or travelling to find wielders.

A home.

He'd never had one, not truly. His survival had always depended on constant vigilance and a blade at his side. Perhaps this could be different.

"I sense that you've made your decision," she said, pushing up from the bed. "We have much to do."

With a firm pull, she opened the cell door and moved past

two guards who watched her with wide eyes. "Hello, gentlemen." She looked back at him and crooned, "Coming?"

He followed her up through the Barracks and out into the brilliant spring day — the lesser pollinating Spirits of Aristaeus' hive floating from flower to flower, leaving small trails of golden powder.

She placed a bare, muddy foot up on the Armoury's steps.

He stopped. "Why are we here?"

"You need a sword, don't you?" she replied and continued upwards without looking back.

The guard's eyes widened as he rose from his chair, tripping over his own feet — a simple wave from Vix and he sat again, resuming his newspaper as if she didn't exist.

He followed on her heels and into the vault that he had just spent a month in solitary confinement for entering.

They came to the vault door. She turned the combination lock left and right, pulled the handle — it opened with little effort.

She brushed a hand along the racks of swords until she found one and lifted it. "May I see my Orb?"

He opened the cinch of his pouch and held out his Orb — a brilliant light humming from it. A jagged crack ran through the middle, splitting it into two uneven pieces.

She moved to a rack of shields and placed one half in the hole at the centre.

He opened his mouth to ask, but she shushed him and placed the other half into the handle of the sword.

It snapped into place and glowed blue, illuminating the etchings: *Noli me sine causa trahere. Noli me sine virtute tractare.* Margot was an excellent teacher; he could translate it: *Do not draw me without reason. Do not wield me without valour.*

He sensed the *mana* within it come to life as Vix held it high. "Kneel, Nikolas Venator." The weapon hummed.

His spine locked, his breath hitched — he had knelt only

once in his life, and the memory of his father's boot pressing into his neck still haunted him.

"Kneel so I can knight you," Vix corrected.

He saw Margot's smile, faint and blurry on the edge of his mind. Her laughter, her warmth. Her body arching beneath him hours ago.

He lowered himself onto the stone floor. Not out of fear, or out of duty. Maybe he wasn't kneeling to be owned.

He was kneeling because he desired a future for the first time.

Vix touched the sword to his shoulder, then to the other. "Pledge your life to defend us. To protect Historia and its people as family."

A family. "I will."

"You may now rise, Nikolas Venator," Vix said. "Rise as the sword and shield of Historia."

The weight lifted off his shoulders. For once, he didn't feel like running away.

The Archival Vault

✷

"Opening the vault is an enormous event. Researchers from every department are coming out to watch it be unsealed," Margot said.

Nikolas rolled his shoulders. His back ached from the three perimeter laps Vix made him do that morning — three laps a day. He smothered a yawn and blinked hard. The days were wearing him thin, but when she talked, he tried.

She slapped his hand. "Are you listening to me?"

Nikolas nodded. "Always."

Margot had been organising the opening for a week now. The various guilds and departments were fighting — he had years of academic politics to learn, and most of it flew straight over his head.

Nikolas would rather kill a pack of Canis than sit through another meeting. They say Spirits are petty, but mortals are worse.

Some days, he felt like saying goodbye and walking out of the shields entirely.

He cleared his throat. "Orion is signing the form tomorrow, then we can make our way to the Vault. There's an access tunnel on the basement level of the museum. Then a downward spiral the whole way."

"For how many floors?" she asked.

"Estimates are forty minutes."

"Of just going down?" She rubbed her temples. "That means it'll be forty minutes of going up as well." She groaned as her head hit the table.

He huffed a quiet laugh, unable to stop himself. "I'd offer

to carry you, but you'd kick me down the stairs."

The look she gave him confirmed it. Nikolas twisted in his seat, cracking his back. "It's brutal. Vix has sent me there twice."

"At least it will be worth it," Margot said, taking a breath. "Getting to see a treasure trove of knowledge be unsealed is exciting."

"Do you know why they want it unsealed?"

"Ley lines and topographical charting." She shrugged. "Orion was studying them before… you know. The explosion." She tucked a curl behind her ear.

"I never got the full story from Vix. She dances around it."

"Do you remember when we were planning the heist? I was translating a diary."

Nikolas nodded — he remembered it was one of her pet projects, picked up to keep her mind busy. "Olivia Brown, right? She died in the explosion, but other than that, I got nothing."

"There is an annual exhibit that covers the incident. Richard was Vix's last bonded."

"Vix doesn't talk about her previous bonds, either."

"Neither does Orion. It's why I translated her diary." Margot packed up her notebook and twisted the cap on her fountain pen, tucking her bag over her shoulder. "I keep it at the house. I have been meaning to show you, but…" She pulled at her sleeve. "Orion keeps me so busy. I know he means well, but I need a break."

Margot's estate was a short walk from the Study Hall. Scaffolding still covered half the building — impressive all the same, she was monitoring the stonemason guild's attempts to replicate the stonework.

"*The Ship of Theseus*. Where does new and old begin?" she mused.

Nikolas chuckled. "You say the weirdest stuff with a

straight face."

She puffed up her cheeks and pushed him. "Rude."

After walking through the front door, Margot slumped her book bag against the wall and began rifling through piles of notebooks — battered covers, scraps of parchment sticking out at every angle, bits of leather string keeping them from spilling open. After several muttered curses and one triumphant squeal, she shoved a notebook into his hands.

Her notes were meticulous, her handwriting elegant, the margins full of observations. He ran a thumb along the ink flourish.

"Your handwriting is beautiful," he whispered.

She turned and tucked a curl behind her ear.

He leafed through the notebook. "*…the desert has claimed two more porters and their beasts, according to reports from Theodore… I fear we may have to weather this sandstorm for… the cave was discovered northeast of the border…*" He flipped to the end of the notebook. "*Orion…*"

Margot slapped the notebook out of his hand. "That's cheating!"

Nikolas took the notebook back and held it high, goading her into jumping for it.

"Unfair," she growled.

"Survival instincts," he countered, though he was enjoying the excuse to watch her glare up at him.

Margot jabbed him in the side.

"*Oof…*" Nikolas crumpled to the ground. "Fu—"

Her knees hit the carpet beside him. "S—sorry, oh fuck… shit, sorry."

A flicker of surprise, followed by pride. She was stronger than she realised, dangerously so — she hadn't even pushed *mana* into that jab.

She'd nearly cracked a rib.

Nikolas lay there for a few more seconds, collecting his

dignity. "It's okay… has Orion put you through physical training yet?" he panted, looking up at her.

Margot shook her head and looked at her hands. "I didn't even…"

Nikolas coughed, letting air expand his lungs. He touched her cheek. "Ask Orion to let you train with Vix."

Her breath caught when his thumb grazed her skin — a small hitch. He withdrew his hand before he lingered.

She nodded. "I will."

Silence settled. She didn't move away.

"I plan to read this at the Vault tonight," Nikolas said. Her gaze flicked to his lips. He sensed her heated thoughts, vivid enough to steal his breath. He leaned in to kiss her.

She bit her cheek and stood. "I have to get back to work. I will see you tomorrow."

Margot walked out again.

He watched her go, jaw tight.

✸

"Olivia Brown" has been chosen as the name for the daughter born on the first day of Cadere's rising. Please join Mr Sean Brown and wife Nicole at the Blacksmith Guild in celebration.

Richard Vale and Olivia Brown of Historia are delighted to announce their engagement. Richard Vale is the Department Head of Mycology, and Olivia Brown is a professor teaching at the Department of Animus Bestiary Studies.

Olivia Brown has died in the explosion.

Nikolas put the news clippings aside as he read Olivia's last diary — it began when she went on an expedition to find the Antikythera Mechanism. Orion was obsessed with finding it.

From what he could gather, Olivia was one of the first Soul wielders born in Historia. When teachers discovered her brilliant mind they trained her from a young age, and after bonding, she assisted Orion with mechanical calculations and astronomical predictions.

A sandstorm trapped her for three days before she came back with the mechanism — the journal entry ending one day after her return.

⁕

Nikolas's back ached from sleeping on a hard bedroll on the cold floor. "I got to the end, and what — Richard blows her up? Why?" he said, stretching. He watched the eager faces of the Library staff as they stood in front of the Vault door.

Margot shushed him and whispered into his mind, *"Richard was secretly jealous of Olivia and Orion's relationship. He had speculated for years that they were sleeping together."*

"No way." He blinked. Focusing his *mana,* he found the thread that connected them and held it tight. *"And they weren't?"* He'd observed how Orion treated Margot — like a teacher mentoring a gifted student, encouraging her to push past her anxieties and worries. It was never —

"I asked once, and he ignored me for a day. So, I did my own digging: Richard was experimenting with a new strain of mycelium. I read his autopsy report. It had burrowed into his brain and driven him mad."

"Interesting."

"They had samples taken of his earwax when he started saying he saw Spinners."

"And the Council went along with his orders?"

Margot shrugged. *"He was the Spirit Protectorate. Orion was… heartbroken, and well, I am sure Vix will tell you her reasoning for sleeping."*

So Olivia Brown was just an amazing woman, taken before her time.

The crowd murmured as Orion walked onto the stage. "Thank you for joining me on this special day. It has been nearly eighty-one years since the explosion that took pillars of this community, and now I hope we can…"

Nikolas gazed over the crowd — researchers who worked during the day, cleaners who worked at night, the teachers, secretaries, assistants, and aides who kept the guilds running. A hush of awe swept through them before giving way to a rising thrill, elation and wonder coursing through the crowd as Orion raised the staff high and whispered, *"Omnia ab uno."*

The metal groaned, and the carvings along the vault glowed, their lines flowing like molten veins across the etchings.

The air thrummed as Orion set the staff into the hole in the door's heart. He turned it clockwise, back and forth, until it sank with a deep, resonant clink.

He withdrew the staff and stepped aside.

The crowd held its breath as the vault stirred, the great door unsealed with a long, hissing exhale.

Screams rippled through the crowd.

Before Nikolas could turn, heat slammed into his back — a blast so violent it stole the air from his lungs.

The world tilted. His feet left the ground. He hit the stone with a bone-rattling crack, vision fracturing at the edges.

But even dazed, he saw it.

A shape burst from the crowd.

Too fast. Too fluid. A blur of limbs. A cloak and sharp steel in its hands beneath black fabric. Researchers toppled as it ploughed through them, shoving bodies aside with feral, single-minded force. Someone shrieked. People fell and toppled over one another. Papers spiralled upward in the heated air, caught in a sudden draft.

"Margot!" he croaked, forcing himself upright.

The figure didn't run toward the exit. It ran toward the Vault.

Straight through the settling dust. Straight past Orion's outstretched hand into the darkness.

His vision caught a smear of motion. He sensed the intent. Not fleeing. Hunting.

His instincts roared awake. He ripped the shield off his back, sword hissing from its sheath as he ran, boot soles slipping on scattered papers. Heat still burned against his spine.

And then the scent hit him.

Fresh blood — too much of it.

The cavern walls narrowed. The crowd fell away. He sprinted into the ancient darkness after the intruder.

Sword drawn. Shield braced. Heart hammering.

Because whatever had slipped inside the Vault wasn't a person. Something ancient had just woken up, and it was already spilling blood.

MARGOT WILSON

Antikythera Mechanism

An unexpected and entirely inappropriate thrill ran through Margot as Nikolas ran into the Vault without hesitating — his sword drawn and a snarl across his face, blood dripping from his forehead. *A study of movement and gore.*

Margot coughed. Stone dust was everywhere — people screaming, some scrambling to help others to their feet, others flat on the polished floor, stunned or bleeding.

"Orion!" she coughed as grit scraped her lungs. "Where are you?"

Her first event as Orion's second was a disaster — people bled and burned on her watch.

"Nikolas and Orion ran into the Vault. Stay here." Vix swept through the chaos, checking people for injuries with terrifying efficiency.

Stay here? Fuck that. Absolutely not.

Margot ran through the circular Vault door — a yawning metal iris set deep into the cavern wall — and froze.

It was an archivist's dream — Orion's obsessions, an entire lifetime's worth of tomes and notes. The Council had been terrified of him, so they had kept the Vault shut while he slept.

Heat hit her first. Then the sound of crackling, hissing.

Flame licked up the stacks, sprinting along paper edges, rolling through the aisles. Smoke blurred into shades of orange and gold.

Someone was burning the Vault.

Anger bloomed at the sight of burning shelves and falling pages — she ran toward the source, the stacks lighting up as flames rolled between them.

"NIK—!"

He burst into view, grappling a man in a blur of motion — Nikolas slammed him into a shelf, the man retaliating with a vicious strike.

"Nik!"

The intruder's head snapped toward her.

Cold metal kissed her throat in a blur of motion. Her neck throbbed with pain. Warm blood trickled along her chest.

Too much blood.

Her vision tunnelled, the edges fuzzing, her heartbeat roaring. A raw, feral instinct snapped into action — she grabbed the man's arm, fingers locking in an iron grip.

She pulled his *mana* into her hands.

He screamed. The sword clattered to the floor. Icy static crawled along her neck — her flesh knitting, the pain subsiding.

Anger surged — that bastard tried to kill her.

She drove her elbow backward, smashing into his ribs. He grunted, stumbling. She spun and aimed for his head — he caught her arm mid-strike, twisting it sharply behind her.

A gasp tore out of her. She would not let him escape.

She stomped hard — once on his foot, again on his side — and when he reeled, she lunged.

Her fingers found his temples.

Sleep.

Her *mana* surged, crackling amethyst. His body went limp, collapsing in a heap — his skull smacking the wood floor with a sickening crack.

She blinked, breath shuddering, fingers going to her throat.

The cut was gone.

"That was amazing," Nikolas panted, stepping to her, hands skimming over her shoulders, her arms, her waist — checking for wounds. "He was a trained Ignian fighter. How did you do that?"

"I—I'm not sure." She held her hand to where the blade had kissed her skin. "I was sure he cut my neck."

His eyes — that grassy, storm-washed green — were wide with awe. He cupped her chin, tilting her head.

"He did. But you healed yourself."

Her breath caught. His lip was bleeding.

She rose on her toes and licked it better. Screw the rules — she had damn near died and needed to grasp life while it was in her hands. His hands cupped the back of her neck, pulling her in deeper.

The flames crackled behind them. Smoke drifted. Somewhere deeper in the Vault, Orion was shouting directions and calling her name.

Margot broke off the kiss.

Nikolas grumbled as she pulled out of his arms and leaned over to inspect the unconscious intruder. "Let's bind him and have a little chat with our new friend."

Her knees wobbled. "Right. Yes. Okay." She nodded, lightheaded, everything too bright.

No — she would not crumble now.

For a few heartbeats, she stood there blinking. She could heal like Sophia — except she had to drain people to do it. Margot remembered the heist, what she'd done to Clara when she was delirious. She pulled herself together and followed.

They located Orion a short while later.

Margot stumbled toward him, adrenaline still burning through her bloodstream.

Orion's eyes flicked over her, lingering on the still-wet bloodstain smeared across her shirt. She sensed something sharp and protective in his glare.

She forced a crooked smile. "You should see the other guy." Her voice came out thinner than she intended.

"Where is the intruder?" His gaze softened, then narrowed toward the Vault behind her.

"Nikolas is handling the Ignian," she managed. "I'm going to change and be with him when he interrogates… if that's okay."

A beat of silence. Orion assessed her the way he always did, then nodded.

She drifted toward the table, eyes snagging on the mechanism. "Is this what Olivia was searching for?" Small, unassuming, no bigger than a book — ancient and delicate, layers of interlocked brass, gemstone inlays, a dial that caught the cavern's light.

"In a sense, she died for it," Orion said.

Margot didn't breathe for a full second. If Olivia had not left to retrieve the mechanism, she would have noticed Richard's symptoms — the sudden violence, the paranoia, the mycelium infection spreading through his brain.

The infection had spread in less than a month.

"So… what happens next?"

Orion's amethyst eyes went distant. "Now my work continues," he said. "Focus on your studies. I expect my report on my desk as soon as possible. Go."

Her stomach dropped, bones aching. But she nodded. "Yes, sir."

Dismissed. Just like that.

Perhaps she needed the push — something to keep her from drowning in what had happened.

☾

The climb from the Vault to her apartment was murder — her legs trembling with every step, her lungs scraping the cold stone air. By the time she made it inside, she barely had the strength to toss her ruined shirt into a corner and drag herself into the shower.

Warm water hit her skin. Her fingers brushed her throat — a faint, thin scar. She willed *mana* beneath her fingertips, coaxing the mark to fade.

She dressed and headed toward the Barracks.

Her feet throbbed with every step. And of course, Emile was waiting, leaning in the doorway with that cocksure grin she fantasised about punching.

"What do you want, Emile?"

"I'm here to escort you." Emile held up his hands.

Much to her disappointment, he led her straight to the cells and knocked three times.

Margot's breath hitched as the door opened.

Nikolas looked *wrecked* — shirt torn, bloody marks bleeding through, hair more dishevelled than usual. Her heartbeat picked up at the sight of his split lip.

"Good," he said, eyes locking onto hers. "You're here."

Her pulse fluttered. She wanted to lick it better again.

Do not lose focus on your studies.

Orion's orders rang in her ears. She set her jaw and rummaged through her bag for a pen or notebook — anything to occupy her hands.

The stranger coughed, his head hanging low, shackles clinking around his wrists. A lazy, cocky smile spread across his lips when he looked up.

"Yes, we were just getting acquainted. And you?"

Margot opened her mouth to answer —

"Don't answer him. Stay quiet and write."

Her jaw snapped shut. She was here as Orion's second, not a stenographer.

Nikolas continued, "She is no one. Answer the question. Who are you? Why did you try to steal the mechanism?"

Margot's head snapped up. Words bubbled on the tip of

her tongue. She blew out a breath of frustration instead.

"I am also no one. Who are you?" the stranger asked, looking at Nikolas.

They talked in frustrating, stupid, long-winded loops — getting nowhere.

Margot studied the stranger's golden skin and molten eyes. Ignians were natural-born warriors, and the man in front of her screamed well-honed danger. She rubbed her palms together.

How could she take him down?

"Water?" the stranger said, tugging at his metal collar. The chain led to a hook on the wall.

She reached out with her *mana* toward his eyes. *Rot. Thick, sweet, and putrid green.*

Her *mana* recoiled. A yellow-green fluid dripped from his ears, the ooze coiling inside him, a growing mass of ichor that turned her stomach — the smell worsening as he twisted his head, more fluid spilling free.

Her stomach lurched.

"We need to step out," she whispered to Nikolas.

She motioned for him to follow and breathed in fresh air once they left the cell. "Did you smell it? The Rot. It's sickly sweet and disgusting."

"Like rotten eggs, but different," Nikolas said.

"In the passageways, there was that smell. I'm not saying they're connected, but we were in Richard's old office when we investigated your Orb..."

"It's worth having a chat with Vix."

She huffed. "The farming guild has complained for months — fungi in the crops, rot spreading faster than expected. Winter will be brutal if we don't fix this."

Fear washed over her.

"I have to stay here," he said. "If you want to investigate without me, you can."

Margot paced the hallway between cells. She didn't need permission to go anywhere.

She gathered her things from the cell and left, making it halfway to the conservatory before she realised he'd said '*without me*'. Her heart sputtered with irritation.

Focus. Focus. Focus.

She set her gaze down the hallway and continued onward.

☾

The oak tree greeted her in the courtyard like an old friend, its ancient, heavy branches stretching overhead. The conservatory air was humid, thick with soil, blooming leaves, and half-feral *mana* — large circular leaves and deep garnet fronds crowding the space, some studded with spikes, others ready to kill with a touch.

For a moment, guilt curled low in her stomach — Nikolas would've loved this place, he always paused near potted plants. She shook her head.

She was here on business.

Theo was knee-deep in dirt, tending to a massive corpse flower whose thick crimson-red bud was ready to bloom, dirt caked to his forearms up to the elbows. He saw her and beamed.

"Is that you, sprout?" He swept her off the ground in a crushing hug.

A startled giggle burst out of her — Theo's joy was contagious in a way that softened even her fraying nerves.

"It's good to see you too," she said, cheeks flushed.

He deposited her back on the ground. She picked a piece of dried mud off her knit sweater.

She always ended up with mud smears or dusty streaks on her clothes when he hugged her.

"What can I help you with?" Theo asked as he wiped his hands on his apron.

"I need information on a species of fungus," she said. "One

that… leaks fluid out of the ears and smells like rot."

Theo paused. "Oh. That."

"That?" she repeated, her stomach sinking.

"Yes. Has the infected person displayed sudden violent behaviour? Irrational thinking? Paranoia?"

"Does talking in circles count?"

"That'll do." Theo nodded. "*Cordyceps variant twelve.* A nasty thing. We haven't had a case in decades. I'll get you an antidote, but I need to check my old notes first."

"Can you meet me back at the cells?" she asked.

"Of course."

He gave her another delightful, bone-crushing hug — one that left more dirt on her clothes — before bustling off to gather supplies.

Margot headed out, her mind buzzing with possibilities. She stopped at the Mess Hall to grab lunch — tucking bread roll sandwiches under her arm, refilling a canteen of water, and stashing it in her bag. She ate her roll while walking, chewing as the weight of the day pressed against her ribs.

Margot ignored her aching feet — she should be used to trekking across Historia by now.

Soul used to have its own headquarters. Apparently, the Magus for Hex and Bone despised Orion so much she refused to give it back.

"You control too much power. I'll give it back to you when I am dead," her note had said.

Margot chuckled and ate an apple as she walked down the hallway.

Orion brooded over it for a week. *At least someone could stand up to him.*

☾

She made it. Finally — a moment to breathe.

Qu landed in front of her in a perfect, graceful crouch, blue eyes glinting with mischief.

She stared at him for several awkward blinks and decided that talking with him would hurt, so she pushed past him.

He launched into a backflip over her, the wind whooshing past her ears, and landed in front of her with a louder, more theatrical thud.

Show off.

She crossed her arms. "What do you want?"

"I have an offer for you," Qu said, his sky-blue eyes doing that thing they did — the one that made her stomach flip and her knees weak.

She scoffed in surprise. "What?"

"Dinner with me? Tonight?" He held out a note, eyes pleading.

"What? No. What about Sophia?" she said, pushing past him. "You know what!" She turned, mustering her anger and pointing a finger at him. "I can't believe you."

A white blur flew in front of her.

Qu had folded the note into a crane.

Her heart gave another confused sputter as she opened it: *I am okay with it. Please hear him out. — S.*

Margot cursed, balling the paper in her hands. The note was in Sophia's handwriting.

She was being ambushed.

"Fine."

A gust of air blew her curls into her face — Qu was suddenly in front of her, smiling.

"I'll meet you at seven?" He reached for her hand.

She stepped back, flustered. He cannot touch her — she can't risk it. "I can't be out later than nine." She checked her timepiece. "I have to go."

☾

Margot reached the Barracks in record time. She handed a brown package of food to Nikolas — his happy chewing hums joining hers as they ate in the hallway's silence. She'd insisted on eating out there. The smell of the stranger still sat low in her stomach, threatening the contents outward.

She didn't want Nikolas to witness that.

Theo wasn't far behind her. He tipped the antidote into the stranger's throat.

The Ignian shot awake with a strangled gasp, coughing. "What the fuck was that?" His voice rasped. "Where — where am I?"

The stranger's aura was now bright as molten lava, no longer infected with ooze.

"Disgusting," Margot muttered as he spat on the floor.

His molten-gold eyes snapped to hers. "Who are you?"

"We're inquiring about that as well," Theo said. "We are Historia. You are free now."

"Historia, interesting. Kit Sun has been looking for you."

"Are you bonded to them?" Margot asked, just to be sure.

"No." He tugged at the collar. "Was this necessary?"

"Yes," Nikolas said, his voice heavy. "If you agree to the Twelve Tables, you'll be free to go."

Margot leaned toward Nikolas. *"Is that wise?"* she whispered.

He answered loudly. "He either abides by our laws or leaves and faces the Interwilds. Those are the rules."

The stranger chuckled low.

Theo's voice echoed off the cell walls. "Within the shields, you are bound to the rules. If you break them, you get tossed out of the shields. Pretty simple, if you ask me."

"I will agree to your terms under certain conditions," the stranger said, laughing.

A Proposition, with Her Ex

☾

Nikolas and Theodore were back at the Barracks, negotiating the terms of the stranger's release. He'd told her twice to go home after catching her checking her timepiece every few minutes. Her foot tapped louder each time the men debated the semantics of what, exactly, privacy was.

She hated being dismissed. But she hated bureaucratic arguments just as much.

Her nerves were frayed by the time she reached her apartment, feet aching from too many hallways.

A suspicious package waited for her, propped against her door like it had been waiting all day to ambush her — she carried the long box to her bed and untied the bow.

A stunning deep-amethyst garment lay inside layers of tissue, silk so dark and luminous it looked as though a slice of night sky had been stitched into existence. *Extravagant. Far too nice for her.*

He had tucked a note at the bottom: *You deserve it. – Q.*

She covered her smile with her hand. She was far too pleased. *Damn it.*

The faint scent of powder and juniper berries drifted up from the note. Of course his letters smelled like him.

Of course he knew what fragrance would make her pulse skip.

Her breath caught as she ran her fingertips along the embroidery — intricate swirls, careful needlework, designs that shimmered whenever she shifted the fabric. She held it up against her body in the mirror. It brushed her shins. It transformed her.

Made her dangerous.

The timing was terrible.

Margot exhaled and rolled her shoulders back. The day needed to be washed off her, wrung out and banished. She showered, scrubbing away dust, sweat, lingering panic, and the echo of Nikolas' bloody lip in her mind.

She cursed when she remembered it.

She sat at her vanity and assembled herself back into something mortal and composed. A sudden thump rattled the balcony doors. She closed her eyes and counted to three.

He can wait.

When she opened the balcony doors, the chilly spring air slipped around her ankles. Qu stood with his back turned, staring up at the translucent rainbow shields shimmering across the night sky.

He always had a flair for the dramatic.

"You couldn't use the front door?" she said.

Qu turned, that smug golden smile spreading across his face. "That would be absurdly boring." His eyes swept over her. "You look lovely."

Her breath snagged — his aura dripped with lust. She forced a small smile, turning her hips so the silk whispered around her shins. "Thank you. You're being too generous."

Margot tucked her hands together, squeezing her fingers to keep them from shaking — breathed in and blew the candle out, shutting off her senses.

"Nonsense," he said, stepping closer. "You're the Soul Protectorate of Historia." He held out his hand. "Shall we?"

She bit the inside corner of her lip, hesitating for one heartbeat, then placed her hand in his. "Where are we—"

Qu scooped her up in a smooth, reckless motion, bending his knees before launching them into the night sky.

Margot squealed — a mortifyingly high sound she would deny until her deathbed — as her stomach dropped and the wind tore at her hair. The city blurred beneath them. The shields shimmered above. And for one moment… she was exactly like the silk clinging to her skin.

☾

Margot's stomach did that awful lurching thing — the same one it did when she misjudged a step on the Study Hall stairs. The brisk wind made her snap her eyes shut. The only warmth she felt was Qu's arms locked around her.

Or rather, she was gripping him for dear life.

"Qu! Put me down!" she shrieked, the wind shredding her words.

His laugh vibrated through his chest and into her bones. "We're almost there. I remember a time when you loved flying with me."

Flying was a generous word. Leaping was more accurate. Aerians were master manipulators of air, but even they were bound by gravity.

Qu glided toward the terrace, knees bending as her heels kissed stone moments later. Margot fixed her hair, trying to pat the panic away with it.

They had landed in the middle of candlelit tables — patrons freezing mid-bite, mid-sentence, mid-judgmental stare.

The server appeared a heartbeat later. "Mr Atticus, your table is ready."

At the sound of his name, dozens of voices shifted into murmurs of adoration — Qu didn't bother acknowledging it. Margot lifted her chin, refusing to appear rattled as the server escorted them through the dining room.

She shrugged off her coat and took her seat inside a private dining room — the sliding mahogany door closing behind them, dimming the world to a warm amber glow.

"So," she said, placing the cloth napkin on her lap. "What is your proposition?"

Qu smirked. "Getting straight to the point, as always. Eat first, then we can talk."

Margot pursed her lips. She was terrible at small talk — it felt like performing a dance she didn't know the steps to, empty chatter about the weather, which council members were secretly sleeping with whom, or whose child had outgrown their shoes again.

"I didn't mean for you to literally wait to talk before we eat," Qu said as the server poured their wine.

"Oh, well…" Her stomach fluttered. "How is your father? He's been absent from council meetings."

Qu's face dropped.

"I only meant that Theo said he's been helping the carpentry guild with the shingles and reinforcing the ridges —"

"My father is fine," Qu said. "Keeping himself busy and out of my hair."

Margot hummed and let the conversation drift. "And Orion has been keeping me busy. I maybe get five hours of sleep."

"He doesn't let you rest?"

Margot shook her head. "He doesn't sleep. He's always working in that damned archive vault."

"You should stand up to him," Qu said. "Tell him you need rest."

She gave a soft, humourless laugh. "It's complicated. The work is important."

Too important to risk disappointing Orion.

The servers brought out their dishes. After a few seconds of indecisive whining, she'd chosen a steak with mashed potatoes and various steamed greens.

She watched with silent glee as the server kept refilling her white wine.

Qu laughed, a bright and dangerous chuckle. "And then, if

I remember correctly, you told James to go fuck himself."

"I think I said something along the lines of, *'A theory? Gravity is also a theory, but you're not going to jump off a building to prove me wrong.'* And then he had the bright idea of writing a formal complaint to my mother." She laughed, the wine going straight to her head. "He was a little shit, even when we were kids."

Growing up trapped in Historia meant lifelong grievances aged like fine wine. You knew everyone, and everyone knew you.

Qu wiped his mouth with a napkin and placed it on the empty plate, his garlic pasta long gone. A heavy, satisfied smile crossed his face.

"I want to find the Aer Orb," he said, looking up through his reddish-brown hair. "I've been searching our archives. I think I can find it."

"Is that your proposition? You want my help?"

Qu nodded. "It's the only way for Sophia to overthrow her father. Her society won't elect her, so I'm going to force their hand."

As the Aerian Protectorate, she would have total authority to break the engagement between her and Qu.

"And why won't they elect her without it?"

He leaned back. "*She* wasn't born a *He*. Aerian society will only elect male leaders, not for lack of trying on my part to convince everyone otherwise."

Margot's stomach tightened. "So why don't you get elected? Or bond with the Spirit yourself?"

"That's Plan B," he said, his aura flickering with grief, guilt, and something heavier. "I never got the chance to… explain how I left Historia."

Her heart thumped. She nodded, letting him continue.

"Do you remember when I asked you to meet with me? It was when the Acerodons started their nightly migration from the Interwilds during Summer."

She nodded. She remembered. It was a few days before he had 'died.'

"I went to ask your mother for your hand."

"We were so young — " *They still were.*

"I didn't care about my father's rules. I wanted to build a life with you." He paused and took a deep breath. "I went to see my father after getting her permission. I wanted to do it properly. Instead, he lashed out and suffocated me. I woke with a bag over my head, on my way to Alces."

As he spoke, a tear slipped free leaving a hot trail down her cheek. "For years, I survived among his herd. I learned to be strong and became an expert in the Twelve Tables. After sending so many, I received a letter from my father. He wanted me back, but under one condition: *no son of his would marry an ungifted mortal.* He had arranged the engagement, since Sophia had been rejecting other suitors."

Ungifted mortal.

That was what she *was*. What she would have been forever if she hadn't touched Orion's Orb. If she'd had her alignment back then, things might have been different.

She wiped her tear, sniffing softly, careful not to stain her new dress. "Alright. I will help you." Heated thoughts flickered through her. "But this doesn't mean you can just slink back into my bed," she smirked.

He returned it with a wicked grin.

Qu kissed her cheek and scooped her up, the dinner in her belly threatening mutiny — she held on with her eyes closed as he leapt from rooftop to rooftop, her cropped hair whipping around her face and tangling in her mouth.

He deposited her back on her balcony. She let him kiss her other cheek and run his hands along her arms.

Margot wanted to clear the air about Nikolas. She reached for Qu's heart — that unique inner space — and saw a flutter of brown moths cloud her vision. She opened her mouth to speak.

Qu blew her a kiss as he walked backward, then shot back into the sky before she could stop him.

Such a flirt.

Her mind was full of tangled threads. She focused on finishing her report a few minutes before midnight — she would look it over once more in the morning before handing it to Orion.

She changed and hung up her new dress. After slipping into bed, she fell into a hard, dreamless sleep.

Strangers in Their Midst

The stranger's name was Stephen, and he was leaving a trail of broken noses, black eyes, and bruised egos in his wake. "I never got your name," He said to Margot, who was doing her best to ignore him — the less he knew, the better. His presence had turned the Barracks into a disaster zone of offended pride. His official role in Historia was to be Nikolas' shadow — he kept him close so the man wouldn't wander off and ignite another fight. "Or shall I just call you silent little girl?"

Margot breathed in, holding the rage simmering beneath her ribs. She hated being called *little* and especially hated being called a *girl.*

She was a *Lady or a Maven.* She would accept nothing else.

"Nikolas," she said sweetly, handing him a book, "can you take this? I'd like to give him another bump on the head."

Stephen lifted both hands in surrender. "All right, all right. I'll go make myself useful somewhere else." He dragged a finger across the welt Margot had given him.

"Don't go far," Nikolas called as Stephen sauntered off to antagonise someone new. "What did you need?"

She lowered her voice. "I was wondering if Vix mentioned the other Protectorates. Maybe something about Vela? Or the Aer Orb?"

Nikolas hummed, running a hand over the stubble along his jaw. "I have an idea. I meant to show you before, but…" He gestured toward Stephen, who was now flirting with Charlotte. "…he is a complication."

"Perhaps Theo can take him," she said, wiggling her

fingers. "Or I could put him down for a nap. I am practicing."

Nikolas laughed, eyes crinkling. "Theo said if you do that too often, you might cause brain damage."

Delighted laughter from Charlotte echoed through the Study Hall.

Nikolas wasted no time. He found a porter, sent a message to Theo — the porter ran off proudly flashing the gold aureus Nikolas had slipped into the wielding's hand at the other kids.

"You're too generous," Margot said, shaking her head. "They'll get smart and raise their rates soon."

Theo arrived quickly, and Nikolas handed Stephen over without ceremony.

With her hand in his, Nikolas led Margot to a quiet corner of the Study Hall. He pulled one book after another from the shelves, sliding each back into place until something clicked.

Excitement bubbled up inside her. "More secret bookcases?" She leaned closer to examine the spines. Nikolas twisted the head of a statue, and metallic clunking rang out.

The door gave way, and Nikolas stepped through. "Vix showed me this when she woke up. She said it was an old meeting place."

It was a glorious space — coloured light flooding through intricate stained glass, a spiral staircase connecting two levels of bookcases, a round table with twelve chairs at the centre. On the wall hung a large oil painting with an inscription beneath it.

Omnia ab uno. "Everything from one," she read.

She recognised Orion, his ebony hair cropped short. Vix sat primly beside him, her bright red eyes stark against ivory skin — in the painting, she lacked the scar on her lip. Maybe it was new. She didn't recognise the other four figures.

"The Council used to be twelve," Nikolas said. "Six Spirits, six bonded. They created the Twelve Tables when Historia was founded, to bring stability and unify Torresium so Spirits wouldn't dominate mortals. Now, Superior Spirits exploit those rules, bonding with as many wielders as they can."

"The Tables never defined how many bonds Spirits could make."

He sighed, leaning back. "Historia couldn't imagine a future where her descendants would do that."

"Did every Spirit originate from Historia?" Orion had never told her the full story — history always seemed to splinter depending on who told it.

"In a way. Historia made Vix, and the Elemental lineages trace their origins back to her."

She stared at him. "How do you know this?"

"Vix told me," he said. "I guess Orion never bothered."

She let out a sigh thick with pain — Orion always let her sit with half-formed truths, scraps of information, until the pressure became unbearable and she went digging on her own. "I'm glad you showed me. You said Historia made Vix?"

Nikolas nodded. "Some of their offspring are the Spirits you study."

"So the other four Spirits are their children?" She looked back at the painting. "Why didn't he tell me?"

It was a family portrait. "That means Vix is Orion's… wife?"

"Was," Nikolas said. "It's been a very long time since they split. Orion can't stand being in the same room as her." He chuckled.

Ex-wife.

No wonder Orion hid away in the vault, working in an inconvenient, isolated place. The puzzle pieces clicked together; it explained the agitation she always sensed when Vix was nearby.

She rolled a pencil between her fingers. "I hate being the last person to know these things. It's embarrassing."

Nikolas sat beside her. "Vela, Aquila, Lepus, and Cetus." He handed her a book and let her study the illustrations. "Vela is a Sylph, an incorporeal sprite that can shift into the form of a hummingdove."

Her eyes locked onto his finger as he licked it and turned the page. "Aquila takes the form of a firebird. On the third floor, near the Ignian Hall, there's a massive stained glass window. That's them fighting a Wyvern."

She knew the image well: the great Ave's hooked beak crushing a Wyvern's neck, flames in the glass coming alive on the Summer Solstice.

His finger slid onward. "Lepus is a tunnel hare. Digs underground pathways and keeps an impressive gemstone and mineral collection in the Vault. Theo never shuts the fuck up about it."

She let out a chuckle as he scooted closer, his arm resting along the back of her chair. "And finally, Cetus. A Selkie. The first halfway people."

"Halfway people?" Margot already knew, but watching Nikolas light up over shared knowledge made her stomach flutter.

When had he become so handsome?

"Clara can explain it better than I can," he said. "They live between sea and land. Known to lure sailors to their doom with their voices."

"Thank you for showing me."

She sensed his heart beating thick with lust; she shifted to stand, but Nikolas pulled her onto his lap.

"What are you doing?" Another giggle slipped free as his hands slid around her and cupped her face.

Her report was done. When she'd turned it in, Orion hadn't even looked up — she had placed it on the desk while he continued fiddling with the mechanism.

A thrill traced her spine.

"Sorry," Nikolas said softly. "I'm being greedy." His eyes were lush green grass, threaded with gold in the light. "Stephen is a terrible influence. He's rubbing off on me."

Margot snorted. "Ew. Don't say that." The sound came out thinner than she had intended.

Her throat was tight. Nikolas' arm rested around her waist, his breath warm against her cheek.

She tried to steady the chaos inside her. Qu had torn open old wounds, and she didn't want to sit with them alone.

She closed the distance and kissed Stephen's name off Nikolas' lips.

He froze for one heartbeat.

A low, needy sound vibrated against her mouth as he lifted her onto the table. Her breath caught as his lips traced her jaw, her throat, the soft place where her pulse fluttered. Scraps of worn parchment slid from the table like drifting snow, pooling around his boots.

Her hands tangled in his hair, pulling him closer.

And his mouth — Spirits have mercy — the way he followed the line of her neck made her arch toward him.

Qu's confession throbbed in her chest like an old bruise; he had asked for her help. Guilt tangled with the heat crawling up her spine.

"Margot…" Nikolas murmured against her skin, his voice rough, wavering, as if he could sense the storm inside her.

Her breath shook. She didn't answer. She couldn't.

His hand slid beneath her blouse, the warmth of his palm dragging slowly across her ribs, making her gasp. He paused, just for a second, searching her face, giving her a chance to pull away.

She didn't.

His hand cupped her breast, thumb brushing in slow, coaxing circles.

A soft, helpless sound escaped her as her back arched into

him. She wanted him.

Her fingers curled in his tie, pulling him closer as the heat between them deepened.

And for one suspended moment, guilt and desire collided, leaving her breathless.

NIKOLAS VENATOR

Is That a Challenge?

✹

A drop of sweat beaded on Margot's skin as she caught her breath. A contented smile ghosted over her lips.

She was so achingly perfect in the way her chest rose and fell beneath him.

He savoured the sound of her moans, let it vibrate against her skin. Her curls stuck to her forehead, her lips swollen from kissing him senseless.

It had sounded like she was thinking of Quentin right before she leaned in and kissed him. Nikolas wanted to scrub Quentin out of her mind, replace every thought with himself. That wildness wasn't for him alone.

Not yet, not really.

Her curls were frizzing again — he particularly enjoyed the sight of her undone, frazzled, and wanting. Her eyes looked glazed and feral. A flicker of hesitation passed through her thoughts again.

Quentin's name kept echoing in her mind.

His jaw tightened, a raw, ugly heat unfurling low in his stomach.

"Is it just me, or is there someone else?"

The moment he said it, he wanted to claw the words back. *Idiot. Fool. Absolute fucking idiot.*

She stopped.

"What?" she stuttered. "No, I..."

Too late. The damage was done. The moment fizzled. Nikolas reached out with his *mana* — the notes of her thoughts wandering back to Quentin. He wanted — no, he needed — to know what she thought of him.

They were not just friends.

He leaned back, hating himself for it.

"I am not a jealous man, but I don't enjoy sharing."

Margot scoffed, shoving her blouse back on, her hands shaking with rage. "So you think I just sleep around with everyone?"

"You know that's not what I mean." His voice rose, frustration crackling beneath his skin. "But I'm curious if you are with that… *Aerian.*"

"Which one? Sophia? No, you mean Quentin." She cursed, flicking her hair out of her collar. "I've told you to stay out of my head."

Her voice dropped. "I thought you wanted this."

Then, softer, "Wanted me."

He stepped toward her. Her eyes pulled him in.

"It's just… right before you kissed me, you were thinking of him and—"

"So you were in my head!"

He swallowed hard. He deserved that.

She spun toward the door and yanked the rope — gears groaned as the mechanism unsealed. Her embarrassment rolled off her in hot, stinging waves.

"I can't help it when I hear your thoughts," he whispered, confessing the truth he had never wanted to speak aloud. *"Your mind is so loud, a cacophony — old regrets, the ache for your mother, the need you pretend you don't have — and I'm just trying to make sense of it.*F"

He caught her hand, the confession spilling out.

"I want to be with you, but I can't do that if you run yourself ragged following Orion's orders or think of other men when you kiss me."

The door clicked open.

Framed by golden stained-glass light, she stood in the doorway. Beautiful, furious, and wounded. Trying so hard not to break. "You want me?"

Of course he wanted her. He wanted to drag her back into his arms and fuck her senseless against the stacks.

"I want a proper dinner, at the very least. But before that, you need to figure out your feelings about Quentin."

The words tasted bitter, but they were true. He wanted more than stolen kisses and guilt.

He hated telling her this now, when her eyes were still glassy with hurt.

"Vix is on a mission to find her children, and she needs me. We're leaving the shields."

She gasped, breath hitching.

"For how long?"

"Around a month."

In the exchange of information, Stephen had given them a lead on Aquila. Much to his surprise, the cocksure Ignian wanted little in return — content to flirt with anything that moved or fill his belly with cider at the local bar, Theo more than happy to indulge him.

Margot slung her book bag over her shoulder.

"I'll wait for you then. It's only fair." She adjusted her skirt, peering out. "I expect you to come back in one piece."

"I'll be sure to find another hidden bookcase," he breathed.

A small, brittle smile flickered across her mouth and didn't reach her eyes. She walked through the bookcase door without looking back.

✸

A few steps away, Stephen was leaning against a stack, reading a small book. "I was wondering when you'd pop out," he said, snapping it shut.

Nikolas ran a hand through his hair. So much for not getting caught.

"Shouldn't you be with Theo?"

"He mentioned something. Tremors?" Stephen said. "A scrawny little porter came out of the corner of my eye, and I nearly blew his head off. Anyway, Theo said to find you and wait. Then I saw you were otherwise occupied, so I made myself busy. Just a little light reading."

Nikolas glanced at the cover. The idiot was reading it upside down.

He rubbed his eyes, clearing the thoughts of her spread in front of him. Margot was a Panthera — he'd thrown the meaty bone of his heart out like prey, aching for her to take it, terrified she might tear it apart instead.

Wanting her was its own danger.

"She has done a number on you," Stephen laughed. "She looked like she was going to eat you alive."

Nikolas gave him a look that shut him up for half a second.

"I'm glad I took your advice and stayed away..." Stephen chuckled behind him. *Advice. More like insistence, backed by threats of brute force.*

Stephen continued on his tangent about a Mantid Spirit that bred by luring in mortal males. "Teeth marks in the neck bones — it was disgusting."

Nikolas didn't know how to handle the nonstop chattering thoughts of the Ignian. Stephen could be friendly and sociable, then switch without warning to a deadly calm Nikolas recognised only as fight or flight, and Ignians only knew how to fight.

The Chief's personal assistant stood nearby at the reception desk, engaged in a rather flirtatious conversation with Charlotte. He was clearly enamoured with her, but her nervous laughter and thoughts suggested she was not. "...So I said to Tyr, put the rodenta down!" he chuckled, animating his hands.

Charlotte laughed along, attempting politeness.

"Yes, funny story… Oh! Nikolas, the Chief requests your presence!" She waved.

Matthew's eyes snapped to him in surprise, then slumped as he gazed over Nikolas' shoulder. "Maya requests to meet our new guest." His darting eyes betrayed his nerves — he puffed out his chest, shoulders squared in typical male posturing. "She has cleared her schedule for the afternoon, so I am here to escort him."

"I will come with, to make sure he behaves himself," Nikolas said. He wouldn't be able to focus, knowing a fight was inevitable.

Typical Ignian tradition.

⁕

Matthew knocked, waited a few heartbeats, then opened the door.

The Chief sat behind her desk, glasses low on her nose, typewriter clacking with ruthless precision. *Ding.*

She slid the mechanism over and continued typing; the silence broken only by the rapid tapping of her fingers.

Matthew cleared his throat.

"As requested."

She glanced up, disregarded them, and kept typing. She rolled the page out and placed it face down.

"Ah. Our new guest."

She rose, the leather chair scraping against stone.

Nikolas stood by the wall, arms crossed, muscles coiled for intervention. He smelled sandalwood and white florals — his mind flickering to Margot storming out, her hurt expression clinging to him like her perfume.

He forced himself not to reach for her thoughts again. Not after the damage he'd done.

Matthew turned tail, mumbling something about supervising the organisation of a supply closet.

Maya gave Stephen a complete, silent dress-down with her

eyes, irritation simmering beneath her calm. She circled him — his golden eyes never left her. "Like what you see?" he snorted, flashing a reckless grin.

"You couldn't handle me."

"I like a challenge."

"I'd like to see you try," she replied, her voice smoky.

Nikolas laughed — Ignian courting always blurred the line between threat and flirtation. Their gazes snapped to him and he lifted his hands. "I'm staying out of it. I'm just here to make sure you burn nothing."

Maya snapped back to attention, arms folded behind her.

"Stephen, if you wish to stay in Historia, you must be inducted into the Ignian society. As the acting Ignian Council member, I will be the one deciding."

Stephen grinned. "So you are challenging me? I accept."

Maya nodded and held out her hand. No hesitation. "Meet in the training arena in thirty minutes."

As Stephen clasped her hand, heat flared — sparks snapping between their palms. He let go first, surprise flashing across his face, followed by the sharp fear of a predator realising the other predator was bigger.

Perhaps he had bitten off more than he could chew. Now he would have to swallow it.

✷

Nikolas sifted the pit's fine, glass-sanded grains through his fingers, listening to wooden staves striking and fighters crying out as they landed blows. He had meant to visit the Ignian Sand Pit before — he trained in the Gymnasium instead. Battles scarred the sandpit walls: a large burn mark, a shadow suspiciously mortal-shaped that reeked of ash stood out.

Stephen rolled his shoulders, muscles stretching across his back as he prepared to fight, shirtless except for loose pants. Much to his disappointment, Maya merely shrugged off her coat and raised her hands, ready to begin.

Nikolas called out, "Begin!"

The next few heartbeats blurred into flaming red trails and bursts of explosive heat that struck in waves — the silica sand absorbing most of the fire, but the air itself growing hot. Stephen hurled flame. Maya flowed through it, dancing within the heat as if born from it.

Nikolas had never seen her move like this — an acrobat wielding fire as her weapon.

With casual ease, Maya paused mid-fight to roll up her sleeves.

"You're quicker than I thought. Why are you here?" she said, strolling toward him, hands lifting again.

Stephen panted, his grin twisting into a sneer. He lashed out, super-heated flame blurring together with waves of dry heat.

"I'm not telling you shit!" he growled.

She had his shirt fisted. He swung again, hurling flame toward her head.

Letting go, she backflipped across the pit and landed with a thud in the sand. Stephen rushed her in a blazing blur.

"Tell me your story, and I'll consider letting you join us," she snapped, rolling him hard into the ground.

Nikolas coughed as the heat became unbearable and moved to the viewing balcony above the pit.

He spotted Vix on the third level, lounging with a few Aquaans.

"Oh! Good, you're here!" she exclaimed, eating a dried fig. "Want one?"

Heat still prickled beneath his collar even from above. Nikolas took a fig and bit in — *damn, that was good.*

"Maya says she can handle it, but Stephen is keeping pace." Below, Maya had Stephen locked in a headlock. "Oh. Maybe not."

"Kick his ass!" Vix shrieked, stomping her foot hard enough to make the Aquaans beside her flinch.

The arena filled rapidly as word spread — the crowd cheering when their Chief gained the upper hand, booing when Stephen pinned her.

"Everyone loves her," Nikolas called to Vix, raising his voice over the roar.

"Well, of course," Vix said. "She was a newcomer, like you."

"I never got her story. She's always so busy…"

Vix cried out, "*No! No!*" and hid her face. "Why don't you just ask her?"

"She's occupied at the moment."

Vix gasped and cringed as Stephen landed a blow across Maya's jaw.

A feral smile broke across Maya's face. She dipped her head back and laughed, palming her bleeding lip.

"You could never be on the Ignian Council," she called, voice echoing through the arena. "You'd burn right through them."

"They're fighting for leadership?" Nikolas asked.

Vix nodded, shovelling more dates and figs into her mouth.

"Maya is undefeated in the Ignian Council. Barbaric, but that's how they elect leaders. If Stephen won, he'd be leader."

Applause thundered through the arena. "I suppose if everyone agrees to it and it works," Nikolas muttered.

Maya slammed Stephen down and pinned him with a boot to his throat. The crowd erupted.

Nikolas leaned on the railing, barely able to hear himself think. He reached for Maya's mind — and froze.

This was the first time he'd ever managed it.

"Why are you here?"

Shock rippled through him; he could hear them. Through

her eyes, he felt her simmering anger, a wild, focused heat aimed at Stephen, broken and bleeding beneath her.

"Kit Sun captured me when I was a poor boy born under his shields and forced me into the Colosseum."

Her pulse slowed. Her breathing steadied. *No wonder Stephen burned so hot. They hadn't trained him; they'd forged him.*

"I rose through the ranks, became one of Kit Sun's prized fighters, seeking that glorious bond with Him. I lost and damn near died."

She reached out and hauled Stephen to his feet. He brushed sand off his clothes.

"An Aerian Spirit healed me and forced me into a bargain. Then I woke up in the cells..."

She looked toward the balcony — and burned Nikolas out. Heat struck him like a slap.

"Take him to the infirmary," Maya ordered.

Matthew moved in quickly. Maya accepted her blazer and adjusted her tie back into place — her shirt scorched in places, but she wasn't winded. Only the split lip and the simmering heat of her *mana* betrayed the fight.

"That was quite a demonstration," Nikolas said, clearing his throat.

"It was overdue," she replied, exhaling. "I focused too much on finding the cause of the rot."

"Vix said it was personal for you. That I should ask, but—" He faltered.

"I suppose I owe you that drink and a life story."

"No — that's not what I meant," he blurted.

"Vix is right," Maya continued. "They're connected. Meet me in my office. What I've uncovered changes everything."

⁕

The cool silence of Maya's office was a welcome contrast to the arena — heat radiating from his skin, smoke clinging to his shirt.

Maya pulled a bottle from the shelf, poured three knuckles of liquor, and handed the glasses to Nikolas and Vix.

"Thank you for meeting with us," Vix said, her voice gentle.

Maya took a measured sip. "I needed a good fight. He's not so bad… like an acquired taste."

A note of sorrow cut through her Ignian calm.

Vix took a small sip of her liquor, moving straight to the point. "Do you have any updates on Aquila?"

Maya's voice settled back into her clipped commander's tone. "Aquila was last seen northeast of Bennu. Stephen didn't give specifics, but I can chart a route that skirts Kit Sun and threads through several villages. We will need to disguise ourselves. We can make it to Bennu and return by the Spring Equinox."

"I just received word he will be happy to host us," Nikolas said.

"Are there any other volunteers?" Vix asked. The silence hung.

Maya's shoulders dropped, exhaustion cracking through her steel. "No, and I will not force anyone to go beyond. We may have to bring lighter supplies or a cart. And we don't have many beasts to spare."

If Kit Sun captured them, the journey back would be more difficult.

"I do not need a beast to carry me," Vix said, crossing her arms with a huff.

Nikolas shook his head. "You stand out too much."

Vix pouted, searching for a reason to be offended.

"They'd skin you for your fur."

Vix pushed her lip before conceding. "Okay. Boring mortal it is, riding on a smelly beast for a month. My children are so ungrateful," she grumbled. The annoyance covered something older.

Something that still hurt beneath it.

When she woke up, Vix had shared her plan at their old meeting location — she wanted them together once more. *'Or at least to check in on them. I cannot reach them.'*

Maya took another sip and sighed. "I was young when I came here, escaping with a small babe strapped to my chest. She's a fireball... loves playing with the other wieldlings in the courtyard. I want the Ignis Orb for her, to give to her when she comes of age."

Vix leaned back. "Well, that's up to Aquila, if she accepts you or not."

Maya blinked, thrown off balance. A polite reminder that her power wasn't enough on its own. "I suppose..."

"Matthew will take over your position while we're away. Theo has a backup plan for Stephen."

Maya tipped back her glass. "Then it's a plan."

✸

The journey to the shield wall was arduous. It had been a while since he'd gazed out into the forest and decided to stay.

Had it been Margot's laugh? Her warmth? Abyss take him. He couldn't sleep at night, remembering the sounds she made.

The gates opened, and Nikolas mounted his beast. Vix shifted in a burst of prismatic light — far too large, far too excited — and his Equus lost its mind.

"Whoa!" The beast reared up on its hind legs.

Her shimmering white coat stood out against the new foliage — fresh shoots of spring, pops of yellow hanging around the maple trees.

"Vix, we discussed this!"

She laughed and screamed with joy as she ran ahead, shifting into different shapes and sizes of creatures, rolling in the dirt, flinging sticks and foliage aside as she leapt through bushes and hid beneath them.

Warm spring air carried the scent of sweet flowers. He didn't enjoy spring; too much pollen clogged his nose. But it meant he could venture out from the underground cities that pockmarked the land.

The ring glinted on his pinky finger, a constant reminder of his new role. "You're sure the shields won't erase my memory?" He turned to Vix — the quiver in his voice embarrassed him.

Soft. His father would have heard it and sneered.

She must have sensed the worry. "On my word, they will not."

Maya gripped her reins tighter, the gold ruby Ignian ring standing out against her warm olive skin. "I received this from the last Ignian Council member when I defeated him." She tugged the reins as her Equus stirred. "He better not have swapped it."

Nikolas held his breath and pushed through. Static ran over his arms and legs, the air leaving his lungs sharply — he gasped as it crackled along his spine and into his tingling fingers.

"It's rather unpleasant, isn't it?" Vix shuddered and transformed into a mortal form — someone, yet so plain she could be no one.

Amazing. A face stitched from familiar pieces of Margot's hair, Charlotte's eyes, and Maya's skin. "I hid the scar. I figured it would cause more trouble than it's worth."

Nikolas respected her choice not to share the story of the scar — she would tell him eventually.

Maya brought Vix's beast up by the reins. "We should get going. Old Town is a half-day ride."

Vix mounted her beast and gave it a smooth pat long its stripes. She wrinkled her nose when it snorted and flicked its head.

✸

They followed the covered path to the cliffs, where the sun and frigid wind beat down on them. As they traced the coastline, the smell of the sea mingled with rotting algae and salty air — the roaring waves crashing against the rocks until they arrived at the edge of Old Town.

The tavern smelled of fish broth and stale ale, and Nikolas' patience was disintegrating. Vix grew impatient, inhaling her pot pie and firing off questions far too loudly. Maya continued to argue with the village head — still haggling over the price to stay for the night. He was charging her double the standard.

He knew it. And she knew it too.

Their stubborn standoff dragged on until Nikolas was ready to lose his mind. "Is she giving you a hard time?" He slid three gold coins forward and ended the negotiation.

The village head's eyes went wide. "As I was saying to your…" He wisely cleared his throat. "We have enough feed for three beasts, and one couple has offered to house you. But I fear that the cost of feed has increased, and we cannot let in unverified travellers."

Nikolas went through his bag and pulled out the book he'd swiped from Margot's reading nook, sliding out the amulet that served as a bookmark. "Do you know what this is?"

"Bennu…" The village head's mouth dropped. "You should have led with that. Fine — three gold aureus."

The couple's quaint and homey house was a treasure trove of memories, personal mementos piled high and scattered, hung on every available wall. The smell of lavender filled the air. Their home felt lived in, loved.

The place Margot would have adored.

Jane worked as a herbalist apprentice. Diana was a carpenter working to fortify their boundaries. After a brief introduction, they went to bed.

Their travelling group settled into the couple's living room.

"I didn't know you worked for Bennu," Maya said, flinging out her bedroll by the hearth.

Nikolas shrugged. "I have done work for many people." And for Spirits who didn't deserve it.

Maya nodded and settled by the fire, curling away.

Vix flopped onto her bedroll, stretching out widely before falling asleep — a bitter pang of envy twisting in his stomach as he watched her twitch, wishing he had that ability.

On his bedroll, he stretched his numb legs and took off his boots. His bones ached, a dull throb after the long day's ride.

When did he become so soft?

He settled down on the lumpy, hard bedroll. He had become too used to Historia's comforts.

His father would have spat. *Weak.*

Burying the memories of his father's words, he fluffed up the rough wool blanket he was using as a makeshift pillow.

Rolling over, he looked through the window left open to the moonlight.

Nikolas imagined her curled in a blanket by her window, book in hand and steaming tea within reach. Spectacles perched on her nose, hair falling in waves.

Was she doing the same? Staring at the stars, watching the same comets that passed through in streaks of brilliant light?

He reached out, aching to do his nightly check on her, and sensed… nothing but the flowing ley lines beneath the stone foundation. The shields were blocking him.

An irrational, yet entirely reasonable, worry filled him. She was okay. She had Orion.

His stomach turned sour.

Should he have said goodbye to her? *No. Goodbyes felt final. And he was nowhere near done with her.*

Not even close.

Bennu

✷

Vix narrated every moss patch and pebble like a bard who'd had too much mead, and left offerings of dried fruits and berries at every crossroad. "For the small ones."

Elemental Sprites and wisps shifted and flitted from one side of the road to the other, observing the offerings. Anxiety rolled through him every time she did it — but Vix had survived centuries longer than he had.

If she wasn't worried, he forced himself not to be.

After passing through several villages and a particularly long cave passageway that involved bartering with two golems, they reached Bennu's boundary. From the city below, he saw the familiar snow-topped cliffs where the two mountains met — the residents used pine trees for wood, crafting elaborate cabins from mountain rock stacked high and finished with logs and mossy sticks.

Vix squealed from atop her beast and shifted into a blur of iridescence, flying toward Bennu. She tackled the Spirit to the ground in her massive Vulpine form, pinning him with delighted yips and yowls.

She licked his cheek. He'd only ever seen Bennu snarl.

The smile was unsettling. "It is good to see you, Bennu! It has been way, way, way, way too long."

Bennu ran his hands through her white fur, talking in a language Nikolas couldn't understand. "...and my bonded, Nikolas, and Maya, an important member of our Council."

She beamed.

Heat crept up his neck. Claim or not, it felt like a chain being slipped over his shoulders. "It's good to see you again,

Bennu."

Of course, he and Bennu went way back.

Bennu had caught him stealing from their apothecary and thrown him in a freezing cell for three days before striking a bargain. *Find fire wielders and bring them here so I may bond with them.* He'd spent a few summers working under Bennu's watchful eye, passing between villages in the Interwilds and Kit Sun to find any wielders who wanted freedom.

Bennu nodded, dusting himself off, and greeted Maya. "Oh! What a *mana* well you have — a good, powerful fire lives within you." He loomed over her.

"Thank you." Maya didn't flinch, but a single muscle in her jaw twitched, the only sign that Bennu was sizing her up like livestock.

"Come inside, we have much to discuss." Bennu clapped Maya on the shoulder, never letting his arm stray far.

They had a habit of only being friendly to fire wielders — and Vix, apparently.

Nikolas followed them to the long cabin, the meeting space at the centre of the city. Vix and Bennu chatted as they walked, centuries of stories tumbling between them as if they'd only been apart a single afternoon.

"I am sorry to hear that you and Orion are taking another break," Bennu said, chewing on dates from the bowl in front of them.

Nikolas didn't react. Vix liked to pretend Orion didn't exist, which meant he must have mattered to her far more than she cared to admit. He sensed the notes of Maya's bewilderment — but she did not let her mask slip. Her face remained neutral.

Vix shrugged, tossing a date into the air and catching it in her mouth, chewing with her eyes closed. "He'll come around. He's keeping busy fixing the mechanism."

"The tremors are getting stronger. We can chart them even

from here."

"It's a pattern that repeats every few years. Discordia is stirring," Vix said, pulling a thick book from her leather bag and letting it thud onto the table.

Bennu snapped their fingers — one of his bonded whisked the book away. "Historia continues to sleep as well?"

"Yes… it pains me to sense them dream so fitfully."

Maya couldn't stop herself from asking, "What happens if they wake?"

Bennu leaned back and gestured for Vix to tell the story. "Historia and Discordia are two Spirits, split from the same whole. The scales will tip in their favour if one is awake while the other sleeps. When they're both awake, it's a terrible time for Spirits — and even worse for mortals."

Goosebumps rose on Nikolas's arms. A bloody end for thousands of mortals was inevitable when Spirits fought against themselves.

He'd seen enough pointless wars to know that much.

"And the tremors are what? Fitful sleeping?" Maya questioned.

"Correct. Theodore has been keeping records of the tremors so we know if they're going to wake. Spirits are bonding with too many mortals. The ley lines of *mana* are flowing in ways I've never seen. I'm afraid the rot is making it worse."

"Caries," Bennu said, disgust and anger rolling with the name.

"I am not familiar with the name."

Bennu steepled his fingers. "Caries is a new player, but his master is ancient. We first encountered him holding a village hostage with his…" They gestured to the imaginary ooze dripping from their ears.

Nikolas recalled the smell of cloying decay, like fruit abandoned beneath fiery skies. "Mind-controlling fungus?"

"Yes. *Fungus.* It connects mortals together like a…shared mind of sorts. A hive-heart," Bennu said, disgust twisting his mouth. "Mortals with no will of their own. We housed as many of the unaffected mortals as we could, but Caries got away. He's a slippery one."

"Any idea where he is now?" Vix asked, digging into a plate of bread rolls another of Bennu's bonded brought out.

"I have scouts who send reports in, but they've seen no signs of his infection for a season."

The strain infected Vix's last bonded too. It seeped its way in… what was he a professor of? *Mycology?* "Could Caries be nearby?"

A slow heat flared in Nikolas's chest. He wouldn't mind carving the fungus out of their skull.

"Are you not seeking Aquila?" Bennu chided. "Isn't that why you accompanied your Spirit this far?"

Nikolas swallowed back a retort. *Your Spirit.* Vix had bonded with him, but she did not order him around like Orion. She respected his boundaries and was a calming — if very chatty — presence in his life. "My apologies. Aquila slipped my mind."

Vix shrugged. "What's a few more days? Time is a mortal concept."

MARGOT WILSON

The Aer Rune

The spiral down to the Vault felt endless, each turn pulling her deeper into cold stone and darker thoughts. Margot felt dizzy, her vision blurring — she opened the flap of her bag and pulled out a canteen of water.

One sip steadied her. She tucked it away and continued downward.

As the minutes stretched, the only things she could hear were her own breaths and her footsteps echoing in a maddening rhythm, the ticking of her timepiece circling round and around. Her calves ached. Relief loosened in her chest when the faint smell of incense drifted through the air.

Frankincense and myrrh were used to keep Spirits from manifesting so deep beneath the ground.

Orion sat at his workbench, surrounded by a scatter of miniature tools, with a brass lamp burning bright over a magnifying glass, his open notebook angled beside him.

As he looked up, she jumped. His glowing amethyst eyes, magnified by the loupe, were twin galaxies spiralling. He lifted the device off his head.

"Good. Let's get started."

She sat beside him with a long exhale, worry settling heavy in her gut. Nikolas hadn't said goodbye. They hadn't parted on good terms, but she'd expected something — a word, a glance, a note. The silence sat heavier than any goodbye she could have imagined.

And hearing it from Emile, of all people — he'd come up to

her smug and cruel, bragging that Maya was taking him beyond the shields '*to cull the weakling.*'

Orion's voice cracked like a whip. "Focus, Margot."

Right. The tremors. She straightened.

"Theodore has given me a significant collection of historical records to sift through. The ones we've been experiencing are minor."

Orion flicked through the detailed report. "Well done. I hadn't considered the variables you mentioned."

She sat up straighter. "The carpentry guild repaired the foundation after a tremor cracked it a few years ago."

He rubbed his eyes and shut the report. "Have it inspected."

She nodded and jotted down a note. "If it's agreeable to you, I'd like a few days off to help a friend." Her pen twisted between her fingers. She hated how small the question sounded.

She saw how Vix respected Nikolas' boundaries, and yet anxiety still curled tight in her stomach.

"Helping a friend? You mean that nonsense with Sophia?" He sighed, scribbling a note. "All right. I suppose you've earned it. Do not make me regret it."

Sophia didn't deserve what her father was doing to her, and Margot refused to be useless again. She broke into a wide smile and hugged him.

He didn't pull away.

"Oh, thank you, thank you…" She flipped through her notes, cheeks warm. "Um… can I ask you a few questions?"

Orion ran a hand through his hair, a smile tugging at the corner of his mouth before being quickly smothered. "I suppose you've earned that too."

Excitement fizzed in her chest — a dozen questions tangled together, but she chose the most important. "Who is Vela?"

"Vela is the youngest. As chatty as her mother, but far

more flighty." His voice gentled. "She shed her mortal form and became a Spirit of pure air."

Margot wrote: *Spirits can shed mortal form.* "Do you know where she is now?"

Orion shook his head. "The Aerian Councillor has the ring. Use it to find them and the Orb."

She leaned back. "May not be that easy. Anthony wants to stay in power."

"Dealing with Council business can be… problematic," he sighed. "So I don't involve myself in their petty power plays anymore." He studied her, brow furrowing as he sensed the spike in her anxiety. "I mean no offence to Sophia, but I've found it's easier to let them settle it themselves."

She bristled, her voice trembling with anger. "They're forcing her, Orion. That isn't tradition, that's control."

"Quentin will let nothing happen to her. He is a perfect marriage candidate."

"He will not marry her," she growled, startling even herself.

Orion laughed, low and sharp. "Because it ruins the little fantasy you built as a girl?"

Her pulse stuttered. Heat flushed her throat, equal parts embarrassment and fury. Mortification slammed into her so hard she wished the floor would crack open and swallow her whole. "*No!*" Her cheeks burned — she forgot he'd watched her entire life and knew her too well. "Fuck, I just want to help them get out of this mess, that's all."

She groaned, her voice thick with frustration.

He kept his gaze lowered. "Do not curse. It's unbecoming."

She clenched her jaw, then whispered, "*Sorry.*"

A brief flash of amethyst flared in his aura. He cleared his throat. "Anthony is a coward. I would find something he values and offer it in exchange for the ring — something he wants more than his Council seat."

"And that would be?" she pressed.

"I do not know him that well," Orion huffed.

Margot's thoughts spun. Piece by piece, she began sketching a plan in her mind.

She wanted her friends back and was prepared to do whatever it took.

The Sylph

☾

With the Spring Equinox fast approaching, the ground had a fresh layer of emerald grass, bright as — *no.* She halted and nearly collided with a mother and her child. She shook her head. *No more of that.*

Sophia's estate sat only a few streets away, but it felt worlds apart from her now. She no longer had meals at her house or saw her for lunch.

The distance between them had stretched tight and brittle, ready to snap.

Sophia was the only person Margot could be her truest self around, and had tended to her for a week after Orion's transfiguration. She owed Sophia; fixing this marriage nonsense was the least she could do.

Lenora opened the door. "Margot! I was not expecting you."

"Sorry to bother you. I was looking for Sophia."

"Yes, of course. Come in." Lenora smiled. "Sophia moved in with Quentin a week ago. I'm surprised she hadn't told you."

Margot's breath snagged. "No... she didn't tell me."

Lenora scribbled an address on a scrap of paper and handed it to her. "Here. I can fetch my porter to guide you?"

Her smile sharpened at the edges.

"That won't be necessary." Margot folded the note and turned to leave.

Lenora's voice lashed out behind her. "Do not come between my daughter and Quentin."

A cold, instinctive flare of *mana* curled under her hands —

she saw a side of Lenora she had never seen: polished cruelty and motherly ambition. Margot folded her arms, masking the anger rising. "I have no intention of marrying him. Don't worry."

"I don't believe a word you say," Lenora said sharply. "Now leave and don't step foot in this house again."

She stopped and scoffed. The impulse hit too fast, and she didn't care enough to stop it. She cracked her knuckles and grasped the orb at her side, connecting to the hollow, echoing space where Lenora's heart should have been.

She sent her a vision: a Corvis, towering and black-feathered, eyes burning red.

Lenora screamed and bolted upstairs.

A giggle slipped from Margot, sharp and unrepentant, leaving the door open behind her.

☾

She looked at the note — an address for an apartment building near the Aerian Society Hall, a private meeting space for their members. She made it halfway through the lobby before a snotty attendant stopped her. "Residents only," he said.

"I am here to see Quentin Atticus."

"Mr. Atticus isn't expecting guests." He snapped his fingers and motioned for her to approach.

"Can you send a message that I am here to see him? My name is Margaret Wilson."

He huffed and sent a porter to see if he was home. She waited nearby, arms crossed, staring at the different auras of the mortals thrumming past her.

Every day, she grew more appreciative of this power inside her.

The attendant's piercing glare made her skin crawl at the back of her neck. *Crazy bastard. What was his problem?*

The porter led her to Quentin's apartment, his shoes

tapping on the ornate marble floor.

She knocked. His scent drifted into the hallway as he opened the door — water dripping from his wet hair, wearing only a loose robe.

Of course, he answered half-dressed. Subtlety was not one of Qu's virtues.

"Can I come in?"

Qu opened the door wider. He tipped the porter three gold coins and whispered to keep quiet. *Of course, he couldn't be seen with her.* Shadows and secrecy had woven their entire history together.

"I wasn't expecting you," he said, rubbing a towel through his hair.

"Orion let me help and gave me good information, so I came straight here." She rubbed her stomach as it rumbled. "I see you took a shower. *That's convenient.*"

Quentin cocked a smile. "I just came from the Wielding Hall." He took the towel from his neck and hung it along a chair. "Aeroball practice."

"Can you put clothes on? You're not being decent," she retorted.

He pouted. "Me? Never." He turned and closed the bedroom door, hopefully putting on clothes.

Trying to appear casual, she wandered around and snooped through the various things he had on display.

He still had this? She hid a smile and picked up a wood carving she'd made for him when she was ten.

Margot sensed his peaking interest and fumbled as she put it down and turned. She winced.

Nice. Not at all suspicious.

He was wearing a loose, buttoned shirt and pants, much less formal than she'd seen him wear lately.

Get your shit together — the absolute last man she should react to was him. She shook her head and stifled a smile. "I still can't believe you're alive." The words slipped out before she could stop them.

He smiled and walked to the sink of his kitchenette. "Many people have tried, and I'm still kicking. Hungry?"

Rifling through her bag, she pulled out her notebook. "I have a few notes Orion gave me." She moved to the couch.

None of Sophia's things were here, no touches that were distinctly hers. "Where is Sophia?"

"She lives next door. I think she's at lunch? I'm not sure."

A cold spike went straight through her stomach. *Fuck.* "Lenora said you lived together, so I just assumed…"

He chuckled. "A real viperid, isn't she?"

Margot realised she was imposing too much and moved to the door. "I'll come back when she's here."

He stood in her path. "You went through all this trouble. Please tell me what you found."

She's too weak for those bright blue eyes.

Margot set her notes down and ignored the sounds of drawers opening and pans being set down. "Vela is a Sylph that has no actual body. They're made of pure air. Orion isn't a noble father; he doesn't know where they are or what happened to them. He just mentioned it being Aerian Council business, but he offered a few suggestions."

The sizzling sound of cooking muffled his voice. "Orion was different before Olivia. I believe he loved her."

She choked. "No way. He's… he can't do that."

"Spirits have bonded with and loved mortals, sometimes allowing them to live longer than a Terran, but those relationships are rare." He scraped delicious-smelling food onto a plate.

She took a plate from him — a medley of chopped vegetables, grains, and sauces. "Olivia was with Richard. She didn't love him."

Qu nodded. "That's because he's cursed. Or so the legend

goes..."

"He's cursed?" she squeaked.

He nodded, taking a mouthful. "Alces used to boast about it. Orion has an extensive rivalry with them, and I mean a really long time."

"So, like... hundreds?" She swallowed.

"Thousands. Tens of thousands."

Margot hadn't thought about how old Orion was. *Eons,* he'd once mentioned. "Damn." She shook her head while chewing. His cooking was delicious.

"Orion suggested we find something Anthony has been seeking in exchange for the ring. Any ideas?"

He ate his food, lost in thought. "I don't know him that well, but I can check with Sophia."

She placed the empty plate down on the table. "Orion gave me a few days off to help sort this whole thing out."

Qu stacked the plates and took them to the kitchen — they rattled against the ceramic sink. Margot wanted to go home and rest her legs. Perhaps a lavender soak in the bath, then slip into bed with a thrilling adventure novel.

She moved to the door. As she reached for the handle, he was a blur of juniper and fresh linen in front of her.

Her heart leaped. She hated the way he always encroached on her personal space as if he had a right to it.

He reached up and kissed her knuckles. "Leaving so soon?"

Heat flared where his lips brushed. "Yes. I am rather tired from climbing. I was going home." She pulled his hand away, letting silence speak for her first.

Qu nodded and moved out of her way. "May I call upon you later? After I inform Sophia?"

"Fine, but if I am asleep, do not wake me," Margot said, rubbing her nose. She grabbed the handle and dashed through the door before he could kiss her knuckles again.

Just an Observation

☾

Margot made it back home in record time and noted it in her agenda. Lately, she'd been pushing her physical limits — ever since watching Maya's effortless, lethal grace in the arena.

Maya was a master of her wielding, with flames coming out of her hands in whipped ribbons of light, heating the air to exhaust her opponent. A reminder of everything Margot wasn't and everything she wanted to be. She'd spotted Nikolas watching the battle from across the arena — seeing him watch Maya with open awe sent a sharp, twisting jealousy through her. The ugly kind that whispered she might be easy to forget.

He could be with Maya; they were well suited together.

She put her book bag down and flicked off her shoes, her heels feeling lighter on the soft carpet. Warm water ran through her fingers as she added lavender salts and soap — the heat soothing her muscles, warming her bones. She turned the Ignis lights down low and lit a few candles, letting the lavender fill her nose as she exhaled.

She grasped her Orb from the side and let her *mana* fill the tub. An amethyst glow flowed through the water, violet ink eddying together. Looking at her hand, the paper cut she'd got an hour ago no longer stung.

Small wounds healed. *The bigger ones… not so much.*

She focused and sensed her inner space, her library filled with fantastical images of creatures. She catalogued everything she'd learned, shelving it for later.

Organising her thoughts was easier than dealing with the

Nikolas-shaped tangle pulsing behind her ribs.

A loud thump and a knock at her window snapped her eyes open. For one fleeting moment, she thought it was Nikolas.

The disappointment stung.

Water flowed over the edge of the tub, and in her rush, pain flared. She gathered what dignity she could, limped to the closet, and pulled on a robe.

She peeked her head out of the bathroom door. In a moment of cruel irony, Qu was at her bedroom window. Of all the people she could've been half-naked, bruised, and dripping in front of, it had to be Qu.

He was temptation wrapped in every bad habit she thought she'd outgrown.

"I was just…" She gestured to her robe. Muffling her pain, she sat on her bed.

He moved toward her. "May I…?"

She wrapped her robe tighter and nodded. He knelt down, his hand cool against her heated skin, healing the blue bruise forming on her kneecap — the pain easing away with that golden light. He looked up at her, sky-blue eyes glowing in the moonlight, hand still holding the back of her knee. "All better."

A flush of roaring blood went straight to her ears. She sat up and moved her leg out of his reach. "Thank you. I was meditating in the tub, and I slipped on the tile." She cinched the tie on her robe tighter, cutting into her ribs.

His touch healed the bruise, but it only made the hollow, lonely ache in her chest flare. He was so close.

She could just lean over; it wouldn't take any effort.

She bit her lip hard. "I should tell you — I am with Nikolas." Her pulse stuttered.

Claiming Nikolas was terrifying, and she still wasn't sure he'd claim her back.

His aura cracked, rage and grief colliding like a storm. "I thought so, and yet… you want to help me?"

"I am doing it to help Sophia." She got up and turned before she could hear his reply. "I am going to get changed. Touch nothing."

Qu made an X on his heart and wisely sat in her reading nook beside her bed.

She changed into dark blue and white striped loose pants and a black shirt, brushing her wet hair out — it now fell just past her shoulders. She glamoured the strands into looser, neater curls that framed her collarbone.

Mortification crawled up her spine when she saw Qu reading a few passages of a rather saucy book. "Oooh, that's a fun one."

He snapped the book closed with a flush on his face. "I didn't know descriptions of men's cocks could get so… detailed. You women read the nastiest stuff with a straight face."

Her hackles rose. Typical Aerian smugness — she refused to let it fluster her. "If you don't like it, don't read it." She leaned down, moving to take the book out of his hands.

He moved it back onto the pile. "Just an observation."

The flash of his cerulean eyes, the heat longing on her lips, made her stomach dip.

"What did Sophia say?" She leaned back, crossing her arms.

"She said she didn't know."

"So then, why are you *here*?" She groaned. "You could've told me in the morning."

"Because…" he said, sitting up from her reading nook chair. "I have a plan, and I know you'd want to hear it."

She shuffled on the carpet, pondering. The lingering warmth of the bath had softened her edges. So she sat down in her living room. "Let's hear it then."

NIKOLAS VENATOR

Kit Sun

✹

Bennu had propositioned Maya more than once to stay with their *kettle*. Every refusal earned the same dramatic sigh, the same kiss to her knuckles. "Next time," they always murmured.

Nikolas' stomach twisted. "She has a daughter," he snapped, then winced, glancing at Maya. "*Sorry about that,*" he whispered, a warm brush of thought against her blazing mind.

Bennu only brightened. "The more the merrier! Bring her. Tell me, does she wield fire too? She must be powerful. Your *Fireblood* is strong."

Maya's jaw tightened. She shot a look toward Vix, who was mid-game of *Debits and Credits* at a nearby table. "*Vix,*" she said with a venomous smile, "walk with me." Vix allowed herself to be dragged away.

Maya's expression was a blazing warning to Nikolas. *Do not follow.*

Nikolas turned to leave, but Bennu glided into his path with predatory ease. "Nik," they crooned. "Stay a moment."

Reluctantly, he did. Bennu sidled up with all the grace of a harpy circling carrion. "Tell me — is she unbonded?"

Nikolas narrowed his eyes. "Why don't you ask her yourself?"

"I have." Bennu pouted, lower lip pushed out. "And I asked Vix too, and neither will answer me."

"I don't know," Nikolas said, voice flat. "And that's her

story, not mine."

Molten orange flashed through golden eyes. "Find out," Bennu said. "Report back."

The invisible threads of their old bargain tightened in Nikolas' ribs, constricting like a snare.

Anger surged, making his fists clench. He shoved Bennu hard in the shoulder.

Reckless. Stupid. "Our bargain was for me to find fire wielders," he hissed, "not to pry into their lives."

He didn't wait for a response and stormed out of the meeting hall, lungs burning, needing air before he did something idiotic.

The cold air cooled his heated skin — he wandered until he spotted Maya standing at a merchant's window, staring through the glass but seeing nothing at all.

"Sorry about that," he whispered against Maya's mind.

The habit had become part of their routine over the journey. First out of necessity, sharing silent warnings while Spirits prowled the dark roads. Then out of convenience, trading thoughts beneath Bennu's ever-listening ears. Now the thread between them was… easy. *Familiar.*

A quiet shorthand neither of them had acknowledged aloud.

Maya could have scorched his mind out at any time. But lately, she'd been lowering those walls of fire.

She didn't turn, but her shoulders shifted, the rigid line easing. "It's fine." Her reflection in the glass looked brittle despite the steel in her voice. "Whenever the subject comes up, I get… angry. And then the whole '*cool, collected Chief*' act goes straight to the Infernum."

Her throat worked, a tiny swallow.

With hands tucked into his pockets, Nikolas stepped beside her. "They push too hard."

She let out a dry, humourless huff. "My fire attracts

predators. It always has."

There was something in the way she said it. *Not wounded. Just weary.* Nikolas wanted to scorch Bennu's questions out of existence.

⁕

Maya led them up the hill toward a squat, warm-lit tavern. *The Stubborn Goat* was quieter than usual — rich cider scents, yeast, wood smoke. A cosy space where people went to relax.

"Come sit. Have a game with me." She dug a worn deck of cards from her bag. "And if I sense you using that little mind-reading trick of yours, I'll burn off your eyebrows."

Nikolas laughed, unbothered. He went through his bag and dug out his pouch of coins. "Joker's Bet? Draw three?"

They slipped into a corner booth — he ordered a crisp apple cider, Maya a hearty stout. She shuffled the deck with practiced fingers, splitting and recombining it in smooth motions.

Vix glided into the booth beside them, a massive glass of white wine in hand. "I am sitting out this one. Bennu has been squawking in my ear all day," she sighed dramatically, taking a gulp.

Maya dealt. Nikolas checked his hand: a pair of fives and a Joker. He tossed the fives into the discard and drew two more. "One aureus says I have two jokers."

Maya drew, cool as stone. "Two aureus says I have one."

They slid their coins into the pot. Maya showed her cards, sweeping the winnings to her side with a smug little flourish. "Try harder."

They played again. Nikolas won.

And again. He won a second time.

Maya's eye twitched. She took a long drink, avoiding his eyes. "My mother was a dancer. My father was the lovesick bodyguard who saved every coin he could to buy her out of a bargain."

Nikolas paused halfway through tossing in his next wager. Maya kept shuffling, not looking at him.

"Of course," she added, voice dry, "the Vulpine Spirit who bonded to her lied and tried to kill my father. But he survived." A tiny, hesitant smile.

Nikolas set down two coins. "One joker."

"They joined a troupe of travelling entertainers…"

"Oh! You mean the circus?" Vix blurted.

Nikolas shot her a look. Vix flinched and retreated into her wine.

Maya chuckled. "A tiny circus, yes. I was born not long after they left. I grew up with them."

She showed her hand — another win — and took a long drink before speaking again. Her voice roughened. "Like every idiotic fire wieldling, I had big dreams. I wanted to dance in the palace of Kit Sun." A whisper of a tear thickened her throat, and she swallowed.

"After a fight with my mother, I ran away. I clawed my way through the palace ranks. No one stops a scrawny kid who's fast enough."

She fanned the next hand but didn't bother looking at it.

"Kit Sun noticed me. Not just my dancing — my fire too." She unclasped her shirt, revealing the burned scar just below her collarbone.

Nikolas' stomach dropped. He'd seen that mark before. Knew what it meant.

Kit Sun had bonded with her. No wonder she clenched her jaw every time Bennu mentioned bonding — she was fighting the pull every day she was outside the shields.

"It turned into a nightmare," she whispered. "I danced and entertained for them…" She took another swallow of stout, washing the memory away. *"Then they got bored."*

She stood to refill her drink. Their card game lay abandoned. When she returned, she continued with a brittle laugh.

"Then I discovered I was pregnant."

She didn't cry, but her voice thinned further.

Nikolas leaned back, gutted. "I... I'm so sorry."

"Don't be. I was young, stupid, and terrified." She spun a coin on the table, gaze fixed on its wobbling orbit. "I ran to the nearest ship. Didn't even think. Only realised what I'd done once we were past the harbour."

"The ship took me to Historia ten months later. And... I stayed."

He stared at her, stunned by how easily her life could have spiralled into tragedy.

"You gave birth on the ship?" Vix said, eyes glass-bright as she squeezed Maya's arm.

"It wasn't terrible. There was an Aerian healer on board, a family of Aquaans who pulled fog over the waters to hide the ship. They all helped me — told me about Historia, about the place that protects mortals." Maya's voice softened. "I had nowhere else to go."

"And your parents?" Vix asked.

Maya shrugged, wiping a tear. "I searched over the years. Last I heard, they retired somewhere warm. But..." The word cracked. "I've always been ashamed."

"Shame is good," Vix sniffed, wiping her own cheek. "Builds character."

Nikolas looked at Maya and recognised the fire she wielded to survive, not to scorch others. She wasn't just strong — she'd clawed her way out with a baby on her hip and built a life with nothing but grit and determination. She was an undefeated Ignian.

The one thing she wanted most was a bond for her daughter.

"We'll find the Ignis Orb," Nikolas declared. He lifted his cider. "For her. For you."

Maya blinked, startled but softened.

Vix whooped. Their glasses clinked together.

For the first time since arriving in Bennu's domain, Maya's smile reached her eyes. Not the practiced one she gave her Council, but something real. The rest of their night drifted between drinks and Vix recounting appalling stories of Orion's history — apparently he'd been on a legendary '*gigantic asshole*' streak for three centuries before Olivia, the first Soul Wielder in generations, tempered him.

Maya clinked her glass against the table and muttered, "Men, am I right?"

Nikolas narrowed his eyes, a spark of offence tugging at his drunken logic. He snorted.

Abyss take him, he was far too buzzed.

Needing air, he rose. Maya rose with him. "I'll walk with you."

Outside, the cold mountain wind slapped the haze out of him. Pine, resin, and cold stone — Bennu's domain smelled of survival and old memories. He exhaled, breath fogging in the chill.

They walked the steep trail back to their cabin. Bennu's best, which meant they'd displaced two soldiers.

Their belongings still hung from the walls, but it was far better than the hay cot in the stables Bennu had offered him. Nikolas went straight to watering the plants on the sill with the earnest excitement of a drunken fool.

"Look, a fresh shoot! It's doing way better here on this window."

Maya leaned beside him, hands braced on her knees. Her grin softened. "You're right. It's glowing." She straightened and stretched. "Want one more drink?"

He hesitated. *Just say no. You're drunk enough. Bad idea wrapped in a worse idea.*

He reached for a glass. "One more won't hurt."

Her laughter was infectious. The liquor burned all the way. "Bennu gave you the good stuff," he coughed.

"They're only polite because Vix is here."

Nikolas shook his head, gaze unfocused. "No… they're right. I can sense your fire. It's a ribbon of flame under the night sky." The words came before he could stop them.

"It's stunning. Beautiful."

Maya froze. Faint heat pulsed off her skin, her mind flaring open just long enough for him to sense the jolt of her surprise.

And her lust.

He jerked back, knocking over a plant. "I'm involved with someone." Margot's name stuck in his throat.

Guilt sliced through the haze.

She nodded, hand half-covering her expression. "You took me off guard."

"It's complicated," he added uselessly. *Understatement of the century.*

They moved onto the couch — Maya curling up with a pillow, Nikolas collapsing beside her, nursing the liquor against his chest like a shield.

"*Margot,*" he whispered, the name slipping out like a bruise he kept pressing. "Orion's bonded."

Maya's eyebrows lifted in understanding. "*Oh.* That makes sense."

"She's had this long… thing with another guy — he's engaged — it's a mess."

"But she's with you?"

"Yes — maybe? I *tol'her* to sort it *al'out.*" He hiccupped. "Now'*m* worried she'll choose *him* once we get *back.*"

Maya inhaled. "That's a tough situation." She tapped his leg gently. "I'm… with someone too… she's flighty, impossible to pin down." She rose, finishing her drink. "I'll be in my room if you change your mind."

He stayed frozen in a drunken stupor. He could go to her

room. Temptation whispered the obvious.

Maya was steady and uncomplicated. A clean break from the chaos Margot ignited in him.

But when he closed his eyes… *Abyss take him*. It was Margot's voice he heard. That soft, stubborn quiver of her bottom lip when she tried to pretend she didn't want him. *'I'll wait for you then'… 'I expect you to come back in one piece…'*

Nikolas pushed to his feet, grabbed his coat, and stepped into the cold mountain night. Maya was striking, kind, and fierce. But Margot — Margot was waiting for him.

He wouldn't betray that fragile trust.

✷

He hiked up the mountain as far as his legs could climb. He needed somewhere quiet.

Somewhere Margot's absence didn't echo so fucking loudly.

He flopped onto the stone, letting its cool weight steady him. He'd spent many nights up here listening to the Aves, letting their distant cries smooth out the chaos inside him.

He snapped awake from a brutal boot kick to his ribs. He wheezed, vision swimming. "Fuck you, Bennu."

Bennu's feathers flickered with irritated flame. "You're late. I was flying all over the city! Get your ass down *now*."

He rolled up with a groan. "Asshole."

"The patrol have been waiting all morning!"

Nikolas laughed, a good, hearty chuckle. "It was worth it, though."

"Is she bonded? Tell me." Bennu crouched low, eyes gleaming with hunger.

Telling Bennu any detail about Maya made his skin crawl. Nikolas looked up at Bennu against the harsh sun, flames bursting around their feathers. "Let's make a bet. If I kill Caries first, you build me a cabin up here. If you kill them first, I tell you if she's unbonded."

"Deal." Bennu crouched, flames coiling around their talons.

"Can I ask you something?" Nikolas called, the question burning since he arrived.

"*What*?" Bennu called down, irritated.

"Why didn't you tell me about Historia?" Nikolas yelled to the giant vulture harpy. "You knew I was wandering half-blind out there."

Bennu's answer echoed off the cliff face. "Because they only guide the worthy ones." They didn't bother to fly him down. They just flew against the blue mountain sky in a streak of crimson flame down to the lakeside.

The sun stabbed straight through Nikolas' skull — he held his hand up against the beating light.

By the time he reached camp, his head was pounding and his mouth was dry. Vix had abandoned the mission and was three games deep into *Checks and Balances* with an Ignian who adored her.

Maya was nearby, drilling a group of wieldlings, her voice sharp and confident again. "Good to see you're alive! Bennu, I take full responsibility." Her hand was on her heart and threw Bennu a flirty eye flutter.

Nikolas tried not to smile.

Bennu huffed. "Fine, but tomorrow the group will leave at dawn, with or without you."

In the cabin, Nikolas finally found solace, escaping his pounding hangover. Exhausted, he fell into bed, a wave of relief washing over him.

Tomorrow would be dangerous. Tomorrow, he'd have to face Caries.

MARGOT WILSON

The Society

The carriage rocked, wheels grinding over cobblestones, and Margot pressed her palms flat against her thighs.

Two steady heartbeats. She could do this.

Sophia's hands had trembled in hers the night they made the plan — small and cold, shaking like a bird in a closed fist. Her life inside Aerian walls was a gilded cage wrapped in grey silk. *No eye contact, that's the first rule. Hands in front, that's the second. An Aerian Lady must be demure, polite, respectable.*

Margot had memorised every rule. She'd memorised the freckles too — the exact scatter across the bridge of Sophia's nose, the faint rose-gold flecks in her hair, even the tiny chin hair Sophia complained about but never plucked.

Intimate details only the people closest to her would noticc.

The glamour slid over her skin now, a second skin she wore the way others breathed. She felt it settle — Sophia's voice humming somewhere at the back of her throat, Sophia's face resting over her own like a mask of warm wax.

Good. Hold it.

She felt naked without her orb. *Stripped.* She felt as though she had left a piece of herself on the hall table, like a forgotten glove. Qu had insisted. *Aerian ladies don't carry a thing.* She'd argued. He'd won.

Qu's warm hands had slipped the fur over her shoulders, letting it curve along her arms and rest at the small of her back. A silver silk garment beneath it that showed off every curve she hadn't asked him to notice.

Heat had pooled low in her stomach.

All for the mission.

Outside, the streets narrowed. The wheels found smoother stone, the carriage slowed.

She was doing this for Sophia. For the girl who'd cried in her lap while reciting rules she'd never been allowed to break.

Quentin folded his hands in his lap opposite her, posture impeccable — every inch the dutiful Aerian heir. He caught her eye and gave a single, quiet nod.

She exhaled.

The carriage stopped.

☾

Quentin offered his hand as if they were stepping into a ballroom rather than a political nightmare dressed in silk.

She placed her palm in his.

The attendant opened the doors. Margot's stomach clenched. *Don't look up. Hands in front.* She slid into her seat, ankles crossed, spine straight. When Qu glanced over and gave an approving nod, relief loosened her shoulders a fraction.

If he believed it, the others would too.

Her blood went cold the moment Anthony entered.

He did not arrive alone.

David Atticus stepped into the hall beside him — tall, sharp, and smelling of iron and cold stone. The air thinned. She tightened the glamour on reflex and let out a breath so slow it barely moved her chest.

David was a man protected by wealth, guild influence, and the Aerian Council's collective greed. An open secret that he'd suffocated rivals and thrown them beyond the shields to be eaten by Canis. He was untouchable and owned half the city's buildings and a sizeable stake in the crafting guild.

She smiled at Anthony the way Sophia would.

"It's good to see you, Father."

He kissed her cheek. "You too, my daughter. It's good to see you dressed so fine! Quentin has been treating you well?"

His breath was wine-sour and warm. She fought the urge to recoil.

"You selected well for me."

David leaned in and kissed her other cheek. "A few years with Alces wised him." He slapped Qu hard on the back. "Eh, boy."

The server escorted them through the luxurious dining hall. The Mess Hall was for workers, for the help. *Just get through dinner.* Qu would distract David afterwards. She would sway Anthony.

Insane. Qu is absolutely insane.

A crisp salad arrived first — round radishes and leafy greens, a sharp drizzle of vinegar dressing. All she had to do was keep her head down and her mouth full.

She could do that.

"So," Anthony said pleasantly, as if requesting more wine, "when can we expect the first?"

The lettuce lodged in her throat. Vinegar burned her eyes. She coughed as politely as possible into her napkin while a cold shock crawled up her spine.

Qu shot her a warning look. "We've been trying, as you requested."

She tipped the icy water back. It did nothing for the panic in her chest.

"Good. Shall we start planning for a wedding on the Summer Solstice?"

Quentin's jaw flexed as he turned to her. "You're excited to begin planning, aren't you, darling?"

"I am."

A light pumpkin soup followed — warm, rich, nutty. The men talked building codes. Orion's tax increases on permits. She bit her tongue twice. Qu's fingers tightened on her knee, once, twice, a third time.

Stay still.

A wave of relief washed over her as David, glancing at his pocket watch, declared the north-side gables required inspection and then made a courteous but swift departure.

Qu suggested the drinking room on the third level. Margot followed — hands folded, eyes down.

Spirits have mercy. Is this happening now?

Qu lunged, ramming his father-in-law-to-be to the floor.

"What are you, what?!" Anthony shouted.

"Shut the door!" Qu barked, grappling until he had him pinned under iron restraints. "Can you wipe his memory?"

Margot froze. "Pretty sure," she admitted.

"Pretty sure?" His voice jumped an octave. He cocked an eyebrow as he tied Anthony to the chair.

There was no more time for doubt. This was the plan. It had to work.

"It works most of the time."

Qu let his head drop.

"Please make it work this time."

She pressed two icy fingers to Anthony's temple.

He shot awake — confusion mixing fast into rage. He jerked against the irons, muffled curses vibrating behind the gag. His aura bucked like a wild creature resisting a leash, a violent spike pressing against her senses. *He wanted to snuff her out.*

"Are you sure that will hold him?"

Quentin didn't look away. "Air wielders need hands. If he can't move them, he can't wield."

"Oh." She blinked, then squared herself. "All right, then."

She drew a two-fingered line down his temples, behind his

ear, along the arteries flowing down his throat to his heart, pushing her *mana* into him and keeping her palm pressed to his chest.

"Anthony. Tell me what you want the most."

His defences were strong. Her vision pulsed at the edges. She kept pushing until he had nothing left but the emotions she wanted. Her *mana* surged through her, sharp and icy.

His stormy grey eyes glazed.

She nodded to Qu, who removed the gag.

"A grandson," Anthony whispered. *"To continue the family line."*

Something inside her rebelled. Sophia didn't deserve to be reduced to a womb.

Qu shook his head. "Keep going."

"Anthony. Tell me what you want. Gold, jewels — do you want the orb?"

Anthony sneered, half-entranced. "I don't want that *thing* to bond with *me*."

Margot leaned back, exhausted. "He wants a grandchild." The word curdled on her tongue.

"Fuck," Quentin hissed, pacing. "Nothing else?"

"No. He's locked down tight."

Quentin rubbed his face. "All right. *Plan Swap*."

Margot lifted Anthony's fingers, trying to open his palm. Anthony had other ideas. He lunged forward with a savage snarl and tried to bite her.

Qu grasped his head. "Do not touch her."

Anthony choked. His lungs seized. He went pale, then blue, and passed out.

She loosened the silver-and-aquamarine ring and clicked her fingers. Qu took off his ring and passed it over.

She held them, one in each palm.

Her vision blurred. Her *mana* was running low — she'd depleted most of her well. *Idiot. She shouldn't have left her orb at home.*

No. She could do this for them.

Stars burst behind her eyes. She pushed through it, cupping one ring in each palm. A violet spark snapped between them. Her body seized, vision pinpricking with white static.

She glamoured Quentin's ring into a replica of Anthony's.

Her knees buckled the moment it was done.

"I've got you," Quentin said, reaching out.

"No. Don't touch me." She couldn't risk draining him.

He fisted his hands, nodded, moved away. She handed him the glamoured ring.

"I don't sense the pull," he said, studying it on his finger.

"Later," she rasped. "Focus on the mess we have now."

"Are you sure you did it right?"

"*Yes,* I did it right." Light-headed, she struggled to get the ring back on his finger. Anthony clenched his fists and snapped forward, teeth flashing.

"Enough of *this!*" She put two fingers to his temples.

His head dropped forward like a stone.

A tingle ran through her body, her head swimming. *Shit.* A heavy tremor followed.

She stared down at her hands — her *real* hands. Her real curls burst through the illusion. The room tilted, the edges of her vision going black, a horrible swooping sensation rolling through her.

The glamour was slipping off her.

Margot crossed the room and leaned against a chair. "He'll wake in five minutes. Or so."

"Tell me what I can do," Quentin said, hoisting Anthony upright against the wall.

"I said I'm fine."

"Please tell me."

She flicked his hands away. "I'm *fine.*"

He sighed and sat beside her, head in his hands.

"My *mana*'s low." Speech felt like pushing through thick fog. "I need to replenish it."

"How long do you need?"

"Longer than five minutes." She chewed her thumbnail. "There's one thing I can do," she said, "but it hurts."

He nodded. "Do it."

Margot looked up at the ceiling, exhaled, and reached for his forearm when he rolled up his sleeve. He wore that cocky grin that did things to her chest she didn't have the energy to argue with.

"Qu. You're going to regret this."

"Just do it. You can't hurt me."

She reached over and wiped that grin right off his face.

"Mother of — *ah!*"

She closed her eyes and pulled deeper and deeper on his *mana,* letting it flow through her, inside her.

She stood in a candlelit conservatory. Beyond white iron windows, a beautiful night sky — juniper and parchment on the air, moths fluttering around her in waves of brown, white, and black, filling the lush tropical green space.

His heart space.

She walked the gravel paths. Circular baths dotted the room, filled with resting moths — others, the size of her hand, flitting along tree trunks. She looked for somewhere to sit.

There were no benches. No garden chairs.

Qu didn't build spaces for rest.

Her name tore through the conservatory — distant at first, then louder, raw, growing until it split the air open.

Pain radiated across her cheek. Qu's voice dragged her back.

Anger bloomed as she held her face. Then guilt, fast on its heels. A bright red welt, the shape of her hand, marked his skin.

"Sorry." She hadn't meant to pull that deep.

He winced and tugged his sleeve down. "Glamour. Now."

Feeling lighter, she shot up and glamoured herself back into Sophia. Her skin tingled all over, raw and overstretched. Qu checked her over once, gave a nod.

"Looking good." He walked to Anthony and hauled him up. "Follow, and be a dutiful daughter concerned for her papa, okay?"

"Demure and doting. Got it."

She followed Qu down three flights, playing the part as Anthony stirred, choking on the water she fed him.

☾

The ride back was excruciating.

Anthony reeked of liquor, body odour, and vomit the entire carriage ride home. Qu held him while he snored, startling awake whenever a wheel hit a bump.

Margot breathed a sigh of relief when the driver opened the carriage door to escort him home.

"He'll sleep it off and be none the wiser," Qu snickered.

"I wiped his memory twice, just to be sure." She waved the fur — she'd sprayed it with perfume before she left, which helped mask the stench. "He pissed himself."

"I'll get it cleaned in the morning." Qu shifted closer to her side of the carriage.

Margot shifted away and stared out the window. The driver was walking back. She was going to be sick.

Keep an eye on the horizon.

The carriage lurched, the rhythmic creak of its wheels filling the air — a harsh wind slicing through her fur as the wheels scraped over uneven cobblestones. She pulled the fur tighter.

Qu moved and shrugged off his coat. Her heart thrummed when he settled it over her shoulders. "Just for the ride home, okay?"

She nodded and kept her eyes on the window, trying not to be sick. Her *mana* bled thin, glamour marbling across her skin, the nausea worsening with each bump.

She made it past the nosy receptionist. Made it most of the way up the stairwell.

The glamour slipped off her like a torn veil.

Qu's warm hands were the last thing she remembered.

☾

The soft brush of fingers woke her.

A bright sky. Yellow leaves flitting down and collecting on the ground. Children on their parents' shoulders in warm coats and floppy knitted hats. Laughter and warm apple pie.

For one awful heartbeat, she thought she'd woken in Quentin's bed.

Then she smelled Sophia's perfume and exhaled.

Endless sky-blue eyes stared back at her.

"Hey, sunshine."

"How long was I out? Did anyone see me?" Margot rubbed her eyes.

"A day." Sophia pressed a finger to her mouth. "I have informed Orion."

Margot reached up and pulled her down tight. "Thank you," she croaked.

She leaned back against the headboard — Sophia's bed, Sophia's pyjamas, soft fabric against her palms. Sophia's perfume everywhere.

"Quentin has been living next door while I healed you," Sophia said.

A blue tinge of worry threaded through her aura. Margot caught it immediately. "What is it?"

"Hm? Oh, nothing..."

"Spill it. You can't lie to me."

"I hate you can do that now." Sophia blew a puff of air at

her. "While I was healing you, Qu let me try on the ring."

Margot sat up straighter. "Did you feel the pull?"

"I told Qu I couldn't feel it." A pause. "But I did."

"So why did you hide it?"

"You don't understand Aerian male pride like I do. He couldn't feel the pull."

"Interesting."

"Will you help me find it? Please, Margot. I can't do this alone."

"Of course I will."

Relief and dread tangled in Margot's chest. If Vela had called Sophia, then everything they'd risked wasn't for nothing.

NIKOLAS VENATOR

Caries

✷

Nikolas fed an apple to his Equus and brushed a hand down its neck. The beast chewed happily, bobbing its head as the chilly spring air puffed from its nostrils in pale mist.

A twig snapped behind him.

His hand flew to his hilt. Steel whispered half-free before his breath caught.

He listened, head tilted toward the sound.

"Just me," Maya whispered as she stepped out from the trees. She had been surveying the village from higher ground. Her boots were muddy, her hair wind-tangled.

"Something's wrong in there. The people are… off. I don't know how else to say it."

"We're on the right track, then," Nikolas said. "We wait for sunset and catch them off guard."

Maya crouched and traced a quick shape in the dirt with a charred fingertip. "Gate's watched. Tavern's blind," she said.

Eiran leaned in too close. "I can take the —"

"No," Maya cut in, flat as stone. "We split into two groups. Nikolas and I infiltrate. The others hang back with Vix and support."

"I can handle this!" Eiran shouted.

Maya smacked the back of his head. "Not with lungs like that."

Finn shifted, uncertainty flickering across his face. Nikolas hid a grim smile. Eiran and Finn were bright, eager, and too damn green. He would not carry two teenage Ignian deaths on his conscience.

Maya wouldn't survive that either.

"Ow," Eiran muttered, rubbing his skull. Finn snickered.

Vix made them hold hands and whispered a protection hymn, soft as breath and old as bone. Then they slipped into the trees.

They moved fast and quiet, keeping low — Maya scouting ahead and pausing until Nikolas caught up. He crouched behind a thick bush and watched the gate.

A large, burly guard stood at the entrance, checking everyone who passed. Maya blended in with a group of hunters arriving with their catch, folding her posture and pace into theirs until she became just another shadow among shoulders and fur packs.

Nikolas exhaled when she made it through.

An older man struggled near the entrance with a stubborn pack-beast. Nikolas stepped in, soothed the creature with a practiced touch, and earned a grunt of thanks. The man ushered him forward.

Nikolas slipped through.

A guard caught him by the collar and yanked back his hood.

Nikolas stilled.

The guard's fingers forced his jaw open, checking something inside his mouth, then released him with a grunt and shoved him onward.

Nikolas kept his head down and walked toward the tavern.

Inside the village, sound felt wrong. Too thin. His boots struck packed gravel too loudly. When he cleared his throat, no one looked up. No chatter. No laughter. Just bodies moving in slow, mechanical rhythms.

A woman swept the street. Her gaze was vacant, her jaw slack.

Nikolas reached out with his *mana* and recoiled.

A high, piercing whine tore across his senses, sharp enough to throb behind his eyes. Something lived inside her mind that was not hers.

Maya waved him over from a corner booth in the tavern. *"This place is worse up close,"* she whispered.

The bartender's head turned toward them.

Nikolas cleared his throat.

Maya tipped back her drink like a dutiful patron. She gagged and slid the cup to him.

Nikolas pushed it back. He lifted it, smelled it, and grimaced. Brine, algae, saltwater — a strip of green seaweed bobbed on the surface.

What kind of mortal drinks this willingly?

They retreated upstairs. Maya had paid for a room for the night, though neither of them intended to sleep. The space was small. The bed was even smaller.

The air smelled of mould and salt.

"This isn't normal," Maya whispered.

"No shit," Nikolas whispered back. *"I tried to read them and got… static. They're thinking in a way I'm not built to hear."*

"What does it sound like?"

"A shrieking whine," he rubbed his head. *"It hurts."*

Maya nodded once. *"Aquila is still being held in the meeting hall. I got a glimpse when I passed the gate."*

"Good," Nikolas whispered. *"We move as soon as it's dark."*

Maya stood at the window, elbow braced on the sill, her stare fixed on the road below as if she could burn answers from the stone.

Nikolas made his mind still and his hands busy. He drew the whetstone along his blade in slow, steady strokes until the rhythm settled him. He lifted the Lucerna Orb from his sword, removed the other half from his shield, and locked the two pieces together.

He closed his eyes and followed its pull downward, through boards and foundations, into the bones of the village.

Ley lines ran below in gold and silver threads, *mana* hummed a distant song. Two rivers met here, a confluence thick with power. And beneath it all, he sensed Aquila's pain.

Heavy chains. A net of sorrow and exhaustion pinning them down.

Maya's hand landed on his shoulder, snapping him back. "It's time."

They stepped outside the tavern.

Three men emerged from the dark, cutting off Maya's path. Those same men who had watched her from across the bar, eyes too hungry, attention too fixed.

Their gazes locked onto her with something that wasn't mortal.

Maya lifted her hands, voice smooth. "I'm not interested. I'm with my husband."

One man reached for her.

Maya twisted away. Flame sparked and curled around her fingers.

The men hissed and recoiled, flinching from the heat.

Maya snapped the flame down to the ground and whipped it around her head. It cracked like a lash, bright and vicious.

Nikolas unsheathed his sword and raised his shield, shifting into a defensive stance. He tried to connect with the men — pain stabbed behind his eyes. The whine returned, a chorus this time.

A screeching wall of noise that made his teeth ache.

The men circled, keeping their distance, hissing and snarling. A pungent stench crept over the mud. Rotten eggs and sulphur.

"So much for not getting noticed," Maya muttered, gagging at the smell.

"I can't control them," Nikolas said. "We may have to

knock them out."

Maya widened her stance and raised a protective ring of flame. It hissed around them, bright enough to paint the alley in orange.

Then a man strolled out of the meeting hall.

Shock-black hair. Chalk-pale eyes that caught Maya's firelight and reflected it back. Shabby dress clothes hung off him in tatters, stained with dirt, patched with moss like he'd been crawling through graves.

The hissing men backed away as he approached, parting around him. He walked through the centre as if the street belonged to him.

Nikolas glanced at Maya. She gave the smallest nod.

Caries.

"We wish to trade for the release of Aquila," Nikolas said, shield still raised.

Caries clicked his tongue. "I'm afraid they're bought and paid for."

"By who?" Maya barked.

Caries's smile sharpened. "By whom. And that's confidential." He inspected the dirt beneath his fingernails. "Now, who are you?"

"We're not important," Nikolas said. "Why did you attack Aquila?"

Maya's flames trembled. She couldn't keep the circle forever.

Caries waved a hand.

One of the men lurched into the fire.

Nikolas met him with the shield and drove him back. Another rushed in, too fast and too close. Instinct took over. He slashed, quick and clean, forcing the man down.

The man hit the mud and did not rise.

Maya pointed, voice tight. "Something's moving."

A pale, skittering thing slipped from the man's mouth,

bone-white and fast. It crawled through the edge of the flame as if the heat meant nothing to it.

Nikolas threw a dagger. The thing twitched, then vanished into shadow.

Caries watched, amused. "I'm on a tight schedule," he said. "Can we wrap this up?"

The third man leapt into the circle.

Nikolas stepped sideways, shield snapping up as Maya's shoulder brushed his back. The impact jarred his arm, but the blow never reached her. The man slammed into the shield and thrashed.

He glimpsed movement again, something unnatural in the man's mouth.

The screeching in his head cut off mid-note as he drove his dagger forward.

Maya's flames lowered. She panted. Her *mana* was running thin.

Three bodies lay in the mud.

Caries still smiled.

More villagers stumbled out of their homes as he lifted his hand again. Faces vacant, mouths slack, drawn by his will.

Nikolas sucked in a breath and shouted, "Vix! Now!"

Moonlight flared overhead, sudden and brilliant.

Caries's smile faltered.

In a wash of silver light, Vix dropped over the wall . She hit Caries like a storm in Vulpine form, jaws clamping onto him as she shook him like prey.

In a blur of sickly yellow, Caries flew and slammed into the log wall with a wet thud, and crumpled.

Striking infected bodies aside with terrifying force, Vix swept her bushy tail across the mud. The villagers toppled, limp as puppets with cut strings.

Then she shifted back into her plain mortal shape, dusting her hands. "He tasted awful," she complained. "I hate mushrooms."

Nikolas exhaled, his chest still shaking with adrenaline. "Thank you," he said. "I mean it."

"I didn't want you to turn into… *that*." Vix nudged a fallen man with her boot. She crouched and pried his mouth open with two fingers, nose wrinkling. "Nik look — his tongue is missing. Disgusting."

His stomach soured. He didn't need to look.

Red flames rippled off Maya as she moved. She crossed into the meeting hall in long strides and got to work on the chains anchoring Aquila to the stone floor.

The Ave was immense, wings folded tight, gold and ruby feathers caked with grime. A hawk's beak marked with patterned waves and dark speckles.

A spear pinned one wing at a brutal angle.

Aquila's ruby-bright eyes tracked Nikolas as he approached. Assessing his intentions.

Nikolas bowed low, the motion instinctive. He waited.

A soft chirr answered him. *Permission.*

He knelt and worked at the bolts embedded in the floor. His fingers slipped once as something heavy struck the outer wall. Again. Again. Outside, Vix was finishing the mess.

He tightened his grip and kept going.

The last bolt clanged loose.

Talons scraped stone as Aquila shifted its weight. Only the spear remained.

Maya braced the wounded wing, jaw clenched. "On three," she said. "One. Two. Three."

Nikolas pulled.

Aquila screamed.

The sound knifed through the hall. Dust shook from the rafters. Her talons gouged the stone as she surged upright.

The spear came free, slick with blood.

For a breathless moment, she loomed over them. Then

Aquila shook herself out, wings snapping, feathers realigning with sharp, practiced control, even through pain.

Nikolas and Maya bowed together.

"Aquila," Vix said as she strode in, wiping her hands on a rag. "It's good to see you."

Fire bloomed.

Aquila's form folded inward, flames curling and reshaping until a tall woman stood where the Ave had been. Ebony-brown skin, similar to Orion's — except she shimmered *gold.* Long limbs with muscle coiled beneath the surface. Ruby hair spilled down her back, wild as living flame.

Turning away, he had a sudden urge to inspect the rafters when those ruby-eyes landed on him.

"What a polite one you have," Aquila said to Vix, voice smooth despite the tremor in it. "Thank you for aiding me."

She swayed.

Vix caught her. Aquila hissed as weight settled wrong on her arm.

Her fingers were bruised and bent, coloured wrong.

"Your bonded?" Vix asked softly.

Aquila shook her head. "Didn't survive the fall." Her throat worked. "We were shot out of the sky."

Maya stepped forward, voice clipped. "The Orb."

Aquila went still.

"Caries," she said at last.

Nikolas moved to where Caries had fallen. Only a smear of yellow residue clung to the wall, seeping into the cracks.

He turned back. "Gone," he said. "And he took the Orb."

Vix pressed water into Aquila's hands. "Come back to Historia with us."

Outside, Maya paced in a tight line, fire snapping at her fingertips. "If we don't follow now, we lose him."

He met her gaze. "Do you feel the pull?"

Maya dragged a hand through her hair. "No."

He looked between them and made the call. "I'll take Aquila to Bennu. You take Vix and hunt him."

Aquila met Vix's eyes and gave a single nod. "I'll return with you."

He faced Maya. "Kick his ass."

Maya didn't smile. She didn't answer. She was already turning, focus locked, a controlled inferno.

Finn had the cart ready, grain and fruit piled high. Eiran brought Nikolas's beast around to the tavern.

Nikolas helped Aquila onto the cart, every movement slow and careful.

As they started back toward Bennu, he glanced over his shoulder.

Maya stood amid the wreckage, shoulders squared, gaze fixed on the road ahead. She didn't look back.

He let her go.

MAYA IYER

It's Always about Olivia

∆

Vix clasped her hand, and *mana* poured in, bright and warming as it threaded through Maya's veins and settled in her lungs. Maya breathed in the crisp air, opened her eyes, and focused that *mana* on her sight.

A hare grazing nearby caught her sight. A trail of yellow ooze stood out on its paw — a bright chartreuse patch against the blue, inky darkness of grass and dirt. She followed the paw prints, nose trailing to the sulphur smell on the breeze.

A rune marker jutted from the soil, half-swallowed by moss. Past that line, the Interwilds began, and sane mortals turned back.

Drawing her dagger, she put up her hood and stepped in.

She kept her breathing shallow, her footsteps light. The drippings of ooze were darker here.

Behind her, twigs snapped. Maya spun.

Vix jumped back with her hands up. "It's just me."

"Almost took you out."

Vix walked in front. Maya kept quiet and low to the ground, creeping through the bushes.

The forest came alive in the Interwilds during the full moon. The leaves of the trees glowed — Maya observed the tree roots soaking in the last remnants of sunlight and drawing it to their core. Fungus stretched out in blobs, lichen and mosses clinging in patches of greyish, greenish blue; in cups of red or crackly yellow or a plush mossy green. Newborn dust motes floated past, sleeping with their wings and knees tucked, flowing together in the dark.

Maya spotted a small clearing and a cave. She went to step out — Vix stopped her, pulling her down and backwards onto the soggy grass.

Thud. Thud. Thud. Something enormous shouldered out of the dark. Vines looped where muscle should be. Rotten sticks jutted like ribs. Rocks ground together under a mossy hide that did not belong to any living thing. One hand dragged a square hammer that gouged the ground with each step.

Maya's throat tightened. *Malleus leaves a trail of devastation in its wake.*

Her heart dropped when it stopped, and Caries walked out into the moonlight. "Malleus! It is good to see you've grown! Eat any interesting villages recently?"

The creature grumbled deeply in the ground. *"Where is my…Aquila…I desire to eat her for dinner."*

The dirt and air vibrated beneath her toes.

Fury rose within Maya, filling her veins and lungs with heat.

Caries bowed. "Yes, of course I am happy to provide."

The creature wheezed, *"Get her…now."* It lumbered over to the cave and settled into one spot.

Heat surged up Maya's spine. Her fingers twitched into flame. Vix's grip locked around her shoulders. A warning, hard and desperate.

Vix pulled Maya away. "That's Malleus, a Spirit of great wrongdoing. Forget the Orb."

Maya wrenched her sleeve free. "Caries is right there."

A voice slid under her skin, close enough to feel. "I would take her advice."

Maya went cold.

"Hello again, Vix."

Vix's face turned pale in the moonlight. "Hello, Richard."

Maya's gaze snapped to Caries. "Richard?"

He smiled. "I now go by Caries."

Vix's eyes went feral. "You are an even bigger idiot than I thought. Did you really shed your mortal form and pledge yourself to Malleus?"

Caries huffed a laugh, adjusting his dirty tie and running a hand along his black hair. "Malleus grants me way more power than you could ever offer."

Vix shifted into her large Vulpine form in a creeping mist — spectacular in the moonlight, her ruby streaks glowing. *"Was it worth losing her?! Losing Olivia?"* She snarled, hackles raised.

Oh, this is personal. She'll have to get the details later.

Confused blinks shifted into a sneer. "It's always about Olivia!"

Maya felt the ground shake and shudder. She turned — the trees were snapping again. Malleus was stirring.

That was her signal.

With Vix's *mana* coursing, she rushed to Caries. Time slowed. Her hands went into his pockets.

There.

She found it in his inner coat pocket, glowing warm through the pouch. She ran back to Vix and held it high above her head. "I got it! Let's go!"

"Climb on my back," Vix cried out, skidding to a halt beside her.

She grabbed fistfuls of fur and pulled herself higher onto Vix's back, settling between her shoulder blades. She splayed her fingers. When Vix lurched forward, Maya's hands tightened.

Vix was so warm, with the softest fur coat.

The trees blurred as Vix ran, the cool night air whipping against Maya's face.

An overwhelming, giddy, childish joy surged within her. *She got the Ignis Orb.*

"I am still one of the fastest Spirits in the whole of Torresium!" Vix howled.

Maya howled with her, up into the moon. So loud she hoped Lunaris could hear her.

The night's burden lifted from her shoulders.

All that unnecessary death — was it worth it? She slumped forward onto Vix's soft fur and ran a bloody hand through it — a mix of translucent rainbow strands, a cream coat, and white frizzy undercoat. She tried to dig her fingers down to the skin, but it was so thick. She closed her eyes as Vix moved through the Interwilds.

Nothing would dare touch her here, carried on top of Vulpecula, the diamond Vulpine.

Bennu's village wasn't far — a half-day journey. The first rays were rising over the linen-streaked mountains when she woke on Vix's back.

Nikolas looked relieved to see her — she got a rare glimpse of his smile when she showed him the Orb. It was a fiery, brilliant ruby the size of her hand. Aquila was nearby, her arm in a sling. Maya passed it to her while bowing.

If you want to gain a Spirit's favour, just stroke their ego.

"Thank you, Maya," Aquila said, her eyes burning a hole right through her soul.

Aquila assessed her the moment she stepped foot into the meeting hall and found her lacking. Kit Sun had bonded to her.

But a small part of her had hoped the shields may have wiped the slate clean.

She decided that a hearty stout was the cure for a lonely, empty heart.

Rheon

△

Maya chugged the stout back. She told no one the truth, not cleanly. Not all at once.

Rather than lying, she handpicked the slices of truth she would voice.

Her parents taught her every trick they knew under their patched canvas tent. Her days were rather repetitive: wake at dawn, travel to an outskirt village, set up outside through the afternoon. They permitted her one break at dinner before she had to dance and beg her little heart out from dusk till past midnight.

She loved it. The heat in her palms. The way faces tilted toward her. Wowing and wooing the crowd with her fire wielding charms as she panhandled while her mother danced.

Naturally gifted, her mother would say to all her guests.

She'd spotted the boy with the Vulpine ears in the crowd outside of Kit Sun. *Never go to the city,* her mother instructed. But, like any stubborn child her age, she ignored her.

Maya waited until her parents and the rest of her troupe were asleep.

It was one of those sultry nights when she rolled off the hammock and breathed in the summer air. She slept in a bed made of old rope above them — the netting dug into her back, so she would often settle for a patch of dewy grass and a thick blanket outside. The air buzzed with humidity, the chirps of insects and croaks of slimy creatures rolling together.

Loud snores came from her father, Arthur. Soft moans

came from her mother, Elora, cuddling on top of his hairy chest. The twins, her brother and sister, were squashing themselves between her parents' arms and legs.

Together, her family made a distorted mortal shape in the back of their caravan under the blankets.

A blur of movement caught her eye in the darkness. A boy around her age, standing beside one of her food barrels. *He must be hungry, we have plenty of food.* She came closer, but he skittered toward the wall. She just wanted to say hello and compliment his nice ears.

Furry and white, glimmering in the moonlight.

He ran into the city.

She couldn't resist the temptation to enter. The lights were too bright. Too enticing to a young, impressionable mind. She'd scrounged up gold aureus for months — a few here, a few there. Her family wouldn't notice. Just one peek, one more stall, one more taste, one more smell.

Soon, she was dizzy with glee. She'd never seen so many beautiful things, so many beautiful people.

Come, try this.

She woke with a sharp slap across her cheek. *Never go into the city!*

Her mother dragged her out of Kit Sun. Kicking and screaming, arguing the entire way. Her mother had a firm grip on her hair, nails matted into the knots, and cut her scalp.

She didn't mean to, it was all instinct, *a drive, a yearn.* When Ignians reach that crucial age, they only know how to fuck and fight. *And oh, she loved to do both.*

The shiny city was a mirage, a fake oasis for weary, thirsty travellers. Kit Sun pulls you in, and only when the trap closes do you realise just how slimy, sticky, and gross everything has become.

She was Kit Sun's personal dancer for many years, quite an

outstanding record considering most don't last a few days. Oh, how she loved to wrap them in her light and pull, the only one who ever dared.

Do it again, they demanded.

She rolled her hips as they grasped her thighs, under the crease of her ass. To have their full attention on you is an addiction, a high so potent she might never leave. It's glorious to bathe in the glow of their *mana.* Until they take it away, starve you of their light, their attention.

Kit Sun had rules. Most were unspoken. One was not.

I will kill anyone who seeks affection from anyone but me.

Of course, no one could be so near Kit Sun and seek another. That would be blasphemy. No touching, no whispering in ears, no late night romps.

Kit Sun preferred to keep select company in their gardens on top of the city. A true Emperor and Empress — a twin-headed Vulpine with twin tails, pure golden fur, and deep ruby eyes that refracted gold.

One half will grant you a vision of how you die. The other half will grant you a vision of when. Only one will answer.

That is their price, and their gift, if you bond with them.

Their gender changed often, depending on their mood. One of her particular favourites was the beautiful mortal woman Kit Sun changed into before *he* came.

A slip of the hand, a glance. She suddenly found herself entangled in the sheets with the man who drew her into Kit Sun in the first place.

Rheon, they will find out.

No, they won't.

His smile was lovely, his eyes a stunning golden colour. Warm skin that was endless — she could stare at him for days and never tire of it.

Her body told her before anyone else did. She knew it was time to leave.

Kit Sun would never stop you from leaving their city. When she reached for the door to leave, it shattered.

She leapt to the side onto hard marble as the ceramic door fell and shattered into a thousand pieces, dust scattering across the floor. The wind blew through the passage, down the stairs, and into the larger city.

She picked herself up off the floor and ran. Even now, she did not know what pushed her forward. Perhaps it was the sheer terror of Kit Sun's wounded eyes as she looked back through the mirage that was her home.

Perhaps it was for a reason that was not entirely her own.

She ran down to the docks. Kit Sun always hated the ocean.

She spotted a Vulpine board a ship. Perhaps it was Rheon calling to her. The Aerian woman on board glanced at her swollen belly and told her about Historia. She is still friends with the Aquaan woman who delivered her child.

Rylea grew fiercely and grew fast. Now she was seeing too much of her younger self in those wild eyes.

Determined, impulsive.

Maya woke up with a rather solid headache. The thumping kind that gave her a dry mouth, yet nothing would quench it. She pushed herself up and flopped back down on her belly.

She groaned.

Sunlight streamed from the window. *Must be mid-noon — she can squeeze in a few extra hours of sleep.* Maya tried to be helpful around the kitchen, the carpentry guild, and the armoury.

They all politely refused and pushed her back to the tavern or to one of the merchant shops.

A knock came from the door.

"Are you decent?" Nikolas said.

Maya sat up. "Yes."

Nikolas poked his head in. "Vix is outstaying her welcome,

we have to leave soon."

"What happened?" She groaned. Vix had a tendency to talk herself into holes she couldn't dig out of. "Did she threaten to eat Bennu's wielders again?"

The unexpected part of the journey had been getting to know Nikolas. He was unfazed by the constant shifting of Vix's whims and fancies — Maya watched him get flighty and nervous when he sensed other Spirits get near, but then Vix just shooed them away or figured out how to satisfy them with gifts of fruit and nuts. When Vix got into fights with Bennu, he smoothed things over.

They worked together by calming the other down.

"No…she picked a fight with one of the stubborn ones, and now Bennu is asking when are we leaving."

She blinked at the bright light. "I am fine with going home."

"Can you be ready by tomorrow morning?"

She nodded. *Her break was over, back to work.*

MARGOT WILSON

Oak Tree in the Conservatory

Why did they use the masculine vowel here? It's supposed to be feminine. She scribbled red ink along the page, critiquing as she went. '*This translation is messy.*' She wrote at the top of the page, sighed, and moved onto the next. She took another from the pile and traced her red pen along, fixing slight errors. "No!" She put a big cross next to a word.

Delia's handwriting was always messy, but this reminded her of a Terra wielder who used a whittled stick and mud mixed with blood to write. '*Needs revision.*' She moved the bound pages to the revision pile.

Juniper berries hit her nose. She sighed, forcing the scent back out as if it might clear her head. She had to revise the pile before noon.

She needed to focus.

The next set of pages were perfectly translated, with neat handwriting. Only one problem. She checked the name: *Amelia Norrington.*

She sighed and wrote, '*Translated into Angloic, not Laetin.*'

Powdered musk and juniper berries hit her nose again. She took off her reading glasses and leaned back, rubbing her eyes. She inhaled the collar of her sweater.

Did he rub off on this one too?

"Hello." Qu smiled, resting his chin on his fist.

Blood rushed to her ears. "How long were you sitting there?"

"Not long, you're cute when you're absorbed in your

work. You get this line in your fore—"

She threw a pencil at him. "Shut up and let me finish this."

He nodded and opened a book.

It wasn't long before she looked up again. Qu was engrossed in his book. He caught her eye.

The smile turned her insides into mush. He looked down at her work. "Keep going, you have one more hour."

She nodded, clearing her throat. The hour stretched.

The last few seconds ticked round on her timepiece. She stretched her shoulders up and cracked her back against the chair.

Her pile of work was done.

She walked across the Study Hall, dropped her work off at the main desk, and got her bag. She sensed a few of the librarians' auras change when Qu walked towards them — lust dripping off their tongues. "Shall we?"

She locked down her senses.

She made small talk on their walk to the Conservatory. Margot sat down on a bench under the oak tree in the centre, its thick limbs stretching wide and high, twisting towards the open sky.

"What did you need?" Qu asked.

She scooted and leaned closer. "For you to take a nap." She pressed two fingers to his temple and laid his head on the bench. Getting to work, she threaded the Aerian ring off his finger and took an identical one out of her pocket.

Margot brushed a lock of hair out of his face and kissed his temple. "*Sorry*," she murmured against his skin.

Walking through the Conservatory, she looked back at him. He looked so peaceful in the soft breeze, the sun filtering along his face.

She spotted Sophia resting near a pruned display of white roses. "Got it," she said, handing Sophia the ring.

Sophia smiled and threaded it on her finger. "I feel it, the pull."

She smiled. "Then let's go get it."

☾

"I don't understand, there's nothing here." Sophia sighed. "We have to keep going North."

"Any more North and we'll be out the shields," Margot said. This was the furthest from the city centre she'd ever been — the buildings scarce and dilapidated, a few barns and brick silos.

A few trees dotted the tall grass plains. Her ankle rolled on a rock — she gasped.

The sun beat down as they climbed over the rocky outcroppings. She sat down and took a drink from her canteen, the cool water soothing her throat.

"I can feel it, just a bit longer."

Her feet ached. A blister burned along her heel. Despite that, she continued onward, scribbling notes of abandoned windmills that were contributing to the growing rodenta problem.

She checked her timepiece and looked at the horizon through a shaded hand — two hours of sunlight left.

"There!" Sophia yelled and pointed to a grain silo.

Rivers of white paint dripped from the hole at the top. The roof caved in and twisted. She looked up at the brick — a ladder extended from the top. Margot pulled on it to test the metal.

It creaked. "We can come back?"

"No, keep going." Sophia grasped a handhold and pulled herself up.

Steeling her nerves, Margot did the same and followed. Rung after rung, she pulled herself up.

She dared to look down and regretted it. The wind whipped her hair and skirts. Sophia disappeared inside the silo — she pushed up from the last rung and peered into the cavernous hole.

Sophia was still. "What is it?"

The shushing noise coming from Sophia made Margot's heart leap.

A ruffle of feathers caught her eye. Her heart was in her throat. Small skulls, a few white spines, sinewy jawbones. A stinking nest made of twisted sticks, rotting branches, and hay in the centre, covered in tiny fluffy feathers. Gross white plaster kept the nest together.

No, that was shit.

Flashes of gold, silver, and gemstones littered the nest. The creature stirred and settled.

Margot could only watch in horror as Sophia crept forward.

She aimed for the back corner, but a twig snapped under her foot. The creature's head popped up and squawked in her face.

Sophia fell on her ass and scrambled backwards through the bones and leftovers of its meal. She screamed to distract it, running, leaping out of the hole.

The Harpy screeched and followed in a rustle of feathers and sharp claws.

Margot ducked as the creature brushed its wings against her head — she gripped the ladder for dear life. Sophia leapt and dodged the winged creature in mid-air.

Margot peered in, looked to where Sophia was pointing, and climbed into the silo. She coughed, pinching her nose from the smell of its last dinner. She pulled at the twigs and branches.

Two chirps drew her attention — the brown fluffy babies looked like a horrific mix between a chick and a mortal babe. Harpy babies lurched, searching for food, biting her arm.

They screeched. She picked one up and tossed it across the nest. It fell clumsily and dug its sharp talons into the sticks and came right back at her, chipping with hunger. They scratched her as she looked for the Orb.

She grasped one by the neck; it was trying to peck out her eye. She tried to focus her *mana* to put the babies to sleep, but it wouldn't work on them. Why wasn't it working on them?

Her eyes snapped to the hole in the silo. A blur of yellow and grey followed by the brownish blur and call of a mother harpy flew by. A smash against the silo walls made her move faster. The flash of aquamarine caught her eye — she grasped it, felt a small tingle of *mana* reach out and reject her, and shoved it in the pouch.

She cinched it closed.

"Got it!" Margot yelled out of the hole.

Sophia was on the ground, deep scrapes and bleeding tears over her arms and face, scrambling away from the harpy.

"HELLO HARPY! COME GET ME!" Margot screamed. Bright yellow eyes and matted wild hair turned up, screeching with browned teeth. She clasped her ears and scrambled away from the hole as it flew up towards her.

A blur of blue and mahogany pushed the harpy to the ground.

"Qu!" She screamed. He was bleeding and scratched as well. Was he fighting it this whole time?

She needed to be on the ground. She needed to heal Sophia while Qu dealt with the harpy.

Looping a leg over the rungs, she made her way down, step by step. The rusty ladder swung in the breeze.

A smash of feathers and bodies landed next to her — her foot slipped on a rung. The rusty ladder detached from the brick. As she fell backwards, she grabbed for the rung.

Her fingers slipped.

No, not like this.

The fall lasted less than a second. Long enough to hear him say it — three words, quiet and certain, as if he'd been waiting for the right moment.

Strong arms enveloped her.

They landed hard. *Too hard.*

The spinning stopped after a few seconds. Rocks dug into her back. Her lungs had no air, pain radiating through her body. Her leg ached. She leaned up — the sharpness of the rocks bit into her hands.

Qu lay next to her. A flash of white hot, piercing fire pain shot through her leg. Sophia screamed, her voice cracking.

She couldn't get up, couldn't move. The pain was…too much. She grasped her Orb and reached for Qu, willing her *mana* to heal him. It wasn't enough.

Tears poured down her face as she lay there, useless.

The Aer Orb. She can get the Orb to Sophia.

"Sophia! Catch!" She summoned every muscle in her arms to flip the pouch high. It thunked onto the rocks. Pain radiated from her ribs.

Hot, acute, burning.

Sophia ran towards it and scooped it up.

She lay there and watched Sophia wrestle with the harpy, flying and leaping in the air like a woman possessed with fury. Her cuts and tears were healing.

The Aer Orb gave her a magnificent golden glow.

Qu's eyes weren't open. Margot reached for him and found nothing.

She already knew before she looked. She still couldn't connect with his heart.

She wanted to see his space one more time.

"No, no…Qu? Open your eyes." Tears fell down her face. "Please wake up."

Sophia screamed and shrieked as she fought and wrestled the harpy. She got a good grip and choked it, crying, wailing. Sophia mustered every fibre of her being when she grasped its jaws and twisted sharply.

The harpy dropped to the ground with a weightless thump.

Margot leaned up, her back aching and her bones screaming. "Sophia! Are you alive? Please tell me you're alive."

"I'm alive," Sophia called out.

Sophia sobbed as she knelt next to Margot.

Static tingles ran through her body. Her back no longer ached, and all of her wounds had closed.

Her leg was still broken.

"This is going to hurt," Sophia said, wiping away her tears. Stiff hands were on her leg — a rush of intense pain as it was pulled into place. She placed a splint against Margot's shin and wrapped it in grey strips from her dress.

"Don't heal me. Heal him." She put a hand on his heart. "He's not breathing."

"There was nothing I could do. He was gone seconds after you hit the ground."

"Wh — what?"

Sophia stopped tying and put her head in her hands. "This is all my fault."

"No, no, he's not gone." She leaned over and slapped him hard. She poured her *mana* into his chest.

He was so cold. She had to warm him up. "Qu, don't fucking leave me again. *Please.*"

Tears poured down her face. Why did he have to save her?

She already knew what he'd said. She'd heard it in the fall — those three words before they hit the rocks.

I love you.

NIKOLAS VENATOR

Her Loss and Devastation

✷

Nikolas never thought he'd welcome the tingle from the shields as they crossed back into Historia. Vix leaped from her beast and shifted into a gigantic snow Ave, massive claws dug into the battlement wall as they trotted up to the gates. Her two flat, wide eyes and small hooked beak looked absurd with those bright red eyes.

Yes, he was glad to be back.

Margot had promised to wait for him.

He made a minor detour, stopping at a bakery for two sweet bread rolls. He couldn't resist the smile on his face. He steadied his breathing.

And knocked.

Sophia answered the door, her mouth opened in shock. He didn't need his senses to know something was wrong.

"Nikolas... Margot isn't seeing anyone right now."

"What happened? Is she okay?"

Sophia paused and looked back. They spoke quietly behind the door. He could smell the liquor and wine seeping out.

They must have been celebrating.

She'd chosen Quentin.

His chest fell. "I will go." He turned, respecting the choice, even as it hollowed him out. The weight of the paper bag felt heavy in his hands. "Can you give these to her?" He held out the package, and she took it.

Nikolas was no one. *No lands, no noble family lineage, no*

crest.

He made it halfway down the hall when Sophia gripped his sleeve. He spun. "What is it?"

The rejection burned through him, sadness coated his stomach. He had to leave before he said something he'd regret. Her eyes were red and puffy. She stammered and talked in circles.

"Just spit it out." He huffed.

"Fuck you. Quentin died."

He reached for Sophia's mind, and the memory hit him.

Quentin. Margot. The rocks.

"Oh… fuck. I just got back, came straight here… I'm sor —"

"Stop, it's okay. Margot is…well, she's suffering, but she's whole." Sophia tucked in her arms.

"Can I see her?"

Sophia sighed and sniffed. "Can you come tomorrow?"

He nodded. "What time?"

She looked at her timepiece and tapped it a few times. Biting her lip. Grief was overwhelming her senses — she was unfocused, staring off at nothing.

He made her choice easy. "Let's go with noon and go from there."

"Good enough for me."

"Tell her I am sorry for me, will you?"

Sophia gathered up her knitted sweater and tightened it around her arms. "I will."

✸

He caught up with Vix at the tavern.

"What happened?"

He passed over a packet of dates. He wasn't sure if it was his business to tell. "Something happened to Margot. They are fine, though."

She gasped, chewing on a date. "No way, what

happened?"

He shook his head, not believing the news. "Quentin passed away saving her. I'm going to get more details tomorrow."

He had mulled the whole thing over several times. Images of Sophia's grief came back to him in waves. Deep cuts. Puncture wounds from massive talons. He'd drained his *mana* and was helpless as they fell.

Aerian women were always the stronger wielders. No one ever said it out loud.

Vix tapped a date on her chin. "Quentin…Atticus?"

"Sophia's fiancee."

She paused for a few seconds. "Oh! Yes, David's boy. Alces herd traded him for a while."

"How do you know what?"

"I hear everything that happens in this city."

"He and Margot had dated, or something…" *He'd had exes too. None had come back to life, though. His were all still dead or pissed at him for running away.*

Vix poured two shots from the bottle the barkeep gave her. "How did he die?" Nikolas opened his mouth to answer, but he hesitated. She continued, "If I don't hear it from you, I'll hear it from someone else."

"He died saving her life."

Vix slammed down the shot. "Ah! A hero's death." She wiped her nose and winced from the burn. "He loved her, right? The best way to die," she said as if she knew what happened and just wanted someone to discuss it with her.

He'd been beyond the shields. Too far to sense her. Too far to do anything but come back after.

He lifted his shot. "To Quentin, who died a hero's death saving the girl I love." He hiccuped.

Vix squealed, "I knew it!" She kicked back another shot.

Death had surrounded him his whole life. There was no

greater way for a man to die, saving the woman he loves. Nikolas could respect that. Own that. Embrace the second chance that Quentin had given him.

Nikolas failed to protect her. He should've been there to catch her.

A plan emerged in his drunk mind.

✷

Sophia answered the door exactly at noon, looking vacant and tired eyed. "Yes?"

"It's noon, and I brought food."

Her eyes shifted to the package of two warm toasted rolls. The smell of fried eggs and salted swine.

The perfect bait. Nothing two grieving ladies needed more in their bellies after drinking themselves into a stupor. He could smell stale liquor when Sophia opened the door.

She lifted the package to her nose and inhaled. "Yes, come in."

"Sophia!" Margot's voice came from the living room as she hurried away.

"Don't come in, please," she whispered into his mind. Her protests came from the bedroom, mostly excuses about how she was a mess.

He chuckled and whispered back, *"Nothing I haven't seen before."*

"Get out!" Margot cried from the bedroom. "I am not decent!"

Nikolas could sense her sorrow weeping from behind the bathroom door. "I'll be here." He sat and leaned his back against it.

"For as long as you need me."

SOPHIA MEYER

Finally Free

✦

Sophia chewed on the warm bread roll Nikolas had given her. He would stay with her. She didn't want to be a third wheel, and could be alone with her thoughts for a minute.

Every waking second was about keeping Margot alive. The first time Quentin died, Margot had tried to follow him. Sophia had stayed at her side for months until her mother forced her to rejoin the Aerian society.

Sky-blooded daughters aren't weak.

So pathetic.

Sophia made her way to the Conservatory, letting the pull guide her steps. No Spirit had shown itself yet. She held her Orb in her lap and sat on the bench — the same one where she'd told Margot to leave Quentin.

The plan had been hers. *Put him to sleep where he used to nap when he was a kid.*

Heat ran through her, a molten gold burn through her veins as she felt *mana* flow — she stroked a thumb over the rune mark on her wrist.

"I hear your pain, my child," the wind whispered. The leaves of the oak tree shook and circled around the trunk, caught up and carried.

Laughter rang out in her head.

Sophia called out, "Hello?"

"Hello, my bonded." The whisper of a voice was icy and crisp, sending chills skittering along her spine. *"I am Vela."*

"I can't see you."

"I can speak to you, that's not enough?"

Her breath caught in her chest. A thousand questions rolled through her mind.

"How have I not heard your name?"

"Aerian males." Vela scoffed. *"They do not agree with my choice of bonding."*

A horrible mixture of guilt and sorrow rolled through her stomach, twisting it into knots. "They refuse to pass the ring to Aerian women, despite us being stronger." Sophia had diminished herself throughout her entire life.

She learnt at a young age to be small. Quiet. Told to not take up space.

"Ah yes, I have watched you grow so big and strong. I'm glad that you found me."

Sophia reaped the benefits while they suffered. She didn't find the ring or have the courage to confront her father. She relied on Margot and Quentin to do it for her. "I don't deserve this."

The corners of her eyes burned. She didn't think she had any more tears left to shed.

"Yes, you do. I am picky, even among women." Vela chuffed.

Vela materialised before her. Shining iridescent eyes. Long gold-citrine hair caught the wind and flowed around her. Insect wings fluttered behind her.

Sophia swallowed.

Beautiful.

She remembered reading the works of Paracelsus when she was a wieldling. She would stare out her window, wishing to be as free and unbound as the Sylphs.

She was finally free. She struggled to take a full breath. The cost was too large.

A weight settled on her shoulders, on her chest. It was unbearable.

"You are too kind." Vela landed, not making any sound with

her bare feet.

Sophia's heart raced. "Sorry, I'll learn to contain my thoughts," she spluttered.

She placed her hands in her lap, returning to that neutral pose that was beaten into her as a young girl.

"Never apologise."

Her head shot up. "Sor—" She snapped her jaw shut.

"We have much to do. I have been watching rot seep in along the edges, growing in the darkness."

"What is it? The Rot?"

"It is a corruption of the oldest kind, my dear. Discordia is awake, and we must prepare for war."

# AUTHOR'S ACKNOWLEDGEMENTS

She is, as always, first. I'd like to thank my tuxedo cat, Pepper, for being my constant writing companion. She dedicated many hours to purring in my arms or between my legs while I typed and assisted me with many ideas.

Second, I'd like to thank my partner, Michael, for supporting me throughout this whole thing. Without him, there would be no world of Torresium. It would've just been just another forgotten idea in a half-completed notebook. He gave me courage and support to start typing away and compiling my notes.

Now it's real.

Third, I'd like to thank my family and friends!

Trina, you're my ride or die. Thank you for listening to my daily rants in the car on the way to work, and for your unending support.

Matt, thank you for getting my cover to where it needed to be. Ange, Kevin, and Chris, thank you for the encouragement in and out of the group chat.

To my Australian family; Sean and Nicole, I love you both.

To Piper; this one is for you, kid.

AUTHOR'S BIO

Anika Nagy is an Australian author living in Halifax, Canada with her partner, Michael. When she isn't losing at video games or satisfying the neediness of their cat, Pepper, she works full time and occasionally fits in time to write. Spirit & Soul is her debut novel.

www.ingramcontent.com/pod-product-compliance
Lightning Source LLC
LaVergne TN
LVHW041108080826
845145LV00007B/1726